Cherished Secrets

by

C. B. Clark

Cherished Secrets

Cover Art by *Debbie Taylor*

The Wild Rose Press, Inc.
PO Box 708
Adams Basin, NY 14410-0708
Visit us at www.thewildrosepress.com

Publishing History
First Crimson Rose Edition, 2016
Print ISBN 978-1-5092-1046-6
Digital ISBN 978-1-5092-1047-3

Published in the United States of America

Her breath caught in her throat.

A small fragment of cloth lay atop her purse, the vibrant colors glowing in the meager, late afternoon light. With a shaking hand, she picked up the cloth. The smooth silk slid between her fingers. Mesmerized, she studied the scrap of torn fabric.

The air in the car was suddenly too thick to breathe. Fingers shaking, she turned the cloth over and jammed her fist in her mouth stifling a scream. Written across the silk in thick, black letters was a single, condemning word. *Guilty.*

She dropped the cloth as if it burned and gulped air. While she'd been traipsing around the forest looking for where the killer had dumped Skye's body, someone had been inside her car and left this piece of Skye's scarf for her to find. The same person could still be here, watching her, waiting.

Her hand shook so much she dropped the keys on the floor twice before finally fitting them in the ignition and starting the car. The engine choked, sputtered, and died.

Dedication

Thanks to my family and friends.
I couldn't have achieved this
without your love and support.

Chapter 1

Carrie Ann Hetherington couldn't believe her bad luck. Stranded in the dark on the side of the lonely, rutted gravel road, with rain pelting on her head, running down her face, drenching her hair, and ruining her new suede coat. "Piece of junk." She kicked the flat tire on the small, red rental car. "Where the hell's the spare?" Her other foot slipped out from under her, and she let out a shriek as she fell, landing with a splash in a muddy puddle.

Icy moisture seeped through her thin, wool pants, raising goose bumps on her arms and legs. "Okay, you win," she shouted into the storm. "You're right. I should've never come back to Cooper's Ridge." As if agreeing with her, lightning crackled overhead. She lifted her hand to brush back the hair hanging in her eyes but stopped short at the muck dripping off her fingers.

What the hell was she going to do now? Cell service didn't reach this far out in the country, so she couldn't call a tow truck. She shuddered at the thought of walking ten long miles to town on dark roads without a flashlight in this downpour.

The deep roar of a diesel engine sounded in the night, echoing off the surrounding forested hills.

She staggered to her feet as a large pickup truck sped around the bend and skidded to a stop, pinning her with twin high beams.

The driver's door swung open and Blake Shelton's voice blasted through the truck's radio into the rainy night. A figure stepped out and slammed the door, cutting off the twang of a steel guitar.

Peering through the rain, she made out a large, masculine shape. "Thank goodness you came by." She tried not to sound too desperate. "My tire's flat. Can you help me, please?"

The man remained a dark blot.

A bright flash lit the sky, and the ground trembled under another crash of thunder. Unease flickered low in her belly. "Mister? Did you hear me? I said my tire's flat." Her voice squeaked. What was wrong with him? Was he some kind of pervert? Would he attack her? Her canister of pepper spray was in her purse in the car. What would she protect herself with? Mud?

He stepped closer.

Holding her muddy hands up to her eyes to block the dazzle of the bright headlights, she squinted at the blur of his face.

"I should have known it was you."

She shivered at the venom in his husky voice. The deep tones and laconic drawl sounded familiar. "Do I know you?"

His harsh, abrasive laugh chilled her. "Carrie Ann Hetherington."

Her unease morphed into shock. "Declan?" He stepped out of the glare of headlights, and a wave of dizziness washed over her.

"In the flesh. Bet you never thought you'd see me again." His gaze roamed over her, and he snorted. "My dog's dragged in cleaner-looking roadkill than you."

She bristled. "It's raining, in case you haven't noticed."

"Looks to me like you fell in a mud puddle." He smirked. "Can't say anyone deserves it more than you, sweetheart."

"Are you going to stand here in the rain all night, or are you going to help?" She glared, stuffing years of bitterness into the look.

He narrowed his eyes and leaned against the side of her small, red, two-door coupe, seemingly oblivious to the cold rain pouring down on him, plastering his dark curls to his head. His long-sleeved shirt clung to his chest, revealing a well-defined set of pecs. He motioned to the dark outlines of dripping trees looming along the sides of the road and the acres of farmland beyond. "What's the matter? Are you afraid, Carrie Ann?"

She shivered at the ice in his voice, but knew he was taunting her. She felt so many emotions about him—anger, betrayal, guilt, to name a few—but not fear. Never fear.

"Come on, you can tell me the truth. You're afraid of me, aren't you?" His gaze was probing. "Like everyone else in town."

"I see you haven't changed." She clasped her hands behind her back before he noticed their trembling.

"Me? Look who's talking? At the first hint of trouble, you ran away like a scared little rabbit."

She straightened, trying to add inches to her five-foot, four-inch frame, and jammed her hands on her hips. "I have no intention of rehashing the past with you, Declan. If you won't help me, leave. I'll wait in my car until someone else comes along." As she reached for the handle to the driver's door of her car, her foot slipped in the ever-deepening quagmire. She grabbed for the door, missed, and yelped as she fell. *Not again. Not with* him *watching.*

In the next breath, she was hauled against a firm chest. A flash of memory thundered through her, of running her hands over this same chest, her fingers twining in crisp, dark hair. Heat rushed up her neck and flooded her cheeks.

****

Declan gritted his teeth against the torrent of remembrances…the swell of her hips, the fullness of her breasts, the smell of her… He cursed, released her as if she burned, and backed away, sucking in a ragged breath. Even though two feet of watery air now separated them, the softness of her curves was still branded on him. His hand shook as he swiped at the rain washing over his face. The last thing he wanted was for her to see the effect she had on him. His eyes narrowed against the downpour as he inspected her.

Her shoulder-length, auburn hair was a tangled mess. Rain sluiced off the planes of her pale, mud-spattered face and dripped from her chin. Smudges of mascara rimmed her eyes. Even in the storm her eyes shone with an intensity he remembered. The darkness hid the color of her eyes, but if he closed his, he remembered their amber lights. Cat's eyes, he'd called them. He balled his hands into fists and squeezed until his nails dug into his palms, hoping the pain would remind him of the hurt she'd caused.

She shivered, her slender body shaking with the cold.

Damn and double damn. He had to do something or she'd catch pneumonia. He swore again for good measure. Bad luck plagued him, especially when she was around. Why the hell had he taken this back road tonight of all nights? With a resigned sigh, he grabbed her hand and towed her behind him toward his truck. "Come on."

She let out a squeal and shoved against him, trying to yank her hand free.

He tightened his grip. Jesus. She hadn't changed a damn bit. He winced as a blow struck him on the arm. "What the hell?"

"Let me go!"

"You might not have any common sense, princess, but I do. I'm putting you in my truck so you can warm up. All right?" He opened the driver's door of the truck and lifted her onto the seat.

The second he released her, she scrambled over to the far side of the cab, her eyes flashing fury.

His gut twisted. He didn't have time for this. Not tonight. Not when he needed to reach Rankin's Farm before it was too late. But he couldn't leave her stranded on the side of the road. He reached into the back seat and grabbed an old shirt he'd tossed on the floor after his last tennis match weeks ago. The shirt wasn't clean, but it was dry. He tossed the crumpled shirt on her lap. "Put this on."

He turned the keys in the ignition, started the engine, and set the heater to high. Grabbing a flashlight from the glove compartment, he slammed the door shut and trudged back to her car.

The small, mud-caked car rested crookedly on the rim. He checked the tire. It was flat all right. Leaning closer, he shone the light. The tread was worn smooth. He ran his fingers over a small, puckered hole in the sidewall, and a chill shot up his spine. He'd seen this before, years ago, when he was a kid, and he and some buddies had gone target shooting at old cars at the dump.

Rain dripped off his hair into his eyes. Had someone taken a shot at her car? He shook off his concern. The tire was bald. A sharp rock, a nail, or a piece of glass could have punctured it. The only way to tell for sure would be to take the tire into a shop and examine the hole.

He opened the driver's door, popped the trunk, slogged through the mud, and peered inside for the spare. Empty. Damn. This night just kept getting worse. Slamming the trunk hard, he retrieved her suitcase and purse, trudged back to his truck and climbed in, tossing her belongings in the back seat.

Silence filled the cab, building until it was thick and coiled as if a living entity.

"You couldn't fix the tire." Her voice sounded small.

"You don't have a spare."

"I know."

He wiped water off his face. "Nice of you to tell me."

"I would have said something if you hadn't tossed me in here like a sack of potatoes."

He switched on the interior light and pinned her with a hard gaze. "Have you pissed anyone else off recently?"

"What?"

"Is anyone, other than me, mad at you?"

"What are you talking about?" Under the veil of dried mud, her face paled. "Declan, what is it? What's going on?" Shadows filled her eyes.

What the hell was he doing? Trying to frighten her? He wasn't even sure someone had taken a shot at her car. "Nothing." He shook his head. "Forget it." He focused on the dark road ahead.

They sat in silence, the tension between them growing with each swish of the windshield wipers.

She giggled.

What the hell? He slid her a glance.

She laughed again, the all-too-familiar sound evoking a slew of bittersweet memories. "Can you believe this? What are the odds of the two of us meeting here, on this road, in the middle of a rainstorm, after all these years?"

He couldn't help himself. A wry chuckle broke through his tight lips. She was right. The happenstance of the two of them finding each other on this isolated road in the middle of nowhere was funny. Ridiculous, impossible, yet funny.

Their gazes met and locked.

His laughter died in his throat. In the sudden silence, the thumping of his heart was louder even than the pounding of the rain on the roof of the cab. How could he have forgotten the unique color of her eyes, or the way her impossibly long lashes framed them? His gaze shifted to her mouth, and the air blasted out of him like he'd been punched in the gut. He swallowed, remembering how sweet those lips had tasted. He tore his gaze away. He didn't need this shit. Not again. "Where were you headed?" He cursed under his breath at the hoarseness of his voice.

"Vivian's."

"Really?" As far as he knew she hadn't been back

to Cooper's Ridge in years. Not since—He ground down on his back molars, cutting off the thought.

"It's complicated."

Complicated. He bit back a snort. She didn't know what complicated was. He turned off the interior light, put the truck in gear, and pressed his foot hard on the accelerator. The truck's heavy-duty tires spun and gripped the slippery road, and the vehicle surged ahead, leaving a spray of mud and gravel in its wake.

As the truck rumbled through the storm, he struggled to think of something…anything other than the woman beside him. He smelled her. He tried not to inhale, but he couldn't help himself. Roses, vanilla, Carrie Ann.

"Are you taking me to Vivian's?"

The soft, honeyed tones of her voice struck him like a fist. God help him. He still wanted her after all these years, after all the anger, all the bitterness.

"Declan?"

His fingers tightened on the steering wheel, the knuckles turning white. He risked a glance at her. She'd put on his shirt, and even though it was far too big, the loose folds didn't hide the swell of her breasts. He swallowed the lump in his throat and thought of the hole in her tire. "Who knew you were coming home tonight?"

"Only Vivian and Leland. Why?"

"Are you sure?"

"What's this all about?" She frowned. "Why do you care?"

She had a point. Why did he care? What happened to her was none of his business, hadn't been for a long time. He refused to look at her again. Afraid of what he'd do. Afraid of himself, afraid of what she might see if he did.

Silence filled the cab, broken only by the heavy purr of the motor and the swish of the windshield wipers. The lights from a few scattered houses appeared as they reached the outskirts of town.

A headache bloomed and worsened with every mile until his head was ready to explode. He longed to rub his aching temples, but he wouldn't show her how seeing her again after all these years affected him. How, suddenly, his whole world had been turned upside down.

He turned off the main street onto Winters Road. A minute later, he swung onto a driveway and drove up to the house he hadn't seen in twelve years. Like a lot of things in Cooper's Ridge, the house hadn't changed. The two-story, Colonial mansion was still painted white, the shutters a dark, hunter-green. Two, white Adirondack chairs sat on the wide, covered, front porch. He caught sight of the porch swing and stiffened, fighting off another surge of memories. "We're here." He reached across, careful not to touch her, and opened her door.

She didn't budge.

The cab light illuminated her pale, tired, mud-streaked face, and his gut tightened. He gentled his voice. "You'd better go in. You must be freezing in those wet clothes."

Her pale hands twisted the thin cotton of his shirt into knots.

"Carrie Ann?"

She faced him, and he flinched under the full impact of her eyes.

"Thank you," she said quietly.

He nodded. He couldn't speak, couldn't move, could only stare at her as if caught under a spell.

A smile curved her full lips, softening her face.

Warmth flooded over him.

"I know it's too little, too late, but I am sorry. Sorry for everything." She released her seat belt, leaped out of the truck, and ran through the rain to the porch. She knocked on the door. It opened, and she disappeared into the house.

He stared at the closed door and gave in to the relief of massaging his aching temples. If he'd chosen a worst-case scenario for tonight, finding Carrie Ann stranded with a flat tire on the road to Rankin's Farm would top the list. He slammed his fist into the steering wheel. He didn't need this shit, not now, especially not tonight.

A rapping on his driver's side window made him jump.

An elderly man peered at him through the rain-streaked glass.

Even before Declan pressed the button and rolled down the window, he knew who the man was.

Leland Winters, Carrie Ann's uncle, stared at him with cold eyes, his short, thinning, gray hair glistening with raindrops. "McAllister."

Declan nodded, hiding a groan. First Carrie Ann and now Winters. Were they ganging up on him?

"Carrie Ann left her suitcase and purse in your truck." Winters gestured at Declan's truck.

Shit. Declan reached into the backseat, grabbed the small suitcase and her purse, opened the door, and handed them to Winters. His throat slammed closed. He might be a fully-grown adult, but he couldn't help feeling like an awkward, insecure kid around the old judge. The bitter taste of resentment filled his mouth at the thought of what this man had done.

"Thank you." Winters' voice was clipped. He assessed Declan, and his mouth tightened into a thin, disapproving line as if the words hurt. "Thank you for bringing her home."

Declan nodded, feeling as if he were a bobblehead doll. "I'll get someone to fix the tire and have her car delivered here tomorrow morning."

"I'd like to compensate you for your trouble. Where do I send the check?"

Declan snorted. "To the devil." He put the truck into reverse and squealed out of the driveway, uncaring that the old man had to scramble out of the way to avoid being sprayed by muddy water.

Chapter 2

Carrie Ann sagged against the bedroom door listening to the squeal of truck tires on the driveway as Declan sped away. She'd known coming back wouldn't be easy. After twelve years, how could it be? Especially since she'd made it clear she hadn't wanted to come back, wouldn't have, if she'd had a choice.

A tap at the door drew her out of her thoughts. *Go away. Leave me alone.* She couldn't bear another confrontation. Not tonight.

"Carrie Ann? May I come in?"

Her heart sank. Resignation set in. She walked over to the bed and collapsed onto the pink satin cover. "Come in."

The door opened, and Vivian Morgenstern Winters strode into the room.

Carrie Ann bit back a gasp. Her aunt had always been slim, but now her body was emaciated, her bones protruding like thin, brittle twigs beneath her crepe-paper skin. Beads of perspiration highlighted her sallow complexion and gaunt face. Her hair, once a thick, lustrous, dark-brown, was streaked with gray. Patches of shiny scalp shone through the wispy strands. The old woman's hands trembled, and she leaned against the desk, clutching the back of the chair as if for support.

She's sick. The astounding thought raced through Carrie Ann, but then Vivian spoke, and all concern for the older woman's health fled.

"Hello, Carrie Ann. It's been a long time." Vivian's withering scrutiny seemed to take in the mud on Carrie Ann's clothes and the damp and dirty patches staining the flowered, satin bedspread. Her mouth tightened. "Leland told me you were caught in the storm. A flat tire? Really, my dear, you should've stuck to the main road. I'd have thought you knew better." She pointed toward the window where rain pelted against the glass. "Especially on a night like this."

Carrie Ann refused to let Vivian upset her. She was no longer a child. Vivian didn't have any power over her. *Yeah, right. So why come back to Cooper's Ridge?*

"Your clothes are soaked. You'll catch a chill." Vivian rambled on, oblivious to her niece's simmering resentment.

Goose bumps prickled on Carrie Ann's arms. She hated to admit it, but Vivian was right. She was cold. While Declan had checked on her flat tire, she'd changed out of her wet coat and blouse and put on the shirt he'd tossed at her. Her nostrils had flared at the familiar scent clinging to the soft cotton. She'd have ripped off the shirt, but she'd been freezing, and the shirt was the only dry clothing she had until he retrieved her suitcase from her car.

She shivered again. "I was going to shower and change into something warmer, but..." Her voice trailed off, making it clear Vivian had interrupted things by her visit.

"I won't keep you long, my dear. I wanted to welcome you back home." Vivian's eyes bore into Carrie Ann's. "Leland told me Declan brought you home."

13

"Yep." The less said on the subject of Declan McAllister, the better.

Vivian's eyes narrowed. "You're still angry at him."

"Of course not." Anger implied she cared, and that Declan still had the power to hurt her. "I haven't thought of him in years. Furthermore…" She paused at the knowing simper on Vivian's face. She was protesting too much, but she couldn't stop, and the words kept spilling out. "I don't have any feelings for him. Not anymore. It's been years. Whatever Declan and I had is ancient history. Besides, what was I supposed to do? He was the first person to come by tonight when I was stuck on that godforsaken road. I needed help. My tire was flat. There wasn't a spare. I didn't want to spend the night in the rain waiting on the off chance someone else would come by."

Vivian raised her eyebrows. "So you don't care for him?"

Carrie Ann rolled her eyes. Vivian hadn't been listening. No surprise. She never had listened. The prickliness between them hadn't changed either. But *she* had. She met Vivian's gaze. "You don't have to play the role of the caring aunt. We both know it's bullshit. You know why I'm here."

Vivian opened her mouth to speak.

Carrie Ann cut her off. "Where're my mother's possessions?"

"You've just arrived, dear. I thought we could visit first and catch up. I haven't seen you in a long time."

"I didn't come back for a family reunion. I'm here because you ordered me to appear."

"You always were so dramatic, my dear. I didn't

14

order you to come home. Goodness me, you're an adult. I couldn't possibly tell you what to do."

Carrie Ann grimaced. *Here we go again.* "Okay, would you mind telling me why you *asked* me to come to Cooper's Ridge to pick up my mother's possessions? Why couldn't you ship the box to me? It would've saved us both a lot of bother."

"You're still hurting, aren't you, my dear?" The lines in Vivian's forehead deepened. "You're so angry. This is my fault. I'm sorry."

Carrie Ann swallowed over a sudden lump in her throat. In all the years she'd lived with this woman, she never remembered receiving a kind word from her. She recalled countless harsh criticisms, angry words, bitter sarcasm, but never an apology.

Vivian's harsh, racking cough broke into Carrie Ann's thoughts. Her aunt's gaze once again traveled over her damp and mud-spattered clothing. Her frown deepened. "Our little chat can wait until tomorrow, when you're more"—her narrowed eyes inspected the stains on the comforter—"presentable, shall we say?"

Carrie Ann almost smiled. This was more like what she was used to. She was tempted to push, to force the old woman to give her the box of her mother's effects now, but past experience had taught her the futility of arguing. Vivian would let her see her mother's possessions when she was ready, and only then. "I guess I'll have a shower then." She pinned Vivian with a hard look. "But we'll settle this first thing tomorrow. I'm not staying any longer than I have to."

Vivian paused with her hand clutching the door handle. "I'm glad you're home, Carrie Ann. I've missed you. Leland and I both have." She shuffled out the door, closing it behind her.

Carrie Ann stared after her. Had Vivian Morgenstern Winters actually said she'd missed her? She shook her head in disbelief. A shiver rippled through her, and she crossed her arms over her chest. A hot shower was just what she needed.

Tugging off Declan's shirt, she lifted the soft cotton to her nose and inhaled. A thousand bittersweet memories assailed her. In the next breath, she threw the shirt on the floor as if the material singed her fingers. Tearing off the rest of her damp clothes, she tossed them on top, hiding Declan's shirt from view. She wrinkled her nose. Was it her imagination, or could she still smell him on her? A shower was definitely in order.

Hours later, sheets tangled around her ankles, pillow damp beneath her face, she awoke. It had been a long time since she'd awakened in the middle of the night with tears streaming down her cheeks. Seeing Vivian, Leland, and Declan resurrected painful memories; memories she'd fought hard to put behind her.

Last week, Vivian had contacted her, breaking twelve years of silence. Her aunt had found a box of Carrie Ann's long-dead mother's personal possessions. The devastating fire, which had killed both her parents when Carrie Ann was five years old, had destroyed everything else. The prospect of learning more about the woman who'd given birth to her was irresistible. Vivian, being Vivian, had refused to ship the box, threatening to throw out the effects if Carrie Ann didn't return to Cooper's Ridge and pick them up in person. Now here she was, back in the one place she'd vowed never to return.

Throwing back the covers, she swung her legs out of bed. A cup of warm milk with brandy would help her sleep. The timbers in the old house creaked and groaned, settling in the cool, predawn air as she made her way down the stairs to the kitchen.

She touched the switch and the lights flickered on. A shiny new fridge and stove with matching stainless-steel dishwasher and microwave gleamed under the bright fluorescent lights. What had once been a dark and dreary room filled with outdated appliances, was now a bright, cheerful, modern kitchen. Some things in the old house had changed.

Crossing to the fridge, she took out a bottle of milk and poured some into a pot that she set on the stove to heat. Now for the brandy.

She turned on the overhead light in the pantry, expecting to see the shelves filled with jars of homemade, canned peaches, tomatoes, jam, green beans, pickles, and boxes of dry goods. She blinked. The pantry was empty. A thin layer of dust covered the two remaining jars of preserves. *What the heck?* Vivian had been a firm believer in preparing for any number of disasters, and she'd always ordered the current cook to stock the pantry with enough food to withstand weeks, if not months, of forced isolation. Another example of her aunt's need for control.

A vision of Vivian's gaunt face and stick-like figure rose before her, and with the image, a frisson of unease trickled along Carrie Ann's spine. Again, she shook off her worry. Whatever was going on with Vivian wasn't her concern.

Hopefully, some things hadn't changed. She stood

on a stool and reached to the back of the top shelf and grabbed the bottle of brandy sitting right where Leland had always kept it hidden. Walking back into the kitchen, she poured brandy into a cup and added steaming milk. Leaning against the counter, she raised the mug and sipped, sighing as the doctored milk coursed down her throat, leaving a trail of warmth in its wake.

The kitchen door swung open and she jumped, slopping some of the hot drink on the floor.

"Oh, Carrie Ann, it's you. I saw the light on and wondered who was up burning the midnight oil." Leland smiled at her.

"You're still awake?" Other than a brief conversation when she'd first arrived, the last time she'd seen Leland had been when he'd driven her to the clinic twelve years ago.

"I don't sleep like I used to." He shrugged. "Too much on my mind, I guess." He pointed at the bottle on the counter. "I see you found my secret stash. Is there enough for me?"

Nodding, she ripped off several sheets of paper towel from the roll on the counter and crouched down and wiped up the spilled milk on the floor.

Leland poured brandy and hot milk into a mug. "You're looking well."

"I'm doing okay."

"I'm glad. How's your daughter? Bonnie, isn't it?"

She hesitated. Anything she said would be passed on to Vivian, but the genuine concern in his faded blue eyes softened her resolve. "She's great. Happy, smart, and fearless." Her pride in her beautiful daughter warmed her.

"If she's anything like her mother, she must be something special." His smile widened. "Vivian and I would love to meet her."

She snorted. "Yeah, right. Vivian's the soul of motherly love."

"She's changed, Carrie Ann. She's not the same woman you knew."

I'll bet. Carrie Ann didn't say the words aloud, knowing they would only hurt him. Leland had always defended Vivian, never seeming to see the harsh, cruel streak that ran through his wife.

Silence settled over them, broken only by the steady ticking of a clock on the wall and the hum of the refrigerator.

"It's good to have you home." Leland's deep baritone was rough. "Your aunt's happy you're here. Seeing you again means a lot to her."

She choked on a swallow of milk. "I don't believe you."

Leland opened his mouth to say something, but took another sip of his drink instead.

Again the incessant ticktock of the clock filled the room.

"I was surprised to see McAllister." He finally broke the thick silence. "He hasn't been back in town for years."

"Declan doesn't live in Cooper's Ridge?"

Her uncle shook his head, his short, silver hair catching the light. "He moved away ten or so years ago."

Whenever she thought of Declan McAllister—and she didn't think of him, not ever—but if her thoughts did happen to wander to him, she pictured him living in

Cooper's Ridge. He'd always said he'd never leave, not until he proved how wrong everyone was about him. "I can't believe he moved away."

"His circumstances were challenging, to say the least. A few months after you left town, his mother killed herself."

She inhaled a quick breath.

"Sad, but you know how she was, always locked in her bedroom, drinking herself into a stupor. God knows what crazy concoction of drugs she used." He sighed. "One night she took too many sleeping pills. The pills and the booze killed her. Declan found her." He scrubbed his hand over his chin. "Old man McAllister smashed his car into a tree a week later. The coroner said his blood alcohol level was double the legal limit."

She fought to swallow, her mouth an arid desert. "He's dead too?"

Leland nodded.

She blinked back the sting of tears. Declan must have been devastated, losing both parents so close together. Even though his relationship with his mother and father had been strained, they were the only family he had.

"Between the accusations he was a murderer and his parents' deaths, the stress was too much. Like the coward he is, he fled Cooper's Ridge. Far as I know, he didn't tell anyone he was going. Slunk out in the middle of the night. One day he was here, and the next he was gone."

"Things must have been bad."

"After…" He seemed to be searching for the right words. "After everything that happened, folks around here made his life pretty miserable."

"Surely, once he was cleared of the charges, things were better. I mean, once people knew he was innocent, they stopped harassing him."

Leland shook his head.

"I don't understand. Why not?"

"When Skye Lawrence's murder wasn't solved and no one was found guilty, people took to blaming McAllister again. You know how everyone always said he was a bad seed, exactly like his old man."

"But that's not true. Declan's nothing like his father." She bit her tongue to stop the flow of protestations. Declan could fight his own battles. He didn't need her defending him. But she couldn't help adding, "Declan's innocent. The sheriff didn't find any real evidence to prove he hurt Skye."

"People react strongly when they're frightened." Leland set his cup on the table and met her gaze. "As far as I'm concerned, they had good reason to be afraid. He murdered that poor girl. I'm only sorry we couldn't prove it."

"It wasn't for lack of trying." Bitterness filled each word. "You did everything in your power to have him convicted."

"I had to, Carrie Ann. I'm a judge. My job is to protect the citizens of this county from dangerous criminals."

"Declan was innocent. He didn't do anything to Skye. Besides, he's innocent until proven guilty. Isn't that what you always told me?"

He smoothed the palm of his hand over his hair. "We've been through all this before. Let's not do it again. I hope we get a conviction this time. I intend to do my best to see the bastard pays for what he did."

She set her cup down with a clatter. *This time?* She opened her mouth, but he raised his hand and stopped her before she could get a word out.

"I don't want to talk about this now. Not on your first night back." He stood and took his empty cup to the sink. "Besides, it's high time I went to bed. I have a full day in court tomorrow. Good night, Carrie Ann."

"Wait." She jumped to her feet, shoving back her chair. Her hand brushed against her mug, and the cup fell, landing with a loud crash on the tile floor, splintering into dozens of tiny shards. She glanced up, a plea on her lips.

The room was empty. He'd gone.

Chapter 3

The next morning, Carrie Ann took a deep breath and braced herself to confront her aunt. Her stomach fluttered at the thought of what was in the box of her mother's effects, forgotten all these years. She knew so little about her parents. Vivian had always refused to discuss them.

A note taped to the fridge informed her Vivian had already left for her clothing boutique. Leland was at the courthouse. She could search the house, but Vivian wouldn't have left the box somewhere she could easily find it. Her aunt would demand, and receive, her pound of flesh before she handed over Carrie Ann's mother's things.

She poured a cup of coffee and reached for the newspaper folded on the counter. The *Cooper's Ridge Chronicle,* published biweekly, was filled with more local gossip than news. Skimming through the pages, she learned two high school classmates had recently given birth, one to a set of twins. A new restaurant had opened, specializing in authentic Asian cuisine. *Gotta love small town papers.*

Amid the results of the recent Fall Fair baking and canning competitions and an ad for Buckner's Pharmacy was a short article with the headline *'Old Murder Case Revisited'.* Her hands shook, rattling the paper, making the printed words almost impossible to read.

According to the article, the long-unsolved murder of eighteen-year-old Skye Lawrence was being re-examined by county officials. Judge Leland Winters was spearheading the inquiry. The article speculated this new investigation would result in the killer of the pretty, high school senior finally being brought to justice.

She clutched the counter, her heart pounding. This was what Leland meant last night. He was involved in the new investigation into Skye's murder.

A knock sounded on the kitchen door.

Her first thought was to ignore it. No one knew she was in town. The person at the door was looking for Vivian or Leland. Another, louder knocking changed her mind. She shoved away from the counter and walked on wobbly legs to the back door, her mind still reeling with what she'd read in the paper.

A tall, lanky man stood on the walkway dangling a set of keys in his hand. A lock of greasy, dark hair escaped a sweat-stained ball cap and fell over his brow. The name 'Ted' was stitched on the chest pocket of his blue, grease-stained coveralls. "Mornin', ma'am. I got yer car." The odor of stale tobacco smoke oozed out of his pores and seeped from his clothing, swirling in the air around him.

"My car?" She blinked, trying to focus. Leland had told her Declan was having her car towed to a garage to have the tire repaired.

"Yep. Tire's all fixed. Mind you, if I was you, I wouldn't plan on doin' much travelin'. If you don't mind me sayin', those tires you got on that there car are ready for the dump." He handed her the keys.

"How much do I owe you?"

"Nothin'."

She wrinkled her brow, anger starting to burn. "Wait a minute. Did Declan McAllister pay you for the repairs?"

"Yep. He was in first thing this mornin' and paid fer the work then." The man scratched his head under his cap. "I gotta say, that McAllister fella is a heck of a lot nicer than I thought he'd be. I mean, everyone in town says he's a killer, but he was downright friendly." He hawked a gob of phlegm into the bed of geraniums beside the door. "And he didn't dicker about the charge either. In my book, that says a lot about a man right there."

"A killer? Who says he's a killer?" She gulped. *Did the people in town still think Declan had murdered Skye?*

"Darn near everyone, ma'am." Once again he scratched his scalp. "I weren't livin' here when the murder happened and all, mind, but I heard 'bout it." His eyes brightened. "You know him, right? I mean he paid for yer tire and all. You two must be friends. Tell me, did he do it? Did he kill that poor gal?"

She gulped, struggling to swallow. *Did he kill that poor gal?* The damning words clamored through her mind. This suspicion is what Declan had faced all these years. No wonder he'd left town. She opened her mouth to defend him, to tell this oaf Declan was innocent, but thought better of it. Did she really want to get involved? Was she willing to risk everything to protect Declan?

Anything she said to the mechanic would be repeated and exaggerated around town. "Look." She eyed his nametag. "Look, Ted, I don't know why Mr.

McAllister paid for the repairs to my tire. He shouldn't have." She reached in her pocket and withdrew her wallet. "I'll pay you."

Ted spat another wad onto the poor flowers. "No, way, ma'am. I ain't takin' yer money. If you've got a problem with the guy, work it out with him. As far as I'm concerned, I've done my job and been paid fair and square."

Damn. She hadn't been in town twenty-four hours and already she was indebted to Declan. Not going to happen. She'd hunt him down and give him back his damn money, as well as a piece of her mind.

"Um, ma'am, I figure there's somethin' you oughta know." Ted shifted from one foot to the other.

"What is it?"

"I promised Mr. McAllister I wouldn't say nothin' to you, but that don't sit right with me. I mean, the way I see things, you need to know, seein' as yer the one drivin' the car and all."

"Know what?"

He rubbed his hand over his chin, the rasp of stubble loud in the morning air. "The flat tire y'all had?"

She nodded.

"Well, you see, ma'am, it weren't no ordinary puncture."

"It wasn't?"

He shook his head. "I wouldn't likely have noticed if that McAllister fella hadn't told me to look fer it, but once I had the tire off yer car and had a good look, I seen the truth plain as day."

"What?" She tapped the toe of her shoe on the tile floor. Would his rambling never end? "What did you see?"

"The hole in yer tire? It weren't caused by no nail." He met her gaze. "I found a bullet hole in the sidewall."

She gaped. "Someone shot my tire? Are you certain?"

"Sure looks like it, ma'am."

"And Declan, I mean, Mr. McAllister, he knows this?"

"He's the one told me to look fer the bullet hole."

"And he told you not to tell me?"

"He didn't want to scare you none." Ted shrugged. "I thought it better you know, but sweet Jesus, look what I've gone and done. Yer shakin' worse than a spring lamb 'bout to be butchered. Maybe I shoulda listened to him. Maybe he was right."

"What..." She gulped. "What about the police? Do they know?"

He shrugged. "Doubt it. Look, you don't need to worry none, ma'am. Most likely some farmer was shootin' at a coyote and the bullet got away on 'im. That's all. Happens from time to time round these parts."

A chill settled over her. *Someone shot at her car last night!* Only Vivian and Leland had known she was coming back to town yesterday. Even if someone else had known, no one could have predicted she'd take the old shortcut through vast stretches of farmland and forest instead of the paved Interstate to Cooper's Ridge.

But someone had known. Someone had hidden on the lonely stretch of road waiting for her to drive by. A quiver of unease rippled along her spine. Someone had been there. *Declan* was there. In the next breath, she brushed her disquiet aside. The puncture in her tire was an accident. Like Ted said, a farmer shooting at coyotes. She rubbed the goose bumps on her arms.

"Look, ma'am. I reckon I shoulda kept my trap shut. I sure as heck didn't mean to scare you none."

She almost laughed. *Really? And he didn't think telling her someone had shot at her car would frighten her?* "It's okay, Ted. You're probably right. I'm sure it was an accident, but thanks for telling me."

"That's the way I see things." He shuffled his feet and scratched his head again. "Well, if that's all, ma'am. I reckon I gotta go. You get those tires replaced before you take a trip, you hear? Come see me, and I'll give you a real good deal."

She closed the door, her head throbbing. *Someone had shot at her car.* The words rang like an ominous refrain through her mind. Why had Declan kept this information from her? Even if the shooting was an accident, she deserved to know.

She jumped at another knock on the door. *What now?* She opened the door expecting to see Ted's oil-stained face.

Instead, a short, wiry man wearing a dark suit and a bright, yellow, power tie grinned at her, exposing a row of gleaming white teeth. "So, it's true. You are back." He chuckled. "Damn, but the Cooper's Ridge gossip brigade is bang on. Nothing gets by them."

"Sheldon Dubrowski?"

He nodded, beaming as his gaze swept over her. "You look damned good, girl."

She couldn't say the same about her old schoolmate. His rust-colored hair receded from his high forehead. Gone were his mouthful of metal and face plastered with an unflattering mix of freckles and pimples, replaced by deep grooves radiating from the corners of his eyes and bracketing his wide mouth.

"Can I come in?" He gestured at the partially open door.

She hesitated. Sheldon had been Declan's best friend in high school. She wondered if he still was.

His blue eyes drilled into hers, the grin fading, but never leaving his face.

Resigned, she breathed deep. "Come on in."

He strolled across the kitchen and dragged out a chair from the table, sat down, and studied the room. "Do you realize this is the first time I've been inside this house?"

"We didn't hang out here, remember?" She shrugged. "My aunt—"

"Ah, yes, your aunt. How is the old boot?"

She couldn't help chuckling. "Can I get you something? Coffee? Tea?"

He shook his head. "I have to get to work. I just wanted to stop by and say hello."

"You heard I was here?" How did he know? Had Declan told him he'd seen her?

"Don't tell me you've forgotten the local gossip mill." He chuckled. "Folks around here knew you were coming home before even you did."

She shook her head. One of the many things she didn't miss. Her Seattle neighbors hardly knew her name, much less cared what she did.

"So, tell me, why are you back?" His eyebrows rose, and he leaned closer, his whipcord-lean body bristling with curiosity. "Now, after all these years?"

"My aunt asked me to come home."

"Ordered you, more likely." His sharp eyes

narrowed. "I wonder why?"

"You tell me. You know more of what's going on than I do." The last thing she wanted was to give him any more fodder to pass on to the town gossips.

"Declan's back too."

"Is he?" She fought to keep her expression impassive. *So Declan hadn't sent him.* Sheldon didn't know about their encounter last night.

"Have you seen him?"

She shook her head, not sure why she lied.

He smirked. "Why would you? It's not as if he'd call you, not after the way things ended between you two."

She grabbed her cup of coffee and gulped down the dregs, shuddering at the cold, bitter taste, but needing the fortification.

He took her hand, holding it between his two warm, moist ones. "Whatever the reason you're back, I'm glad. If you need anything, anything at all, don't hesitate to call."

She yanked her hand away, resisting the urge to wipe her palm on her pants. "Thanks, but I'm not staying long. I'm hoping to leave town tomorrow."

"That's too bad." He shook his head. "Say, have you heard I'm working with my dad? Seems I like accounting." He mock bowed. "Sheldon Dubrowski, Certified Public Accountant, at your service." His mouth twisted. "Who knew? What are you doing these days? I hear you live in Seattle. Are you married? Do you have any kids? Come on, tell me all your news. I'm dying to know." His keen eyes watched her.

Yeah, right. Like she'd risk telling him anything. "How do you know I live in Seattle?"

He shrugged. "I heard it somewhere. Is it true?"

Instead of answering, she said, "We all change, Sheldon. Life changes us. We get older and grow up."

"It's the pits, isn't it?" He rose and walked to the door but halted with his hand on the knob. "By the way, did you hear the news?"

"News?"

"I thought Leland would have told you. I assumed it was the reason you were back."

"What are you talking about?" Her heart started to pound. She knew what he was going to say.

"They've reopened Skye's murder investigation."

"I read the article in the paper this morning." She fought to keep her voice calm, not wanting to give him the pleasure of seeing how rattled she was.

"Exciting news, isn't it? Declan's back in town, and he's hired some hotshot private detective to look into the old case. He's determined to clear his name. I don't blame him. Man, the way the people in this town talk about him, you'd think he was already tried and convicted." He swelled with importance. "I'm meeting Declan later. He's going to tell me all about the investigation."

She clasped her hands together to stop their shaking.

"It would be great if they finally found out who murdered Skye." His eyes shone. "Of course, unlike most people in this town, I've always known Declan was innocent."

She opened her mouth to speak, but words failed her.

"I know you two had your problems, and you left town when all the trouble blew up," he continued, "but surely you don't think he's guilty. Do you? I mean, you knew him better than anyone."

Her paralysis released its hold. "Look, I have to get ready. I'm meeting Vivian."

A dozen heartbeats passed as he searched her face. "I have to go too," he finally said. "Money to make, you know?" He gripped her hand in a tight squeeze. "Nice to have you back. Let's get together before you leave. It'll be like old times. Call me." With a wave, he left, closing the door behind him.

She sagged in a chair listening to his retreating steps on the brick-lined path. A car door slammed, and an engine rumbled to life.

Call me. Not likely. Why had he come? His visit wasn't just to reconnect with an old friend. He'd been Declan's friend, not hers. No, he was here on a fishing expedition. The questions were—why, and who'd sent him?

Chapter 4

Carrie Ann opened the heavy glass door to Vivian's small boutique and stepped inside. Rich, perfumed air mingled with the muted strains of classical music. A pair of well-dressed, older women looked over racks of over-priced, designer dresses, blouses, and slacks.

The sales clerk bustled over, a smile pasted on her middle-aged face. Her smile faltered when she took in Carrie Ann's faded jeans and scuffed leather boots. "Good afternoon. May I help you?"

"No, thanks." Carrie Ann waved the woman off. "I'm here to see Vivian."

Once again, the sales clerk perused Carrie Ann from head to toe. Her mouth pursed as if she'd sucked on a lemon. "I'm afraid *Mrs. Winters* is busy. Let me check and see if she has a moment for you."

"Don't bother. I know the way."

The clerk's pucker tightened, but she didn't try and stop her as Carrie Ann wound her way through circular racks of clothes and artfully posed mannequins to the back of the store.

When Carrie Ann was a teenager, Vivian had made her wear some of the clothes she sold in her high-priced ladies' clothing boutique. Carrie Ann's face burned at the memory. The styles were conservative and matronly, far too old for an awkward girl trying to fit in

33

with her peers. It had been one more bone of contention between her and Vivian.

Past the dressing rooms was a small, recessed door with 'Vivian Morgenstern Winters' etched in elaborate calligraphy on a discreet, brass plaque. Without bothering to knock, she opened the door.

Vivian sat behind an antique, gold-trimmed, French provincial desk clicking at a computer keyboard and frowning at the screen. Her gaunt face lit up when Carrie Ann stepped through the door. "Carrie Ann, how nice to see you. Come in and sit down, my dear." She indicated an elegant, fragile chair more appropriate for a boudoir than an office.

Carrie Ann sat as directed. The opulent office hadn't changed. Four copies of paintings by Monet, with their depictions of vibrant, flowered fields and French countryside, provided a splash of color against the cool green walls. The floral, cloying scent of Vivian's favorite perfume filled the air.

Squirming on the uncomfortable chair like she was fifteen again, waiting to be scolded for some misdeed, Carrie Ann tried to take the offensive. "I want my mother's effects." She scowled at the quaver in her voice.

Vivian's sharp gaze swept over her. "You're pale, my dear. Is something wrong? Did you read the newspaper I left on the kitchen counter for you? Is that why you're so upset?"

"I saw the article on Skye Lawrence's murder investigation, if that's what you mean."

"What do you think?"

"I don't think anything." The lie slipped from Carrie Ann's lips. It was becoming a habit. "Why should I? Skye Lawrence's murder investigation has nothing to do with me. Not anymore."

"Don't play games with me, Carrie Ann. You never were a good liar." Vivian's long, red nails tapped on the desk. "I know how much you cared for Declan, how much you still care."

Carrie Ann blew out a breath and gave up all pretext of disinterest. "Is it true? Is the sheriff looking into the case again?"

Vivian nodded. "Leland is in charge of the effort. It turns out, we might have been wrong all these years."

"You mean someone other than Declan was responsible for Skye's murder. I always knew he wasn't guilty."

"You may have, but most people in town don't believe he's innocent. Declan's returned to town and hired a private investigator in an attempt to prove his innocence." Vivian sipped water from a crystal goblet on her desk and dabbed at her lips with a lace handkerchief she'd tugged from her sleeve. "If this private investigator finds anything, and the evidence holds up, everyone will know Declan's innocent once and for all."

Carrie Ann blinked. When Skye's beaten and bloodied body had been discovered, circumstantial evidence had linked Declan to Skye and the crime scene; enough to substantiate the sheriff's suspicions. Declan had been hauled in for questioning. Nothing had come of the interrogation, and he'd been released after spending a night in the local jail. No thanks to Vivian and Leland, who'd done everything in their power to convince people of his guilt. "I imagine the thought of him being cleared pisses you off."

Vivian flinched as if Carrie Ann had struck her. "On the contrary, my dear. I intend to do whatever I can to help him prove his innocence."

"I don't believe this." The words exploded out of her. "I always knew Declan didn't hurt Skye, but you were so certain he was guilty, you did everything short of sending him to the gas chamber. Now you're telling me you think he's innocent?"

Vivian dabbed her forehead with her hankie. "Come on, Carrie Ann. You really can't blame me. The McAllisters were bad news. You know as well as I what they were like. The whole town knew. His mother locked herself in her bedroom, living on a steady diet of prescription drugs and alcohol." She inhaled a shaky breath. "His father was a drunk, and when he wasn't drinking, he was sitting in jail for one petty crime or another. Declan's reputation wasn't much better. He had a temper like his father. Look at all the fistfights in which he was involved. Seems to me he was suspended from school for fighting several times over the years."

Carrie Ann jerked upright, ready to defend Declan against Vivian's unfair accusations. Declan didn't have a temper, at least, not one fueled by alcohol. His anger only erupted when he was protecting someone. But she pressed her lips together and kept silent. What was the point? Vivian wouldn't believe her.

"I couldn't in good conscience allow you to become involved with a loose cannon like Declan." Vivian inclined her head. "You were my responsibility, and you were just a child." Her hand shook as she patted at the moisture gleaming on her ghostly face. "When that poor girl was found murdered, and Declan was the prime suspect, I had to ensure your safety. I didn't want you to end up like her. I thought if he were locked in jail, you'd be safe." She turned pleading eyes on Carrie Ann. "What I did was wrong, I see that now, but I did it for you."

"Wrong?" Carrie Ann glared at her. "I left Cooper's Ridge because of you, because of what you did." In their determination to railroad Declan, Vivian and Leland had hammered at her night and day trying to convince her of his guilt, until she didn't know which way was up. After a while, head pounding, exhausted, sick at heart, she hadn't been able to stomach anymore of their pressure. She couldn't fight them and everyone else in town, not with her world falling apart.

"I thought I was doing the right thing." Vivian's voice was a mere whisper.

"All you've ever cared about was what your prune-faced, tight-assed friends thought. You didn't give a damn about me. I was an embarrassment you wanted to get rid of." Carrie Ann gripped the arms of her chair, her nails digging into the carved wood.

Tears streamed down Vivian's face, marring the perfect makeup, revealing the ravages of age. "I wanted what was best for you."

Carrie Ann's anger raged. "All these years Declan's had to live with a dark cloud hanging over him, knowing everyone in town thinks he's a murderer. Hell, their unfair suspicions drove him away from the only home he had." She glared at Vivian. "You played a big part in the way he was treated."

Vivian blew her nose with shaking hands. "I'm not proud of what I did, but I'm trying to make up for my actions." She wiped her eyes and met Carrie Ann's gaze. "I'd like you to help him."

"You want *me* to help him?" Carrie Ann rubbed her forehead trying to quell the clamoring alarm bells. "I get it now. This is the reason you wouldn't give me my mother's possessions unless I returned to Cooper's Ridge. You want me to help you ease your guilt over the way you screwed up Declan's life. I bet you don't even have a box."

"Of course, I have a box. I told you. Your mother must have stored her things in my attic before she left home years before the fire. Mary Beth found the box last month when she was cleaning."

"Where is this box then? Show it to me."

"I will, but first, you need to listen." Vivian rose and tottered around the desk until she stood over Carrie Ann. She grasped her niece's hand. "What Leland and I did to Declan was wrong, but you were wrong, too."

Carrie Ann yanked her hand away. "What the hell are you talking about? I didn't do anything to him."

"You were as much a part of this as Leland and I were."

"You're wrong." Carrie Ann spluttered. "I didn't try and have him convicted for a crime he didn't commit."

"No, but you left immediately after he was taken in for questioning. Your leaving town was as good as announcing to everyone you thought he was guilty."

"But—"

"I realize mitigating circumstances were involved, my dear, but the people in this town saw your actions as a confirmation of Declan's guilt."

Silence filled the small room.

Carrie Ann's head throbbed. *"Mitigating circumstances?"* All her anger and resentment spewed out in those two words. "That's what you call it?"

"The point is," Vivian continued as if Carrie Ann hadn't spoken, "Declan needs help. He's lived with the taint of guilt far too long. We must assist him in whatever way we can."

Carrie Ann jumped to her feet. The tiny chair skittered across the polished hardwood floor and struck the wall with a crash. "Then *you* help him."

Vivian stumbled back and sagged against the desk. "Believe me, I've tried. When I heard he'd come back to town, I tried to contact him, but he refused to talk to me. He won't accept my help, but he will accept yours."

Carrie Ann thought of her encounter with Declan on the dark road and shuddered. "What makes you think he'd accept my help? He despises me."

"Yet he helped you when you had a flat tire." Vivian sighed. "You must realize he doesn't hate you, my dear. Declan loved you far too much to ever hate you. He may be angry with you, but hate—" she shook her head "—never. You are the best one to help him. He needs you."

Carrie Ann frowned. Vivian had always disliked Declan. Hell, she'd destroyed his life. Now she was supposed to think Vivian had had a change of heart and wanted to help? "What's in this for you?"

"Is it so hard to believe I want to make amends?"

"Yes," she said simply.

"Whatever you think of me isn't important right now. Declan needs a friend, someone he can trust; someone who knows he's innocent."

"He has Sheldon Dubrowski."

Vivian waved away the suggestion. "He needs

you."

Carrie Ann shook her head. "Whatever was between Declan McAllister and me was a long time ago. I'm sorry for what he's been through. I'm glad they're reopening the case. I hope he can prove his innocence, but there's nothing between us. There never will be." She inhaled a deep breath. "Now, may I see my mother's things? I'd like to get back to Seattle as soon as possible."

Vivian watched her with piercing eyes. "I'd hoped Bonnie would be with you."

"You can't be serious. This is the last place I'd bring her. She doesn't know anything about you, Leland, or Cooper's Ridge, and she never will."

Vivian's face paled. "I'd like to meet her one day."

"If you'd had your way, Bonnie wouldn't exist." Carrie Ann's eyes burned with unshed tears. "You have no right to be part of her life, no right at all."

Vivian looked as if she'd aged ten years in the past few minutes. Deep lines carved across her forehead. Her shoulders hunched forward, shrinking her emaciated frame. She stepped toward Carrie Ann, but stumbled and clutched the desk to stop her fall.

A stab of alarm struck Carrie Ann. "Are you okay?"

With visible effort, Vivian straightened, squaring her shoulders into a parody of her usual rigid bearing. "Careful, my dear, you almost sound like you care."

Anger blazed through Carrie Ann once again. "I've had enough of this *family* reunion. Hand over my mother's possessions."

Vivian raised a skeletal arm and pointed at a cardboard shoebox sitting on a shelf in the corner of the office.

"That's the box you found?"

Vivian nodded.

Carrie Ann walked over to the small, rectangular box. The original white of the cardboard had dulled to a soft yellowish-gray. One corner was crushed, part of the lid torn. She ran a finger across the top, and the accumulated dust of years stuck to her skin. She lifted the box off the shelf, surprised at the weight. Her hand shook as she raised the lid and peered inside.

A stack of Polaroid photographs, their once vibrant colors faded, lay on top. Beneath them, a small book with its red, faux-leather cover cracked, and the tiny, brass lock tarnished. Her mother's name, 'Caroline Jane Morgenstern,' was inscribed on the cover in faded, gold-colored letters. She reached for the diary, anxious to read her mother's thoughts, but stopped.

Vivian watched her, a faint smile on her haggard face. "I wanted you to have her things. You have so little of hers."

Carrie Ann placed the lid back on the shoebox and wiped her stinging eyes. No matter what Vivian had done in the past, she'd given her this box of her mother's personal possessions. She wouldn't forget the simple act of kindness by her aunt. "Thank you. This means a lot to me."

Vivian nodded, tears glinting in her faded eyes.

Carrie Ann breathed deeply. Time to leave, but she had one more task to complete before she put Cooper's Ridge behind her forever. "Do you know where Declan's staying while he's in town?"

"I've heard he's at the Blue Horizon Motel." Vivian beamed. "Does this mean you're going to help him?"

"No. I have something of his I want to return before I leave town." She headed toward the door.

"You need to tell him the truth," Vivian called after her. "He has a right to know."

Carrie Ann stopped and turned and faced Vivian. "You were the one who convinced me to keep quiet. Don't you remember?"

"I remember, all right. I remember every sad detail. I want to make amends…to both of you."

Once again Carrie Ann's anger flared to life, and she flung open the door.

"Either you tell him, Carrie Ann, or I will."

She slammed the door behind her and rushed through the store, almost knocking over a rack of those dreadful, Parisian-designed dresses in her need to escape. She hurried out the front door, her breath rasping in her chest.

Hurtling down the sidewalk, she clutched the shoebox, the rush of traffic on the street, and the people who stopped to stare as she passed, a blur.

****

Carrie Ann turned onto the driveway of Vivian and Leland's stately Colonial home and switched off the car's engine. She grabbed the shoebox from the seat beside her and climbed out of the car. Time to put the past behind her and return to her life with Bonnie in Seattle.

"Ms. Hetherington?" A man stepped out of the shadows of the oak trees lining the driveway. His broad shoulders strained a black, knee-length raincoat. Salt and pepper hair receded from his high forehead. His cold eyes watched her with an unsettling intensity.

Backing toward the security of her car, she asked, "Yes?"

"I'd like to talk to you." He held out a massive ham of a hand. "Jessup Caruthers."

Uncertain whether she should shake his hand or run for help, she hesitated, but her innate politeness kicked in, and she nervously placed her hand in his.

His grasp was surprisingly gentle. "We need to talk." He released her hand and stepped back.

"We do? About what?"

"Declan McAllister."

"Declan?" Her stomach knotted.

"I'm sure you're aware the local authorities are re-examining Skye Lawrence's murder. I'm a private investigator." He reached into his coat and drew out a slim, black wallet, flipped it open and revealed a photograph of him on a state-authorized private investigator's license. "Mr. McAllister hired me to look into the case."

Her fingers dug into the sides of the cardboard shoebox. "I'm afraid I can't help you. I told the police everything I knew twelve years ago when they questioned me." She stepped around his bulk, moving toward the front door of the house.

"Don't you want to know what really happened?" He followed her onto the porch and stood behind, his bulk looming over her.

Her hand shook as she fumbled with the key. "I told you. I can't help you." The key slipped from her numb fingers and fell on the porch.

Caruthers bent down and grabbed the key. His eyes bore into hers.

"May...may I have the key, please?" She hated the

tremble in her voice.

"I can't force you to talk to me, Ms. Hetherington, but if you care anything at all for Declan McAllister, you'll help me clear his name once and for all."

"Please, leave me alone." All she wanted was for him to stop regarding her with those cold, accusing eyes and leave.

"Declan was right." He stared at her like a hawk watching a mouse. "You wanted him found guilty."

"No, I—"

"You were so angry he dumped you and took another girl to the high school prom, you lied to the police to get back at him." He leaned closer, forcing her back a step. "Isn't it time you grew up?"

She shook her head, wanting him to stop, but he lobbed another barb.

"You made up the story you told the sheriff." He sneered. "What's the saying? Hell hath no fury like a woman scorned?"

She willed away the imminent tears.

"Tell me, after what you did to him, how can you live with yourself? Do you have any idea the hell he's been through? Even if you don't care about Declan McAllister, the real killer's walked free all these years. Doesn't Skye Lawrence deserve justice?"

Tears filled her eyes and leaked down her face. She hadn't lied to the sheriff. She'd wanted to, but not to incriminate Declan—to protect him.

"Come on, Carrie Ann. It's not too late to tell the truth." His gaze tunneled into hers. "What did you really see when you drove out to the old farm the night Skye Lawrence was murdered?"

"I told the truth."

He snorted.

"I told the sheriff what I saw." Tears blocked her throat. "I knew what I had to say would hurt Declan, but I—"

"You what?"

She swallowed. Vivian and Leland had forced her to tell the sheriff what she'd seen. She hadn't been strong enough to stand up to them, not then, not with what was going on in her life. Even though she knew she was casting guilt on the man she loved, she'd told the sheriff exactly what she'd seen that night. Her damning statement had been the basis for Declan's arrest and subsequent interrogation. The townspeople's suspicions of him were her fault.

If she'd kept quiet... She shook her head. Too much time had passed for regrets. Besides, more than Declan's tarnished reputation was at stake now, much more. Wiping her tears, she faced Caruthers. "I'd like you to leave." She held out her hand for the key.

Seconds ticked by as she waited, pinned by the force of his steely gaze.

After a dozen heartbeats, he nodded. "This isn't over. I'll be back." He dropped the key into her palm and strode across the porch and down the steps. A car door slammed, followed by the roar of a motor and the squeal of tires as he drove away.

The sharp edges of the key dug into her palm. Her legs wobbled. She staggered over to an Adirondack chair and collapsed onto the hard, wooden surface.

"Are you all right, Carrie Ann? Did he hurt you? Should I call the sheriff?"

Swiping her damp face, Carrie Ann met the inquisitive eyes of the woman hovering over her. "Mrs.

Higgensdorf." Her heart sank.

Mary Higgensdorf had lived next door for as long as Carrie Ann could remember. Her husband had died years ago, and ever since his untimely death, she'd lived for gossip...the juicier the better. The old woman's pudgy cheeks were flushed, and her button nose twitched with excitement. "Are you sure you're okay, dear? It looked to me like that man was threatening you. Who is he? Is he the private detective Declan McAllister hired? He has a lot of nerve coming here and bothering you, though, I've heard he's been questioning people all over town." Her beady-eyed gaze raced over Carrie Ann.

Carrie Ann steadied her breathing. The last thing she wanted was to give Mary Higgensdorf any fuel for the grapevine. "I'm fine. It's nothing to worry about."

The old woman's mouth tightened, her red lipstick bleeding into the innumerable, tiny lines radiating from her lips. "It's wonderful you're back. Your aunt has missed you something fierce. I was telling Louise Jorgensen down at the Handy Mart the other day, it was a real tragedy you left town so long ago and never returned." Her bosom heaved, and her cheeks flushed.

A fierce pounding hit Carrie Ann's temples, worsening with each word the woman uttered, like nails pounding the lid of a coffin.

"But, my dear." Mary Higgensdorf barely paused for breath. "I must tell you, I couldn't have been more shocked than when I saw you get out of Declan McAllister's truck the other night. You could have blown me away with a breath. Is he the reason you're back in town? Are you here to help him in his foolish quest to prove his innocence?" She made a loud tsking sound. "I mean, I ask you, does anyone really think he's innocent?" She peered at Carrie Ann. "He may have escaped prosecution, but we all know he killed that poor girl."

Past experience had taught Carrie Ann the futility of reasoning with the interfering, old woman. Once she set her mind on something, she was a force to be reckoned with. But no matter Carrie Ann's feelings for him, Declan didn't deserve to be treated like a criminal. "The sheriff must think he has a good reason to re-examine the case."

Mrs. Higgensdorf set her hands on her ample hips. "Come on, Carrie Ann. That boy was always trouble, like his father and his father before him. Those McAllisters have always been trouble." Her nose wrinkled in disdain. "He did it, mark my words. Declan McAllister murdered Skye Lawrence as sure as I'm standing here. You ask me, he should be in jail, not living the high life in Dallas. Now he's back in town, no one's safe. Not while he's walking around free and clear." She shuddered. "I swear I haven't slept a wink since he showed up."

Unable to stomach anymore, Carrie Ann jumped up and faced the old woman. "Declan *is* innocent." Her voice gained strength as she vented her outrage. "People like you drove him away. You hounded him and hounded him with your baseless accusations until he couldn't stand the hatred anymore. And why?" She sneered. "Because his dad was a drunk? Declan's nothing like his father. He never was."

Mrs. Higgensdorf stared at her, her eyes bulging, her mouth opening and closing like a fish gasping for air. For once, she didn't have anything to say. She blinked, her thin eyelashes fluttering on her now-pale cheeks.

The pungent aroma of fried onions and boiled cabbage assailed Carrie Ann when she stepped closer. "Go home, Mrs. Higgensdorf. Lock your door, close your curtains, and stop sticking your nose into other people's business."

The old woman patted Carrie Ann's shoulder. "Oh, my dear, I'm so sorry. I didn't realize. You still love him, don't you?" She shook her head. "You foolish girl. He broke your heart once. Don't let him do it again."

"Goodbye, Mrs. Higgensdorf." Carrie Ann huffed out a weary sigh and turned toward the door.

Mrs. Higgensdorf, her voice strident, called to her. "What's in the box, Carrie Ann? Is it your mother's? I heard Vivian found some of her effects. Who'd have thought after all these years—"

"Go home, Mrs. Higgensdorf." Carrie Ann unlocked the front door and stepped into the hushed quiet of the big house. She closed the door behind her, leaned against the solid, cool surface, and breathed.

Why hadn't she kept her mouth shut? Mary Higgensdorf was probably already on the phone spreading the word Carrie Ann Hetherington had come back to town to help Declan McAllister prove his innocence. Before the day was out, the entire town would have her sleeping with him. As if that would ever happen.

Chapter 5

Declan lifted his soda and drank, grimacing at the saccharine-sweet taste. He leaned against the shiny, cracked, vinyl back of the bench seat. The High Five Bar and Pool Hall was busy for a Thursday night. Most of the booths were filled, and a crowd stood at the bar demanding service from the lone bartender. Smoke hung in a thick haze, dulling the low wattage lighting even more and making his eyes water. Apparently the sheriff was too busy to enforce the indoor no-smoking bylaws in Cooper's Ridge.

The battered wooden door opened, and Sheldon stepped into the bar. He glanced around the room, spotted Declan at the back table, waved, and shouldered his way through the mob. "Hey, man, good to see you," he shouted over the buzz of conversation, the sharp crack of billiard balls, and twang of honkytonk music emanating from a pair of oversized speakers set against the far wall by a tiny, rickety-looking stage.

Declan stood and shook his friend's hand and then they sat, facing each other across the scarred, wooden table.

Sheldon signaled the harried waitress for a beer for himself and another soda for Declan. He swung back to Declan. "So, the prodigal son returns. Finally."

Declan ground his teeth. Everyone felt the need to comment on the all-too-obvious fact he was back in town. "Didn't you think I would?"

"I wasn't sure. You can be one stubborn cuss when you want."

"I should have done something years ago. This mess has been hanging over me far too long."

"Well, you're back now." Light reflected off Sheldon's scalp, visible through his thinning red hair when he nodded. A deep furrow ran between his thick, red brows, and a myriad of tiny lines extended from the outer corners of his eyes as if he spent a lot of time squinting over numbers. "I'm glad you are."

The years had taken a toll on Sheldon, but Declan wasn't the same man he'd once been either. He couldn't recall the last time he'd slept through the night without waking in the throes of a nightmare; a nightmare that didn't end when he awoke.

"Declan?"

He shoved his dark thoughts away and turned his attention to Sheldon. "Sorry. What were you saying?"

"I asked if you'd talked to the sheriff yet."

Declan shook his head. "First, I want to meet with the private investigator I hired and see what he's found. The sheriff's going to need some serious convincing before he'll even begin to look elsewhere for a suspect."

The waitress bustled over with a large, frothy pint of beer and a glass of soda.

"Hey, Tanya." Sheldon flashed her his one-hundred-watt, toothy grin. "Busy tonight."

She cracked her gum and cocked a hip. "Big football game over at the high school. Our team won."

"What?" Sheldon chuckled. "The other team didn't show up?"

She chortled, a deep throaty sound. "Better not let anyone hear you. In these parts, dissing the local team's grounds for murder."

Declan cringed at her choice of word, but when she didn't glare at him and continued her teasing banter, he relaxed. Maybe everyone in town didn't know about his past. He'd been gone ten years after all. Maybe to some people, what had happened prom night twelve years ago, was old news.

"Hey, have you met my friend, Declan?" Sheldon pointed across the table.

The waitress turned her sharp-eyed gaze on him. Her face would have been pretty if her skin wasn't plastered with so much caked-on makeup and her eyelashes clumped together with layers of thick, black mascara. "No, but I know who he is. You're quite a celebrity around these parts, Declan." She popped her gum. "Everyone's talking about you."

Declan didn't have to scan the room to know she told the truth. From the moment he'd walked into the bar, all eyes had been on him. He'd known he'd face distrust and antagonism when he returned to town; he hadn't counted on how much the censure would bother him.

"What are they saying?" Sheldon craned his neck as he peered around the bar.

Declan glowered. What was with the man? He knew damn well what the topic of the bar patrons' chatter was.

Tanya picked up his empty glass and set it on her tray. "They're saying y'all had something to do with some poor girl's death a while back."

Declan bit back a gasp, startled at her candor.

"What do you think?"

She shot him an assessing gaze. "I don't pay much attention to gossip. I make my own decisions about people."

"Thanks, I think."

"Hey, Tanya, quit gabbing and get your sorry butt back here," the bartender hollered at her.

She turned on her heel and flipped him the finger. "Enjoy your drinks," she called over her shoulder to Sheldon and Declan, and strutted, hips swaying, back to the bar.

Declan lifted his soda and drained half the contents in a single swallow, hoping the icy liquid erased the bitter taste in his mouth.

"So"—Sheldon shrugged—"people are talking. What's new, right?" He flashed a grin. "This *is* Cooper's Ridge after all."

Declan grunted.

"I saw Carrie Ann today," Sheldon said.

Declan sucked in a breath.

"I heard she was in town, so I stopped by her aunt's place." He held up a hand as if to forestall any words of protest from Declan. "I know, I know, she's a bitch and you hate her. Hell, I don't blame you one little bit. She done you wrong, buddy."

Declan didn't say anything. He had no intention of discussing Carrie Ann with Sheldon or anyone else.

"I have to say, man, she looks damn good."

Declan scowled, but he couldn't help thinking Sheldon was right. Even covered in mud and drenched with rainwater, Carrie Ann was beautiful. He was still pissed at the kick in the gut he'd felt when he'd seen her standing in the road. It had taken all his willpower not to kiss her, or at least touch her, to see if she tasted as sweet as she used to, or if her skin was as soft. But he couldn't forget what she'd done, and it was as if a layer of ice had formed around him and suddenly, keeping his distance was easy.

Sheldon was still speaking. "I can't believe after all these years, this private dick of yours thinks he can find any new evidence."

"I've heard he's pretty good."

"He'll have to be. The sheriff and his crew didn't find much when they searched the crime scene years ago."

"You mean, they didn't find proof pointing at any one person, and that left me as their fall guy." Declan rubbed his stomach, pressing hard to ease the all-too-familiar painful twisting deep in his guts as he relived the nightmare memories of the law's injustice.

"They sure were gunning for you, especially Judge Winters. He was furious when the sheriff had to release you."

"The sheriff had to let me go. He didn't have a choice. The charge wouldn't stick. How could it when there wasn't any hard evidence against me?" The knot in Declan's gut tightened. "Part of the reason the local authorities agreed to take a second look at this case is their hope they'll find something to finally pin Skye's murder on me."

"But they won't, right? You must be stoked." Sheldon leaned across the table. His beer-scented breath washed over Declan. "I mean, if this private investigator comes through, we'll finally know who killed Skye, and you'll be in the clear."

"I sure as hell hope so."

"You know, your friends never thought you had anything to do with her murder. They believed in you."

Declan's mouth twisted in a sneer. "Yeah? Well, where were all these friends twelve years ago? Where are they now?" He met the stare of a bearded man wearing a ball cap with the local football team's logo stenciled across the sweat-stained peak, slouched in a chair at a nearby table. Randy Martin. They'd been in the same grade in high school.

Randy nudged the beefy guy sitting beside him. His dark brows furrowed in a vee as he said something. The other man eyed Declan, and then they both glared.

Declan turned away, his gut churning. He should be used to this. He'd faced the same distrust and hatred since the moment he'd become the prime suspect in Skye Lawrence's disappearance and murder. The fact he'd been cleared of the crime was irrelevant. As far as the people in Cooper's Ridge were concerned, he was guilty. They didn't care that no real evidence against him existed. He was the prime suspect. He'd been dragged into the police station for questioning; therefore, he must be guilty.

"Well, when your investigator finds out who murdered Skye, everyone will know the truth." Sheldon nodded. "They'll be eating crow for years trying to make it up to you."

Declan smiled at his friend. Through all the hell of these past years, Sheldon had stuck by him. When he'd moved away, they'd kept in contact. And now he was back in town. Being seen with him, the local pariah, couldn't be good for Sheldon's business. Yet, here he was.

Sheldon had suggested they meet at the High Five

for a drink. Declan hadn't wanted to, but Sheldon had insisted. He said he wasn't going to let Declan hide like a criminal. He had to get out and meet his accusers face-to-face. Ice cubes clunked as he swigged more soda and drained the glass. He never had been able to refuse his friend anything.

Sheldon tapped Declan's empty glass. "I see you're still not drinking booze. That's crazy, man. Have a drink with me. One beer won't turn you into your old man."

Declan licked his lips. He wanted a beer, could almost taste the bittersweet ale, wanted nothing more than to lose his mind in an alcohol haze, at least for a while. But he wasn't going to have a beer. He'd promised himself years ago, he wouldn't drink like his old man. He'd broken his pact only once—the night Skye was murdered. And look how that had turned out. He heaved a sigh. "I'd better take off. I have some paperwork to finish tonight."

"Always the busy executive." Sheldon emptied his glass. "How's the business doing anyway? Still raking in the dough?"

"Still making money." At least the work side of his life was going well. Business was good, very good.

"Who'd have thought people would spend a small fortune to have you buy and sell stocks for them?"

"Lucky for me they do. The private investigator I hired doesn't come cheap." Declan stood and tossed some cash on the table. "Thanks, Sheldon." He waved a hand indicating the empty glasses. "I needed to get out."

"Hey, what can I say? You're my friend, man. We go back a long ways."

"Good night." He turned to leave.

"I'll see you tomorrow?" Sheldon called after him.

"I don't know. I'm going to be pretty busy these next few days."

Sheldon nodded. "I'll call."

Declan threaded his way through the crowd toward the door.

"Hey!"

Someone grabbed his arm. He stopped and faced a burly man with watery, red eyes. Spittle flecked the corners of his mouth.

"You're the asshole who killed that poor, sweet, high school gal, aren't you?" the man slurred.

Declan shook off his hand and turned to leave.

"What? Are you too chicken to fight someone your own size? You only like to hurt women?"

He forced himself to keep walking.

The bar had grown silent. Someone had turned down the music, and even the clink of glasses had ceased.

Walk away. Walk away. He took another step and then another. The door and escape seemed miles distant.

"How did it feel when you wrapped your hands around her throat and squeezed the life out of her?" the man taunted. "Did she beg you to stop? Did you get a kick out of hurting her, you asshole?"

Declan whirled and faced his accuser. "What did you say?" he bit off. He had the satisfaction of seeing the other man's face pale.

The drunk stumbled back a step, before steadying himself against his friend. He studied the ring of bright-eyed spectators, puffed out his chest and sucked in his large belly. "I asked what it felt like to murder that girl." His red-streaked eyes glared at Declan.

"And you're asking me this because?" Declan kept his voice neutral, but his insides seethed.

The other man blinked. "What sort of monster are you?" he sneered.

Declan shook his head in disgust. Once again, he turned and walked away.

The drunk called after him, his slurred words carrying over the strains of country western music. "Better lock up your daughters and wives, fellas. Declan McAllister's back in town. Ain't no female safe now."

Fire burned in Declan's belly, and he clenched his jaw until his teeth ached, but he kept walking, placing one foot in front of the other toward the red Exit sign. He ached to punch the drunken jerk in the face, smash his fist again and again until his jowly cheeks were a bloody pulp. Oh, yeah, he wanted to hit him. But he was going to walk out of the bar. He couldn't beat up everyone who accused him of Skye's murder. Half the town would be in the hospital.

He reached the exit, kicked open the battered door and stepped into the parking lot. As the door closed behind him, he sucked in the fresh night air and contemplated the sky, trying to cool the fire heating his blood. Stars twinkled in the clear night, so distant, removed from human troubles. He envied them.

Why had he come back? No one gave a damn about the truth. As far as the people in this town were concerned, he was guilty—as good as tried and convicted. No matter what proof he offered, no matter what the Sheriff's Office ruled, to the people of

Cooper's Ridge, he'd always be the guy who kidnapped and murdered Skye Lawrence. After all, he was a McAllister. Like father, like son. Right?

A hand gripped his arm. He spun, fist cocked, ready to strike, adrenaline coursing through him. He drew back at the last second. "What the hell, Sheldon? Do you want to get punched?"

Sheldon released his hold on Declan's arm and stumbled back a step. He gestured toward the bar. "I couldn't let you leave like that." He held out a cigarette. "Here."

Declan shook his head. He'd smoked when he was in high school, but quit cold turkey years ago.

Sheldon pulled a lighter from his shirt pocket and lit the cigarette. He blew a cloud of fragrant smoke into the night air.

The music from the bar throbbed. Laughter and voices once again raised in heated conversation reached them.

Sheldon broke the silence. "Joe Phillips' an ass."

Declan nodded. He couldn't agree more.

"No, I mean it. He's a blowhard. He's in the bar all the time, drinks too much, and gets into a fight more nights than not. You can't listen to what he says."

"Don't worry. I've heard worse. I expect I'll get even more hassle now the case has been reopened. I can handle it."

"I never doubted you, you know? Not once."

Tears burned Declan's eyes. "I know, man. I know." He turned and walked toward the far end of the dimly lit parking lot where he'd left his truck. He couldn't help the wave of despair flooding him. Sheldon might have stood by him, but he knew damn well he was the only one who had.

The one person who should have believed in him, the one person who should have stuck by him through the whole sordid mess hadn't. The one person he'd counted on had deserted him when he'd needed her the most. He'd never forgive her.

Chapter 6

Declan swerved around another deep pothole. The truck skidded on the loose gravel, the rear end swinging wide. He gripped the steering wheel as the heavy vehicle shuddered and bounced over a series of washboards.

He'd been on his way out to the old farm on Getty's Road the night he'd run into Carrie Ann and her flat tire. Earlier that day, he'd received an anonymous text instructing him to go to the farm. The person who texted him said he'd meet him at the farm at eight o'clock, and promised proof of who murdered Skye Lawrence.

Chances were the text was a cruel trick, but Declan couldn't ignore it. He'd jump through the fires of Hell if the slightest possibility existed to prove his innocence. Running into Carrie Ann had ruined his plans.

After he'd dropped her off at her aunt's house, he drove to the old farm, but the place was deserted. Whoever texted him was long gone. If it weren't for Carrie Ann, he might be holding evidence to point to Skye's killer. A part of him knew he was being unfair. She hadn't shot out her own tire, but he couldn't stop blaming her. This whole damn nightmare was her fault.

Incredibly, he'd received another text a few hours ago saying there was something to be found at the farm.

The entire scenario seemed like a joke, and at first, he'd decided to ignore the text. But he couldn't get it out of his mind. What if the person was telling the truth? What if some sort of clue to who murdered Skye existed? He couldn't risk the possibility the anonymous texter was telling the truth.

He steered the truck through a puddle spanning the width of the road and turned left onto a narrow lane. The path to the farm was more track than road, winding through thick underbrush, almost vanishing in places where heavy vegetation covered the gravel.

Rankin's deserted farm had been the party place of choice back in high school. He and the other kids from town had gone there after every hometown football, basketball, or baseball game, either to celebrate a win or cry over a loss. The rough, little-used road made it clear the kids didn't go there anymore. They'd more than likely found a place closer to town.

The track opened onto a small clearing, and he stopped before a dilapidated barn and turned off the engine. Tall grasses and tangled patches of wild rose and hawthorn bushes held a stranglehold on the land. Trees and brambles formed a nearly impenetrable barrier separating the dense forest beyond.

How the hell was he going to find anything here? He didn't even know what he was searching for. Still, he had to look even if he had to crawl on his hands and knees and examine every inch of this damn place.

Twelve years ago he'd slunk from town, his tail between his legs like a beaten mongrel. Anger and bitterness had plagued him every day in the years since, plus nightmares at night. He'd had enough. He was through living like a criminal. Determined to clear his name, he'd hired the best private investigator he could find and returned to Cooper's Ridge to right the past wrongs.

He opened the truck door and stepped into a mud puddle. Cursing, he shook the water off his boots and scrambled to drier ground. Silence surrounded him, broken by the creak of the barn door as it swung in the breeze. A crow, its shiny black eyes watching, cawed from atop a lone, dead pine in the middle of the clearing. The bird called again, its cry haunting as it spread its wings and flew into the forest, black feathers gleaming in the feeble morning sun.

A chill rippled along his spine. This was the last place anyone had seen Skye Lawrence alive. He closed his eyes against the onslaught of painful memories.

He'd brought her here to celebrate their graduation from high school. It had been the perfect evening, except for one thing—he was with the wrong girl. Almost every senior student had been at the party, drinking, dancing and making out. But then Skye vanished, and the nightmare began, made even worse when her beaten and bloodied body was found in the nearby woods two days later.

He rubbed his hands over his face, trying to scrub away his guilt. Contrary to what everyone suspected, he hadn't killed her, but he had let her down. Because of him, she'd left the party alone and walked into a murderer's clutches. He couldn't change the horror of her untimely death, but finding out who killed her would be a step toward his salvation.

The dilapidated red barn was still standing, but judging by the sagging roof, not for long. An old tire swing attached by a fraying rope to a branch on the dead pine swung back and forth in the breeze, a reminder a family with children had once lived in this desolate spot. He crossed the overgrown yard to where the old farmhouse had stood. A pile of weathered boards almost hidden beneath a thick tangle of scrub was all that remained. He kicked a piece of scorched wood. A crushed beer can lay half buried in the muck beneath the wood.

The wind had risen, and the barn door squeaked and swayed on long-unoiled hinges, the sound grating on his jagged nerves. Any evidence remaining after all these years had to be in the barn.

Crossing the muddy yard, he stopped and listened.

The roar of a vehicle's motor filled the air and a small, red car bounced and shuddered over the rough, gravel lane and screeched to a stop. The door opened and Carrie Ann jumped out. She stomped toward him, ignoring the mud splashing her high-heeled, black, leather boots. Her shoulder-length, auburn hair gleamed like burnished copper; two red spots flamed in her cheeks.

His gut spasmed. God, she was stunning, especially now when she resembled an avenging Valkyrie. "What the hell are you doing here? Are you following me?" he demanded.

Her eyes blazed, the amber lights flashing gold. "Leland told me you were here."

"You drove ten miles on a muddy, gravel road to see me. Should I be flattered?"

She withdrew a crumpled white shirt from her purse and tossed it at him.

He caught the shirt. It was the one he'd given her to wear the night she'd had her flat tire. A vision of her wearing the shirt flashed before him, and he bit back a groan. She hadn't been wearing her bra under the thin cotton shirt. He'd noticed. Man, had he noticed. The thought of her bare skin against his shirt, took his breath away. Still did. "You didn't have to drive all the way out here to give me this. You could have kept my shirt. It would give you something to remember me by." He forced a wolfish grin, knowing he was baiting her, but unable to stop.

"I'm on my way out of town, but I wanted you to have this." Again she reached in her purse. This time she held a handful of crumpled bills. She threw them at him.

The money landed in the mud at his feet. "What's this for?"

"Ted from the garage told me you paid for having my flat tire repaired."

"I don't want your money."

"I pay my own way." Her voice was tight. She worried her bottom lip, white teeth digging into soft, pink flesh.

Remembering how sweet her lips tasted, he gulped for air.

The crow cawed from the nearby forest. The barn door creaked. They faced each other like two combatants ready for a showdown.

Finally, she spoke. "Ted told me about the tire."

Damn.

"He found a bullet hole in the side wall which is why the tire was flat." Her eyes narrowed. "Why didn't you tell me?"

Double damn. "The night was dark, and it was raining. Remember? I couldn't be sure."

"But once you knew, why didn't you tell me then? Didn't you think I had a right to know?"

He opened his mouth to say something trite, but changed his mind at the fear shadowing her eyes. "I didn't want you to worry. It was probably an accident. There are lots of farms around where you had your flat. Some farmer was likely shooting at a coyote."

"Ted said the same thing."

"He's right."

"You should have told me anyway."

"What would you have done? Called the police? Told them I shot your tire?" He took a step toward her. "That's it, isn't it? You'd like nothing better than for me to be arrested for shooting out your tire." Another step. "I don't believe this. After all these years, you still want to get back at me for taking Skye to the prom. Isn't it time you got over it?"

She paled.

Two more steps.

Her hands fluttered to her throat.

Cold settled over him and sank deep into his bones. She was afraid. Of him! For a brief second he wanted to reassure her he'd never hurt her, but then he remembered what she'd done, and he kept walking closer.

She backed away, stumbling on the uneven ground until she bumped against the hood of her car.

Why the hell was she so frightened? He'd never done anything to cause her to be afraid of him. The truth hit him like a bolt of lightning, and he staggered, almost losing his balance. She thought he'd done it. She believed he'd kidnapped and murdered Skye. All these years, he'd harbored the belief that despite all the anger and betrayal, after everything she'd done, somehow Carrie Ann, the girl he'd given his heart to, believed in his innocence. But now, here, once and for all was proof. Like everyone else, she thought he was a murderer.

Something inside him broke. A fury overtook him, anger so hot he was amazed the earth beneath him didn't scorch. He glared at her, his fists bunched at his sides, afraid of what he'd do if he lost control. "Why the hell are you here? If you're so damn afraid of me, why the hell did you come all the way out here by yourself?"

A tear trembled on her eyelashes. "I wanted to return your shirt and pay you for having my tire repaired."

"Come on, Carrie Ann. You didn't drive all the way out here to give me this." He shoved the shirt in front of her face. "What's the real reason you're here?"

"I wasn't going to come. I didn't want to, but…" Her voice faded.

He narrowed his eyes. "But what?"

"I thought you might need help."

"Help?" He snorted. "From you?"

"Leland said you were here looking for evidence in Skye's murder."

"How would Leland know?" He hadn't told anyone of the text he'd received or of his intentions to come out here. Was the old bastard having him followed? He wouldn't put it past him.

What she'd said hit him, and he forgot Leland Winters. "You drove all the way out here to *help* me?" She was lying. She'd made her feelings more than clear years ago, when at the first hint he was a suspect in

66

Skye's murder, she'd run away. "I don't believe you," he ground out. "You don't give a damn about me. You didn't twelve years ago, and you sure as hell don't now."

Her full lips tightened, and she shoved past him, her eyes flashing. "You don't know anything. You have no idea what things were like for me."

"For *you*? Oh, lady, spare me. You weren't the one accused of kidnapping and murdering a friend. You weren't the one the whole town thought was guilty. Hell, most of them *still* think I am." He thrust his fingers through his hair. "Skye's life wasn't the only one destroyed that night.

"I was eighteen years old and as far as this town was concerned, I was no better than my old man. Like father, like son. Everyone said it. The sheriff didn't have any physical evidence against me, but I was treated like a felon. For weeks, my name was in all the papers and on the news every night. I was the 'prime suspect in Skye Lawrence's murder'. Hell, I couldn't even go to her funeral for fear of being attacked by a lynch mob." He stopped, breathing hard, spun on his heels, and stomped toward the barn.

A car door opened and slammed shut. An engine roared to life, but he didn't turn to watch. The noise faded until once again he was surrounded by silence.

Chapter 7

Carrie Ann's hands shook on the steering wheel as she swerved to the side of the road and turned off the motor. Squeezing her hands into fists, she winced as her nails dug into her palms. It was a mistake to come here, but the last thing she wanted was to be beholden to Declan.

She hadn't planned on offering to help him, but Leland's dogged belief in Declan's guilt had changed her mind. When she'd told Leland she was leaving town, he'd seemed pleased. With Skye's murder case being reopened, people would be talking again and a large part of the conversation would center on her.

Leland believed Declan's case was hopeless. It was only a matter of time before the sheriff found the proof he needed to convict Declan once and for all. Leland had snickered and told her Declan had driven out to the old Rankin farm on a foolish quest to prove his innocence. "As if any evidence would be there after all these years," he'd sneered.

She hadn't defended Declan. What was the point? As far as Leland was concerned, Declan was guilty and deserved to be punished. Nothing she said would change his opinion.

But she couldn't get the thought out of her mind of Declan, all alone at the desolate farm, searching for something he'd never find. Leland was right. Any evidence from that terrible night would be long gone, either taken by the authorities, or destroyed by time.

Yet Declan searched.

Forty-five minutes later, after bumping along the muddy and rutted road, she'd driven into the overgrown clearing.

Declan had been standing amidst the ruins of the old farm, the wind tangling his dark curls.

She'd almost turned around and left. Should have, in hindsight. But the bleak expression on his all-too-handsome face portrayed his loneliness and isolation. Heart pounding, she'd opened her door and stepped out of the car.

He hadn't been happy to see her. His brow had furrowed, and he'd clenched his teeth so tightly a pulse beat in his jaw.

For a brief moment, she was afraid, but then she saw the hurt hiding beneath the anger, transforming his eyes into black coals. Her fear fled, replaced by guilt. She'd wounded him far more than he'd ever know. He was angry with her now; if he knew the full truth of what she'd done, he'd despise her.

A car horn blared, drawing her out of her thoughts.

A blue sports car pulled a U-turn in the road ahead and parked on the shoulder. Sheldon Dubrowski stepped out. He grinned and waved as he jogged toward her.

She slid her window down. "What are you doing here, Sheldon?" No one used this back road; yet, here he was.

"Hey, Carrie Ann. Do you need some help?" He leaned through the open window, his face inches from hers, his warm breath reeking of stale cigarette smoke.

"Do you have another flat?"

Her eyes narrowed. "How did you know I had a flat tire the other night?"

He blinked. "What do you mean?"

"Come on, Sheldon, I heard you. How did you know about my flat tire? Who told you?"

He shrugged. "You know how things are in this town. People talk." He wrinkled his brow. "I heard you're heading back to Seattle today."

"Why am I surprised?"

"It's Cooper's Ridge." As if that explained everything. He waved a hand at the acres of empty fields and thick forests surrounding them. "What are you doing out here? This isn't the way to Seattle. This road's a dead-end. The only place it leads is to the old Rankin Farm." His gaze sharpened. "You remember the farm, don't you? We used to party there in high school."

"I was at the farm." She gave in to the inevitable, knowing he'd find out anyway.

"Really? I haven't been there for years. Not since...you know." His freckled face turned serious. "Why were you there? No one goes to that old place anymore. Not even the kids. Some folks say the farm's haunted." He shuddered. "Not that I believe in that hocus-pocus baloney, but there's no way you'd catch me there alone." Once again, his sharp gaze swept over her. "Why were you there?"

"I wanted to see the place one more time." She hoped he'd let it go.

His eyes narrowed. "Really? Did you see Declan?"

"Declan?"

He nodded. "He told me he was going to the old

farm this morning. He said he wanted to check out something. You must have seen him."

She shook her head, once again lying to him. The last thing she wanted was for him to start spreading rumors she and Declan were having a secret tryst. What next? Would the town gossips ferret out the truth she'd worked so hard to hide all these years? "I didn't see anything except for an old barn and a bunch of weeds." She could tell he didn't believe her.

"Really?" His gaze sharpened. "Are you sure?"

She sighed. "What do you want, Sheldon? I have to get going."

"Do you want to go for coffee, you know, to catch up?" He grinned, the sudden flash of white teeth blinding. "The Perked Pot still serves a pretty mean cup of joe."

"I can't. I really am on my way out of town."

"You're sure?"

She nodded.

"Okay, but I'm taking a rain check." His grin spread. "The next time you're in town. You owe me a cup of coffee."

"Sure." She knew she'd never come back.

He started to return to his own vehicle, but stopped and turned back. "Are you sure you didn't see Declan?"

She threw up her hands. "Okay, you win. I saw Declan. He was at the farm. Are you happy?"

He retraced his steps and leaned in the window. "And?"

"I saw him. That's all. I saw him, and then I left."

He reached through the window and traced a finger down her cheek. "You've been crying."

She leaned away from his touch. "It's nothing."

She turned the key in the ignition and started the engine.

He raised his eyebrows but backed away from her car.

She shifted into Drive.

"I don't believe you, Carrie Ann," he called over the noise of the motor.

She pressed her foot on the gas pedal.

He shouted through the open window. "You can run away, Carrie Ann, but the truth is more than clear. You're still in love with him."

She jabbed her finger on the window control button and rolled up the window silencing any further comments, and jammed on the gas. The car surged ahead, skidding on the loose gravel as she swerved around his car, missing his rear bumper by inches. She glanced in the rearview mirror.

He stood where she'd left him, a wide grin wreathing his homely face.

His last words echoed through the car, the refrain pounding into her head with each condemning syllable. *You're still in love with him.* She gripped the steering wheel, her foot pressed hard on the gas pedal. The little car raced down the rough road, bouncing over the deep ruts.

He was dead wrong. She didn't love Declan. Not anymore. Too much guilt and too many lies separated them. He'd broken her heart once. She'd barely survived. If she hadn't had Bonnie to care for, she wouldn't have.

A siren's blare rent the air.

She glanced in her rearview mirror.

A sheriff's car, lights on the roof flashing red and

blue, was gaining fast.

She looked at her speedometer and swore. Easing her foot off the gas, she slowed and pulled over to the side of the road.

The sheriff's car parked behind her, and the siren died, the lights still flashing their warning. The door opened and a uniformed sheriff's deputy climbed out. He was heavyset. His paunch hung a good three inches over his belt, straining the buttons on his tan shirt. Settling a hat on his balding head, he checked for his gun in the holster at his side and lumbered toward her.

She reached for her purse, withdrew her wallet, and opened her window.

The deputy leaned in, his sharp gaze roaming over first her, and then the car's interior. "You're going somewhere in a mighty hurry, ma'am."

She forced a smile. "Was I speeding, Deputy?"

"I clocked you at sixty miles an hour. The speed limit for this road's forty."

Her cheeks hurt from smiling. "I'm sorry, Deputy. I didn't know. I'm really sorry." She widened her smile.

His mouth tightened, his eyes hidden behind the mirrored lenses of his sunglasses. "Let's see your driver's license and insurance."

She showed him her license and reached in the glove compartment for the insurance papers. The small space was empty. She flipped her visor down. Nothing. Where the hell was her insurance?

"Ma'am?" The furrow between his thick brows deepened. One hand rested on the butt of the revolver on his hip. "Your insurance?"

She forced a laugh. "I don't know where the papers are."

He stared at her.

"I don't. You see, this is a rental car. I was certain the rental car company gave me the insurance papers, but I can't find them. I paid for insurance. Honest."

"Wait here."

She watched in the rearview mirror as he returned to his patrol car. He left the driver's door open and spoke into his police radio.

The damn rental car company! Served her right for going with the cheapest one in town. She'd have a word with them when she returned to Seattle. They'd rented her a car with bald tires, no spare or a jack, and they hadn't given her the insurance papers she'd paid for. She rubbed her aching temples. She should have left town when she'd planned. Why had she gone out to the old farm? It wasn't as if Declan appreciated her offer of help.

"You need to follow me, ma'am."

She jumped. She hadn't heard the deputy return. "Follow you? Where? I'm on my way to Seattle."

He shook his head. "You ain't goin' nowhere today. Leastwise, not Seattle."

"But—"

"Follow me back to town." His eyes narrowed. "And don't try any funny business. Cooper's Ridge may not be Seattle, but we sure as crikey know how to deal with criminals."

She gulped. "Criminals? I'm not a criminal. I told you. This is all a misunderstanding. I *have* insurance. I paid for it. You can call the rental company. They'll tell you."

Her pleading didn't faze him. "Follow me." He turned and strode to his car, climbed in, and slammed the door.

She groaned. Just what she needed, returning to town escorted by a sheriff's deputy's car. The gossips would have a heyday. She started her engine, and with a sinking heart, followed the police car back to Cooper's Ridge and away from Seattle. At least the siren wasn't blaring.

Chapter 8

Declan rubbed the back of his aching neck. His eyes burned from the puffs of fine dust raised with each step. For the past two hours, he'd used a rusty pitchfork he found in the old barn and sifted through the straw scattered across the hard-packed, dirt floor. He'd climbed the rickety wooden ladder to the loft and ripped apart moldy hay bales covered with caked-on mounds of dried bat shit, careful not to dislodge any loose boards. One misstep risked a fifteen-foot plunge to the floor below. He'd even knelt on the filth-encrusted floor in the back corner of the cavernous barn and lifted each faded red brick in the six-foot high stack of old building material and checked beneath. Nothing.

He wiped the damp from his brow. He was a fool. The text message was a prank, someone's idea of a sick joke. Whoever had written the text was having a good chuckle. He'd wasted the better part of a day searching...for what?

A gust of wind blew through the open barn door stirring the scattered piles of hay and raising swirls of dust. Over by the horse stall, beside the pile of bricks he'd just searched, something flickered in the breeze. He stepped closer, his heart starting to pound.

Crouching, he squinted into the gloom. A tattered scrap of cloth hung from a rusty nail that was embedded in an old, weathered board. How had he missed this?

When he'd restacked the old bricks and moved them away from the wall, he must have bumped the horse stall and dislodged a loose board, exposing the small piece of cloth fluttering in the slight breeze.

He leaned closer studying the tattered rag, sucked in a sharp breath, and fell back on his butt. He squeezed his eyes shut, but the design on the cloth was seared onto his eyelids. Jumping to his feet, he ran to his truck and retrieved the pair of work gloves he kept in a toolbox in the backseat.

Back in the barn, his hands shook as he unhooked the rag from the nail. The cloth, no more than six-by-eight inches, was gold with vibrant splashes of green and teal blue dancing across the glossy surface. He'd never forget the colorful pattern. How could he when every word, every gesture, every second of the night was seared into his brain, every single bit of minutia locked-in.

He hadn't forgotten a detail from the moment he'd driven up to Skye's clapboard house in his rusty, old, pickup truck, to when she stepped out of the back room in all her prom finery. She'd found a vintage, designer scarf in a secondhand shop and wore it, twisted in an intricate knot around her slender throat. She made him touch the soft, silken fabric, and he remembered admiring the rich colors.

After the dance, before they'd headed out to the farm for the party, she changed into jeans and a sweatshirt, but kept the scarf wrapped around her neck. If he closed his eyes, he could see her fondling the delicate scarf, running her hands again and again over the silk as if making sure it was still around her neck.

He stared at the piece of silk in his hands. The

lustrous colors and unique design were identical to the scarf Skye had worn. On shaky knees, he staggered out of the barn and examined the cloth in the afternoon light. His heart stuttered as he ran his gloved fingers over the ragged edges. It looked as if the remnant had been torn from a larger piece of fabric. Was it a part of Skye's scarf? Was that possible?

He rubbed his forehead, trying to ease the tightening band of pressure. This couldn't be from Skye's scarf. Impossible. If this was a piece of her scarf and it had been in the barn all this time, the colors would have faded. Dust would have covered the fabric with a layer of dulling grime. Even hidden behind the old board, the cloth would have yellowed.

The investigators had searched the barn looking for clues to Skye's murder. Why hadn't they found the scrap of cloth in the course of their investigation? If this really was a section of Skye's scarf, only one answer made sense—the person who'd texted him had left the cloth for him to find.

He turned the cloth over and froze. A faded, rust-colored smear marred the gold. Blood? The roiling in his gut left little doubt. A horrific scenario flashed through his mind—the murderer luring Skye away from the party on one pretext or another, attacking her, hitting her, again and again until she stopped fighting and lay still. Such a violent attack would have resulted in blood splattering her scarf.

The sheriff had to see this. The forensic specialists would be able to tell if the brownish smear was blood and confirm the scarf was Skye's. DNA evidence might still be on the fabric and point a finger at the murderer.

One thing was for sure. Whoever had hidden the

cloth in the barn was the murderer. No one else would have had access to Skye's scarf. The killer had dragged her into the forest and covered her in dirt, but before he buried her, he'd taken a souvenir. He'd ripped off a piece of her scarf and kept it all these years.

But why bring it out of hiding now? Acid burned deep in his gut, and the pounding in his head ramped up. Of course. He'd been played. The killer wanted him to find Skye's torn scarf. If Declan showed up at the Sheriff's Office with a piece of Skye's bloodied scarf, the sheriff would arrest him on the spot. He'd take it as proof Declan had murdered her. He wouldn't believe an anonymous text had led Declan out here to find the scrap of cloth. The sheriff would toss him in a cell and throw away the key. He'd never get out this time. As far as the law was concerned, they'd have all the evidence they needed to get a conviction.

He didn't have a choice. The scarf might contain evidence to help find the real killer. He had to turn it in to the authorities. He had to think of Skye. She deserved justice. But what if there wasn't any DNA evidence on the scarf? Was he prepared to spend the rest of his life in jail?

His gut churned. He'd been tricked, all right...by a master. The bastard who'd texted him had played him like a bad tune, and Declan had been stupid enough to walk right into his trap. Now, what the hell was he going to do?

A car drove into the clearing, coming to a stop beside his truck. Sheldon opened the door and stepped out, a grin on his angular face. "Hey, buddy, how's it going?"

"What the hell are you doing here?" Even to

Declan's own ears, his voice sounded sharp. First Carrie Ann and now Sheldon. Did the whole damn town know he was coming out here?

"I thought you might want some company."

"Who told you I was here?"

"Carrie Ann. I was driving around, and I saw her parked on the side of the road a ways back. She told me she saw you." Sheldon's gaze sharpened. "She was upset. I think she'd been crying."

Declan flinched as if from a blow. He shouldn't have been so hard on her, but seeing her opened old wounds. When he was around her, all he could think of was making her hurt as much as he hurt.

"What's that you have?" Sheldon's gaze fixed on the piece of fabric clutched in Declan's hand.

Shit. He'd forgotten. "Something I found in the barn."

"What is it?"

Declan heaved a breath. Might as well get this over with. Everyone was going to know once he showed the sheriff what he'd found. "I think it's a piece of Skye's scarf, the one she wore prom night."

"What?" Sheldon's eyes widened. "No way."

He nodded.

"But how…?" Sheldon's voice broke. He met Declan's gaze. "Oh, man. This isn't good, is it?"

"It gets worse." He turned the cloth over and held it for Sheldon to see. "I think this is blood."

Sheldon gulped, his Adam's apple bobbing in his thin throat. "Are you going to show this to the sheriff? You have to, don't you? I mean, it's evidence, right?"

Declan's head throbbed.

"Oh, man. This won't look good," Sheldon

continued. "You having a piece of Skye's scarf after all these years. This is what Sheriff Atkins and Judge Winters have been waiting for." He rubbed the back of his neck. "Why did you come out here on your own? You should have brought that expensive P.I. you hired with you. At least he could have backed you up and say he saw you find the scarf in the barn."

Declan glared, putting all his anger and frustration into the look, though Sheldon was only voicing aloud what he'd been thinking. He should never have come out here on his own. He should have asked Jamieson Caruthers to search the old farm with him, but Declan hadn't really believed he'd find anything helpful, and he hadn't wanted to waste the private investigator's time on a fool's errand. Now, who was the fool?

"Easy, man." Sheldon patted the air. "I'm on your side, remember? I'm just telling you what the sheriff's going to think."

Declan sucked in a steadying breath. "Sorry." He rubbed his aching eyes. "I'm just so fricking pissed. I was set up. Someone's gone to a lot of trouble to make damn sure I go to jail for a murder I didn't commit."

"You mean, you're being framed? Come on. Who'd do that?"

"I don't know, but I sure as hell intend to find out."

Silence hung in the air. Even the wind had died.

"So what are you going to do?" Sheldon nodded at the scrap of fabric. "You could throw it away and pretend you never found it. No one would know. I sure wouldn't tell anyone."

"I can't do that." He held up the cloth. "This might help find Skye's killer."

"But it makes you look guilty as hell."

Declan nodded, the movement increasing the jabbing pain in his head. "You're right, but if there's the slightest chance this will point at her killer, I have to turn it in."

"I could give the scarf to the sheriff." Sheldon bounced on his toes. "I could say I was out here looking around, and I found it. You'd be in the clear."

A lump formed in Declan's throat. He placed his hand on Sheldon's bony shoulder. "You're a good friend, but I can't let you do that."

Sheldon's face flushed. "You helped me out in high school. I'd have been beaten to a pulp if you hadn't stood up for me." His blue eyes glistened with tears. "I owe you, man. I'd do anything for you."

"I'll see the sheriff gets this." Declan's voice was a hoarse croak. "But I won't let him walk all over me again. I'm not a penniless kid anymore. I know my rights."

"Okay, man. If you're sure." Sheldon paled and his eyes widened. "You know what this means, don't you? The murderer was here...recently." He shuddered and peered warily around the deserted homestead.

"Don't worry, we're alone. I checked."

"Carrie Ann was here."

"Yeah, she was." Declan schooled his expression, hoping Sheldon wouldn't guess how the mere mention of her name upset him.

"What did she want?"

"She wanted to return some stuff to me."

"And she drove all the way out here to return something? What was it? It must have been important."

"It wasn't."

"So why'd she come?"

Declan shook his head. That was the six million dollar question. "I don't know."

Chapter 9

Carrie Ann followed the deputy's car back to town. The flashing red-and-blue lights attracted attention. A lot of attention. As they paraded down Front Street past all the main businesses in town, heads craned for a closer look at the car being led to the Sheriff's Office.

The hope she wouldn't be recognized faded when she glanced out her window. Three women stood on the sidewalk pointing at her and talking excitedly as she passed. One woman had her cell phone out and was speaking into it. Another held her phone in the air, filming.

Carrie Ann's heart sank. Man, she hated small towns.

The deputy put on his cruiser's blinker and turned down Edwards Street, but instead of stopping at the Sheriff's Office, he drove past.

What the hell?

The cruiser continued down Edwards and turned onto Winters Road.

She tightened her grip on the steering wheel. She should have known.

The deputy swung onto her aunt's driveway and stopped in front of the house.

She parked beside him, leaped out of her car, and marched toward the deputy's vehicle. "What the hell is this? You told me you were taking me to the Sheriff's

Office."

The deputy climbed out of the cruiser. He placed his hat on his head and stood watching her, a bland expression on his jowly face.

"What's going on?" She could feel her blood pressure rising. "Why are we here?"

The door to the house opened, and Vivian stepped onto the porch.

"Here she is, Mrs. Winters." The deputy gestured at Carrie Ann. "I brought her in like you asked."

"Thanks, Beau."

"Well, I reckon I don't deserve too much credit. I was on a call to the old Rankin Farm out on Getty's Road when I spotted her."

"The Rankin Farm?" Vivian frowned. "What in Heaven's name was she doing out there?"

"I don't rightly know, but I aim to find out. I'm headin' back out to the old farm as soon as I finish up here. Seems someone phoned in a report of suspicious activity."

Vivian crossed the porch and faced Carrie Ann. "I'm glad you're back. You left so abruptly, we didn't get a chance to finish our business."

Carrie Ann's anger flared. "I'm not a kid anymore. You can't do this. You don't control me." Spinning on her heel, she strode back to her car. She opened her door, but paused when the deputy called out.

"Er, ma'am, I'm afraid you're not free to go."

"What are you talking about? I'm not under arrest. I have every right to go wherever I want."

He removed his hat and scratched his scalp. "You see, ma'am, there're these little issues of you exceeding the speed limit and driving without insurance." His fat lips stretched in a wide grin. "Both are serious offenses in this county. You ain't goin' nowhere."

She opened her mouth to argue but gave up. He had her dead to rights. She had been speeding, and she couldn't find the insurance papers for her car. "Okay, write me a ticket. I'll pay the fine."

He eyed her for a long, drawn-out minute. "I don't know, ma'am, you were goin' mighty fast."

"Maybe we can make a deal, Beau," Vivian cut in. "Write Carrie Ann a ticket for speeding. Make the fine a big one. I'll guarantee she pays."

Carrie Ann's face burned. She didn't need Vivian to deal with this. "Enough." The word came out as a shout.

Vivian and the deputy stopped their negotiating and turned to stare at her.

She took a steadying breath. "Look, I'll pay the fine. I'll do whatever I have to, to get out of this damn town." She glared at the deputy. "Tell me how much."

His gaze shifted between Vivian and her.

"My aunt has nothing to do with this." Her anger boiled over when he glanced once again at Vivian.

Vivian nodded.

"Okay, fine." He reached into the open window of his cruiser, removed his ticket book and began writing on it. When he finished, he handed Carrie Ann the ticket.

She gaped at the amount and bit back a gasp. The fine was steep, probably way too much, but she didn't dare argue. She'd pay the damn thing and leave. She climbed into her car, but before she could turn the keys in the ignition, Deputy Beau tapped on her window. She rolled down her window.

"Where you goin'?"

She fought the urge to yell. "To the Sheriff's Office to pay the fine you just handed me."

He shook his head. "No, you ain't."

She rubbed her pounding head. "Okay." She spoke as if addressing a small child. "I sped. You gave me a speeding ticket, and now I'm going to pay the fine." She pasted a smile on her face.

"You don't have any insurance, lady." This time he laughed. "You ain't goin' nowhere."

You ain't goin' nowhere. If he said those words one more time, she'd scream.

"You can't drive this car until you get insurance." He crossed his arms over his beefy chest. "It's the law."

She wanted to smash the smug expression off his pudgy face. An image of being locked in the town jail flashed before her, and she grimaced. "Okay, you win. Where can I buy insurance?"

He grinned, enjoying this. "Nowhere. Leastways not today, or tomorrow, or maybe even the next day. Thelma Buick, who owns the insurance place in town, is away right now. Her daughter's havin' a baby over in Fullerton. Ain't no tellin' when she'll be back."

She let his words sink in. He had her. She wasn't going anywhere. Still shaking her head, she climbed out of the car, walked around to the trunk, and yanked out her suitcase and the weathered shoebox. She walked past the deputy, up the stairs to the porch and stopped and glared at Vivian. "You win." She stuffed all her bitterness into the two words.

"This isn't a game, Carrie Ann. No one wins."

Carrie Ann laughed, the sound hard and brittle. "You always do, Vivian. You always do."

Back in her room, she punched in the familiar number on her cell phone. Although she'd talked to Bonnie mere hours ago, it felt longer. She'd never been away from her daughter this long. Listening to the phone ring she pictured the scene at the other end of the line. Bonnie, with her unruly mop of blonde curls and freckled nose would be in her room reading or playing a video game. Or maybe she had a friend over and they were listening to music or watching television.

Janine, Carrie Ann's best friend, and the woman looking after Bonnie, answered the call. "I wondered when you were going to phone."

"How are things?" Carrie Ann fought to speak through the thickening lump in her throat. Janine's voice was a soothing balm in her ear.

"Never mind us. How are you doing?"

Tears stung her eyes. "Okay."

"Is it as difficult to be in Cooper's Ridge as you thought it would be?"

"Worse."

"Do you want to talk about it?"

Carrie Ann shook her head, but realized her friend couldn't see her. "It's…ah…it's complicated."

"I'm listening."

In spite of her tears, she smiled. Janine was a good friend. She'd met her after moving to Seattle when she was pregnant with Bonnie. Janine was also a single mom, and the two of them had hit it off right away. Over the years she'd confided in her, and Janine knew how difficult it was for Carrie Ann to return to Cooper's Ridge, the risk she was taking by being here.

"Carrie Ann? Are you still there?"

She grabbed a tissue and wiped her eyes. "Yeah,

I'm here," she choked out.

A long silence descended, and then Janine said, "Come home."

"I can't. Not yet."

"Why not? I can tell you're hurting."

She couldn't begin to explain the emotional roller-coaster she'd been on since she'd arrived in Cooper's Ridge. "There's something I have to do first. I'll tell you about it when I get back." Before Janine could argue, she asked, "How's Bonnie?"

Janine hesitated, but then said, "You can ask her yourself. Here she is."

The sound of fumbling, laughter, and her daughter's voice echoed through the line. "Mom, when are you coming home? I miss you."

"I miss you too, kiddo. I miss you so much." She wanted nothing more than to hold her daughter and smell her sweet, familiar scent.

"Are you finished your work?"

When Carrie Ann decided to return to Cooper's Ridge, she'd told Bonnie she had to go away on business. She hated lying, but if she'd told her the truth, Bonnie would have insisted on coming with her. A prospect that made her stomach curdle.

In the past year, Bonnie had begun asking questions about her father. Carrie Ann told her he'd died before Bonnie was born. A lie. She'd also said neither she, nor Bonnie's father, had any living family. Another lie. Bonnie could never know of Cooper's Ridge. The town held too many secrets. Carrie Ann wouldn't risk destroying the comfortable life she'd worked so hard to build. A life built on lies and deception.

"Mom?"

She forced herself to focus. "I'm here, kiddo."

"You weren't listening."

"I am now. Tell me what you've been up to. Did you study for your math test?"

"Mom," Bonnie exploded. "You always ask me if I studied. I told you. I don't *need* to study for math. I know all that stuff. Multiplication and division are easy as long as you know your facts, and you know I know them. You drill me on them every night." A brief silence ensued. "At least you do when you're home."

Carrie Ann smiled. Bonnie always aced her math tests. Numbers came easy for her. Unlike Carrie Ann who struggled to balance her checkbook each month. Where had the child inherited her math skills? She ignored the obvious answer. Just as she ignored the fact Bonnie's dark brown eyes and matching dimples were an exact match to her father's. DNA and genetics were all in the no-go zone, as were so many topics.

She chatted with Bonnie for another twenty minutes, listening to the details of her busy, young life. She loved her daughter more than she could ever have imagined. Raising a child alone hadn't been easy, but she was proud of the job she'd done. Bonnie was a happy, secure, wonderful child.

After she hung up the phone, she sank onto the bed in the room where she'd spent most of her childhood and gave into the loneliness surrounding her. She missed her daughter. She missed Janine and her other friends. She missed her comfortable apartment in Seattle. She even missed her job as an executive assistant in the realty company where she worked. As soon as she resolved the insurance issue and paid her traffic fine, she'd leave this damn town and never come back.

A knock at her bedroom door drew her out of her thoughts. Sitting up, she steeled herself to face Vivian and her gloating triumph. "Come in."

The door opened, and Leland walked into the room. "I'm glad you're here, Carrie Ann. I wanted to talk to you." He wandered around the small room, picked up a book lying on the shelf, flipped through the pages, and then replaced the book. Lifting an old basketball trophy from the dresser, he squinted as he read the words engraved on the small, brass plaque on the base. He crossed the room and stood before a faded poster of her teen heartthrob, Kirk Cameron. "Vivian hasn't changed a thing in here since you left. Nobody is allowed in this room. She won't even let the housekeeper clean it, and insists on doing the cleaning herself."

Carrie Ann snorted. "Right. I can see her wielding a dusting cloth."

"It's true. Believe it or not, your aunt loves you."

Again she snorted.

"Why do you think she begged you to come home and is doing her utmost to keep you here?"

"Because she likes to control people."

He sat down on the bed beside her and took her hand. "You don't understand her, Carrie Ann, not really. You never have."

She snatched her hand away and jumped up. "Come on. I lived with her for eleven years. I grew up hearing her never-ending criticisms. Nothing I did was ever good enough. I was a constant disappointment. So, don't tell me what I know or don't know."

"She loves you. She always has."

"Yeah, and she treated me the way she did because she loves me." Tears burned her eyes.

"We need to talk."

She heard the quiet gravity in his voice and her head started to throb. This conversation was heading to a place she didn't want to go. Not now, not today. Not ever.

Leland patted the bed beside him. "Please?" The bright, afternoon light streaming through the window highlighted the lines time had carved across his face. His short, thinning hair was more white than gray. For the first time, she realized he was an old man.

Her anger faded. Her fight wasn't with him. He'd stood between her and the full brunt of Vivian's controlling ways on more than one occasion. He'd always been kind. "What do you want to talk about?" Resigned, she sat on the edge of the bed beside him.

"How is Bonnie?"

"Great. I just talked to her. You should see her—" She stopped, realizing what she'd said. Leland would never meet Bonnie.

"She sounds lovely," he said. "I'd like to meet her one day."

She closed her heart to the sadness darkening his faded, blue eyes. "I've told you, you and Vivian will never see her." She gentled her voice, not wanting to hurt him any more than she already had. "I'm sorry, but Bonnie will never come to Cooper's Ridge. She doesn't know you and Vivian exist, and she never will."

"You're still angry over what happened. The situation has changed. Vivian's changed. She's not the same woman."

She laughed, the sound brittle in the quiet room. "I told you when we were outside the Women's Clinic, and I refused to have the abortion she so desperately wanted, I'd never let Vivian into my life again. I meant what I said."

"Yet, here you are."

She turned from his probing gaze. He was right. Here she was. Vivian beckoned, and she'd come running. In spite of the vow she'd made all those years ago, she'd come back to Cooper's Ridge.

"It wasn't my idea to bring you back here. Vivian wanted to see you. She wants to make amends." He shrugged. "I told her now wasn't the best time, but you know Vivian. Once she makes up her mind, nothing stops her." He squeezed her hand. "But you're here now, and we have to deal with this McAllister issue."

She blinked. "Declan?"

"He's not the punk from the wrong side of the tracks anymore. I've checked. He runs a successful investment firm in Dallas and is well thought of in the business community." Leland rubbed the back of his neck. "He has money now, and money is power. When he decided he wanted to try and clear his name, he spoke to the State District Attorney. She agreed to look at the case again."

Carrie Ann wasn't surprised at Declan's success. He'd always been smart and determined. That's why she'd been shocked when after the sheriff had taken him in for questioning in Skye's murder, he hadn't defended himself. He hadn't retained a lawyer, not even a court-appointed one. He'd taken all the slurs and insults the townspeople had hurled at him without a fight. His inaction was as effective as if he'd admitted his guilt.

"Carrie Ann?"

She returned her attention to Leland. "I'm glad Declan's trying to prove his innocence. He should have fought harder years ago. I hope the private investigator he hired finds something to help him."

Leland's eyes met hers and held. "McAllister's guilty. By the time this investigation draws to a close, he'll be charged with first-degree murder and will be looking at spending the rest of his life in prison." He scrubbed a hand over his face. "Promise me you won't get involved with him again. Don't forget what he put you through. I was there. I saw what he did, how hurt you were, how his betrayal changed you."

"You don't have to worry about me. I'm leaving town as soon as I can."

"Why did you go out to Rankin's Farm this afternoon?" He looked concerned. "You knew Declan would be there."

She flushed. Why *had* she gone out there?

For some crazy reason, she'd felt sorry for Declan and had decided to help him, but she wouldn't tell Leland.

Not when Declan had thrown her offer of help in her face. "I wanted to return something of his."

"Did he find anything?"

"Like what?"

"I don't know. He was trying to find something to prove his innocence. I wondered if he had."

"What could possibly still be there? After all these years?"

He shrugged. "You never know." Without another word, he rose and walked out of the room.

She stared after him, her headache now a fierce pounding.

Chapter 10

The tires squealed as Declan swerved onto the brick-paved driveway and slammed on the brakes. Leaping out of the truck, his feet thudded on the brick path as he strode toward the house. He cleared the steps and pounded on the door.

It opened before he had to bang again.

Vivian stood in the doorway, her frail body blocking the entrance. "What do you want?" Her cool tone made it clear how unwelcome he was.

No surprise. He'd never been welcome in this house. Not once during all the years he'd dated Carrie Ann had Vivian had a kind word to say. More often than not when he'd come to pick up Carrie Ann, Vivian had made him wait on the porch until Carrie Ann appeared. She was probably afraid he'd steal the family silver. Her attitude had angered him then. It still did. "Where is she?"

Her gaze was almost feral in her perfectly made-up face.

She wasn't going to let him in. He could tell by the way her body tensed. She may have kept him out years ago, but not now. He was here to confront Carrie Ann and nothing would stop him. He'd shove his way in if he had to.

To his surprise, Vivian stepped aside and opened the door wide. "She's upstairs in her room. Wait here.

I'll get her."

"Don't bother." He rushed past her and up the stairs, taking two steps at a time.

He reached the top, paused, and surveyed the long corridor. Four doors flanked the hall, all closed. She was behind one of them. He strode down the hall and rapped on the first door. No answer. He opened the door and peered inside. The room held a king-sized bed and a collection of ornate, antique furniture, all painted white. A familiar, cloying perfume filled the air. Vivian's room.

He strode further down the hall to the next room and stopped, his heart beating a trip-hammer in his chest. This was the one. Carrie Ann's room. He sensed her behind the closed door. He raised his hand to knock, but hesitated. What the hell was he doing? Meeting her on the road the other night was bad enough, and their confrontation at the old Rankin place had swamped him with a flood of memories, memories he neither wanted, nor needed.

But he had to know, and so, not bothering to knock, he inhaled a deep breath and opened the door. The room was dim, the curtains drawn. His eyes took a moment to adjust, but then he saw her lying on the bed, and he slipped into the room and moved toward her.

She was asleep, her auburn hair spread across the pillow in silken waves. Long, dark eyelashes rested on her sleep-flushed cheeks. Her mouth was open, her lips full and pink.

Memories of kissing those soft lips, touching her, loving her, assailed him. He bit down hard, blocking the groan threatening to escape. Sweat dampened the palms of his hands, and he wiped them on his jeans. Why the hell was he here mooning over her like a lovesick teenager? He turned to leave before he did something he'd regret.

She stirred, and the bed creaked.

He kept walking and didn't look back.

"Declan, what…?"

Every instinct urged him to get the hell out while he could. Hating himself for the weak fool he was, he stopped, turned and faced her.

She was sitting up, her hair tousled around her shoulders, her eyes wide, their amber light luminous in the dusky room.

His gut tightened.

She brushed back a lock of hair. "What are you doing here?"

He swallowed, his mouth desert dry. Why was he here? But then he remembered, and he glared at her. "Why did you come out to the farm this afternoon?"

Her eyes were too big for her delicate face. "I wanted to return your shirt and pay you the money you gave Ted to fix my tire."

He snorted. "You didn't drive out there to give me a few dollars and a ratty old shirt."

"I told you. I thought you might want help."

She was lying. She wouldn't help him. She hadn't all those years ago, and she sure as hell wouldn't now. "I'm supposed to believe you drove all the way out there to help me? *Me*?" He glared at her, daring her to lie again.

Rising, she crossed to the window, opened the drapes, and let in the last remnants of the day's light. She turned to face him. "Believe what you want. I'm telling you the truth."

"Why?"

"Why what?"

"Why do you want to help me?"

She shrugged. "I don't know."

"We both know how our relationship ended."

Her eyes turned wounded and dark.

His heart shuddered, but he held firm and tore into her again. "I know what you did."

She faced him, her hands on her slim hips, matching patches of red rising on her cheeks. "Oh, really? And what is it you think you know?"

"You texted me and told me to go to the old farm." She opened her mouth, but he cut her off before she could spout any more lies. "You wanted me out there."

"Why would I want to lure you out there?" Her eyes widened. "Oh, I get it. You think I texted you with some stupid message about having evidence in a twelve-year-old murder so I could be alone with you? You think I still care for you." She rolled her eyes. "Man, you have some inflated ego."

He took out the piece of torn silk he'd found in the barn and showed it to her. He'd placed the scrap of cloth in a clear plastic bag to protect any possible DNA evidence remaining on the silk. "You wanted me to find this. And you arranged for the police to show up. You hoped they'd find me with it. Caught red-handed, as they say."

She leaned closer. "What is it?"

"Oh, come on. Do you expect me to believe you have no idea what this is?"

She shook her head.

"I found this in the barn, behind a piece of wood, hooked on a nail." His eyes bore into hers. "Where you hid it."

She gaped. "Me? You think I put *this* in the barn? It's a piece of cloth. Big deal."

He held out the bag. "Look at it. Look closely."

She took the bag from him and held it to the light streaming through the window. She studied the cloth for several minutes and then shook her head. "I still don't understand."

"It's a piece of Skye's scarf, the one she wore the night she was killed."

Her hand holding the plastic bag trembled. "Are you sure?"

"Do you think I'd ever forget?" He grabbed the bag from her. "This was ripped from her scarf."

She stared, her face pale. "Who put it there?"

Her shock seemed real, but he kept at her, the need to attack raging through him. "The question is where did you find it?"

"Me? You think *I* hid a piece of Skye's scarf in the barn?"

"You told the sheriff you went out to the farm after everyone was gone. Maybe you found part of her scarf lying on the ground. When her body was found, you realized what you had. You've kept the scarf all these years, hoping you could use it someday to get back at me."

Stop! The warning blazed through him. But he couldn't. Even though he knew every word out of his mouth was ridiculous, he couldn't block them. "You hid the scrap of silk in the barn, and you texted me. You told me to go out to Rankin's Farm and look for it. Then you called the sheriff's department, hoping a deputy would find me holding a key piece of evidence.

Lucky for me, I left before they arrived, or I'd be in jail right now."

A pulse beat in her slender throat. Her eyes flashed, the amber turning gold, reminding him of an angry lioness. She stomped closer, stopping when her sock-covered toes bumped the front of his boots. "Do you actually believe I set you up?" Every muscle in her slim body tensed. "Where would I have found a piece of Skye's scarf? I wasn't even at Prom." She poked him in the chest, emphasizing each word. "Remember? I. Stayed. Home. I never attended Prom because my *boyfriend* broke up with me and took another girl." She glared at him, disgust written across her face.

He fought the urge to rub his chest where her finger had stabbed. "If you didn't hide the piece of scarf, who did?"

"How the hell would I know? Did you stop to think this…" She jabbed the bag. "This has probably been in the stall since the night she was murdered? The murderer left it."

He shook his head. "The fabric's too clean. This hasn't been in the barn longer than a few days."

Her eyes flashed fire. "You're a piece of work, you know that? You're so desperate to prove your innocence, you're willing to blame anyone you can."

All the anger, all the pain of the past twelve years reached critical mass and exploded out of him. "You try living my life, lady. Do you think it's been easy knowing everyone thinks I'm a murderer?" He spit out the words, tasting the bitterness and hurt he'd lived with these past years.

Tears filmed her eyes, sparkling on her eyelashes. "Living in this town couldn't have been easy. Leland told me how people treated you after Skye's murder. How they all thought you were guilty." A single tear slid down her cheek and trembled on her chin.

Her tears added fuel to his anger. He didn't want her pity. He wanted to wound her like she'd hurt him, and so he charged on. "Well, you got what you wanted. The sheriff was all over me the night Skye disappeared. He was so certain I murdered her, he was practically salivating."

"I…" She wiped her face. "I was upset, true, but I had nothing to do with the sheriff arresting you."

"I heard different."

"What do you mean?"

"You told the sheriff you saw me at the farm after everyone had left."

"Do you think I wanted to tell him? He called me in for questioning. I had to tell the truth." She turned pleading eyes on him. "I didn't want to. I knew how bad what I had to say would make you look, but Leland and Vivian hounded me until I did. When I was questioned, no one knew she'd been murdered. We all thought she'd run away." Her shoulders slumped. "I wanted to help find her. I didn't know…I didn't…" Her voice died. She looked beaten, but she kept her gaze fixed on his.

His anger vanished, leaving him weak. He'd come here looking for a fight, wanting to take his frustration out on her. Now look at her. She was right—he was a piece of work. He leaned closer, so close the warmth of her body seared his skin. He wiped a tear from her cheek, his hand lingering, savoring the softness of her skin.

Their gazes connected and held.

His heart thudded as he contemplated her mouth, the lips full and inviting. Sweat trickled down his sides. He bent his head. Their lips touched, all the anger of seconds earlier morphing into something else, something sweeter. He groaned.

She stiffened, and he jerked away as if she'd slapped him. "Sorry," he croaked, though for which of his many sins he was sorry, he wasn't sure. He didn't know what else to say. He'd already said more than enough. With heavy steps, he turned and walked out of the bedroom, closing the door behind him.

Chapter 11

Carrie Ann stumbled back to the bed and collapsed on the rumpled blankets. Using a tissue, she wiped her wet cheeks. She'd expected Declan's anger. Even his outrage and accusations hadn't surprised her. What shocked her, what pierced her soul, was the hurt in his dark eyes, the pain so similar to her own.

When he'd touched her, something inside had shattered, leaving her open and vulnerable to a riot of emotions. The desire in his eyes had startled her, but she'd wanted his kiss, reveled in the warm press of his lips against hers. The touch of his tongue seeking hers, his familiar taste, and she wanted more, so much more. Then thoughts of Bonnie had intruded, and she'd stiffened and turned away.

A knock at the door set her heart racing with a wild surge of hope. Declan! He'd come back. She stood and faced the door, her mind whirling with everything she hadn't said.

The door opened and Vivian shuffled into the room. Her aunt's sharp-eyed gaze slid over her, taking in Carrie Ann's tearstained face and rumpled clothes. The lines bracketing Vivian's mouth tightened, and she shook her head. Expelling a loud sigh, she sat on a chair by Carrie Ann's old study desk and crossed one thin, nylon-clad leg over the other, smoothing her wool skirt over her bony knees.

Carrie Ann sank back on the bed. "I'm tired, Vivian. Can we do this another time?"

"I'm tired too, but I have something to say to you, and it can't wait."

"Of course it can't."

Vivian's thin hands fluttered, fussing with her skirt, smoothing a strand of loose hair, and back to her skirt again. A deep cough racked her thin body. Her face paled as she inhaled a shaky, torturous breath. Under the layer of artfully applied makeup, Vivian's face was white and gaunt. Lines etched across her forehead, and a deep furrow ran between her perfectly shaped brows. She resembled an old woman, frail and worn. Only her eyes retained the furious energy she'd always possessed. Vivian cleared her throat. "I heard you and Declan arguing."

"Were you listening at the door?" Eavesdropping had been a favorite trick of Vivian's on the rare occasions Carrie Ann had been allowed to have a friend over.

Vivian sniffed. "I didn't have to. Your voices carried all the way downstairs." She coughed again, a deep, phlegmy hack. Withdrawing a white, lace-edged handkerchief from the sleeve of her blouse, she dabbed at her mouth. "Declan's been through a rough time. I feel responsible for what happened."

"You should. You helped point the finger of blame."

"I know." Vivian struggled to sit up straighter. "You had a part to play in this too, my dear."

"Me? I wasn't the one who urged the sheriff to charge Declan with Skye's murder. I wasn't the one sleeping with the county judge and whispering lies

C. B. Clark

about Declan in his ear. I didn't try to railroad a boy into jail just to get him away from my niece."

Vivian paled but held her gaze steady. "I'm not proud of what I did, but at the time, I thought I was doing what was best for you."

Carrie Ann laughed, the taste bitter in her mouth. "Me? What good did you do me? Declan and I had already broken up before Skye was murdered."

"You would have found your way back to each other. You two were too much in love to stay apart for long." Vivian spread her hands on her lap. "I couldn't allow you to get together again."

"*You* couldn't allow it? You thought it better I destroy the baby I was carrying because you were convinced the father was a murderer?"

"I'm admitting to my mistakes, Carrie Ann, but you're responsible for your own choices."

"I was sixteen years old."

"Old enough to have a mind of your own. Even though you were certain Declan was innocent, you still allowed me and Leland to convince you to leave town and to terminate your pregnancy."

Anger soared through Carrie Ann, the heat scorching. She jumped to her feet. "Bonnie! Her name is Bonnie."

Vivian's eyes softened. "I know, dear. And she's a lovely child. You've done a wonderful job with her. You're a good mother."

"How do you know anything about her?" She'd been careful to keep Bonnie away from Vivian and Cooper's Ridge.

A glint of the old, determined Vivian shone in her aunt's eyes. "You don't think I wouldn't keep track of

106

you, do you? All these years? You're my niece, dear, my only surviving relative. In spite of what you believe, I do care for you."

"How—"

Vivian cut her off. "Declan has suffered enough, don't you think? I believe he's innocent."

"Leland doesn't agree with you."

Vivian's face hardened, and she turned away. "Leland has his own agenda." A heavy silence hung over the room. "After Declan is cleared, I will tell him about Bonnie."

"You have no right."

Vivian's eyes were hooded. "I do, Carrie Ann. I have every right. It's called human decency. The man deserves to know he has a daughter."

Panic filled Carrie Ann, and her blood turned to ice. If Declan discovered he had a daughter, he'd want to meet her. Bonnie would know her mother had lied to her all these years. "Please, don't do this."

Vivian stood and smoothed the wrinkles from the front of her skirt. "Then you tell him. Far better he hears it from you than from one of the town gossips." Vivian's gaze fixed on her. "You know they'll find out. They always do." She walked out of the room.

Carrie Ann rubbed her aching temples. She'd been so young when she found out she was pregnant. She didn't want a baby. Not then. She had plans, none of which included bearing a child at sixteen. She'd wanted to go to college, earn a degree in medicine and become a doctor. Declan was going to work for a year so he could pay for college. He had dreams of earning a Business Degree and starting his own company.

They were in love. They wanted to get married and

have children eventually. But not at sixteen, not before she'd even finished high school. Even so, they might have figured a way to have it all…baby, college, and marriage, but before she could tell him of the pregnancy, they'd had yet another fight.

Her stomach knotted as memories assailed her. The problem started like it always did—an argument over Skye Lawrence.

"How many times do I have to tell you?" Declan's dark eyes flashed. "Skye and I are just friends." He yanked out a crumpled pack of cigarettes from the back pocket of his faded jeans and tapped out a cigarette. Using a cheap, plastic lighter, he flicked a flame to life with his thumbnail and lit the end of his cigarette. He sucked in a deep drag and expelled a cloud of smoke. "It's not easy for her. Her old man's always hassling her." His face hardened. "Skye won't admit it, but I'm sure the bastard hits her."

Carrie Ann threw her hands up in the air. How could he not see it? "Skye likes you. She really likes you." Her insides twisted when she thought of just how much Skye liked Declan. The tall, thin girl threw herself at him every chance she got. She was always touching him, brushing his hair off his forehead, or rubbing her pointy breasts against him like a cat in heat.

He narrowed his eyes. "Are you saying you don't trust me?"

"Of course not. It's Skye I don't trust."

He picked off a fleck of tobacco from his bottom lip. His gaze zeroed in on her. "You're not still mad about what happened at Joey's party, are you? I told you that was nothing. Skye was upset about something her old man had done. She was crying. What was I supposed to do? I couldn't ignore her."

Carrie Ann couldn't stop a snort of disbelief. "And that's why you two were wrapped in each other's arms like a couple of pretzels?"

He tossed his cigarette into the river. "I don't know how many times I have to tell you. Skye and I are friends."

Unable to look at him another second, she turned her back. Fury razed through her like a wildfire. How could he stand there and lie? Didn't he know Skye had told her what really happened that night? That Declan and Skye had made out?

She jumped when he touched her arm. His fingers burned her skin, and she snatched her arm away. "Don't touch me. Don't you dare."

"Come on, Carrie Ann, don't do this. Please." Once again, he stroked her arm. This time she didn't pull away. How could she when his lightest touch set off an explosion of sensation that left her desperate for more? She turned and burrowed into his arms.

But then an image of him kissing Skye rose before her, and she stiffened and wrenched free of his embrace. "No!" She scrubbed her hand over her mouth, wiping away his taste. "We're not doing this. Not now. Not ever again." Her chest heaved as she struggled to breathe through the constriction blocking her throat. "You lied to me. I'll never forgive you. Never."

"Carrie Ann." His voice was a hoarse cry as he reached for her.

She backed away holding her hands in front of her, stopping him. "We're over, Declan." Her voice hitched up an octave. "Do you hear me? We're done. I never want to see you again." Her heart shattered as the pain drove her to her knees.

"Don't do this." He crouched before her, his face close to hers. "Please."

She shook her head, her hair whipping around her face. "It's over." She covered her face with her hands as tears streamed down her cheeks.

His harsh breathing was loud in the quiet glade.

She fought back a deluge of tears, waiting for him to leave, so she could sink into the looming pit of despair.

"Okay." He blew out a loud gust of air. "If that's what you want."

Peeking through her fingers, she watched as he stood and walked away, disappearing into the forest. A sob broke free, and she sagged on the ground.

And that was it. Just like that, their relationship was over. In spite of all the hurt and anger, they might have found their way back to each other, but he'd done the unthinkable and asked Skye to Prom. Carrie Ann had found out she was pregnant the same day.

Her world fell apart. Pregnant and alone at sixteen. For days she didn't eat, didn't sleep. She sat alone in her room crying, until the tears dried up. She had to do something. Her breath hitched in her throat as she recalled the awful morning she'd gone to Declan's house to tell him of her pregnancy. Even though he'd betrayed her, he deserved to know she was carrying his child.

Her heart had thudded in her throat as she knocked on his door. She'd forced a smile when his mother opened it, her dark hair tangled, a stained nightgown floating like a shroud around her too-thin body.

"Carrie Ann." Mrs. McAllister blinked at her through puffy, reddened, bleary eyes. "Declan's asleep." She stumbled and swayed, clutching the doorframe for support.

"Can you wake him? I need to talk to him."

Mrs. McAllister peered at her. A frown settled between her brows. "Are you okay? You don't look so good."

"I'm fine," Carrie Ann lied, swallowing back bile as another bout of morning sickness threatened to engulf her. "Please, just get Declan."

"Are you sure? Because if you're feeling poorly, I got some pills you should try. They'll fix damn near anything that ails you." She giggled and stumbled as she lost her grip on the doorframe.

Carrie Ann grabbed the woman's skeletal arm, steadying her.

The older woman giggled some more, the girlish sound a stark contrast to her ravaged face and lifeless, pale eyes. A livid, purple bruise stained one cheek, and her bottom lip was swollen, a crust of dried blood at the corner of her mouth.

Carrie Ann shuddered at this sign of Declan's father's handiwork. "You should go back to bed and rest, Mrs. McAllister. Let me help you."

A flash of clarity lit the older woman's eyes. "You're a nice girl, Carrie Ann. Declan's lucky to have you in his life."

A lump rose in her throat. "Can I come in and see him?"

The clarity was gone, the puffy eyes once again vague and unfocused. "He's not alone. They're sleeping."

"They?" Carrie Ann asked, though her stomach roiled.

"He and Skye Lawrence. They've been here all night." Mrs. McAllister cackled. "Don't know what they been doing, but they sure was quiet. I ain't heard a thing." A dreamy look flashed across her face. "I didn't hear nothin' all night." She turned and staggered back into the hall, vanishing into the gloom, leaving the door gaping open.

Tears filled Carrie Ann's eyes. Declan and Skye had spent the night together. A sob shook her shoulders, her stomach heaved, and she hunched over and spewed vomit into the weeds beside the steps.

The next days had passed in a daze as the world she knew shattered into a million pieces. Skye had gone missing, and then her body was discovered in the forest behind Rankin's Farm. The sheriff and his deputies had questioned everyone who knew Skye and who had been at the prom party. Declan became the prime suspect, and Carrie Ann had been called in to testify.

Left with no other option, she'd gone to Leland and told him of her pregnancy, asking him for help. He, of course, told Vivian, and the situation spiraled out of control. Vivian took over. The next thing Carrie Ann knew, she was outside the Heartland Women's Clinic in Seattle preparing to have an abortion.

But she hadn't gone through with the operation. For the first time in her life, she stood up to her aunt. She refused to have the procedure and had walked away, losing herself in the anonymity of the city. That night was the worst and the best night of her life. Choosing to go through with the pregnancy, to give birth to her daughter, was her singular, shining moment.

One she never regretted.

Life as a single mother hadn't been easy. She'd coped the first, difficult year alone in the big city with the fistful of cash Leland had shoved in her hand when she opened the car door and announced she was leaving.

She'd struggled to survive at first, finding work at a fast food restaurant until the baby was born. Placing Bonnie in a subsidized day care facility, she worked during the day and went to school at night, earning her high school diploma. Next, she'd taken a secretarial course and found a position as an administrative assistant with an established real estate firm. Now she had a nice apartment in an attractive area of Seattle. Most importantly, she had Bonnie.

Maybe she'd been wrong not to tell Declan he had a daughter, but she made her choice long ago. The past couldn't be undone. How could she explain to Bonnie her long-dead father had come back to life?

She couldn't tell Declan he had a daughter, but she could try and do something to help make up for her deception. If she found Skye's murderer and proved Declan's innocence, it might ease the burden of guilt weighing her down.

Declan wouldn't like her helping him. He'd made his feelings more than clear. Too damn bad. She was doing this for Bonnie, not him.

Chapter 12

Declan opened the door to Rosie's Café and stepped into the stifling heat of the small restaurant. Diners, eager for Rosie's famous Tuesday night special of homemade pierogies and Polish sausages, turned and stared. Conversation ceased and all gazes followed him as he threaded his way through the tables to where Jessup Caruthers sat alone at a table in the back corner.

"Sorry I'm late." Declan slid into the booth across from the burly investigator.

"No problem. I've been enjoying the food." Caruthers pointed at the empty plate before him. "It's not bad, not bad at all. You should try the sausages. They're the best I've tasted in years."

Declan's stomach churned at the overpowering aroma of fried onions and grease. The last thing he wanted was food. "What have you found?"

Caruthers glanced around the crowded diner and nodded his chin at a nearby table where two young men and their dates made no secret of their eavesdropping. "Are you sure you want to do this here?"

Declan eyed the two couples. Sliding out of the booth, he strode over to their table, a phony smile pasted on his face. "Hey, how you doin'?" He almost chuckled when their faces paled.

The bigger guy sputtered and choked on a sip of beer.

The other man drew his girlfriend closer as if protecting her from Declan.

Anger burned deep in Declan's gut. "Do y'all have nothin' to talk about?" He laid on a thick Texas drawl. "You're mighty interested in me and my friend over there."

The dark-haired woman whimpered, her hand covering her mouth.

"Hey, man, we don't want any trouble." The big guy's last word ended on a squeak.

Declan nodded. "Good. Then we'll be fine, won't we? You'll mind your business, and I'll mind mine." He stared at each of them until they met his gaze.

Their heads bobbed in unison.

"Y'all have yourselves a nice evening." He turned and walked back to his booth and sat down. Damn. Putting them in their place felt good. Damn good.

Caruthers pulled a face. "It's been hard for you, hasn't it? All these years with a cloud of guilt hanging over your head."

"Small towns can be a bitch." *And then some.* "Even if you're officially cleared of all suspicion, the taint of having been a suspect stays with you. Guilt's like a bad odor. It clings to you. People have to accept you're innocent, but they never really believe you're clean." He took a deep breath. "So, what do you have?"

The P.I. opened a leather briefcase on the seat beside him. He removed two pieces of legal-sized paper and placed them on the table in front of Declan.

Declan scanned first one page and then the other, his heart sinking with each word. When he finished, he met Caruthers' gaze. "What the hell? I thought you told me you had some new evidence. I already know what's in here. Hell, half the town knows this."

"Take it easy. Give me a minute to explain."

Declan sucked in a steadying breath, fighting to overcome his crushing disappointment. "I'm paying you good money, and this is what you bring me?" He crumpled the papers in his hand. "This is useless."

"The report's only preliminary." Caruthers placed a hand on Declan's arm. "Hear me out."

Declan closed his eyes and breathed. After a minute, he opened them. "Okay, you have five minutes to convince me you're worth your fee."

Caruthers nodded. "Fair enough. I talked to the sheriff and the County judge." He paused. "You must have done a real number on Leland Winters' niece back in high school. He's pissed right off at you."

Declan grimaced. "It's a long story."

"I've studied all the files pertaining to the case, and I examined the coroner's report," Caruthers continued. "Skye Lawrence was brutally beaten and strangled to death." He dug in his briefcase, drew out a manila folder, and placed it on the table. "This is a copy of the coroner's report."

Declan's hand trembled as he opened the file. He examined the photo on the top of a small stack of papers and swallowed back vomit. He slammed the file shut. Too late. The image of Skye's beaten and bloodied body was seared onto his retinas. What sort of monster would cause another person so much pain? The people in this town thought *he* was the monster. He met Caruthers' gaze. "My God. I had no idea."

"The attack was brutal, all right. The wounds inflicted on her body are some of the worst I've seen. The killer was enraged. He wanted her to suffer."

Declan struggled to swallow.

"The killer knew her." Caruthers sounded certain. "This attack was personal."

Declan's hand shook as he slid the file folder across the table. "Who could do this to another human being?"

"I don't know. Not yet. But I intend to find out. One thing about small towns—we know all the suspects."

"You think someone in Cooper's Ridge hurt her?"

Caruthers tapped a thick, callused finger on the file folder. "This was an act of passion. The killer knew her. I'd stake my reputation on that."

Declan gulped, at a loss for words, but then a thought occurred to him. "This explains why the police were so certain I killed her. Doesn't it?"

"Yep, there you were." Caruthers pointed at Declan. "The perfect suspect. You knew her. You were strong enough to inflict a lot of damage. You were known to have a temper, and your ex-girlfriend's evidence puts you at the crime scene around the time Skye was murdered." He shrugged. "You had means, motive, and opportunity." He shaped his hand into a gun and pointed at Declan. "Bang! You're guilty."

"But I explained everything to the sheriff. I took Skye to the party, but like a jerk, I ignored her. I was so torn up about breaking up with Carrie Ann, all I wanted was to get drunk and forget. Skye didn't like being ignored, so she took off." Declan ran his hands over his face, trying to erase the haunting images. "I don't know where she went. All I know is she was beside me one minute, and the next she was gone. I figured she'd found someone to take her home. I wasn't good company, and I sure as hell couldn't drive, not after what I drank."

"The police didn't believe you." Caruthers sounded matter-of-fact. "They were so busy trying to pin the crime on you they didn't look at anyone else. Their lack of due diligence was a technicality, but their sloppy work opened the door for us to push to have the cold case re-examined."

"Do they have another suspect?"

"Not yet, but the fact their investigation was so biased was enough to force them to take another look at the case."

"What good does all this do me if we can't find the murderer?"

"We will, but it's gonna take some time. You have to trust me on this."

Declan rubbed his burning eyes. "It's been twelve years. I don't know how much longer I can live with this hanging over my head."

Caruthers placed his hand on Declan's arm and squeezed. "We will find the murderer, Declan. I promise you, I won't give up until we do."

Their gazes met and Declan nodded. A tendril of hope unfurled inside him. For the first time in a long time, he wasn't alone.

"One more thing, something the police kept back from the public," Caruthers said. "The killer strangled her with her scarf."

The air whooshed out of Declan. He stared at Caruthers, his heart pounding so hard he feared it would explode. He scanned the room and winced. He and Jessup were the center of attention. With a shaking hand, he withdrew the plastic bag containing the scrap of cloth from his pocket, and shielding it with his hand, he slid the bag across the table. "Don't let anyone see. I found this today."

Caruthers' eyes narrowed. "What is it?"

"A piece of Skye's scarf."

The investigator's mouth tightened. He slipped the bag onto his lap and examined it beneath the cover of the table. His gaze met Declan's. "How do you know?"

"She wore it prom night. The scarf was new, and she couldn't keep her hands off it. Her constant fussing drove me nuts."

Caruthers turned the bag over exposing the faded, rust-colored smear. "Looks like blood."

Declan nodded.

"Where did you find this?"

"In the old barn at the Rankin Farm."

Caruthers' forehead furrowed, his dark eyebrows forming a deep vee above his crooked nose. "You'd better start talking. And your story better be damned good."

"I know how this looks, but two days ago I received a text. The person who texted said he'd meet me at the farm. He had proof I was innocent. I was on my way out to the farm when—" Declan stopped, not wanting to rehash his encounter with Carrie Ann on the dark and muddy road. "Anyway, I didn't get there, but he texted me again and said he'd left something for me to find. I drove out there today and found that." He nodded at the bag in Caruthers' hand.

Caruthers heaved a breath and smoothed the palm of his large hand over his short spikes of graying hair. "Not smart, Declan. Not smart at all. You should have called me. I'd be able to state we found the scarf

119

together."

"I made a mistake. Going out there was stupid, but when I received the text, I wasn't thinking. I just wanted to find a clue to the murderer."

The P.I. rubbed his face, the scratch of stubble loud even in the noisy restaurant. "Tell me exactly where you found the scarf."

Declan explained how he'd searched the barn until he'd found the scrap of cloth hidden at the back of an old horse stall, behind the pile of bricks.

"Please tell me you used gloves when you touched the cloth."

Declan nodded.

"Well, that's one thing, I suppose." Caruthers shook his head. "This doesn't look good. You're the prime suspect, and you're in possession of the murder weapon."

"I'm turning the scarf into the sheriff as soon as we're done here. I wanted to run it by you first." A pulsing pain throbbed behind Declan's eyes.

Caruthers rubbed his face again. "Okay, let's think here. We have to assume the person who texted you was the killer. No one else would have known about the scarf."

"I don't understand. Why did the killer take part of her scarf?"

"It happens. Sometimes murderers keep mementoes of their victims."

"But why leave it for me to find?" The pounding in Declan's head revved up another notch. He rubbed his eyes to ease the painful pressure. "That's the part I don't get. Why me?"

"I don't know. Either he wants to further implicate

you in the murder, or he wants you to find him."

"Why would he want to get caught? Now? After all these years?"

Caruthers shrugged. "I've heard of stranger scenarios. Guilt can be an awful burden. Whatever his reason, there's a positive angle to this."

"Positive angle? Seriously?"

"The killer feels threatened. You being back in town triggered something and made him act after all this time. He'll make a mistake, and when he does, we'll get him."

Declan pointed at the plastic bag in the investigator's big hands. "What do we do now?"

"I'll take this to the authorities. They'll have their experts examine the cloth, and we'll see if this stain really is blood, and if so, whose blood." He regarded Declan. "You'd better be prepared for them to interrogate you. They'll want to know exactly where you found this, who told you to look for it, all the details. And they won't be gentle."

Declan nodded.

"Stick to the truth, and you should be okay. I don't think this is enough to arrest you." Opening his briefcase, he slid in the bag.

The truth. Declan bit back a snort. He'd told the truth twelve years ago, and look what being honest had achieved—a night in the local jail and the disgust and anger of every man, woman, and child in this damn town.

"One thing puzzles me." Caruthers placed his hands on the table and spread his big-knuckled fingers wide. "I've never understood why you went back to the farm the night Skye Lawrence disappeared."

"I've been through all this with you."

"Tell me again."

Declan hated thinking of that night, but if the slightest chance existed they'd find who murdered Skye, he'd rehash the painful memories again and again until he was blue in the face. He took a deep breath and began. "It was the after-party on prom night. We were all standing around a bonfire. Everyone was having a good time, talking, dancing, making out. Most of us were drinking or smoking weed. You know what those high school parties were like."

"But this wasn't a typical party. Not for you."

Declan shook his head. "I didn't drink, not ever. I still don't. I saw what booze did to my old man. No way was I going to turn out like him. But I was so torn up over Carrie Ann, when someone offered me a bottle of whiskey it was as if something came over me. I couldn't get enough of the stuff." He met Caruthers' gaze. "Turns out, I'm not so different from dear old Dad after all."

"Where was Skye at this point?"

Declan shrugged. "All I wanted was to get plastered and forget Carrie Ann. Skye got pissed off and left."

"What time was this?"

"I don't know, eleven o'clock, maybe closer to eleven-thirty. All I remember is looking up, and she was gone." He scrubbed his hands through his hair. No matter how many times he recounted the events of that terrible night, it never got any easier. Each retelling brought back the overwhelming burden of guilt. "If I hadn't been such a jerk, if I'd gone after her, she'd be alive today."

Cherished Secrets

"But you didn't."

Declan swiped a hand over his eyes. "No, I didn't. What sort of man lets a woman wander off alone in the dark miles from anywhere? Who does something like that?"

Silence hung heavy over the table. The rattle of dishes and the voices of the other diners seemed muted.

Declan grabbed Caruthers' untouched water glass and drained the water.

"You were a kid." Caruthers shook his head. "You made a stupid mistake. We all make mistakes. What you do about them is what counts."

"It's my fault she's dead."

"So do something. Stop feeling sorry for yourself and find her murderer."

Declan sagged against the seat back. Caruthers' words were like fists pounding, driving the air out of him. "I'm trying. What else can I do?"

"For starters, keep talking. Tell me exactly what happened next."

The pain in his head now a screaming crescendo, Declan swiped his arm over his damp forehead. "I guess I passed out because the next thing I knew, Sheldon Dubrowski was shaking me, telling me it was time to leave. I was so drunk I hadn't noticed almost everyone else had left. Only the hardcore drinkers and stoners were still hanging around. I searched for Skye. She wasn't there." He met Caruthers' gaze. "I figured she'd caught a ride home with someone else."

"Okay. Your friend woke you up." Caruthers' voice was calm and steady, his face expressionless, giving no hint of what he thought of Declan's actions. "What did you do next?"

"I was too drunk to drive, so I left my truck and caught a ride to town with Sheldon. He drove me home."

"But you went back out to the farm again. Why?"

Declan rubbed his eyes. *Would this God-awful pounding never end?* "I don't know. It was stupid."

"Go on."

"I woke up in bed after an hour or so, one thought on my mind—find Carrie Ann. I had to tell her I was sorry. I wanted to beg her to give me another chance, to take me back." He picked up the saltshaker on the table and rolled the small glass bottle in his hand, watching the salt crystals slide from one side of the container to the other. "I walked over to her place. The lights were off, but I knew she hadn't gone to Prom, so she had to be home. I knocked on the door, but Vivian wouldn't let me in. I told her I wouldn't leave until I saw Carrie Ann, but she threatened to call the sheriff."

He wiped his brow. "I knew she'd never let me near Carrie Ann. The old battleax was thrilled we'd broken up. She'd have done anything to keep us apart."

He swallowed, his throat dry, desperate for more water. "I caught a ride out to the farm. I wanted to get my truck and drive around until I cooled down and figured out a way to get Carrie Ann to forgive me."

"You don't remember who gave you the ride?"

Declan shook his head. "I was too drunk. I'd filched a bottle of rum from my old man's stash and begun to work on it." He shrugged. "I was so pissed I'm amazed I could still walk. The rest of the night's a blank." Self-loathing filled him. That night he'd proved he was a typical McAllister. Give him booze, and he turned into an animal. People around him ended up

124

hurt…or dead.

"Come on, Declan, who picked you up and drove you back to the party? You must remember."

"Don't you think I've tried to remember? My recollection is a complete blank. I figure someone passing through town picked me up and drove me out there."

"Why do you say that?"

"If someone from Cooper's Ridge had given me a ride, they'd have come forward when they heard what happened to Skye. Wouldn't they?"

"Maybe." Caruthers tapped his fingers on the table as he sat deep in thought. "Maybe not." He studied Declan. "What happened once you arrived at the farm?"

"I told you, I don't remember. I must have found my truck somehow and started driving around. I woke up the next morning feeling worse than shit. I had a cut on my head, and the front end of my truck was buried in a haystack in the middle of some farmer's field." He rubbed his face. "When I returned to town the next afternoon, the sheriff was waiting for me at my house."

He closed his eyes, remembering his surprise at learning Skye was missing. No one had seen her since the party the night before. He was even more shocked when the police made it clear they thought he had something to do with her disappearance. At first, they'd questioned him at home, but when they'd found her body the following day, they'd hauled him into the police station, and the real grilling began.

Over the next two months they'd questioned him repeatedly. No matter how often he'd protested his innocence, no one believed him. At one point, he'd even been held overnight in a cell in the basement of the Sheriff's Office before being released for lack of evidence.

"Why didn't you hire a lawyer? The police were hounding you. They wouldn't have been able to if you'd had legal representation."

Declan's mouth twisted. "Lawyers cost money. I didn't have any, and my parents sure as hell weren't offering to help. Besides, what was the point? The sheriff was so damn certain I murdered Skye, not a single lawyer in the County would have been willing to help me. Even if one had stepped forward, I wouldn't have hired him. Skye was dead because of me, because I was wasted. I deserved whatever they threw at me."

Caruthers' eyes narrowed. "So why are you now trying to prove your innocence? What's changed?"

"I finally stopped feeling sorry for myself. Finding out who murdered Skye and putting the killer behind bars for the rest of his life is more important than my hurt feelings and bruised ego."

"You probably should contact a lawyer."

Resignation washed over Declan, and he nodded, Caruthers' warning clear. Now he'd found a piece of Skye's scarf, he'd need some serious legal help if he planned to stay out of jail.

Caruthers placed the file folder in his briefcase, closed the lid with a snap and slid out of his seat. "Any thoughts on who might want to frame you for this?" He grabbed his coat hanging on a hook at the end of the booth and raised his heavy brows. "Well? At this point, I'll take any suggestions."

Declan shook his head. "I wasn't the most popular kid in those days, but I can't think of anyone who'd hate me enough to do this to me."

"Think harder. Someone in this town has a serious dislike for you."

Declan wet his lips. When he thought of who'd want to see him suffer, only one name came to mind—Carrie Ann Hetherington.

As if reading his mind, Caruthers said, "My investigation would be a lot easier if your ex-girlfriend would talk to me. Any chance of you putting in a good word for me?"

Declan snorted.

"That bad, is it?"

"You have no idea."

Chapter 13

Declan watched the private investigator walk out of the restaurant. The other diners stopped eating and broke off their conversations to watch him, too. The glass door swung closed behind the burly investigator, and their attention swiveled back to Declan.

From the second he'd stepped out of his truck when he'd arrived back in Cooper's Ridge three days ago, he'd faced a wall of fear, distrust, and outright animosity; part and parcel of being the town pariah. He'd experienced the hostility before, and he'd expected it again. He hadn't come back for a holiday.

Even though no one in Dallas knew of the cloud of suspicion hanging over his head, he did. After years of acting like a gutless pussy, he needed to move on with his life. To do that, he had to find Skye's murderer and clear his name.

He threaded his fingers through his hair, trying to ignore the suspicious glances directed at him. His stomach rumbled with hunger, but he wouldn't eat. Not here. The waitress hadn't approached his table in all the time he'd been in the small café.

He watched as she served plates of steaming pierogies and sausages to a table of two, bustled over to another group of diners, took their food orders, and cleared dirty dishes from a nearby table, all the while ignoring him. He was tempted to demand she take his order, but being right wasn't worth the hassle. He grabbed his coat from the seat beside him and stood to leave.

The door to the café opened, and Sheldon strolled into the restaurant. After a quick glance around, he caught sight of Declan, waved, and hurried over. "I heard you were here." He took off his jacket and hung it on the same hook Caruthers had used and slid into the booth.

Declan sank back onto his seat. "Let me guess...the Cooper's Ridge gossip brigade."

Sheldon grinned. "Who else?"

Secrets didn't exist in this damn town. Declan let out a discouraged breath. Everyone knew what everyone else was doing. Except regarding one person. He thought of his conversation with Jessup Caruthers. Someone in this town had a secret—a big secret. Someone in Cooper's Ridge was a vicious murderer.

"Have you eaten?" Sheldon asked.

He shook his head.

"Let's order. I'm starving."

"You go ahead. I was just leaving." Declan pointed at the waitress who stood behind the counter, arms crossed over her sagging bosom, watching them, making no move to take their order. "I don't think they want my business."

Sheldon looked where Declan pointed. His cheeks flushed. "This is not right, man." He rose from the booth.

Declan held out his hand to stop him. "Forget it. It's not worth it."

"You're not a criminal. You haven't been charged with anything, let alone convicted." Sheldon's voice rose. "This is bullshit!" He glared at the other diners.

Most stared back, but a few turned away as if uncomfortable with what was happening.

Declan let out a discouraged breath. *Life sure has changed.* Now Sheldon was sticking up for him. In elementary school and all through high school, he'd been the one who'd protected Sheldon from an unending stream of bullies. Sheldon attracted trouble, like flies to a dead fish. Maybe it was his loud mouth, or his cocky attitude, but whatever the reason, he was often on the bad side of the worst kids in school. He reminded Declan of one of those toy dogs people carry around in their purses, small, yappy, and ready to bite at the slightest provocation.

"What?" Sheldon demanded, still shooting daggers with his eyes at the other diners. He pointed at a heavily bearded man seated at a table near the front of the restaurant. "Do you have a problem, Ewan?"

Declan grabbed Sheldon's arm, stopping him from charging over. "Let it go," he said quietly.

Sheldon's eyes gleamed in his eagerness for battle. "Are you sure? I mean, this isn't right. You don't deserve to be treated like this."

"Let it go."

Sheldon mouthed an obscenity and sank back on his seat. "Okay, if you're sure. But it's not right. It's just not right."

They sat in silence as the conversations of the other diners gradually resumed, though Declan still felt the burn of their condemning gazes. His thoughts turned to his recent confrontation with Carrie Ann. He could have handled the situation better, but for some reason, he'd felt the need to burst into her bedroom and start hurling one accusation after another. Not cool. Definitely not cool.

He didn't really believe she'd texted him and hidden the torn piece of scarf for him to find. He'd needed to take his frustration out on someone, and she was the obvious choice. All his pain and devastation led back to her.

"Hey, man, are you listening?"

He rubbed his head in an attempt to erase the image of her wounded eyes when he'd accused her of trying to set him up. "Sorry, what were you saying?"

"I asked you why you came back."

"I told you. I want to clear my name."

"I understand, but why now, why after all these years?"

"Don't you think it's time?"

"You've made a life for yourself in Dallas, a good life. You own a successful business. No one in Dallas knows what happened in this little backwater town. No one cares. Even if they were to find out about Skye's murder, it's ancient history. You were never charged with any crime. You're innocent. You know it. I know it. Isn't that enough?"

Declan shook his head. "You have it all wrong. If someone found out, where would I be? My business is built on trust. Who would trust a man with their hard-earned money if he has a murder charge hanging over his head?"

Sheldon tore a paper napkin from the metal dispenser on the table and folded the napkin into a fan shape. "Why now? Why not five years ago?"

Declan sighed for the hundredth time today. "I guess you could say, I finally saw the light."

"You found religion?" Sheldon's attempt at humor fell flat.

"I finally realized this wasn't just about me. Somebody murdered Skye. Her killer's been walking around free and clear for twelve years. If I'd stuck up for myself back then, if I'd retained a lawyer, maybe the police would have considered other suspects. They might have even caught the guy who killed her."

"I doubt it, man. They had a real hard-on for you. They weren't interested in looking at anyone else."

"Even so, they would have had to at least make an attempt to dig deeper into the case. Instead, I rolled over like a cowed dog, and let them beat me again and again. I played right into the killer's plans."

Sheldon pressed a hand on Declan's arm and squeezed. "You've gotta stop blaming yourself, man. You were a kid. Everyone was against you, even your damn parents. What else could you do?"

"I could have thought of Skye, instead of feeling sorry for myself. She was my friend. She deserved better."

"You're here now."

Declan nodded. "I intend to find who murdered her and see the bastard pays for what he did."

"And this has nothing to do with Carrie Ann? Her being back in town is a coincidence?"

Declan scowled. Did this have anything to do with Carrie Ann? She was all he'd thought of since the first night they'd run into each other. Her name lingered on his every breath. Night after night he lay awake tortured by visions of her laughing, talking, loving. Even now, when he should be focusing on finding Skye's murderer, an image of a pair of cat's eyes surrounded by long, dark lashes floated before him. He felt the weight of Sheldon's sharp gaze, and a flash of heat burned through him. "This has nothing to do with Carrie Ann." He tried to put force into his statement. "Absolutely nothing."

Sheldon smirked. "Really? And you actually believe that?"

Declan bit back another sharp denial.

Silence hung between them as Sheldon continued to fold and refold the paper napkin. "I hate to bring this up, man, but what if you can't find the evidence you're looking for? What if, after all this, nothing changes?"

He didn't like to think what would happen if he struck out and nothing changed, but what Sheldon suggested was a real possibility. He'd known coming back to Cooper's Ridge and finding Skye's murderer after all these years, was a long shot. He could still end up the prime suspect. "That's not an option. I'm not leaving Cooper's Ridge until I find her murderer."

"But—"

"Look around you." Declan pointed at a group of women sitting at a table in the far corner of the restaurant who were sneaking peeks at him and talking in excited whispers.

A man glared from another table.

"People think I killed her. I intend to prove them wrong."

"Well, then I guess we'd better find the evidence to clear you."

Declan's throat thickened. "Thanks, buddy. Before I finish in this town, the truth will be out. Everyone will know Declan McAllister is an innocent man."

****

Carrie Ann took a deep breath and opened the front door.

Jessup Caruthers' broad frame filled the doorway.

"Thanks for coming, Mr. Caruthers." She stepped aside and ushered him into the house.

"Jessup, ma'am. Call me Jessup."

She met his stony gaze. Something flickered in his eyes, and she shivered. He'd stop at nothing to get to the truth. Declan had chosen wisely when he'd hired this man to help him. "Okay, Jessup." She took his coat, hung it on the hall coat stand, and led the way to the living room. They were alone. She'd waited until Vivian and Leland had left for work before she'd called him.

Jessup's gaze was cool and assessing.

She pointed to a floral-patterned, stuffed chair beside the fireplace. "Sit there, if you like."

He squeezed his long legs and broad shoulders into the tight space, dwarfing the small chair.

She perched across from him on the edge of a matching chair. "Thank you for coming."

He nodded.

She wiped her damp palms on her pants. "You wanted to ask me about Declan."

His penetrating gaze met hers.

She shuddered, wishing her palms would stop sweating.

"Why are you willing to talk to me now?" he asked. "The last time I approached you, you refused."

"I've changed my mind."

"Do you mind if I ask why?"

She squirmed on the chair, crossing and uncrossing her legs. "Declan didn't kill Skye Lawrence."

"Okay, so what made you change your mind?"

"I didn't change my mind. I've always known he was innocent."

"So, I ask you again, why have you now decided to talk with me?"

"I don't feel right standing by while an innocent man is wrongly accused." She shifted in her chair.

"But you were okay with doing the same thing twelve years ago."

"I was a child. I didn't understand what my leaving town would mean for Declan...what would happen...there were things...stuff...going on in my life..." Her voice died away as she realized what she'd almost said.

"What *things*?" His blue eyes were unblinking.

She fought the urge to run, to escape his probing gaze. "Look, this isn't getting us anywhere. I agreed to tell you what I know. Let's get on with your questions."

Again the infuriating nod, as if he'd read far more into her words than she'd intended. "Tell me what happened the night Skye Lawrence was murdered."

She took a deep breath. "Okay," she began. "Declan and I had a fight a few days before Skye disappeared." She met his gaze and shivered. It was as if he listened with every cell in his big body. "We broke up, and he asked Skye to Prom. I was upset, and didn't go. I couldn't face him with her on his arm, knowing everyone was talking about us, feeling sorry for me." She shrugged. "You know how things were in high school. Everything was big drama."

He didn't speak.

After a few heartbeats, she continued. "Anyway, I was pretty broken up over what had happened. I locked myself in my bedroom, ate a box of chocolates and cried myself to sleep." Her mouth twisted in a grimace. "I thought it would help ease the pain." She met his gaze. "It didn't."

He nodded, a glint of understanding softening the hard lines of his face. "You didn't go to the after-party at the farm either?"

She shook her head.

"But you did go to the farm later, after everyone had left."

She puffed out a breath. "I was in bed. It was late. Sheldon Dubrowski called me. He told me Declan was drunk, and he'd driven him home from the party. He was in bad shape. Sheldon was worried Declan would do something foolish."

"Why?"

She turned away from those all-seeing eyes. "You have no idea what Declan's life was like. His dad was the town drunk. He drank all the time, and when he was drunk, he used Declan and his mother as punching bags. It was awful." She shuddered. "It's why I was so worried when Sheldon told me Declan was drunk." She rubbed her damp palms on her pants again as if she could erase the memory. "He didn't drink. He saw what alcohol did to his father, and he didn't want to be like him."

"But he had a temper like his father."

She shook her head. "He'd get angry sometimes, but only if he saw someone mistreating someone else. Declan always stuck up for the underdog."

"So he was a saint."

"I didn't say he was perfect. Declan had a lot to overcome. He was in fights...lots of them, but he always had a good reason. Not everyone understood that."

"What happened after Sheldon called you?"

"Declan showed up at my house. He was hammered. I heard him pounding on our door, but Vivian refused to let him talk to me. At first I was glad she wouldn't let him in. I didn't want to see him, but after Sheldon's call, I was concerned. I knew Declan was upset." She swallowed over a lump in her throat. "Later, I snuck out, and *borrowed* Vivian's car and drove over to his house. He wasn't home, but Sheldon had told me Declan had left his truck at the farm. I knew he'd want his truck. When he was upset, he'd go for long drives to cool down."

"So you drove out to the farm?"

She nodded.

"What time was this?"

"I don't know…late…around three in the morning, I think."

"Did you pass any other cars?"

"I don't think so. I wanted to get to the farm before Declan left. From what Sheldon told me, he was way too wasted to drive."

"Did you see Declan?"

She nodded. "He was in his truck. I honked my horn, hoping he'd hear me and stop, but he didn't. I followed him, but he drove too fast and I lost him."

"Did you see anyone else? Any other cars? Anything?"

She shook her head.

"You do realize your testimony is one of the main reasons Declan's the prime suspect in this case?"

Tears burned her eyes. "Don't you think I know

what I did?"

"But you told the sheriff you saw Declan alone at the farm, and in the process you had your revenge on the boy who dumped you."

She jumped to her feet, anger, hot and heady, overwhelming her. She was tired of the guilt, tired of taking the blame. "We're done here."

He stood, towering over her. "Prove me wrong. Help him. Help Declan prove his innocence. Help us find the murderer."

"Don't you get it? I'm trying to help. It's the reason I'm talking to you now."

"Did Declan tell you he found a piece of the scarf Skye wore the night she disappeared?" he asked.

"He accused me of hiding it."

"Did you?"

"Of course not."

He narrowed his eyes.

She kept her gaze on his, refusing to look away.

"Okay." He nodded. "I've tried to talk to people in town, but they clam up as soon as they find out I'm working for Declan. You grew up here, you know these people. They trust you. As far as they're concerned, you're another one of his victims. They'll talk to you."

Ever since she'd arrived back in town, she'd avoided her old friends, but maybe Jessup was right. They might know something they hadn't told the sheriff, something they didn't realize was important. She'd be risking a lot. If anyone found out about Bonnie, she didn't know what she'd do. But she'd deserted Declan once. She wouldn't let him down again. "Okay, I'll try."

"Good girl." For the first time since she'd met him,

he smiled. The smile transformed his face, and for a minute, he looked almost approachable. He turned and strode out of the living room.

She hurried after him. "I'm not the only one who thinks he didn't kill her."

He halted, his hand on the door handle, his gaze locked on hers.

"My aunt believes he's innocent."

"The more the merrier." He opened the door and stepped onto the porch. "I'll be in touch." He walked down the brick path to his car.

Her mind whirled. They had to find who murdered Skye and clear Declan once and for all. She picked up her coat and purse from the hall closet. She'd called the rental car company first thing that morning and convinced them to fax her copies of the insurance papers. The shocked expression on the sheriff's deputy's pudgy face when she'd showed him the papers was comical. He'd had no recourse but to tear up the citation he'd written the previous day and return her driver's license.

But he'd gotten in one last jab as he'd reminded her of the money she owed the county for her speeding ticket. She'd paid the exorbitant fine, trying to ignore his all-too-obvious gloating.

Jessup had asked her to meet with some of the old gang and see if one of them remembered anything new about the after-party on prom night. But first, she had something to do.

Chapter 14

She knocked on the scuffed motel room door. Flakes of peeling paint showered onto the worn hall runner. Declan's truck was in the parking lot. He had to be here. Maybe he was in the shower. His naked body, warm water cascading over firm muscles, the soap— She cut off the thought and knocked again.

"He ain't here."

She turned.

A short, stocky woman watched her from the open doorway of a room two doors down. Graying, frizzy, shoulder-length hair puffed around a heavily lined face. A cigarette hung from her thin lips. Thick glasses did nothing to hide the inquisitive gleam in her brown eyes. A cleaning cart stood beside her filled with towels, toilet paper rolls, and sample soaps.

"Pardon me?" Carrie Ann asked.

"I said, he ain't here. You missed him." The other woman sucked in smoke and blew a perfect smoke ring, then another.

"Do you know where he is?"

The cleaning woman puffed on her cigarette. Smoke swirled in a cloud around her. Ash fell unnoticed at her feet. "Do I look like his mother?"

"Any idea when he'll be back?"

The woman shoved aside the cleaning cart and shuffled toward her, squinting against the smoke blowing in her face. "What business is it of yers?"

"He's a friend of mine." Carrie Ann mentally crossed her fingers at the falsehood. She was pretty certain Declan wouldn't consider her a friend. Not anymore.

"He doesn't have any friends in this town from what I hear." The other woman's gaze traveled over Carrie Ann, beginning with her feet, moving up over her legs and on to her chest, finally resting on her face. "Yer a pretty one, ain't ya?" She shuffled closer, smelling of smoke and stale sweat. "Yer the gal I heard about, ain't ya, the one who broke his heart? The whole town's talkin' about you comin' back after all these years. You two gettin' back together like they say?"

Carrie Ann's head throbbed. "This is ridiculous," she muttered and turned and walked along the walkway and down the stairs to her car.

"Where ya goin'?" The housekeeper's round face peered over the railing as she hollered down at Carrie Ann.

"You don't know where Mr. McAllister is, so—"

"I never said that."

Carrie Ann ground her teeth. "Well, which is it?"

"He took the path over yonder." She pointed a flabby arm toward the far side of the motel parking lot. "He was carryin' a fishing rod, so I guess he was headin' for the river. Good fishin' there, I hear tell."

The cleaning woman's eyes burned a hole in Carrie Ann's back as she walked across the motel parking lot to the dirt path leading into the trees. The news she was looking for Declan would be all over town in a matter of minutes. More fuel for the fire.

The air was cool under the trees, and she was glad

she'd worn a warm coat. The overgrown trail led through a dense growth of old oaks and tall grasses. The traffic noise of the busy road running by the motel faded, replaced by the sound of birds singing in the tall trees. The path climbed a knoll and opened into a small clearing overlooking the river. She stopped to catch her breath and surveyed the scene below.

A frisson of awareness rippled along her spine, and she grabbed the trunk of a tree, holding on as an onslaught of memories threatened to knock her to her knees. The trees were taller, the bush thicker and overgrown, but the familiar scents of fresh water, damp earth, fir resin, and fish told the tale.

This was *their* spot. The place she and Declan had sought refuge when life with her aunt, or his parents, became unbearable. Countless times they'd sat under the shade of these trees by the rushing water and talked for hours. She closed her eyes as memory after memory assaulted her—first kisses, falling in love, loving him, loving each other, and then, the harsh words and accusations of their final argument, the bitter void remaining.

Opening her eyes, she saw him, and her fingers dug into the rough bark.

Declan sat on a large, gray boulder on the bank of the river, fishing rod in one hand, the line dangling in the clear, rushing water. His dark hair gleamed like a raven's wing under the late morning sun. His back was hunched, his shoulders bowed, an aura of loneliness surrounding him.

A lump thickened in her throat. He'd paid a high price for what had happened so long ago. She'd been hurt too, but she'd come out the winner. She had

Bonnie.

He didn't turn around when she scrambled down the bank, though he must have heard her even over the play of water on rocks. He still didn't look up when she sat on a flat boulder beside him. The only indication he was aware of her presence was a tightening of a muscle in his jaw.

She stared at the rush of water, frothing white against the jumble of rocks. For the most part, the Jordan River was shallow and fast-flowing, filled with sharp rocks and sweepers, but if you knew where to look, hungry trout lurked in hidden, deep pools.

"How'd you find me?" His gaze was fixed on the line extending from his rod into the clear pool. A pulse beat a rapid tattoo in his rigid jaw.

"The housekeeper at the motel told me you were here."

Water splashed over the rocks. A crow cawed from somewhere deep within the forest. Sun filtered through the overhanging branches of a tall cottonwood. The steady drone of insects filled the strained silence.

"Do you remember the first time we came here?" He still didn't look at her, but his face softened, and a small smile played about his mouth.

"I fell in." A smile of her own started breaking through. "I thought I was going to drown."

"Until you stood up and found the water was only up to your knees."

"How was I to know?"

For the first time since she'd clambered down the bank, he looked at her. "Isn't it time you told the truth?"

Her heart skipped a beat. *He knows! He knows*

about Bonnie! "What do you mean?" She bit her tongue to stop the flow of excuses and apologies.

His eyes met hers. "You did it on purpose."

"Did what?" Vivian was right. She should have told him he had a daughter before this. She braced for his outrage.

"You deliberately fell in the river so I'd have to save you."

Relief washed over her, and a nervous giggle burst out. "Okay, I fess up. I was trying to get your attention. How was I to know you'd sit there and do nothing?"

"I was laughing too hard to do anything else." He chuckled. "You looked like a drowned cat."

"I guess almost drowning wasn't the most subtle way to get you to notice me, but in my defense, I was fourteen."

"You didn't have to do anything to catch my eye, and you know it." He smiled, lines radiating from the corners of his eyes, eyes warmed to a chocolate brown.

Her breath caught in her throat. She'd been in her sophomore year when she saw him standing on the school steps. Her knees had weakened at the sight. A year ahead of her in school, he was tall and leanly muscled, with long, curling, black hair and piercing brown eyes, impossibly good-looking. She'd spent the next three months trying to get him to notice her.

One day, after her last class, she was at her locker, and there he was, leaning against the adjacent locker, grinning, white teeth gleaming, eyes filled with promise. He'd asked her if she wanted to go for a walk, and he'd brought her here, to this spot. They'd been inseparable ever since, until—Her smile vanished.

Silence settled over them, heavy with bittersweet

memories. She brushed away a fly, shifted her bottom on the hard rock, and counted the number of cottonwoods in the secluded clearing. Twelve.

His face was closed, his mouth tight. The knuckles on the hand holding the fishing rod were white.

The silence grew, each second piling one more brick on the impenetrable wall between them. She swatted another fly and once again adjusted her bottom on the uncomfortable rock. "Any bites?" she blurted, unable to stand the silence a second more.

He shook his head. "I don't have any bait on the hook." He picked up a flat pebble and tossed it in the water, watching as the rock skipped across the small pool. "Do you ever regret it?" His voice was a husky croak.

"Regret what?"

"The fight we had…" His voice grew faint, the rest of what he said lost in the rush of water. He stared into her eyes. "Do you remember what we fought about?"

"Skye," she said at once. "We always argued about her."

"You were wrong, you know. She…" His brows drew together. "She was so alone. Her family was like mine, maybe worse. We understood each other. She needed someone on her side, someone who'd stand up for her. I was her friend, her only friend. I wanted to help her." He coughed, blinking his eyes. "Nothing happened between us, not what you thought anyway."

"You spent the night with her."

"What?" His gaze shot to her.

"After we broke up, I went over to your house. I wanted to talk to you. Your mother said you and Skye had spent the night together in your room." Her

C. B. Clark

stomach twisted, the pain of the shocking revelation as fresh today as twelve years ago.

"You came to my house? Mom never told me."

"She wasn't in very good shape. I doubt she remembered I was ever there."

"What did you want to talk to me about?"

"Nothing. It's not important anymore." She cringed, waiting for a bolt of lightning to strike her at her blatant lie.

He narrowed his eyes. "Are you sure?"

Her heart in her throat, she nodded. *Tell him. Tell him now, before it's too late.* Too late? It was already too late. Neither Bonnie nor Declan would forgive her if they found out the truth now. "I'm sure."

He flipped another rock into the river. "That night, the night Skye spent in my bedroom, her older brother had been arrested for dealing drugs, and her old man took his anger out on her. She came to me, her face bruised, one eye black and swollen. She was scared and didn't know where else to go."

"Declan, what did you do?" Her heart thudded. She knew him, knew he wouldn't have stood by and let Skye's father beat her.

"I did what needed to be done, what I should have done months earlier." His mouth narrowed to a thin line.

"You went over to her house, didn't you?"

"The old man was drunk, passed out on the couch, but I didn't care. I dragged his sorry ass off the couch and pounded the shit out of him." He sucked in a shaky breath. "By the time I was done, he promised he'd never touch Skye again." Picking up a pebble, he tossed the small round stone from one hand to the other. "I always wondered if he was the one who killed her."

"Didn't the sheriff question him?"

"He had an airtight alibi. He was playing cards at Mickey's Roadhouse. A dozen people saw him. He couldn't have done it."

She sagged, suddenly exhausted as another layer of guilt was added to her already overwhelming burden. She'd gone to Declan's house to tell him of her pregnancy, but hadn't because she'd thought he and Skye were together in his bedroom having sex. Instead, he was out doing what he always did—protecting a friend. Because she hadn't trusted him, he'd never learned he had a daughter. "I'm sorry," she choked out. "I thought..." She couldn't finish. She'd thought he'd betrayed her, and she'd punished him by not telling him about her pregnancy. She was still punishing him.

"It's sad, isn't it?"

The rumble of his voice broke through her self-flagellation. She sniffed back tears.

"Neither of us was willing to get past our anger and stubbornness. Because of our hurt pride and damaged egos, we let *us* end."

Her eyes watered. "I'm sorry about your parents. Losing them both so close together must have been awful."

He stared at the river, his throat working. "Ever since I was a little kid, I knew my mother wasn't like other mothers. She was always tired, always sad, always locked away in her bedroom." He shrugged. "I guess I wasn't surprised when she finally killed herself. I knew she'd do it one day."

Carrie Ann blinked back tears, wanting to comfort him, but uncertain whether he'd welcome her touch.

"My dad's death shocked the hell out of me. I figured the old fucker was too ornery to die." His eyes reflected his pain and anger. "Who would have thought he'd kill himself because Mom was gone. I didn't even know he liked her. They sure as hell never showed they cared for one another. Unless yelling and beating someone black and blue is a sign of affection."

"I thought your father died in a car accident."

His harsh laugh sent chills rippling along her spine. "I saw him, you know. That night. He was so drunk he couldn't stand upright, but as usual, he was itching for a fight. I was home, so I was the lucky one. He blamed me for what happened to my mother. He said she couldn't stand to live with the shame of having a murderer for a son." He ran his hand over his face as if trying to scrub away the painful memory. "I hit him, punched the bastard's face as hard as I could.

"For once, he didn't strike back. He glared at me, his nose bleeding all over his shirt, his eyes wild, accusing me of killing Skye." He turned red-rimmed eyes on Carrie Ann. "I wanted to hit him again to shut him up." He shook his head. "Instead, I did what I always did. I ran out of the house and took off in my truck."

She blinked back tears, never taking her gaze off him. His face was pale, his eyes unfocused. He was lost in his private hell, and she wasn't even sure he remembered she was here.

"Usually he passed out on the couch and slept it off, but somehow he managed to stagger out to his truck." His voice was flat, emotionless. "The next thing I knew, the cops were at the house telling me he'd had an accident." He snorted. "Accident, my ass. He knew exactly what he was doing. He took the coward's way out. He wanted to die, and he wanted me to know I was the reason he'd killed himself. He wanted me to pay for what he thought I'd done."

Her heart ached. He'd been through so much. No wonder he was so bitter.

He sighed and straightened his shoulders. "I can't change what my parents did, what choices they made, but I sure as hell can try and change what happens to me. I didn't kill Skye, and I fully intend to prove I'm innocent, and in the process, find out who did kill her."

"I'm sorry I told the police I saw you at the farm on prom night."

He reeled in some of the fishing line, his hands steady on the rod. "I told them the truth when they questioned me. I hadn't done anything wrong. At first, I didn't know Skye was missing, let alone dead."

"I never thought you killed her."

He stopped reeling and faced her. "You had a funny way of showing it. You left town right after the first time the police took me in for questioning. I know. I tried to call you."

She bit down on her bottom lip. She couldn't tell him the real reason she'd left. She was four months pregnant the night Skye was killed. If she'd stayed any longer, her pregnancy would have shown. People would have known. Vivian would never have allowed her niece's unplanned, teenage pregnancy to become fodder for the town gossips.

"Vivian made me leave. She didn't want anyone to think I was involved with the murder." She shrugged. "You know how she was, always wanting to protect her precious family name."

"And you left? Just like that? Because she told you to?"

Heat flared, and she knew her cheeks were a bright red flag attesting to her lie. "I was sixteen years old, and Vivian was overpowering. Leland stood by her side, parroting everything she said. The two of them worked on me until I finally agreed to do what they wanted, anything to get them to stop. Besides, our relationship was over. You'd made it clear you didn't want anything to do with me."

A bright flash fractured the dull morning light, followed by an earthshaking boom as if the gods mocked her deception. She shuddered. Dark thunderclouds scudded across the sun turning the sunny day into twilight.

"Looks like we're in for a storm." Declan reeled in the last of his line. "We'd better get going."

A smattering of fat drops pebbled the water. In the next second, a gust of wind tore at her hair, and rain pelted down in sheets. She shivered and clasped her coat around her.

"Come on." He took her hand and hauled her to her feet.

They ran to a tall fir tree and crawled beneath the branches, and huddled in the nest of dry needles. The thick branches offered protection from the storm. Only a few raindrops dripped through gaps in the boughs.

Shivering, she brushed back damp strands of hair.

He wrapped his arms around her, drawing her close to his warm body.

Her first instinct was to relax against his broad chest into his warmth, but his all-too-familiar scent of leather and forest enveloped her along with a plethora of heady images. She stiffened and backed away.

His eyes were bright even in the dim light. "What are you afraid of, Carrie Ann?"

She couldn't speak, couldn't think. He was too close.

He put his hand on her chin and turned her until she was forced to look at him.

The air rushed out of her at the spark of heat turning his eyes the color of melted chocolate.

His gaze shifted to her mouth.

A wildness took hold of her, an urge to take what she wanted; to stop thinking for once and act. She leaned toward him and pressed her lips to his. The first taste of him was a shock, but then she was home, and she pulled him closer, welcoming him back.

He deepened the kiss, cupping the back of her head, caressing her damp hair with his long fingers.

Sensation pounded through her as years of lies and resentment receded, and she forgot everything but the way he made her ache for more. In the next instant, the warm press of his lips vanished, leaving her gasping for breath. "What is it?"

He eased away, a shock of cold air separating them. "We're not doing this." His voice was cold. The closed expression on his handsome face told her the truth better than words. Kissing her was a mistake.

She licked her lips, tasting him. *Another mistake.* "I should go." Ducking under the branches, she stumbled into the clearing. The storm had blown over as quickly as it had appeared, and only a smattering of drops dripped from the trees. She ran, slipping and sliding in the mud, her one focus to get away from him.

"Carrie Ann, wait."

She ignored him.

He caught her arm, stopping her. "I'll walk you back."

She didn't look at him, was afraid to, but she didn't fight his grip on her arm. Like a child, she let him lead her along the path back to the motel parking lot.

Chapter 15

Declan exhaled a deep breath. After squelching through mud and puddles of water on the slippery trail, they finally broke out of the wet brush and crossed the cracked pavement of the motel parking lot. A few more steps and he'd be safe from the overriding temptation to take her in his arms and once again taste her sweet lips.

After the path narrowed, he'd been forced to follow behind her on the long trek to the motel. A mistake. One of many this day. All he could think of was her slim hips and shapely butt as she hurried ahead of him. He tore his gaze away, but then her fall of auburn hair caught his attention, and he wanted to run his fingers through the silken strands.

Her car loomed ahead and all fantasies of rediscovering her naked body fled. "What the hell?" His gut twisted in a tight knot. All four tires of her rental car were flat. Cursing, he bent down and examined them. A deep gash gaped on the tread of the worn rubber of each tire.

"What happened?" Carrie Ann's voice was a thin squeak.

"Someone slashed your tires."

"What? Who'd want to wreck my tires?"

"Someone who knew you were coming to see me." He walked around her car to where his truck was parked and cursed out loud again. The same asshole who'd slashed her tires had keyed his truck. On the driver's side, across the door and extending onto the side of the truck bed, someone had scratched the shiny black paint. *Murderer* was written in large, block letters.

He heard her gasp, but kept his gaze fixed on the condemning word. *Murderer.* For the hundredth time since he'd come back to Cooper's Ridge he wondered what the hell he was doing here. Everyone thought he was guilty. Nothing he did would change their opinions. The best thing he could do was get the hell out of this damn town.

He glanced at Carrie Ann's car. All four tires were flattened, the vehicle resting on the rusty rims. His anger redlined. He was willing to face the accusations people threw at him, but this nightmare didn't involve just him anymore. Someone had wrecked her car because she was with him. He drew his hands into fists, wanting to pound whoever had done this, to smash their narrow-minded faces until even their own mothers didn't recognize them.

She touched his arm.

The heat from her hand seeped through the thin material of his damp shirt, soothing, easing some of his fury.

"So this is what it's like for you." Her voice was quiet. "People hate you enough to want to hurt you." Tears shone in her eyes and glistened on her long lashes.

He fought the urge to wipe the tears, but then he caught sight of her flattened tires, and his anger flared again at the malicious damage. Whoever had done this would stop at nothing to show him, and anyone connected with him, contempt. A chill settled over him. What if he hadn't walked her back to her car? What if the creep who'd damaged their vehicles was still hanging around? "You're leaving town. Now."

Her face was pale, fear written across her fine features.

Good. She should be afraid. Fear would make her realize the seriousness of the situation. Fear would make her listen.

She shook her head. "I don't think so."

He blew out an angry puff of air. "The asshole who did this is probably the same jerk who shot out your tire. Next time, he might not just wreck your tires. He might hurt you." He rubbed the back of his neck. "I have enough on my plate. I can't be worrying about you too."

She stared at him for another long moment, and then she smiled. The small, tight smile didn't reach her eyes. "Well then, it's a good thing you don't have to worry about me, isn't it? I can look after myself just fine, thanks."

His gut tightened, and all his anger at the person who'd wrecked their vehicles found a target and exploded out of him. "Why do you have to be so damn stubborn? Why can't you leave town and go back to where you've been hiding all these years? I don't need your help, and I sure as hell don't want you here." His breath heaved in and out of his chest as if he'd run a marathon.

"You're a real piece of work," she sneered, her disgust for him plain. She turned and started to walk away.

"Where are you going?"

She kept walking.

He was tempted to let her go, but whoever damaged their vehicles might still be lurking, and so he hurried after her. "Wait. I'll drive you home."

She stopped, turned, and faced him, her eyes blazing like molten gold. "Go to hell." She started walking away again, but not before he saw the tears building in her eyes.

The air whooshed out of him as if she'd punched him. He took a step after her, but stopped. He'd done enough. More than enough.

At the side of the road, she dug out her cell phone and made a call.

He stayed where he was and watched her until after a long wait, a black, four-door sedan slowed and pulled over to the curb beside her. When she opened the passenger door and the interior light shone, he recognized Leland Winters' grizzled face behind the wheel.

She climbed in without looking back, and the car pulled into the stream of traffic and drove off.

He released a breath. She was safe. For now.

He rubbed his jaw, the rasp of beard loud in the cool, afternoon air and regarded the vandalized vehicles. His anger resurfaced, and he yanked out his cell phone and called the sheriff. He wouldn't have bothered calling the authorities if only his vehicle was involved. He could deal with the damage caused by the scratching of his truck's paint, but he wanted the authorities to know someone had done this to Carrie Ann's car. He wanted them watching her and keeping her safe.

While he waited for the sheriff to arrive, he vowed

he'd find whoever did this and make him pay. No one threatened Carrie Ann, no one. Not when he was around. She wasn't his responsibility anymore, but suddenly, finding the person who'd slashed her tires was more important than clearing his own name.

****

He stood on the porch and pounded on the door. Carrie Ann wouldn't be happy to see him. He scowled at the understatement.

The door opened and light spilled onto the porch. Vivian didn't act surprised to see him, and she opened the door wider. "She's upstairs."

He raised his brows in question.

"Go on." She turned and walked down the hall, disappearing into what must be the living room.

He shrugged and stepped into the house, closing the door behind him. Crossing the foyer, he headed up the stairs to the second floor. At the top step, he paused, sucked in a steadying breath, and like a soldier preparing for battle, marched down the hallway and rapped on Carrie Ann's door. As soon as she called out, he opened the door and walked inside.

She lay on the bed, her head and shoulders propped up by a mound of pillows. Her eyes widened as she glanced up from the book she'd been reading. "What are you doing here?"

He walked over to the desk and picked up the same chair he'd sat in the day before. Swinging the chair around, he sat down, resting his arms on the chairback.

Her brow knitted. "You don't listen very well. I told you to leave me alone."

"I thought you'd want to know about your car."

"Leland already told me. You called the Sheriff's

Office. They're looking into who slashed my tires and keyed your truck."

He nodded.

"I guess I should thank you."

"For what?" He wrinkled his brow, confused by the unexpected peace offering.

"You also had the repair shop tow my car. Ted called and told me. He'll have my tires replaced by tomorrow morning." Her mouth curved in a semblance of a smile. "He likes me. I'm his biggest customer. You didn't have to phone Ted about my tires, you know. I would have looked after it."

He shrugged. "What can I say? I like to help damsels in distress." He fought to keep his voice light. The sheriff hadn't offered much hope of finding the culprits who'd damaged their vehicles. He believed a bunch of kids out drinking and looking for trouble had caused the damage. The sheriff's theory was bullshit. The attack was personal. No question, but the violence in the act frightened Declan.

"What about your truck? How are you going to get rid of the…uh…the writing?"

"My truck's in the body shop. They have to repaint the exterior, but the truck should look as good as new when they're done. I'm driving a rental now."

She put her book down and sat up. "You've told me about my car, and I've thanked you. We don't have anything else to say to each other. Goodbye."

The chill in her voice stung. He scanned the room for suitcases or signs of packing. "Doesn't look like you're planning on leaving town anytime soon."

"What I do is none of your business."

"That's where you're wrong."

She raised her brows in question.

"Your tires were slashed because you were with me. The person who did that won't stop with vandalism. You and I have a long history together. Everyone in town knows about us." He rubbed his hands over his face and frowned. He needed a shave. "Someone shot your tire out the night you came back. The same person slashed your tires today."

"You think so?"

"Someone in this town has a serious hate-on for me." He met her gaze. "And for you too, now."

Her face blanched. "Am I in danger?"

He nodded.

"That's crazy. Who'd want to hurt me?"

"I don't know who's responsible. All I know is someone doesn't want us to find out who murdered Skye."

"I don't have anything to do with this. Not anymore."

"Sure you do. Think." He met her gaze, trying to make her see what was so evident to him. "You came back to town the same time as I did. You arrived here with me, in my truck and—"

"That was a coincidence," she blurted. "I had a flat tire. You were the first person to come by and help me. No one saw us together. It was dark and there was all that rain."

"Someone did."

She opened her mouth to protest, but then her face paled. "Mrs. Higgensdorf."

"Is that the nosy old biddy who used to live next door?"

"She still does. She saw you drop me off." She

groaned. "She probably told everyone she knows."

He didn't say anything, just allowed her time to think the situation through and reach the same conclusion he had.

Her eyes widened. "You think people believe I came back to town for *you*?"

He scowled. Was it really so farfetched? "Looks that way."

"My tire was shot out because someone doesn't want me here? Are they trying to warn me away?"

He nodded.

She stared, her eyes large in her pale face.

Cat's eyes. The thought floated through his mind, distracting him, but he remembered the danger she was in and focused on her words.

"I haven't talked to you in twelve years."

"I know you haven't, but does everyone know we haven't been in touch?"

She shivered and crossed her arms in front of her chest. "You think someone's following me?"

"I don't know, but we can't be too careful."

Her eyes narrowed. "*We*?"

He tried a smile, but his mouth was too stiff. "You're not going anywhere on your own. From now on, as long as you're in this town, I go where you go."

"I'm not going anywhere with you."

He stood and slowly walked toward her, his gaze fixed on hers.

She drew her knees to her chest and pressed her back against the headboard.

He stood over her. "Someone is out to cause trouble. I'm not going to let them harm you. Until you leave town, you're with me." He held his breath, knowing she'd fight him on this.

She jumped to her feet and shoved him aside, storming across the room. "I am not *with* you. I don't need your or anyone else's protection. I can look after myself."

"You don't get it, do you? You think this is a game?"

She shook her head, but said nothing.

He rubbed the back of his neck where tension had begun to gather in a tight knot. "Did you ever stop to consider if I didn't murder Skye, the person who did kill her is still in town? He's the one who vandalized our vehicles."

"You think the murderer's someone from here?"

"The P.I. I hired thinks so. It makes sense. Someone local murdered Skye. The killer is willing to do anything to stop us from finding out the truth. He has the best reason of anyone to want to drive me away before I find any new evidence. He framed me with the piece torn from Skye's scarf. He shot out your tire and then slashed your tires. He knows if he threatens you, I'll back off. He's using you to get at me."

She sank onto the desk chair and studied him for a long time. "Who is this person? Someone we know?"

"Probably."

She smoothed her hair back, her hand shaking.

He crouched before her. "I won't let anything happen to you. I promise."

Her eyes were clear amber in her pale face. "Why? Why do you care?"

He knew what she was asking, but he didn't have an answer, at least not one he was prepared to share with her. "I care because we used to be friends." He leaned closer, wanting to brush a stray curl off her forehead.

She flinched.

He dropped his arm to his side and stood. His voice was wooden as he reassured her. "It's okay. You don't have to worry. What happened at the river today won't happen again. Kissing you was a mistake. One I don't intend to repeat." He headed for the door, but stopped and glanced back at her. "Let me know if you decide to leave the house. I'll come and get you."

Her cheeks flushed, and her eyes flashed golden fire.

He hurried out of the room and closed the door behind him.

A loud crash reverberated, and the door shook as something hard hit the solid wood.

He expelled a breath. The conversation had gone better than he expected. At least she hadn't thrown anything at *him*.

Chapter 16

Carrie Ann shrugged on her coat and picked up her car keys from the bench in the front foyer. Her reflection in the hall mirror caught her eye, and she shook her head. In spite of her best efforts wielding blush and mascara, the dark circles under her eyes stood out in her pale face. No wonder. She hadn't slept.

Declan's visit had unsettled her. His certainty someone was out to harm her was ridiculous. She agreed with the sheriff. Her tires had most likely been slashed by teenagers high on drugs or alcohol and looking for trouble. Petty crimes like car vandalisms happened all the time. Even in small towns like Cooper's Ridge.

The keying of Declan's truck was the senseless act of kids being stupid. They might have been babies when Skye was murdered, but they'd have heard the grisly story from their parents. It wasn't every day someone in Cooper's Ridge was murdered. The vandals had probably thought it a real thrill to scratch *'Murderer'* on Declan's truck.

"Where are you going?" Vivian shuffled down the hall toward her.

"Out." Carrie Ann bit her bottom lip. She'd hoped to avoid her aunt. Earlier this morning she'd called someone she'd known in high school. Marie Faulkner had been a good friend once upon a time. She'd attended Prom and the after-party at the old farm the night Skye had disappeared. More important, she was willing to talk. Carrie Ann had phoned three other old friends, but not one of them would talk to her about Skye's murder. They hadn't come right out and said they wouldn't, but she'd seen through their feeble excuses. At least Marie had agreed to meet her.

She glanced at her watch. "Look, Vivian, I have to go." She opened the door.

"Where's Declan?" Vivian frowned at her.

"Declan?"

Vivian placed a hand on her arm. "He told me what happened to your car. He thinks you're in danger. You shouldn't go out by yourself."

"He's overreacting."

"After what happened to your car and Declan's truck yesterday, I would think you'd be more concerned."

"I'll be okay." She tugged her arm to break free.

Vivian tightened her hold. "You're not going anywhere alone. If you won't let Declan help you, I'll get Leland. He'll go with you."

Was that fear in the old woman's eyes? Carrie Ann shook her head. Couldn't be. Vivian wasn't afraid of anything. "I'll be fine. See you later." She opened the door, stepped onto the porch, walked down the steps and along the brick path to her car. Ted had delivered her car earlier in the morning. He'd grinned like a Cheshire cat when she paid him. His business had taken a definite upturn since she'd come back to town.

A car horn honked, or rather, beeped, and a pint-sized, silver, two-door car stopped at the end of the long driveway. The driver's door opened, and a familiar figure climbed out.

"What are you doing here?" she demanded.

"I told you I was driving you today." Declan walked around and opened the passenger door of the silver car. "Come on. Get in."

"Are you kidding me? You don't honestly think I'm going anywhere with you?" She looked pointedly at her watch. "I'm late, so I'd appreciate if you'd move your tin can out of my way so I can leave."

He grinned, flashing even, white teeth. "This car is kind of small, isn't it? Franco's Deals on Wheels didn't have much of a selection."

She inhaled a sharp breath. "Please move." She hated to beg, but she was determined to meet Marie before the woman changed her mind about talking to her.

Declan didn't budge. He stood and waited as if he had all the time in the world, an infuriating grin plastered across his handsome face.

Cursing under her breath, she marched over to the small car. She slid into the passenger seat, strapped on her seat belt, and crossed her arms in front of her, staring straight ahead.

He closed her door and sauntered with an obvious swagger over to the driver's side. The tiny car bounced and shimmied as, grunting and cursing, he contorted his large body to fit behind the wheel. "Damn."

In spite of her determination not to look at him, she snuck a peek and bit back a giggle.

He was wedged into the seat, his long legs crammed on either side of the steering wheel, knees up by his chest. His head almost brushed the roof like a circus clown driving a child's toy car.

He grinned, a matching set of dimples dancing in his lean cheeks. "I know. It's a tight fit, but this baby's a hybrid. She gets forty miles to the gallon." Somehow, juggling his knees and the steering column, he managed to put the car into reverse, and they backed out of the driveway.

Her shoulder brushed against his, and she inched away, pressing against the passenger door's hard vinyl, putting as much space as possible between them.

"So, where are we going?"

"Hector's Casa." She tried not to growl.

The car bounced over a pothole, and their shoulders rubbed together. A tremor of awareness sparked along her spine, and she jerked away, holding her body stiff.

"Why are we going to Hector's?"

Hector's Casa was a small, Mexican restaurant on the outskirts of town along the old highway. The restaurant was out of the way, but Marie had wanted to meet in the old diner, probably because no one was likely to see them. "I'm meeting someone."

"Who?" His voice was level.

She hesitated, but realized she was being childish. After all, she was doing this for him. "Marie Faulkner."

He glanced at her. One dark brow quirked.

"I want to ask her about the night Skye was murdered."

His brows rose higher.

"I know." She shrugged. "It's a long shot, but she was at the party, and she might have seen something."

He steered the car to the side of the road and turned off the engine. He studied her face. "Why are you doing this? Why are you trying to help me?"

"I really don't know." At the moment, she definitely regretted her decision.

"Well, this is not happening. It's too dangerous. I won't risk you getting hurt."

"*You* won't risk it? You don't have a say in this. It's my choice. I want to help."

A pulse ticked in his jaw. "Why?"

The space inside the car shrunk, all the air sucked out. She closed her eyes. "I didn't help you twelve years ago. I should have." Opening her eyes, she stiffened.

His face was mere inches from hers. His features had softened, the lines of strain melting away until he was once again the boy she'd fallen in love with. His dark irises glowed with an inner fire.

Time slowed as she waited, frozen, locked in his torrid gaze, knowing what was coming; afraid, yet aching and desperate.

He lowered his head, and his mouth captured hers in a searing kiss.

Her lips softened, opening at his unspoken demand. She forgot they were stopped on the side of the road, and anyone driving by could see them. She forgot her hurt and anger and focused on his taste and touch. The kiss deepened. The snick of her seatbelt release vaguely registered, and then she was in his arms.

He clasped her closer still until she was on top of him, her hips straddling his. His smell, the heat radiating from him, were familiar, yet excitingly different. The last time they'd embraced he'd been a boy, all lean muscle and bone. Now her eager hands found a man's body, muscles honed by years of hard work and determination.

A horn blared and reality intruded like a splash of icy water. She wrenched away, her face flaming. Scrambling back to her side of the car, she fumbled to re-buckle her seat belt.

He chuckled. "Apparently, finding enough room to make out is a serious glitch with this model." He pointed to where his knee jammed the horn. "It's a mighty tight squeeze." He fought to free his long legs.

His struggles would have been comical if her heart weren't racing. "This…us…this…can't happen."

His gaze met hers and slid away. "Why not?"

Yes, why not? She studied his rugged face and soft lips. Heat coursed through her, but then she remembered Bonnie. *She was why.* "I'm going back to Seattle in a few days. I have a life there, one that doesn't include Cooper's Ridge or you."

Minutes ticked by. His gaze roamed over her face as if he were searching beneath the surface for answers. Without a word, he started the car and pulled away from the curb. His face was closed, his mouth tight. If this were a cartoon, steam would be rising from his ears.

But it wasn't a cartoon, and it wasn't funny. Nothing about the situation was the least bit humorous. Silence hung heavy for the remainder of the drive to the restaurant. She bit down on her bottom lip to stop the trembling and froze. Her lip was tender and swollen as if his kisses had seared her skin.

They arrived at Hector's Casa, and he steered the tiny car into the lot and turned off the engine. "I'll wait here for you. Marie will be more likely to talk if I'm not there."

"Okay." Her voice was a thin waver. As she

crossed the parking lot to the front door of the restaurant, a tremor of awareness prickled along her spine. She didn't have to look to know he watched her. Every cell in her body tingled with the heat of his gaze.

The mouth-watering aroma of chiles, salsa, and cilantro assailed her when she opened the door to the small restaurant and stepped inside. The place hadn't changed. Dust-covered sombreros and colorful piñatas hung on the white, plaster walls. Tired centerpieces of faded, plastic, red flowers decorated each table. Mariachi music played from hidden speakers.

It was too early for the lunch crowd, and the place was quiet. Marie was the only customer. She sat in the back corner of the restaurant at a table almost hidden behind a large, brightly colored, ceramic pot and drooping, plastic fern. A teapot and cup and saucer were on the table in front of her.

Carrie Ann hurried over. "Sorry I'm late."

"I thought you weren't coming. I was just about to leave."

"I'm glad you didn't." Carrie Ann's smile fell flat in the face of Marie's scowl.

Marie hadn't changed since high school. Her long, straight, blonde hair, parted in the middle, framed her angular face. Cornflower-blue eyes, surrounded by artfully applied layers of varying shades of eye shadow, examined Carrie Ann. She held a set of car keys in one hand, drumming them on the scarred, wooden tabletop.

"Thanks for meeting me," Carrie Ann said over the jangle of the keys.

"I wasn't sure I was going to."

"Why not?"

Marie bit her lip, and the keys rattled on the table,

picking up speed. "People are saying you and Declan are together again and that's why you're back in town."

"They're wrong."

"He was never cleared of Skye's murder." Marie frowned. "He's still the prime suspect. You should be careful."

"I told you, we're not together. Our relationship was over a long time ago." *Was it?* Her face heated as she remembered the kisses they'd shared mere minutes earlier.

"I heard no one will talk to you. They don't want to help a murderer."

Carrie Ann placed her hand over Marie's, silencing the incessant clatter of keys. "But you're here."

"You and me." Marie shrugged. "We were friends. I haven't forgotten."

Carrie Ann squeezed her hand. "Thank you."

Two bright spots of color rose in Marie's rouged cheeks, and she smiled wistfully. "It's been a long time. A lot has changed. I married Tommy Salston right out of high school. We have three kids now." She patted her swollen belly. "And another one on the way."

"Congratulations." Carrie Ann fought back her dismay. *Tommy Salston, really?* He'd been captain of the basketball team and a class-one bully in high school. He'd made Sheldon's life miserable with his constant teasing and insults. She couldn't remember the number of times Tommy and Declan had come to fisticuffs.

As if reading her mind, Marie said, "Tommy's changed, you know. He's not like he used to be. He grew up. Like we all did."

Carrie Ann nodded, hoping her friend was right.

"So, what about you?" Marie asked.

"Me?"

Marie sipped her tea and watched Carrie Ann with bright, inquisitive eyes. "Tell me, what's going on with you these days? Are you married? Do you have any kids?"

Carrie Ann licked her dry lips. This was why she'd never come back—too many questions. Questions she was determined not to answer. "I'm not married, and I don't have any children. Not yet." Her cheeks heated at her lie.

"You'd better get at it." Marie pointed a finger. "The old, biological clock is ticking. We're not getting any younger."

Carrie Ann forced a smile and changed the subject. Time to get to the point of this reunion before Marie asked any more probing questions. "You know why I asked to meet you?"

"You said you wanted to prove Declan didn't murder Skye."

Carrie Ann nodded.

"Why?"

"Because he's innocent."

"How can you be so sure? The sheriff thinks he's guilty. So does pretty well everyone else."

"I know him. He could never hurt anyone."

Marie's eyes narrowed. "You're still in love with him, aren't you?"

Carrie Ann's breath burst out in a gasp, but before she could deny Marie's claim and tell her how ridiculous it was, the waitress appeared and asked what she wanted. Glad for the distraction, she took her time perusing the menu and ordered a coffee.

Marie asked for more hot water, and the waitress left.

They were silent while they waited for her to return with their order. The question Marie had asked Carrie Ann hung in the air like a phantom.

Once her coffee arrived, Carrie Ann picked up her cup and sipped the steaming brew. The coffee was good, strong and dark. She blew out an exasperated breath. "Look, I already told you. Declan and I are *not* together. I'm helping him, that's all. I can't stand by and watch an innocent man be accused of something he didn't do."

Marie still didn't look convinced.

Carrie Ann tried again. "As soon as this is over, I'm going back to Seattle. Declan and I will never see each other again."

Marie eyed her for several long seconds. "You wanted to ask me something?"

"You were at the party at Rankin's farm after the prom, weren't you?"

Marie nodded. "I went with Tommy. It was our first date."

"Did you see Skye?"

"She and Declan and a group of other kids were standing around the fire drinking and goofing around. Tommy and I joined them. Skye was pissed. Declan was drinking from a big bottle of whiskey, which was odd because I didn't think he drank. At least, I'd never seen him drink before."

"He didn't drink because of what alcohol did to his father."

Marie rattled the keys on the table again, but as if aware of how annoying the clanging was, she stopped and stuffed them in her coat pocket. "Everyone was drinking, dancing, and having a great time, except Skye and Declan. He looked awful." She sized up Carrie Ann. "You guys had just broken up. I guess he was pretty upset."

Carrie Ann nodded.

"Skye was plain pissed off. She knew he was pining over you, and she didn't like it. I don't blame her. He pretty well ignored her all night. I'd have been furious if Tommy had tried that shit with me." A smile tugged at the corner of her mouth. "Mind you, I wasn't paying much attention to them, or anyone else. I was too busy trying to impress Tommy."

"Did you notice what time Skye left the party?"

"The police asked me the same question when they interviewed me after her body was found in the woods. I didn't see her leave." She met Carrie Ann's gaze and shrugged. "I drank too many beers. You know what it was like. We'd finally graduated, and we were all letting loose. We were crazy."

Something in the way Marie phrased her response twigged at Carrie Ann. "Are you sure you didn't see Skye leave? Think. It's important."

Marie chewed on her bottom lip. "I don't know, maybe."

"What?" Carrie Ann sat forward on her chair, hope flaring.

"I'm not sure. It was dark."

"Come on, Marie, you have to tell me."

Marie's eyes took on a distant look as if she were seeing the party in her mind. "Tommy and I were leaving to go for a drive." Her face flushed. "You know, we wanted to be alone."

"But you saw something," Carrie Ann persisted.

"Look," Marie said, "I was pretty drunk, and I was really into Tommy. I wasn't paying attention to much else. I'm not even sure the girl I saw was Skye. I didn't mention seeing her to the sheriff because I wasn't certain."

"I'm not the sheriff. This isn't a court of law. Tell me what you saw. Please."

"A guy and a girl were hanging out by the cars. The girl might have been Skye. I'm not sure. She had long, straight, dark hair like Skye, but lots of girls wore their hair the same way then."

"Who was with her, Marie?" Carrie Ann prodded. "Who was the man with Skye?"

Marie worried her bottom lip and looked anywhere but at Carrie Ann.

The urge to lunge across the table and grab Marie by the collar and shake her to make her tell what she'd seen was overwhelming. Carrie Ann squeezed her hands together and inhaled a steadying breath. "Marie, please."

Marie lifted her cup and gulped tea. As if reaching a decision, she set the cup on the table, dabbed her mouth with a paper napkin, and faced Carrie Ann. "Sheldon Dubrowski."

"Sheldon?"

"You can't go to the sheriff with this," Marie pleaded. "It was dark, and I was drunk. I might be wrong."

"Did Tommy see Sheldon with Skye?"

Marie tapped her mouth with one red-tipped finger.

"Come on, Marie, please."

"I don't want to get anyone in trouble." She

clenched and unclenched her hands. "I hate being pregnant. I'd kill for a cigarette right now."

"Marie, please," Carrie Ann urged. "What if it were Tommy? What if he were the one accused of a murder he didn't commit? Wouldn't you want someone to help him?" She took a deep breath. "Do you want whoever murdered Skye to get away with the crime?"

Marie's brow creased.

Carrie Ann pressed on. "Whoever murdered her is walking around free, has been for the past twelve years. Don't you think it's time the killer paid for his crime?"

Marie peered around the small restaurant and leaned over the table. Her breath fanned Carrie Ann's face. "Okay, but you can't tell anyone." Her voice was hushed. "Tommy would kill me if he knew I talked to you. He's never liked Declan, and he's positive he's guilty."

"Tell me what he saw."

Marie took another sip of tea, swallowed, and set her cup on the table. "Tommy saw them. We've never discussed it, but he must have seen them because I remember he made some remark about Sheldon getting Declan's leftovers."

Carrie Ann's heart pounded. "Did you see Skye get into Sheldon's car? Did she leave the party with him?"

Marie shook her head. "Look, I have to go. The babysitter can't stay long."

"Come on, Marie. What else did you see?"

Marie struggled out of her seat and shrugged on her coat. "Like I said, most of that night's a blur, but I'm pretty sure I saw Skye get into Sheldon's car. They drove away together." She picked up her purse and slung the strap over her shoulder. "Nice seeing you again, Carrie Ann. Don't get involved with Declan. Even if it turns out he didn't kill Skye, he's still a McAllister, and you know what they're like. Trouble follows them like stink on a fish." She waddled out of the restaurant.

Carrie Ann sipped her coffee, her mind whirling. Sheldon and Sky…together? Why had Sheldon never told anyone? He could have been the last person, other than the killer, to see Skye alive. Why had he kept quiet all these years?

There was only one way to find out. She tossed some bills on the table and hurried out of the restaurant.

Chapter 17

Declan turned down the radio as Carrie Ann climbed in the car. "You look like you're on a mission. What did you find out?"

"Marie thinks she saw Skye and Sheldon together."

"So?" Declan shrugged. "They were friends."

"This was the night of Prom."

"Like I said, they were friends. I was a jerk that night. She was upset. He was probably trying to make her feel better."

She blew out an exasperated breath. "You don't get it, do you? They left the party together in his car."

He blinked. "No way. Sheldon would have told me."

"What if it's true?"

"Is Marie certain the guy with Skye was Sheldon?"

She nodded, but then hesitated. "She was drunk, but she's pretty sure it was him."

"Pretty sure. In other words, it could have been anyone."

"Tommy Salston saw them too."

Declan sniggered. "I saw him that night. All Tommy could think about was getting into Marie's pants. Little green men could have been doing cartwheels and flying a spaceship over his head, and he wouldn't have noticed."

She pinned him with her gaze. "If Sheldon and

Skye left the party together, he was the last person to see her alive. Maybe he noticed someone hanging around when he dropped her off. Maybe the person he saw was the murderer."

"I don't believe it. Sheldon would have said something."

"You have to at least ask him."

His chin jutted stubbornly. "He would have told me if he knew anything."

"Look, you don't have to come with me, but I'm going to ask him if he drove Skye home the night of Prom."

His brow furrowed, but he nodded. "Okay, let's go, but I gotta tell you, this is a waste of time."

"Good. We'll find out the truth together."

The drive across town didn't take long. They parked across the street from a four-story, red brick building. Sheldon's father's accounting firm hadn't changed, except for a large, gleaming, brass plaque announcing the offices of Dubrowski and Son Accountants, Incorporated, posted above the door on the brick wall. The last time she'd seen the accounting firm's sign, there'd been no mention of a son.

They climbed out of the car and crossed the street to the wide, glass-fronted, double doors. Holding the door open, Declan gestured for her to enter ahead of him.

The lobby was expansive. Gleaming, marble floors reflected bright streaks of sunlight shining through a bank of floor-to-ceiling windows. An entire rainforest had been felled to panel the lobby walls in polished hardwood. Works of modern art added splashes of vibrant color to the dark wood.

A circular, wooden reception desk dominated the open space. An attractive blonde sat behind the desk, her attention focused on a computer screen in front of her. As they approached, she looked up, a welcoming smile pasted on her carefully made-up face. "Good morning. Welcome to Dubrowski and Son. May I help you?"

"We're here to see Sheldon," Declan said.

The woman's eyes narrowed. "Do you have an appointment?"

He shook his head.

"I'm afraid Mr. Dubrowski Junior is busy. Perhaps you'd like to make an appointment. I believe he has some time available a week from next Thursday."

"Tell *Junior* a couple of his old friends are here to see him." Declan was quietly insistent. "I'm certain he'll fit us in."

The receptionist assessed them for a long minute. "What did you say your names were?"

"Declan McAllister and"—he shot a look at Carrie Ann—"a friend."

The receptionist's eyes widened, and her face paled beneath her makeup. Her hand trembled as she picked up her phone and placed a call. She turned away and covered her mouth so they couldn't hear what she said. After a few seconds, she swung back toward them, a strained smile affixed to her pretty face. "Mr. Dubrowski Junior will see you. You may go right up."

"I thought he would." Declan led the way across the lobby to the elevator. He pressed the button, and the doors whooshed open.

They stepped inside and began their ascent. Strains of classical music filtered from speakers placed high in the burnished, steel walls.

"Sheldon's done well for himself." Declan's tone was admiring. "The art in the lobby alone must have cost a fortune."

"And to think this was the last place he wanted to work."

"Sheldon hated accounting, but he knew he'd end up working for his dad." He shrugged. "You know what his father was like. Sheldon didn't really have a choice."

The doors opened, and they stepped into a large reception area.

Another circular desk faced them manned by a clone of the woman in the main lobby. She rose to greet them, her mouth pursed in a moue of disapproval. "Mr. Dubrowski Junior is waiting for you." She led them down a wide, carpeted hallway to a polished, mahogany door. A small, brass plaque set in the door announced this was Sheldon's office.

Carrie Ann eyed the heavy, wooden door. *Another tree in the rainforest gone.*

After a quick tap, the receptionist opened the door and ushered them in.

"Hey, you guys. Welcome to my lair." Sheldon rose from behind a large, glass-and-brass desk. He and Declan shook hands, and then Sheldon turned to her. "Carrie Ann, what a nice surprise." He grinned, his teeth gleaming white, leaning in for a hug.

She sidestepped, evading his embrace.

He raised his brows, but after a beat, flashed another wide grin. "Come and sit down. Can I get you some coffee, tea? A drink?"

She shook her head. "This isn't a social call."

His eyes narrowed, but he chuckled. "And here I thought you missed my charming personality." He indicated two dark-brown, leather chairs situated in front of his desk. "Sit down then, and tell me why you're here."

She ignored his false good humor and remained standing. Before she could demand answers, Declan cut her off.

"We'd love to sit, wouldn't we, Carrie Ann?"

She hesitated, but then sat down in the leather chair. She'd let Declan take the lead. At least, as long as he asked the hard questions.

Sheldon walked behind his desk and sat in the padded, leather chair facing them. He crossed his thin legs and studied Declan, and then her. "It's...ah...it's weird to see you two together again." His red brows rose. "*Are* you together?"

Declan turned to her, his gaze piercing.

She gulped and glanced away.

An uncomfortable silence settled over the room.

Sheldon uncrossed and re-crossed his legs, his fingers playing with the knife-sharp creases in his black, dress pants. He coughed and asked, "So, what brings you two here?"

Carrie Ann took a deep breath, preparing to ask him why he'd lied, but once again, Declan beat her to it.

"Tell me about prom night," he said.

Sheldon's brow wrinkled. "What do you mean?"

"Did you see Skye?"

The furrow between Sheldon's brows deepened. His gaze swung between her and Declan. "Of course I did. I was with you guys most of the night. Remember?"

"Did you see her later, after she left the group by the bonfire?" Carrie Ann got to the point.

"What is this?" His eyes narrowed. "You guys are making me nervous."

"Answer the question," she said. "Were you with Skye after she left the bonfire?"

"With her?" Sheldon's face paled. "What do you mean?"

"Tell us the truth." Her frustration with his prevaricating mounted, making her voice sharp. "When was the last time you saw Skye?"

Again, his gaze swiveled between Declan and her.

"Come on, Sheldon." Declan was less confrontational, but unyielding. "Tell us what you know."

Sheldon sank back in his chair and blew out a puff of air, shrinking into his fancy designer suit and yellow power tie. He yanked a folded, yellow handkerchief from his coat pocket and wiped his gleaming brow. "She was upset." A crease formed between his brows. "You were drunk, Declan, and so busy feeling sorry for yourself, you totally ignored her. I wanted to help." He shrugged. "You know, make her stop crying."

"What happened then?" Declan's voice was cold.

"I offered to drive her home."

"Christ, man! Are you kidding me?" Declan jumped to his feet, and leaned across the desk, towering over Sheldon.

Sheldon yelped and scrunched into his seat, holding his trembling hands in front of him as if warding off a blow. "I didn't think it was a big deal. I mean, when she first disappeared, I thought she'd run away or something, so what difference did it make?

182

She'd come back when she was ready. She'd left before without telling anyone, don't you remember?"

"But she hadn't run away. Not this time," said Declan.

"I swear, man, I didn't know. But when they found her body—"

"What?" Declan demanded. "When they found her body, what? You didn't think it important to tell the sheriff she'd left the party with you? You'd rather they think your best friend murdered her?" Declan's hands were clenched, his body taut and vibrating, ready to spring.

Carrie Ann placed a restraining hand on his arm.

His muscles tightened and bunched beneath her touch, but he didn't shake her off.

"Let him talk, Declan," she said. "Give him a chance to explain."

He blew out a ragged breath. "Okay, but he'd better tell the truth this time." He strode over to the large picture window as if needing to put some distance between himself and Sheldon.

"Come on, Sheldon," she urged, "it's time you told us what really happened."

Tears shone in his eyes, and he swiped at them with his handkerchief. "I never meant for you to take the blame, Declan. You gotta believe me, man."

Declan's face remained closed and hard, his eyes narrow slits in his rugged face. "What happened?" he bit off.

"Like I said, I saw her leave the fire, and I followed her. She was crying. I tried talking to her, tried to calm her down, but she wanted to go home." He wiped his face again. "I offered to drive her. I mean, I couldn't just leave her, not after the way you'd treated her. She was too upset." He blew his nose, took a deep breath, and continued. "I had every intention of driving her home, but then…" His voice faded to a whisper.

Carrie Ann leaned closer, straining to hear.

"After we'd driven a few miles, I pulled over to the side of the road." His eyes were pleading. "I wanted to make her feel better. I didn't mean anything by what I did. It was just a few kisses."

"What the hell did you do?"

She flinched at the harsh accusation in Declan's voice.

"I didn't do anything," Sheldon said. "I told you. I'd never hurt her. I was only…" He shrugged. "I guess I got a little carried away and she…" His Adam's apple bobbed in his thin throat. "She got out of the car. I tried to convince her to get back in. I told her I wouldn't touch her again, but she wouldn't listen." The sound of his ragged breathing filled the room.

"What happened next?" Declan's frigid voice rang out, harsh lines carved into his ravaged face.

Sheldon wiped his eyes again. "Skye ran down the road a ways, I guess to get away from me. I didn't know what to do. I hoped she'd come back, and I could drive her home like I'd said I would. I couldn't leave her. It wouldn't be right. I'm not a jerk. You know I'm not, right?" At that moment, he resembled a dog begging his master for forgiveness for chewing his favorite slippers.

The smell of his sour sweat filled the room, and Carrie Ann wrinkled her nose in distaste.

Declan's eyes were cold, his face granite.

Sheldon wiped his watering eyes and continued

speaking. It was as if he'd kept his guilt and anxiety bottled up inside all these years, and once he started talking, he couldn't stop. "I was going to get out of my car and try and talk to her again, but then a vehicle appeared, and she put out her thumb like she was hitchhiking. The car stopped, she climbed in, and they drove away. I didn't see her again." He snuffled. "You gotta believe me, man. I didn't hurt her. You know me. I wouldn't hurt a mouse."

"Did you see who was driving?" Carrie Ann asked.

"It was too dark. I couldn't see anything."

"You saw the car, though. What model was it?" Declan's voice was shards of ice.

"I don't know. Like I said, it was dark. I couldn't tell."

"Come on. You can do better," Declan said. "Was it a car, a truck, a van? A two-door, four-door? What?"

Sheldon scrubbed his hands over his face. "I don't know. Honestly. You have to believe me."

Declan's lips curved in a tight, hard smile, his eyes bleak. "Believe you? After this? Never again."

Tears glistened in Sheldon's blue eyes. "I'm sorry. I'm really sorry. I didn't know she'd get hurt. I didn't know—"

"Come on, Sheldon." Carrie Ann refused to let him off the hook. "You must remember something." If he was telling the truth, the person who'd given Skye a ride was the last person to see her alive, and Sheldon had seen his vehicle. "Think."

"I don't know," he whined, his lower lip trembling. "It was a car, a two-door, I think, dark color, navy, maybe black. All I can tell you is the car had so much fancy chrome, it gleamed even in the dark." He stood

185

and stumbled across the room to a glass-fronted cabinet. Removing a bottle and a crystal water glass, he filled the glass to the rim with whiskey. His hands shook and liquor spilled on the carpet. He slurped the amber liquid, coughing and sputtering, and wiped his mouth with his sleeve.

The booze must have given him courage because he straightened his shoulders. "I'm sorry, Declan. I should have told you this years ago, man."

Declan studied him for a long, hard moment, and then turned and headed toward the door. He paused with his hand on the brass handle and spoke over his shoulder. "You'd better be ready to answer some tough questions. I'm going to tell the sheriff what you told me."

Sheldon nodded and gulped the rest of his drink. "Of course, I'll talk to him. It's the least I can do."

Declan flung open the door and strode out of the office.

"Declan." Sheldon's voice was pleading as he called after him. "I'm sorry, man." Sheldon sagged on a chair and ran his fingers through his thinning red hair. He faced Carrie Ann, his eyes red-rimmed. "I really messed up, didn't I?"

"You should have told the truth long ago."

"I'll make it up to him. You know I will." He slumped like a rag doll, his legs splayed, his expensive suit rumpled, tie askew.

Pity filled her, but she bit it back. He didn't deserve her concern. Not after what he'd done. "You just lost the only friend you've ever had." She shook her head. "I hope lying to him all these years was worth it." She followed Declan out of the office.

Chapter 18

"Have you told him?" Vivian asked.

Carrie Ann glanced up from the sandwich she was eating.

Vivian stood in the kitchen doorway watching her.

"What are you doing home? Shouldn't you be at the store?" Carrie Ann frowned. It was almost noon and Vivian was still in her nightgown.

"I decided not to go in today." Vivian tightened the sash of her silk robe around her narrow waist. A stray lock of lank, gray hair lay across her forehead. Her face was pale, her sunken eyes bloodshot and rimmed with dark circles.

"Are you okay?" A flash of unexpected concern hit Carrie Ann. "You don't look so well."

"Of course, I'm fine." Vivian coughed, a wet, phlegmy wheeze from deep within her chest. "I'm tired, that's all. I didn't sleep well last night." She tottered forward a few steps, but then the fire returned to her eyes, and she straightened and marched into the kitchen. "I asked you a question, Carrie Ann. Have you told Declan about Bonnie?"

Carrie Ann choked on a bite of sandwich. Coughing, her eyes watering, she grabbed the glass on the table and gulped down water. "I already told you. I'm not going to tell him."

Vivian pulled out a chair from the table and

perched on the seat. "He deserves to know."

"It's too late." Carrie Ann wiped her streaming eyes. "Bonnie thinks her father's dead. How can I now tell her he's alive?"

Vivian was silent for several heartbeats. "I heard Sheldon Dubrowski is talking to the sheriff."

"This town is something else." Carrie Ann shook her head. "Everyone knows what everyone else is doing."

"Exactly why you need to tell Declan. You don't seriously think no one knows about Bonnie, do you?" Vivian reached out, but stopped just short of touching Carrie Ann. "Think what will happen if he learns about Bonnie from someone else."

Carrie Ann's stomach clenched. She'd thought of nothing else. Her aunt was right. Far better for Declan to hear the truth from her, but too much time had passed, too many lies had been told. How could she explain the sudden appearance of a daughter he never knew he had?

She and Bonnie were a team. When Bonnie had started asking questions about her father, Carrie Ann had done the only thing she could—she'd lied and told her daughter her father was dead. Over the years she'd embellished on the lie, expanding the tale until it was a tragic love story cut short by sudden death. Bonnie believed her. Why wouldn't she? Mothers didn't lie to their children. After all these years, how could she tell her daughter her father was alive and well? "I'm not going to tell him."

Vivian opened her mouth, but Carrie Ann cut her off. "And you're not going to tell him either."

Vivian watched her for a long moment. "I hope

you realize how wrong you are before it's too late." She stood, swaying, clinging to the table. Her face lost what little color it had.

Carrie Ann grabbed her arm, holding her steady. "Are you okay?"

A long minute passed before Vivian inhaled a shaky breath. "I'm fine. I appreciate your concern, my dear, but you should worry about your own life, not mine." On that biting comment, she shuffled out of the room.

Carrie Ann watched her go, unease filling her. The old woman was ill. But then she shook her head. It was probably just the flu. Vivian would be back to her usual robust self in a few days. She was too ornery to get sick. She'd tell whatever illness dared to attack her to go to hell like she did everything and everyone else.

Picking up her plate, Carrie Ann threw the unfinished sandwich in the trash. She was going out to the old Rankin Farm. Something deep inside, an intuition, sixth sense, whatever you wanted to call it, something told her the answers she was looking for were at the deserted farm.

Most people in town believed Declan had met up with Skye when he went back to the old farm to get his truck the night of Prom. He'd been drunk, and he and Skye fought. In a blind rage, Declan had killed her and hidden her body in the woods.

That version of events didn't pan out anymore. Now they knew Sheldon had left the party with Skye. Later, she'd climbed into a vehicle with someone who'd stopped and picked her up. That person had to be the murderer and someone from Cooper's Ridge. A stranger wouldn't have known about the old farm and its isolation. The killer could have hidden her body any number of isolated spots. Instead he'd chosen the farm.

The back door opened with a bang.

She jumped, her hand going to her chest to still the rapid beating of her heart. "Leland! You startled me."

He strode into the kitchen, chuckling. "I didn't know I was so frightening. I decided to come home for lunch and check on Vivian. She wasn't feeling well this morning." His brow furrowed. "What's going on? You're pale as a ghost." He sat in the chair Vivian had vacated. "Something you want to talk about?"

He'd always been a good listener. When she was a child and upset with Vivian, Carrie Ann often ranted to him about the unfairness of her aunt's autocratic dictates. Leland had listened, never judging, just being there for her. She took a steadying breath. "You heard about Sheldon?"

He nodded. "I just left the Sheriff's Office. Sheldon was talking to the sheriff."

"I can't believe what he did. Declan was his friend. How could Sheldon let him suffer all these years, knowing what he knew?"

"He was afraid, I guess. If we'd known Skye had left the party with Sheldon, the investigators might have looked at other suspects. Sheldon would certainly have been one of them. His father wouldn't have liked his only son being a major suspect in a murder investigation."

"What happens now?"

Leland ran his hand over his gray, bristly hair. "The sheriff will look into the matter. But, since Sheldon didn't see the car Skye Lawrence got into clearly, I don't know what good his information will do."

"He described the car."

"A lot of people own dark-colored, two-door sedans. Even I do, and have for years."

"So this doesn't help Declan?"

"This new information will make it more difficult to convict. Any good lawyer could claim reasonable doubt. A jury would probably believe him."

She picked up her glass and drank some water, trying to ease the dryness in her throat. "Someone must have seen something. After he murdered her, the killer drove back to the farm and hid her body. How could he move around so freely without someone seeing him?"

"It was late. You know what Cooper's Ridge is like. The streets roll up at eleven." He rubbed the stubble on his jaw. "Declan's private investigator was at the Sheriff's Office. He turned over a piece of fabric he claimed Declan found in the old barn at Rankin's Farm."

The breath hitched in her throat. "What did the sheriff say?"

"This doesn't look good for McAllister. Only the killer would have had a piece of the poor girl's scarf."

"But Declan said he found it in the barn."

Leland chuckled. "And you believe him?"

"Yes, of course I do."

He shook his head, sadness filming his eyes. "My poor girl, you've never stopped loving him, have you?"

She opened her mouth to protest, but he squeezed her hand and cut her off. "Don't worry. I won't tell anyone."

"There's nothing to tell."

"You do realize, McAllister's going to jail for this.

Believe me, you don't want to be involved with him when that happens. That's no life for anyone. You have to think of Bonnie."

"But he didn't kill Skye. I know he didn't."

"And who's going to believe you?"

"But what about Sheldon's statement? We now know Skye left the party well before Declan went back there."

Leland's eyes darkened. "Sheldon is Declan's friend, and as a result, his testimony will be perceived as tainted."

"Tainted?"

"Don't you think it's a bit too convenient that after all these years, Declan's best friend comes forward with information that removes some of the suspicion from Declan?"

She jutted her chin. "It wasn't like that. We had to force Sheldon to tell us what happened. He wasn't lying. Not this time."

"Well, we'll find out either way." He stood up. "Any more chicken? I'm starving."

She pointed to the plate of sliced meat sitting on the counter and headed for the door.

"Where are you going?" Leland asked.

"Out to Rankin's Farm."

"Why in Heaven's name would you go all the way out there?"

"I want to see where the killer buried Skye's body."

"Why? How will seeing the burial site help you?"

"I don't know."

"The sheriff and his investigators combed the entire farm and the surrounding forest after Skye's body was found."

"I know it's foolish, but I have to do something. I can't sit here and wait until they arrest Declan."

"Is he going with you?"

She shook her head.

"I'll go with you. You shouldn't go alone."

"No, you should stay here with Vivian. She's not looking well."

His gaze held hers. "Be careful. You're a long way from help if you get into trouble out there."

A frisson of foreboding rippled along her spine, but she pasted a smile on her face. "Don't worry about me. I'll be fine."

****

Carrie Ann surveyed the wall of trees and shivered. She tugged her coat tighter against the chill of the cloudy afternoon. Gusts of wind blew dried, yellow leaves across the desolate clearing. The barn door swayed and creaked on its rusty hinges.

For the hundredth time since she'd left town, she questioned her decision to come out here alone. What if Declan was right? What if someone was out to stop her from finding Skye's murderer? What if someone had followed her?

A raven croaked from somewhere deep within the gloomy forest. She shivered again, trying to ignore the prickling sensation of being watched. *Stop being silly.* She'd come here for a reason, and she'd better get on with her search before the rain hit.

Crossing the clearing, she skirted the old barn, heading for the thicket of trees. Wild raspberry bushes, masses of brambles, and a tangle of red willows created an almost impenetrable barrier to the forest beyond. She scouted along the edge of the bush until she found the remnants of a trail leading into the trees. The path wound through the thick undergrowth. Fir trees towered over her, their branches swaying and creaking in the rising wind.

Hearing the splash of running water, she thrust aside the snarl of thorny bushes to expose a small opening. She stepped through into a clearing. Dim light filtered through the branches revealing a carpet of lush, green grass. A stream bisected the meadow, burbling over moss-covered rocks.

Tattered strips of faded, pink flagging tape fluttered from where they'd been tied to the tree trunks by the long-ago investigators. The thick mat of grass nearly obscured the oblong depression in the middle of the secluded glade.

In spite of the cold, sweat beaded her brow. This was where the killer had buried Skye's body. Twelve years ago the trees would have been smaller, the bush not as thick, but the little clearing would still have been hidden from view.

Crouching down before the dip in the ground, she picked up a handful of sandy soil, sifting the fine earth through her fingers. Skye's battered and bloody body had been covered by a thin layer of this dirt and left for the scavengers. Tears stung her eyes. No one deserved to die like Skye had, beaten and strangled, and dumped in the forest.

Two lives had been destroyed the night Skye was murdered. One senseless attack and two young people's lives had changed forever. Skye was dead; Declan forced to live under a cloud of suspicion.

A fat raindrop plopped on the ground, followed by

another and then another, raising tiny puffs of dust in the dirt. Taking one last look at the small depression in the ground, she turned toward the trail to her car.

A branch cracked in the dense thicket of trees.

She froze, straining to hear over the rain and rising wind. "Who's there?" Her voice was a thin squeak.

Another snap, followed by a furtive rustle of bushes.

She gulped, wishing she'd thought to bring a weapon. The hairs on the back of her neck rose. She wasn't alone. Someone or something was hiding in the dark woods watching her.

In the next second, she was up and racing along the trail to the barn, ignoring the branches scratching her face and tearing at her clothes. Bursting out of the trees, she ran to her car, stumbling over the rutted ground. She opened the door and leaped in, hitting the automatic lock button.

Her chest heaved as she peered through the rain-spotted windshield at the crumbling ruin of the barn looming over her, the red paint on the old boards faded to umber, the windows dark and vacant. Another shiver rippled along her spine. *Stop being foolish. No one's here but you.* The noises she'd heard in the forest were from a squirrel or a deer seeking shelter from the rain. Lots of animals lived in the dense woods.

She released a shaky laugh and reached for her purse on the seat beside her for a tissue. Her breath caught in her throat. A small fragment of cloth lay atop her purse, the vibrant colors glowing in the meager, late afternoon light. With a shaking hand, she picked up the cloth. The smooth silk slid between her fingers. Mesmerized, she studied the scrap of torn fabric.

195

The air in the car was suddenly too thick to breathe. Fingers shaking, she turned the cloth over and jammed her fist in her mouth stifling a scream. Written across the silk in thick, black letters was a single, condemning word. *Guilty.*

She dropped the cloth as if it burned and gulped air. While she'd been traipsing around the forest looking for where the killer had dumped Skye's body, someone had been inside her car and left this piece of Skye's scarf for her to find. The same person could still be here, watching her, waiting.

Her hand shook so much she dropped the keys on the floor twice before finally fitting them in the ignition and starting the car. The engine choked, sputtered, and died. Her heart hammered as she tried again. *Come on. Please, please start.* The engine rumbled to life. Relief flooded through her, and she pressed her foot on the gas. The car leapt ahead.

She sped along the rough track to the main road, the small rental car bouncing over the deep ruts, the back end slewing first one way and then the other. *Guilty.* The single, searing condemnation followed her like a haunting call. She pressed harder on the gas trying to escape the word and what it implied.

Careening around a sharp corner, she clung to the steering wheel, fighting to keep the car on the road. The vehicle skidded, bouncing over a series of washboards. She glanced in the rearview mirror. The road behind her was dark. Releasing the breath she'd been holding, she eased her foot off the accelerator.

Rounding the next bend, she entered a straight stretch and cast another quick look behind. A set of headlights shone in her rearview mirror. Her heart stuttered. Once again, she pressed down on the gas pedal. The little car shook as it sped over the gravel road, the motor roaring.

The vehicle behind loomed larger in the rearview mirror.

Her car was no match for the powerful, black SUV roaring down on her. The gleaming, chrome, front grill resembled sharp fangs ready to devour her.

The distance between them narrowed, and a terrifying realization hit. The big vehicle was going to ram her.

At the last minute, the SUV veered from behind and moved into the lane beside her.

As the SUV drew level, she risked a glance, but the dark, tinted windows made it impossible to see the driver. *Come on, pass.* The SUV held a steady pace, matching her speed.

She slowed, knowing she couldn't outrun the more powerful vehicle.

The SUV slowed.

She slowed even more. Maybe the driver of the SUV was drunk and out for kicks, thinking it'd be a big joke to scare her. Mission accomplished. Her hands shook so much she could barely hang onto the steering wheel.

Suddenly, the SUV surged ahead, swerving into the lane in front of her, nearly clipping her bumper. The brake lights flashed, and it skidded to a stop.

She jammed on her brakes, screaming as her car slid on the loose gravel, stopping mere feet from the SUV's shiny, rear bumper. Her heart pounded at the near miss.

All was still and silent for five long seconds, but

then with a roar of its engine, the SUV's tires dug into the gravel, and the vehicle reversed, crashing into her with a deafening screech of metal on metal.

Her head slammed against the headrest, then she flew forward, the seatbelt cutting into her shoulder and waist. A loud bang filled the car as the airbag inflated. She smashed into it, the air in her lungs expelling in a violent burst, and the world went black.

Chapter 19

Every swipe of the wipers fueled his anger. Why the hell hadn't she called him? She shouldn't have gone out to the Rankin Farm on her own. Didn't she realize how dangerous the situation was? Declan pressed down on the gas pedal, forcing the tiny rental car to go faster.

He'd been at the police station being questioned by Sheriff Atkins when Vivian had called and told him Carrie Ann had gone to the farm on her own. He'd immediately halted the interview and run out of the police station to his car, ignoring the sheriff's protests. Leaving in the middle of the interview was not smart and would make him appear guiltier, but he had to go. Carrie Ann could be in trouble.

He swerved around yet another puddle. Headlights loomed ahead, rushing toward him. Relief washed over him. The speeding car had to be Carrie Ann's returning from the farm. No one else would be foolish enough to be on this remote road in a rainstorm.

His relief turned to confusion, as instead of slowing, the vehicle blasted by in a spray of muddy water and gravel. He slowed the car and turned and squinted through the rain-streaked rear window, but with a flash of red taillights, the car vanished around a curve in the road. All he'd been able to make out was a large black SUV going like a bat out of hell.

Why was the other vehicle going so fast? His gut

tightened, and once again, he jammed his foot on the gas. The little car surged ahead, the motor screaming in protest. He crested the rise of a hill. A single, bright light shone in the distance where no light should be. The knot in his stomach tightened, and he pressed harder on the gas pedal.

Carrie Ann's car, its front end crumpled, one headlight shining up at the rain-filled sky, the other broken and dark, lay ahead. The car's rear end was mired in the ditch.

He jammed on his brakes, barely waiting for the car to skid to a stop before he leaped out. Two strides took him to the driver's buckled door. He wrenched at the door, yanking, until with a protesting scream of warped metal, the door opened. The interior light flickered, and his heart stopped.

Carrie Ann was strapped in her seatbelt, her head hanging down, her chin resting on her chest. A thin drizzle of blood leaked from the corner of her mouth and dripped onto her sweater.

His hand shook as he touched her cheek. Warm. *Thank God.*

She moaned, her dark lashes fluttering against her too pale cheeks.

"Carrie Ann, can you hear me?" His heart beat so loud he barely heard his own voice.

She moaned again.

The pitiful sound crushed something inside him, and he fought the overriding urge to wrap his arms around her and ease her pain.

Her eyes fluttered open, and she raised a trembling hand. Another groan filled the night.

"Are you all right?" He cursed. Stupid question. Of

course she wasn't all right.

She winced with pain, her eyes bleary and unfocused. "Declan?"

"It's okay. I'm here." He choked over the thick lump in his throat.

A look of relief washed over her pale face. "What happened?"

He blinked back tears. "You were in a car accident. Don't you remember?"

Her eyes were too large for her elfin face. "An accident?"

He crouched before her, wiping the blood from her chin with the pad of his thumb. "Where are you injured?"

"My neck hurts." She touched the back of her neck and grimaced.

"Don't move. I'll call an ambulance." The second he said the words, he cursed again. *Stupid.* He couldn't call for help. There wasn't any cell phone service here. "I don't want to move you. Wait here while I go and get help."

A look of terror crossed her face, and she reached for him. "No, don't leave me. Please don't leave me."

He grasped her quavering hand, rubbing the icy skin between his hands. "Don't worry. I won't leave you." *I'll never leave you.* The thought rocked him back on his heels. Undoing her seatbelt, he prayed he wasn't doing more harm than good. With infinite care, he eased her from behind the steering wheel and into his arms.

She rested her head against his chest and clung to him, her arms looped around his neck. "Why are you always rescuing me?" she whispered, her amber eyes fuzzy with pain.

He swallowed, his mouth dry. "Habit, I guess."

She lifted an arm and caressed his beard-roughened cheek. "Thank you."

His skin burned where she touched. Her delicate fragrance wafted in the damp air. The soft mounds of her breasts pressed against his chest. He clasped her tighter.

She yelped and grabbed for the back of her neck, her face blanching.

He loosened his embrace. *Get a grip, man. She's injured.* Careful not to stumble on the uneven ground, he carried her to his car and eased her onto the passenger seat. Closing the door, he strode around to the driver's side and slid in beside her.

The glow from the lights on the dash, and the heat spewing from the vents, created an intimate atmosphere, protected from the rain and the wind buffeting the tiny car.

She closed her eyes and rested her head against the headrest. A bump the size of a golf ball swelled on her forehead.

His heart skipped a beat thinking how close he'd come to losing her. "What happened?" he husked.

She opened her eyes. "I was at Rankin's Farm. A vehicle must have followed me when I left. I tried to outrun it, but the SUV was going too fast." She hiccupped a sob. "When it passed me, I thought it was over, that I was overreacting, but…"

A chill settled over him. "But what?"

"The SUV stopped right in front of me." Her lower lip trembled.

He scowled. Was she saying what he thought she

was? Had someone deliberately smashed into her? His blood boiled. He opened his mouth to demand she tell him all the details, but her pallid complexion and sunken eyes revealed the heavy toll his questioning was taking on her. He dialed back his anger and softened his voice. "It's okay. You don't have to tell me now. We should get you to a doctor."

"No doctor, please. I'm fine."

"What do you mean? Of course you have to see a doctor. You've been in an accident. You might have a concussion."

She grabbed his arm, her grip surprisingly strong. "I have to tell you what happened."

One glance at those amber eyes, and he was lost. Despite his certainty she should see a doctor, he found himself nodding. "Okay, no doctor. For now."

She swiped a shaking hand over her eyes. "The SUV backed into me." She blinked back tears. "I couldn't get out of the way."

"Are you saying this wasn't an accident?"

"The other car crashed into me on purpose."

The other car crashed into me on purpose. Her words reverberated between them. He remembered the speeding SUV he'd passed. Fire burned low in his belly, dissolving the icy pall of fear filling him from the first moment he'd seen her mangled car on the side of the road. This was no accident. It was a deliberate act of violence. She could have been killed. The thought left him breathless, fueling the fury roaring through him.

The driver who'd hit her had to be the same person who'd shot out her tire the night she arrived in town, and slashed her tires in the motel parking lot. The bastard had upped the ante. No longer content to simply frighten her; he wanted to hurt her, to stop her from finding out who killed Skye. He tightened his hands into fists. He'd kill the bastard.

"Declan?"

Her soft voice broke through his fury.

"Who would do this to me?" Her voice was barely audible.

The fear on her ashen face shattered his heart. He didn't want to frighten her any more, but he refused to sugarcoat the truth. The more afraid she was, the more careful she'd be. "The jerk who rammed your car was most likely the same person who killed Skye."

She flinched as if he'd hit her. "There's something I haven't told you."

"What?" He wasn't sure he wanted to know what etched the fear deeper into her pale face.

"There's a cloth."

"What cloth?"

"The one someone put in my car when I was at the farm."

"I told you not to go there alone, and now you tell me someone put something in your car?"

"I sensed someone watching me, and when I returned to my car, a piece of Skye's scarf was lying on the passenger seat on top of my purse."

The world tilted, and he gripped the steering wheel to hold steady. "Are you sure the cloth you saw was part of her scarf?"

"It looked exactly like the piece you showed me, the one you found in the barn."

He clenched his jaw. Skye's killer had been at the farm when Carrie Ann was there alone.

"There's more." Her voice was small.

More? What more could there be? Wasn't it enough the killer had left part of Skye's scarf in Carrie Ann's car as a warning, and then rammed into her, trying to kill her?

"Something's written on the silk."

"What?" He braced himself, his fingers digging into the seat's cheap upholstery.

"*Guilty* is written in large, black letters on one side."

He jolted upright, banging his head against the roof of the car. What the hell was the killer's game? Why place a piece of Skye's scarf in the old barn for him to find, and another in Carrie Ann's car? "Where's the cloth now?"

"It was on the passenger seat." She sat up, but fell back with a groan, rubbing the back of her neck. "I have to get it. The sheriff has to see it."

"You stay here. I'll find the cloth." He opened the door to a blast of freezing rain. Welcoming the cold and wet, he trudged to her car. Using the illumination from his car's headlights, he examined the front of her car. The fender was dented and part of the hood smashed. He crouched down and peered closer. A long streak of black paint was embedded in the front bumper's red, heavy-duty plastic.

Fury thundered through him. He'd kill this bastard when he found him, but first he had to find the piece of Skye's scarf in Carrie Ann's car. The killer's fingerprints could be on the fabric.

Leaning in the driver's open door, he studied the interior of the car. Nothing was on the passenger seat, and the light was too dim to see if anything was on the floor. He tramped around the car, slipping and sliding on the muddy grass at the edge of the ditch. Yanking open the passenger door, he crouched down and peered inside.

Her purse lay on the floor, but no scrap of vibrant silk. He searched under the seat, ran his hands over the upholstery on the back seat of the car, and felt under the rear seats, but all he found was a small wad of gum and an old candy bar wrapper. Where was the cloth?

But then he saw it. The force of the collision had wedged the small piece of silk into the narrow crease between the two front seats. Hands shaking, he struggled to ease the cloth free. By the time he held the scarf in his hands, he'd managed to put his fingers all over it. His DNA was probably imprinted into every fiber of the smooth silk. Too late to worry about that now. Besides, once he showed this to the sheriff, his ass was fried. No way would the sheriff believe Declan wasn't involved in Skye's murder. No way in hell.

The cloth was smaller than the piece he'd found in the barn, but the gold and teal design gleaming under the interior light was the same. His gut twisted, and he swallowed back the sour taste of bile. He held the cloth to the light and stared at the word inscribed on the back. *Guilty.* An icy cold settled in the pit of his stomach. *Guilty.* What the fuck was the bastard up to?

He shoved the cloth in his coat pocket and hurried through the driving rain to his car and climbed in the driver's seat.

"Did you find it?"

He nodded.

Her breath rushed out in a loud whoosh. "Where is it?"

His mind in turmoil, he pinched the bridge of his

nose.

"Declan? Where's the piece of scarf?"

Her voice reached him as if from a distance. He patted his coat pocket. "In here."

"Is it hers?"

"Yep."

"You're sure?"

Again, he nodded.

Silence filled the tiny car, broken only by the drumming of rain on the roof.

She grabbed his arms, her fingers clutching the thick wool of his coat. "Why did someone leave that in my car? What was the purpose?" She lurched up. "Oh, my, God. If we turn this in to the sheriff, he'll think you put it there. What are we going to do?"

Her questions, one after the other, hammered at him. One word stood out—*we*. He turned to her. "You're not going to do anything."

She opened her mouth to protest, but he cut her off. "You're not going to tell anyone about this." He pressed his hand against his pocket where the piece of torn scarf burned like it was on fire.

Her eyes widened. "What are you saying? I have to tell the sheriff. What if the killer's fingerprints are on the material?"

"Don't you see? There won't be any fingerprints. Only mine. This guy isn't stupid."

"We still have to turn it in. It's evidence."

He nodded, knowing with a sick certainty she was right. They did have to give the piece of Skye's scarf to the sheriff. Anger raged through him. That's what the killer wanted. He was banking on Declan finding Carrie Ann and the piece of scarf. He knew they'd turn the cloth into the authorities. The bastard also knew if Declan were found in possession of another section of the murder weapon, the sheriff would arrest him on the spot.

Carrie Ann's grip on his arm tightened. "He's trying to frighten me, isn't he?" Her voice rose. "He put the scarf in my car so I'd know he was watching, know he could hurt me whenever he wanted."

The implications of what she said struck him full force, and for a moment he couldn't breathe.

"But why?" She waved a hand weakly. "I don't understand. We're no closer to finding Skye's killer than we were when we started."

"You must have made him nervous when you talked to Marie and found out Sheldon had seen the killer's car."

Her face was ghostly white. "His plan's working." She reached for him. "I am afraid, very afraid."

That made two of them. He took her in his arms, holding her, trying to stave off the numbing fear chilling him to the bone.

Chapter 20

A thousand frightening thoughts raced through Carrie Ann's mind, adding to the pounding in her head. Was Declan right? Had the person who'd murdered Skye been driving the speeding SUV? Had he been trying to kill her? Or was the accident another warning? Why had he placed the scrap of Skye's scarf in her car? To whom did the word *Guilty* refer? Carrie Ann shuddered and slid a glance at Declan.

A deep furrow ran between his dark brows. His mouth was a thin, unforgiving line. A pulse in his jaw beat a rapid tattoo. Where she was frozen with mind-numbing fear, he bristled with simmering rage.

The car slowed, and he swung off the main road into the parking lot of the Blue Horizon Motel. He turned off the engine, and a weighty silence settled over the car, broken only by the ticking of the cooling motor and the patter of rain on the car's roof.

"Why are we here? I thought we were going to the Sheriff's Office."

The silence continued.

"Declan?" She placed her hand on his taut thigh. The rigid muscle quivered beneath her gentle touch. "What are we doing at your motel? We have to tell the sheriff what happened and give him the piece of Skye's scarf." She shivered at the cold bleakness in his eyes.

Placing his much larger hand over hers, he closed

his eyes. His chest expanded as he sucked in a deep breath and slowly released it. When he opened his eyes again, the coldness was gone. The muscle in his leg stopped vibrating. "We need to talk."

"I've told you all I remember of the accident. I couldn't see the other driver; his windows were tinted."

He ran his fingers through his hair, rumpling the glossy curls. "We need to talk. About us."

The air whooshed out of her. "*Us*?"

"Come on. You're freezing. Let's get you someplace warm." He climbed out of the car, walked around the hood, and opened her door.

Her body was frozen in place. What was he thinking? What about the piece of scarf?

"I'm not going to hurt you, Carrie Ann." He crouched down, his eyes level with hers. "Do you trust me?"

She opened her mouth to speak but no sound emerged from her tight throat. She did trust him. Even after the hell they'd been through these past years, she trusted him.

He must have read her answer in her eyes because he said, "Good. Let me help you out of the car. We can go to my room and talk. Just talk. It's warm and quiet. No one will bother us." He grasped her arm.

Finally freed of her paralysis, she shook her head. "I can walk on my own."

He studied her for a long moment, and then stood and backed away.

Wincing with even the slightest movement, she climbed out of the car and gripped the open door, waiting for the wave of dizziness to ease. The incessant pounding in her head rose to a new level, and she squeezed her eyes shut, willing the pain away.

"Oh, for Christ's sake. You're so damn stubborn." He scooped her in his arms, ignoring her weak protests, and carried her across the parking lot, up the stairs to the door of his motel room. Cursing under his breath, he fumbled with the key card until it slipped into the lock, and the door opened. He stepped inside, kicked the door closed with his foot, and flicked a switch, flooding the room with what felt to her like a thousand watts of fluorescent light.

From the vantage point of his arms, she surveyed the small room. A queen-sized bed, covered with a hot-pink-and-vivid-orange floral bedspread dominated the room. Four overstuffed pillows leaned against the white-oak-veneer headboard. Matching curtains covered the room's single window. A combination heater and air conditioner unit sat below the window. The floor was covered with a worn, brown carpet, the walls painted a tired yellow. A faded print of a French street scene was bolted to the wall above the bed. An open door led to what must be the bathroom.

"The room's not much, but the price is right. And it's clean." Declan set her on the bed and removed a beige woolen blanket from the bottom drawer of a battered dresser and covered her legs. He walked over to the heater and turned a dial. The machine clanked and hissed, and with a loud whump, rumbled to life, and the first faint wisps of warmth belched forth.

He dug in the pocket of his snug jeans and pulled out his cell phone and punched in numbers.

"Who are you calling?" she asked.

"A doctor."

"I don't need a doctor."

211

He stopped hitting numbers and studied her. "You look like hell."

"Thanks." She couldn't help but smile at his bluntness. "But I'll be fine."

His eyes narrowed. "Are you sure? You were in a bad crash, and you were unconscious when I found you. You could have a concussion."

She nodded and bit back a moan as another swell of pain flared in her neck at the movement. "I'm sure." The last thing she wanted was for someone to see her and Declan together in his motel room. Even a doctor would be bound to talk, and the town would be abuzz with even more wild speculation. "Do you think you could find some ice or something for my neck? And maybe some painkillers."

"Were you always this stubborn?"

"Of course. Don't you remember?"

His dimples deepened as the corners of his mouth twitched. "I'll see if I can round up some ice, but don't get your hopes up." He headed toward the door.

"I'm sure this isn't the type of place where you're used to staying."

"This isn't Dallas, that's for damn sure." He opened the door. "Cooper's Ridge doesn't offer a lot of choice of fine accommodation." He shrugged. "I hoped to keep a low profile by staying here."

"How's that working for you?" The second his truck crossed the county line, everyone in town would have known he was back. It wouldn't have mattered where he stayed.

He flashed a grin and stepped out the door, closing it behind him.

The room felt empty and cold after he left, and she

huddled under the blanket. Her head pounded, and her neck ached. She shouldn't be here, not in his motel room, and certainly not lying on his bed. The room spun when she sat up. The pounding in her head increased, but she fought through the pain and edged to the side of the bed. Her legs wobbled when she stood, and she sank back on the bed with a groan.

"What the hell are you doing?" Declan stood in the open doorway scowling, a plastic bag in his hand. He slammed the door and rushed over to the bed. "You're in no shape to be moving around." He plumped the pillows against the headboard and raised his dark eyebrows. "Well, are you going to lie back down?"

"I'm fine. I don't need to lie down." She shifted her legs, preparing for another attempt at standing. "I shouldn't be here. I should leave. I need to call the sheriff."

He crossed his arms over his chest and watched her, a stern expression on his all-too-handsome face. "You're not going anywhere. At least, not yet."

She opened her mouth to protest but was too sore to argue with him. "Did you find any ice?"

"Ice, I'm afraid, is one of the many amenities this motel lacks. I drove to the store down the block and picked up an ice pack." He took out the small pack, squeezed the plastic to activate the chemicals inside, and placed the cooling pack behind her neck.

The relief was instant, and she lay back as the icy cold soothed the tightness.

"Here, take these."

She opened her eyes.

He held a glass of water in one hand and two small, white pills in the other. "What are those?" she asked.

"Painkillers. They should help."

She tried to hide the shaking of her hand as she took the pills and drank from the glass, but she could tell by the tightening of his mouth, he was all too aware of her discomfort. She closed her eyes again and waited for the ice pack and pills to do their work.

"How are you feeling?"

She opened her eyes at the sound of his husky voice, blinking in the bright light. "How long was I asleep?" She rubbed her eyes, her voice a sleep-fogged croak.

"An hour or so. I didn't want to let you sleep too long in case you have a concussion. Are you feeling any better?"

She raised her head. There was tenderness, but not the stabbing shards of pain she'd experienced earlier. The agonizing pounding in her head had eased to a dull throb. "I do feel better. Thanks." She glanced at her watch, shocked at the time. "I have to go."

"Why?"

Their gazes met and held, and just like that it happened. Acute awareness arced between them, the air in the room charged with sudden sexual tension.

"Because…" She coughed, trying to clear the thickness clogging her throat. "Because I shouldn't be here."

His pupils dilated, drawing her into their chocolate depths. "You shouldn't be here in my motel room, or you shouldn't be in my bed?" His voice was rough, his breathing labored.

She shivered and drew the blanket to her chin as if the thin wool would protect her from the heat between them.

His lips curled in a sensual smile. "Let's get you out of those damp clothes."

She gaped. "What?"

The dimples in his cheeks danced. "You're cold and your clothes are still damp from the rain. A warm shower will make you feel better." His grin widened. "What did you think I meant?"

She flushed, warmth rushing along her neck.

"I promise I won't peek." His eyes twinkled. "There're clean towels in the bathroom. The one good thing about this dump is there's plenty of hot water." He removed a white, terrycloth robe from a hook beside the door and handed it to her. "When you're undressed, toss me your clothes. I'll hang them to dry by the heater."

Lying in his bed fully clothed was bad enough, but naked and showering in his motel room was asking for trouble...Declan McAllister trouble.

She shivered again, but whether from the cold or the hunger smoldering in his brown eyes she couldn't tell. As if in a daze, she took the offered robe and tottered on wooden legs into the bathroom, closing the door behind her.

The room was tiny, but clean. A pile of neatly stacked, fluffy, white towels sat on a chrome and glass rack above the toilet. The shower was spacious and inviting. The thought of hot water cascading over her body was too much to resist. She turned on the water, stripped off her damp clothes, and stepped into the shower.

She froze at a loud knock on the bathroom door. "What is it?" She leaned out of the shower and snatched a towel from the rack and wrapped the thick cotton around her naked body.

"Pass me your clothes."

"Wait a second." Stepping out of the shower stall, she grabbed the pile of discarded clothing on the floor, and holding the towel tightly to her breasts, opened the door just enough to pass her clothes to him. She slammed the door shut, clicking the flimsy lock in place. An image floated in the rising steam—Declan sharing the warm humidity of the shower, his naked, muscular body pressed against hers, clouds of vapor rising around them—

Stop! Think of Bonnie. Think what will happen if she learns you've been lying about her father. She shuddered, dropped the towel, and once again stepped under the hot, cleansing spray.

But she couldn't stop thinking about him waiting in the room on the other side of the thin, wooden door. The attraction between them burned as hot as ever. From the first night when he'd stopped and helped her on the road, she'd fought the temptation. But each time she saw him, desire flared anew, and she found herself kissing him, touching him, and wanting so much more.

She angled the spray until the warm water pelted her face and stung her sensitive skin. If she didn't get a grip and stop letting her libido control her, she'd destroy everything she'd worked so hard to build these past twelve years. Being here, alone with Declan in his motel room, was a mistake. A big mistake. As soon as she retrieved her clothes, she'd get dressed and get the hell out of here before anything she'd regret happened.

She turned off the water, dried herself, then put on the terry cloth robe, cinching the sash at her waist. The robe was made for a man Declan's size, and the arms hung well past her fingertips, the hem reaching almost to her ankles. She inhaled, savoring his distinctive scent still clinging to the soft fabric. A vision of his naked body wrapped in the robe rose before her. She gulped as another wave of heat infused her.

Enough! The warning coursed through her like a dousing of icy water. Taking a deep breath, she unlocked the door and stepped out of the steamy bathroom. "Thanks for the shower, but I have to go, I—" She stopped, the rest of her words forgotten.

In the time she'd been in the shower, the small motel room had undergone a transformation. The bright, fluorescent, overhead light was off, and the two bedside lamps lit, lending the room a warm, intimate glow. The television was tuned to a soft rock music channel. Her stomach rumbled at the heady aroma of hot, spicy food.

"I hope you like Mexican." Declan gestured toward several grease-stained, cardboard cartons on the desktop. "I ordered some enchiladas and refried beans from Hector's while you were in the shower. I thought you might be hungry."

"It smells delicious." She sniffed, inhaling a heady mix of refried beans, salsa, and fresh cilantro.

"Good." He beamed. "Come on. There's lots." He dished up a heaping plate of food and held it out to her.

She'd made a vow in the bathroom to leave, but the meal smelled too wonderful to refuse. Besides he'd gone to a lot of trouble. It would be rude to leave so soon. "Thanks." She took the plate and settled on the only chair in the room. She wouldn't go near the bed. Not again.

He withdrew two bottles of beer from the mini

fridge and handed one to her.

Again she wanted to refuse, but she accepted and smiled her thanks. The icy liquid slipped down her throat like silk, spreading fingers of warmth throughout her body. She took a bite of food. It was delicious, pungent, but not too spicy.

They ate in silence; the only sounds the music playing in the background and the gentle clicking of their plastic knives and forks.

When she finished, she tossed her paper plate in the garbage, picked up her bottle of beer, and sat back, watching him inhale a second plate of food. He'd always had a healthy appetite, but the copious amounts of food he ate never affected him. As a teenager, his body had been lean and lanky. He was a man now. The broad width of his shoulders strained the thin fabric of his shirt, which did nothing to hide the hard planes of his chest where it tapered to a flat stomach. The well-developed muscles in his arms flexed as he ate. She licked her lips and nodded. He was a man, all right.

Warning bells clamored. She should leave, but her body refused to budge. What harm could a few more minutes do? She took another long sip of beer and watched him, enjoying the view. His hair was a tangle of glossy, dark curls; his face all angles and sharp bones, his firm chin hinting at his stubborn pride. Fine lines radiated from the outer corners of his eyes, adding to his rugged, good looks. Her gaze shifted to his mouth. His lips were soft and full. Those lips—

"What are you thinking?" He was staring at her.

She gulped. "I…I…" she stuttered, her face burning. "Nothing," she finished lamely.

His lips, the ones she'd been studying so closely,

curved in a knowing smile.

Her face heated even more.

"It's time we talked," he said. And just like that, the mood in the room shifted. The lines bracketing his mouth deepened as he frowned.

"Talk?"

"After you get dressed, I'll take you to the sheriff. You can tell him about the vehicle that crashed into you, and we'll give him the piece of scarf I found in your car."

She sucked in a quick breath. *The scarf!* She'd forgotten all about it. "Is it still in your coat pocket?"

He nodded.

"What if..." She swallowed, and breathed in a lungful of air. "What if we didn't show it to the sheriff? What if we hid it? Pretend we never found it."

His eyes narrowed. "What are you saying?"

She tightened her grip on the bottle of beer. "If the sheriff finds out we have another piece of Skye's scarf, he'll arrest you."

He opened his mouth to speak, but she cut him off. "You know I'm right. He'll charge you with murder." Her insides knotted. What was she doing? Was she actually suggesting they suppress evidence in a murder?

He shook his head. "I can't let you do that."

"But—"

"That's obstruction of justice. You'd be committing a crime."

Again, she started to speak, and again, he stopped her.

"I appreciate the offer, but there might be evidence pointing at the killer on the cloth." He jutted his chin. "I couldn't live with myself if the killer got away because

I was afraid."

A protest died on the tip of her tongue. She knew that look. He'd made up his mind. Nothing she said would make a difference. "Okay, but I'm telling the sheriff the truth. Someone else put that piece of scarf in my car. I'm not letting you take the blame."

He hooked his thumbs in his belt loops and smiled. His eyes crinkled. "You are something else."

Once again the vibe between them altered, and she blinked, her chest tight.

"Back in high school, when we broke up, I was upset." He shrugged. "More than upset. I was furious, and I wanted to hurt you like you'd hurt me. It was why I asked Skye to the prom."

"I was hurting too." Hurting? She'd been devastated; especially, once she'd found out she was pregnant with his child. He'd deserted her when she'd needed him the most.

"I'm sorry. I shouldn't have asked her, but I knew if I took Skye to the prom you'd hear about it. I wanted you to feel as bad about our breakup as I did. I guess I thought you'd come crawling, begging me to take you back." He smiled sheepishly. "What can I say? I was a teenage boy with a broken heart." He ran his fingers through his hair, rumpling the gleaming locks. "I should have tried harder to make our relationship work."

"We were kids," she said, her throat thick. "We didn't think through our actions."

"Being young isn't an excuse. We wouldn't be where we are today if I hadn't been so damn stubborn."

Tears stung her eyes. So many secrets, so many lies lay between them, creating an insurmountable barrier.

He shook his head. "Do you ever wonder what

would have happened if we hadn't broken up?"

She couldn't count the times she'd lain awake at night and thought of how different her life would have been if they'd stayed together, if he hadn't taken Skye to Prom, if Skye hadn't been murdered. But all those life-changing events had happened. Declan had created a life for himself in Dallas, and she had Bonnie.

But she couldn't tell him any of that, so she faced him and prepared to tell the second biggest lie of her life. "No, I've never thought what our lives would have been like if we'd stayed together. What would be the point? Life is what it is. I've moved on and so have you."

His gaze captured hers and held, as he slowly advanced until he towered over her.

The air sizzled between them.

"I don't believe you, Carrie Ann. You can't tell me you're not feeling what I'm feeling." Taking her hand, he drew her to her feet and pulled her close.

The bottle of beer in her hand slipped and crashed to the floor, spilling frothy liquid across the worn carpet. They ignored it. Her breasts brushed against his chest, her thighs against his. Her heart hammered in her chest, threatening to burst free.

"You can't tell me you don't feel anything." His voice rumbled through her, igniting deep vibrations in every cell. "I see the desire in your eyes. You want me. You want this."

Acting on overpowering need, she leaned into him, brushing her lips against his, a mere breath at first, but then deeper and deeper still.

His arms tightened, and he drew her closer. The rapid staccato of his heart beat in sync with hers.

The kiss deepened. A moan filled the air. Had she moaned? Had he? Did it matter?

She stood on tiptoe and rubbed her breasts against the firm wall of his chest, reveling in the sensation of soft flesh against hard muscle.

Her nipples hardened into aching points. She stroked his back, his shoulders, tangling through the silky hair at the back of his neck, as she reacquainted herself with his lean hardness. All so familiar, yet so different.

A whisper of unease trembled through her. *Stop. Now. Before it's too late.* She edged away from his heat until a breath of cool air separated them.

He loosened the tie at her waist and slid his hands inside her robe and rubbed the small of her back, his callused fingers sliding across her skin, raising goose bumps. His lips found the sensitive spot below her earlobe, and she mewed in delight, silencing the warning sirens.

She wanted this. Needed this. To hell with tomorrow. To hell with consequences.

His fingers fumbled as he opened the robe, exposing her nakedness to his fervid gaze. "You're so damned beautiful," he husked, his eyes liquid chocolate. "So beautiful." He cupped her breast in his hand. His thumb flicked across the sensitive nub.

She moaned and arched her back.

He lowered his head and took her other nipple in his mouth.

The moist warmth enveloped her, and she caught her breath. Electricity, wild and fierce, arced between them. When he flicked his tongue across the sensitive tip, she wrapped her arms around his neck and hung on, lost in a haze of desperate need. Her one thought, *more, give me more*.

Chapter 21

She opened her eyes, blinked at the strange surroundings, and then remembered. Everything. Heat burned up her neck and seared her cheeks. She was in Declan's motel room. In his bed. After a quick glance at the empty space beside her she blew out a breath. Her relief was short-lived as she peeked under the covers and saw her naked body. She groaned.

Sitting up, she held the thin sheet against her breasts. Muted daylight filtered through the edges of the floral curtains covering the window. The sounds of the shower running drifted from under the closed bathroom door. She sank back on the bed.

He'd be out soon. What would he say? What should *she* say? She shifted, tugging the sheet tighter and bit back a groan. Her body ached in places she hadn't thought of in years. The reality of last night sank in, and a knot tightened in her stomach. Maybe she could sneak out before he finished showering.

She climbed out of bed, tugged the top sheet free and tiptoed across the room to the heater where her clothes were hanging.

The door to the bathroom opened, and a cloud of steam billowed out.

She yelped and grabbed at the sheet, holding the rough cotton like a shield in front of her nakedness.

Declan stood framed in the doorway, a white towel

slung low on his narrow hips.

She swallowed, her mouth dry. She'd been wrong. He didn't have a six-pack. Oh, no. The hard, defined muscles in his abs were definitely a solid eight-pack.

His mouth curved in a sensual smile. "Good morning."

She gulped. "Hey."

Not hiding the fact he was mentally stripping the sheet from her naked body, he caressed her with a heated gaze. His grin deepened. "Do you want to order breakfast, or—" He arched his dark eyebrows, making his unspoken suggestion clear.

She tightened her hold on the sheet. "Er...no, thanks. I'm not hungry."

"Are you sure?"

"I should go."

His heavy-lidded gaze was full of sensual promise.

"I really have to go."

After another long minute, he nodded. "Let me get dressed, and I'll take you home." He walked back into the bathroom, leaving the door open. The sound of fabric rustling on bare skin drifted into the bedroom.

She patted her cheeks, struggling to cool her burning skin. Grabbing her clothes, she yanked them on. Her fingers fumbled with the snap on her pants, the catch on her brassiere, and the buttons on her blouse. She ran a hand over her hair and was waiting by the door when he exited the bathroom a few minutes later, fully dressed. She swallowed, her mouth dry. How did he look so damn good in faded jeans and a rumpled T-shirt with the dark shadow of beard on his rugged cheeks?

"Ready to go?" He tilted his head.

She nodded.

He stepped closer, his boots brushing the tips of her shoes.

Her breath caught in her throat, as she waited, half-hoping, half-fearing he'd kiss her.

He caressed her cheek as he cupped her chin, the rough tips of his fingers sending chills rippling along her spine. His gaze settled on her mouth.

Caught under the power of his torrid gaze, she couldn't breathe.

He lowered his head, and his warm breath fanned her face, igniting a fire within.

She closed her eyes, reveling in the riot of sensations rippling through her. In the next breath, he released her. Her eyes flew open amid a flood of disappointment.

"We didn't do much talking last night." His mouth quirked. "I guess we had other things on our minds. But we do need to have that talk, Carrie Ann."

Her skin tingled where he'd touched her. "Not now. I have to go." She needed time to think, to consider the ramifications of what had happened.

His steady gaze demanded answers to questions she was afraid to hear. "Okay," he finally said, "but this isn't over, not by a damn sight. I'm not letting you walk away. Not this time. Not without a fight."

Legs wobbling, she took his hand as they left the motel room and walked along the landing, down the stairs, and across the parking lot to his car.

A door of one of the motel units slammed, the noise echoing loudly in the still morning air.

She glanced back and groaned.

The cleaning lady she'd met a few days earlier

stood outside one of the rooms, her cart beside her. A cigarette dangled from her mouth, smoke curling from the tip. The woman grinned and gave her a thumbs-up sign.

Carrie Ann flung open the car door, diving into the seat, trying to escape the housekeeper's knowing smirk.

"What's wrong?" Declan folded his large body into the seat beside her.

She pointed toward the motel. "Someone knows we spent the night together."

He looked in the direction she pointed and shrugged. "You didn't think we'd be able to keep this a secret, did you? You know what this town's like. Before we reach your aunt's house, everyone will know we're back together."

The air rushed out of her. *Back together?* Were they? She rubbed her forehead trying to ease the rising ache. She had to tell him. Now. Before it was too late. She couldn't keep the fact he had a daughter from him any longer. He'd be furious when he found out, but would he forgive her? And what of Bonnie? She'd lied to her too. Would her daughter understand why? Would *she* forgive her?

"I care for you, Carrie Ann. A lot."

His deep voice cut through her turmoil. "What?"

"You heard me."

She closed her eyes, unable to meet his gaze, certain he'd see her deceit.

"Carrie Ann, look at me. Please."

Reluctantly, she opened her eyes.

"I know this isn't easy for you. A cloud of suspicion's hanging over me. Once the sheriff sees the piece of Skye's scarf we found, things are going to get even dicier." He rubbed the back of his neck. "I don't expect you to come running back to me, not the way things are, but I promise you, I will clear my name. I'll find proof I didn't murder Skye, and I'll see her murderer pays for what he did."

"Declan—"

He placed a gentle finger over her mouth. "Don't say anything. Not yet." He clasped her hand in his.

The warmth of his touch took her breath away.

"All I ask of you is a promise."

"A promise?"

He nodded.

She couldn't think, not with his thumb drawing small, intimate circles on the center of her palm.

"Promise you'll wait for me until I clear my name. Once I find Skye's killer, I'd like you to give me a chance to make up for my past mistakes, to give *us* a chance." His gaze bore into hers. "Promise you'll think about what I've said."

Her heart leaped. His words were the answer to so many prayers. In the next breath, her happiness vanished. What was she thinking? Once he found out he was a father, and she'd kept that a secret, any hope she had of renewing their relationship would end.

He lifted her hand and brushed his lips over her knuckles, his breath hot on her skin. "I know this is a lot to take in." His mouth twisted in a ragged smile. "All I want is for you to tell me I have a chance, and once I clear my name, I can come to you. We'll see what happens then."

Her hand burned where his lips touched. "I don't know what to say."

He searched her eyes. "Tell me you'll wait for me."

"Of course I will. No matter how long it takes, I'll wait." The second the words were out of her mouth, she regretted them, but it was too late.

He drew her to him, his arms enfolding her in his warmth. "Thank you," he breathed, and touched his lips to hers.

Her world spiraled out of control, and she returned his kiss, opening her mouth, inviting him in.

When he drew away, his chest was heaving, his breath rasping. "Wow." He grinned, flashing a row of even, white teeth.

She smiled back. "Yeah, wow." Again, her inner voice shrilled a warning. Again, she ignored the alarm. Being with him felt too good, and Bonnie wasn't here. She was in Seattle. Seattle was a long ways from Cooper's Ridge. Somehow she'd figure a way to tell him he had a daughter. But now...she pressed her mouth to his.

When they finally broke apart, they were both breathing hard.

She glanced through the windshield and cringed.

The cleaning woman was still watching, a knowing smirk wreathing her pudgy face.

Declan's grin widened, and he honked the horn and waved as he started the car and sped out of the parking lot.

She glanced back at the motel, and the housekeeper waggled her fingers at her. Carrie Ann waved back. What difference did it make if the whole town knew she and Declan had spent the night together? A kernel of happiness unfurled in her chest, and she grinned.

"Why are you so happy?"

"It's a good day."

Their gazes met. He chuckled. "It is a good day, isn't it?"

They drove to Vivian's house in comfortable silence. She refused to think what the future held. Right now, right this moment, life was good. A rush of warmth washed over her when she slid a glance at Declan. Her heart soared. He'd always been the one for her. The only one.

Her cell phone buzzed from inside her purse. The muted ringing had stopped by the time she fished out the tiny phone. She studied the caller ID, and her blood chilled. Janine. The calls missed icon flashed like an alarm indicating she'd missed three calls, and three voicemails awaited her.

With shaking fingers, she punched in her security code and listened to the voicemails. Each one was an urgent plea from Janine to call her as soon as possible. Carrie Ann bit hard on her bottom lip. She'd set the phone on mute the previous evening when she'd gone to Declan's motel room and had forgotten to turn the ringer back on this morning. How could she have been so careless? Something must have happened to Bonnie.

"Is everything all right?" Declan asked.

"I don't know. I have to make a call." Her fingers were clumsy, and she misdialed twice before the call finally went through. She held her breath as the phone rang and rang. A thousand scenarios flashed through her mind, each one more frightening than the one before.

"About time you called," Janine said when she finally answered the phone.

"Is everything all right? How's—" She stopped and bit her lip, sliding a glance at Declan. He was watching the road as he drove, but he was listening. But she had to know how Bonnie was. "Is she okay?"

"Can you talk?" Janine asked.

"Not really. Did something bad happen?" Is Bonnie safe was what she wanted to ask, but couldn't, not with Declan sitting mere inches from her.

"Oh, God, is that what you thought? No, no, Bonnie's fine."

Carrie Ann's breath whooshed out of her. "Are you sure?"

"She's fine, Carrie Ann, but there's something you need to know."

Bonnie was safe. Nothing else mattered.

"Carrie Ann, are you still there?"

She nodded, but then realized, Janine couldn't see her. "Yes, I'm here. Is anything wrong?"

Declan placed his hand on her thigh, the warmth of his touch spreading tingles along her leg.

Their gazes met. "Everything okay?" he mouthed.

She nodded. "Can it wait, Janine? Now's not a good time."

"No, it can't wait." Her friend's voice was strident. "You need to know—"

"Janine?" Carrie Ann's gut clenched. "Janine? What is it? What's happened?"

No response.

Carrie Ann looked at her phone, and shards of ice sliced through her. No power. She jabbed her finger again and again on the power button. *Damn. Why hadn't she charged the darn thing?*

"Carrie Ann? What is it?" Declan asked.

"My phone's dead." What had Janine been about to say? What was so urgent it couldn't wait? She pressed her hand to her stomach, trying to ease the lump of dread that had settled there. "I need to use a phone."

"My cell's in my pocket." He lifted one hip and scrunched sideways as he fished in the pocket of his jeans. The car swerved, jerking one way and then the other, as he contorted his big body.

At any other time his antics would have been comical, but all she could focus on was her desperate need to call Janine back. "Come on, Declan," she urged.

He gave up on his efforts to retrieve his phone and settled back in his seat. "We're almost at Vivian's. Hang on." He pressed his foot on the gas, and the little car surged ahead.

Five minutes later, he wheeled into Vivian's driveway and turned off the motor. "Give me a second, and I'll get my phone for you."

She shook her head. She couldn't use his phone to call Janine. He was right here. He'd hear everything. "No, it's okay. I'll use Vivian's phone." She reached for the door handle.

"I'll call you later," he said. "We need to figure out what we're going to do next. We should have called the sheriff last night but…" He let the rest of what he was going to say hang in the air.

Heat rose in her cheeks. They should have done a lot of things last night, instead of what they actually did. "I'll phone him this morning." She opened the door. She had to call Janine. Now.

He placed a hand on her arm, halting her rush out of the car. "Look, I know you're in a hurry, and I hope whatever has you so upset works out, but I'm worried about you, and I don't want you going out by yourself.

It's not safe. Whoever crashed into your car last night meant it as another warning. The next time, and believe me, there will be a next time if you remain in Cooper's Ridge, you might be seriously injured."

She met his gaze, and a rush of warmth flooded her at the concern in his eyes. "I'll be careful."

"Pack your bags and go back to Seattle. Today."

"But—"

"Listen to me, Carrie Ann. I'm going to clear my name. To do so, I have to find Skye's killer. I can't figure out this mess if I'm worried about you."

She opened her mouth to protest, but he placed two fingers over her lips, silencing her.

"Go home. You'll be safe in Seattle." His gaze bore into hers. "I promise, I'll come to you when this is over."

Her first thought was to refuse. She wanted to stay and help him find Skye's murderer, but the lines of worry marring his handsome features made her hold her tongue. She nodded.

"Promise?"

She nodded again.

He traced her jaw, his fingers trailing a line of fire. "I'll miss you."

Her heart thudded. "You'd better figure this out quick. I'm not waiting forever."

He laughed and drew her to him, pressing his mouth to hers.

The kiss deepened, and her heart raced, her pulse beating a rapid tattoo.

"Mom!"

She jerked away from Declan and gaped through the windshield. Her heart stopped.

Bonnie stood on the steps, a grin wreathing her freckled face, dimples dancing in her cheeks. Her brown eyes gleamed, her curls a wild tangle of gold. "Mom," she called again and ran down the steps to the car.

"Mom?" Declan frowned. "You have a daughter?"

Chapter 22

Declan stared, openmouthed, as the young girl ran toward Carrie Ann's side of the car and flung the door open wider.

"Mom, where have you been? I've been waiting all night to see you." She threw herself at Carrie Ann, landing on her lap, wrapping her arms around her neck.

"Bonnie? What are you doing here?"

He released the breath he'd been holding ever since he'd heard the girl call Carrie Ann Mom. "Is this your daughter?" He already knew the answer, but had to ask. "You have a daughter," he repeated, reeling as if he'd been sucker punched.

Carrie Ann buried her face in the child's blonde curls, refusing to meet his gaze.

"Carrie Ann?" His voice cracked. "Is this your daughter?"

The girl regarded him curiously. Her eyes were a surprising shade of dark brown for her fair hair and pale skin. "Hi," she said. A shy smile curved her mouth, a matching set of dimples forming in her cheeks. She looked to be ten or eleven years old, all legs and arms, losing the chubbiness of childhood, teetering on the cusp of adolescence.

"Hi." He held out his hand. "I'm Declan."

She placed her small hand in his and shook. "Bonnie."

"Bonnie," he repeated. "Carrie Ann? You never told me you had a daughter."

Carrie Ann bit her bottom lip; a gesture he knew meant she was nervous. "I…" Her voice was thin. "It never…er…it never came up."

He nodded, though he didn't understand at all. "You have a daughter." No matter how many times he said the words, they didn't sink in. Okay, she had a daughter. Not a big deal. But why hadn't she told him? Did she also have a husband she'd forgotten to mention? Was last night all a lie?

"Mom, come on. Aunt Vivian and Uncle Leland are waiting for us."

"Aunt Vivian?" Carrie Ann sounded stunned. "You've met Vivian?"

Bonnie nodded, her curls dancing. "She and Uncle Leland showed up at our apartment in Seattle and told me they were my aunt and uncle. They said you'd asked them to come and get me and bring me here. Janine didn't want me to go, but they showed her some important papers and said she had to let me go with them. Janine was real upset, but after they talked awhile, she said it was okay." She furrowed her brow. "It's all right, isn't it? I mean, they're so nice, and Janine told me I could go with them."

Carrie Ann's mouth opened and closed, but no sound emerged.

"Mom?"

She hugged Bonnie. "Of course it's okay, kiddo. I missed you too."

"Aunt Vivian and Uncle Leland are so nice. They let me stay up late last night while we waited for you to come home." She studied Carrie Ann. "Where were you? I waited a really long time, but they said I had to get some sleep, and I'd see you in the morning. I've been waiting for you on the porch ever since I woke up."

A flush of red suffused Carrie Ann's pale face. She glanced at Declan and quickly looked away.

"How come you never told me I have an aunt and uncle?" Bonnie's brow wrinkled. "I thought you said all our relatives were dead."

Declan blinked at this surprising news. "Go ahead, Carrie Ann. Tell your daughter why you've never told her she has an aunt and uncle. I'd like to hear too."

If possible, Carrie Ann's face paled even more. "Uh, I'll explain everything to you later, honey. Right now, say goodbye to Declan. He has to leave."

Bonnie nodded and leaped off her mother's lap. "Bye," she chirped and grabbed Carrie Ann's hand and tugged, trying to drag her from the car. "Come on. Let's go."

Carrie Ann cast a frantic look at him and climbed out of the car. She hurried after Bonnie along the walkway and up the steps to the house.

Mother and daughter. His mind whirled. *Carrie Ann had a daughter.* The phrase reverberated through his mind. *A daughter!* He threw open the door and jumped out of the car. No way was he leaving without getting some answers. She had some explaining to do, for damn sure. He ran up the steps to the porch and blocked the door with his foot, stopping it from closing.

Carrie Ann whirled to face him. "Declan!" Her eyes were filled with fear. "What are you doing? You need to go."

Her panic hit him with a jolt. She was afraid. Of

him. After last night! Fury blazed through him. "I'm not going anywhere. At least, not until I hear all about your daughter."

Her amber eyes filled with shadows. "Don't do this, please." Her hand trembled as she brushed back a strand of auburn hair.

"Why are you so frightened? What's going on, Carrie Ann? Does your husband know you're here having a fling with your high school boyfriend?"

"Husband?" Her brows drew together. "What are you talking about? I'm not married."

A breath he hadn't known he'd been holding, expelled in a rush. *She wasn't married.* "So what's this about, then? Why are you so afraid? It doesn't matter to me if you have a daughter. I like kids."

Tears shimmered in her eyes, and she shook her head. "Go, just go, please."

He stared at her, trying to make sense of her distress.

"Mom," wailed Bonnie, tugging on her mother's hand. "Come on. Aunt Vivian's waiting. She has cookies. Chocolate chip cookies."

Carrie Ann turned to her daughter. "You go on, honey. I'll be right with you." She released the girl's hand.

"Promise?"

Carrie Ann's lips curved in a stiff parody of a smile. "You bet. Give me a minute."

"Okay." Bonnie turned and raced away.

Silence surrounded them once the girl disappeared into the room at the end of the hall.

Carrie Ann wouldn't meet his eyes. She crossed her arms in front of her as if she needed protection from something. Him? Again he felt a punch in the gut. "So, you have a daughter." His voice cut like a knife through the thick wall of tension between them.

She nodded, still not meeting his eyes.

"Why didn't you tell me?"

She didn't answer.

The silence deepened, growing and stretching until it was a living entity, rearing over them.

Finally, she looked up.

Their gazes met.

Her eyes were deep bruises in her pale face. "I guess I didn't know what to say."

"It doesn't matter, you know. Your having a child doesn't change anything between us."

Her bitter smile didn't reach her eyes.

"What is it?" He couldn't figure it out. "What's wrong? Surely you don't think I care you have a daughter?"

She regarded him with those hollow, dead eyes. "You need to leave."

"What?"

"I said, leave." Her voice was dismissive, her eyes flat. She headed down the hall.

"Carrie Ann," he called after her. "I'm not going anywhere until you tell me what's going on."

She stopped and turned to face him. "I'm leaving for Seattle this afternoon like you wanted. Don't try and contact me."

"What?"

"I hope you find Skye's murderer and clear your name, but this...us...it's over. I don't want to see you ever again." She turned her back on him and continued walking down the hall until she disappeared into the room at the end.

He stood frozen, his mind blank.

"I'm glad she finally told you." Vivian stood above him on the hall stairs.

"Told me what?" His brow furrowed.

"You met Bonnie?"

He nodded.

"What do you think?"

He shrugged. "She's a cute kid."

"And you're okay with the situation?"

"What situation?" he snapped and rubbed his aching head. He couldn't deal with Vivian now.

Childish giggles erupted from down the hall.

"Carrie Ann's daughter, of course." Her eyes narrowed. "She did tell you, didn't she?"

"Look, Vivian. Now's not a good time." His headache worsened.

Her mouth compressed in a thin, tight line. "Come with me." She took his arm, and hauled him behind her down the hall and into a spacious room where sunshine streamed through two large, French doors and danced across gleaming, hardwood floors. A fire crackled in a massive, brick and tile fireplace.

Carrie Ann and her daughter sat on a burgundy, leather couch. Bonnie was showing her mother something on a small, laptop computer. Carrie Ann laughed at something the child said, the sound brittle and forced.

The clink of ice cubes in a glass drew his attention, and he glanced across the room.

Leland sat on a matching, burgundy leather chair. The old man's brow was furrowed, his body bristling. "What are you doing here, McAllister?"

Carrie Ann stiffened. "Declan." She sounded desperate. "I told you to leave."

"And I invited him to stay." Vivian tightened her hold on his arm, and propelled him into the room. She walked him over to the chair beside the one Leland was in, and with surprising strength, shoved him into it.

He sat, too shocked at the events of the past half hour to protest.

Vivian took a seat on the couch beside Bonnie and Carrie Ann.

They sat like a frozen tableau.

Carrie Ann stared at him as if he were her worst nightmare.

Leland scrutinized him as if Declan were a bug he'd like to squash.

Even Bonnie watched him, her brown eyes wide in her freckled face.

Tension thickened the air.

Vivian broke the icy silence. "Carrie Ann, don't you have something to say to Declan?"

Carrie Ann's face grew even paler, her eyes deep hollows in her delicate face.

The hairs on the back of Declan's neck prickled. He had a bad feeling about where this was going, a real bad feeling.

"Carrie Ann?" Vivian prompted.

Carrie Ann chewed on her bottom lip.

He'd had enough. Standing, he scowled at Leland, then Vivian, and finally, Carrie Ann. "Would someone tell me what's going on?"

Carrie Ann whimpered and huddled into the couch cushions.

"Mom?" Bonnie's voice was a thin wail.

Carrie Ann held her daughter close as if protecting her from something or someone.

Him?

Leland's deep baritone cut through the silence. "You should leave, McAllister." He looked pointedly at Bonnie. "Now's not the time to get into this."

"I don't agree." Vivian spoke before he could respond. "It's time you told Declan the truth, Carrie Ann."

The pounding in his head beat a fierce tattoo. "Tell me what?" His frustration made his voice sharp.

"I can't," she whispered. "Not now, not with Bonnie here."

"She's old enough to hear the truth." Vivian rested her hand on Bonnie's coltish leg. "Go ahead, Carrie Ann."

"I don't want her to find out like this." Carrie Ann took Bonnie's hand in hers. "You know I love you, honey, right?"

The girl nodded, her lower lip trembling, tears glistening in her dark eyes.

"You trust me." Carrie Ann's voice was thick with emotion. "Right?"

"Mom, are you okay?"

Carrie Ann ran a hand over the child's golden curls. "I'm fine. You don't need to worry. Go with Uncle Leland and eat your cookies. I'll be with you soon."

"I'm scared, Mom." Bonnie hurled herself into Carrie Ann's arms. "What's going on?"

"It's okay, kiddo. Everything's fine."

Leland put down his glass, stood, walked over to Bonnie, and held out his hand. "Come on, Bonnie, let's go dig into those cookies. I hear they're delicious."

Bonnie sat up and wiped a hand over her tear-streaked face. "Are you sure, Mom?"

Carrie Ann nodded. Tears shimmered in her eyes. "Go on."

"Okay, but don't be long, or we might eat all the cookies before you get there." Bonnie leaped off the couch, took Leland's hand, and skipped out of the room.

Silence echoed in the spacious living room. Vivian perched on the couch watching Carrie Ann like a bird of prey.

Wiping a hand across her eyes, Carrie Ann took a deep breath, brushed her hair off her forehead, and met his gaze.

He flinched at the raw pain in her eyes turning the amber a deep, burnished gold. "What is it? What do you have to tell me that's so awful? What are you afraid of?"

"There's something you need to know, something I should have told you years ago."

Once again there was the prickling sensation on the back of his neck, but he kept his mouth shut and nodded.

Her gaze met his, and then skittered away. She inhaled a deep breath. "Bonnie is your daughter."

The air rushed out of his chest in a whoosh. "What? Impossible." His voice cracked.

"She's yours."

"Mine?" He couldn't think. "But..." He rubbed his forehead. "How could she be? I mean, you weren't pregnant. I would have known. You would have told me. Wouldn't you?"

"I couldn't."

"You couldn't tell me you were pregnant with my child?" A thought occurred to him and he glared at her. "How do I know you're telling me the truth? You've lied to me all these years, how do I know what you're telling me now is the truth?"

"It is."

He searched her face.

For the first time since they'd arrived at the house, her gaze met his, open and honest.

He struggled to swallow over the thick lump in his throat. "How old is Bonnie?"

"Eleven."

His chest tightened as he did a quick calculation. They'd last been together almost twelve years ago. Was it possible? He visualized the child's blonde curls and dark eyes, eyes the same color and shape as his. He remembered the matching dimples in her cheeks when she smiled, dimples like his. He sank back on the chair as the truth hit him. "Bonnie's my daughter," he croaked.

Carrie Ann nodded.

His mind whirled. He had a daughter. He had an eleven-year-old daughter. Even more incredible, he was a father. A *father*. Him. He ran his fingers through his hair, a thousand questions on the tip of his tongue. "Why didn't you tell me?"

"I wanted to. I was going to, but we had that big fight and broke up." She shrugged as if those few words explained the situation.

"You still could have told me. I would have helped you. Surely you knew I would."

She stared, her eyes wide, her face ashen. "I told

you what happened. Remember? I went to your house, but your mother said you'd spent the night in your bedroom with Skye. I was too upset to tell you then."

He frowned. They'd discussed all this the other day when they were sitting in their spot by the river. He'd told her he hadn't slept with Skye, and how he'd beaten the crap out of Skye's father for hurting her. He opened his mouth to reassure her once again, but then he remembered what this was all about, and his anger returned with a vengeance. "Why didn't you tell me you were pregnant?" Surely she knew he would have looked after her, helped raise the baby. He jumped to his feet. "Answer me, damn it! Why did you keep your pregnancy a secret from me?"

She shook her head and wiped at tears leaking from her eyes, streaming down her cheeks. "I couldn't tell you."

"You couldn't?" he snarled. "You thought it better to keep your pregnancy a secret; to never tell me I had a daughter? You thought lying to me all these years was right?" He took a step toward her, his hands clenched at his sides. "You lied to me. Worse, you took something precious from me. Something I can never get back." He fought to hold his fury at bay, but it was a losing battle. He wanted to hit something, anything.

Vivian's voice cut through his outrage. "She didn't tell you because I told her not to."

He spun toward the old woman. "You? You told her to keep my baby from me?"

"Of course I did. You were accused of murder." She lifted her chin. "I couldn't let my niece give birth to a murderer's child. What would people have thought?"

He turned back to Carrie Ann. Tears streamed

down her face and dripped off her chin onto her blouse. For a heartbeat, he felt sorry for her, but he hardened his heart to her misery. "You took my daughter from me." Each word was a sliver of ice.

"I'm sorry, so sorry."

"It was for the best, given the circumstances, believe me," Vivian said.

He glared at her. "Stay out of this, old woman." He glanced back at Carrie Ann. "You agreed with her?"

"I was young, I—"

"Were you ever going to tell me? I mean, if I hadn't seen Bonnie today, would you have told me?" He waited, but he knew the answer. Guilt was written all over her face. She'd planned to keep his daughter a secret forever. A red haze covered his eyes, dimming his vision. "I've had enough of this bullshit." He turned and stormed out of the room.

She called after him, but he didn't stop. He had to get away from her before he did something he'd regret. He heard footsteps running after him down the hall, but he didn't slow. He flung open the door and burst outside, sucking in great gulps of cool, fresh air.

"Declan."

He didn't want to, knew it was a mistake, but he couldn't stop himself; he turned and faced her.

She stood in the open doorway, tears staining her ravaged face. "Please, don't do this. We need to talk."

He hardened his heart against the raw pain in her voice. "We've already talked."

"What are you going to do?"

"Get in touch with my lawyer." He turned and stalked away, trying to block out the sound of her sobs.

Chapter 23

Carrie Ann cupped her hands under the tap and splashed cold water on her face. Grabbing a towel, she dried her skin and scanned the mirror above the bathroom sink. Her hair, a tangled mass, framed her pale face. Swollen, red eyes looked back at her.

Her secret was out. An image of Declan's outraged face rose before her, and she closed her eyes trying to block the memory. He'd been shocked, disillusioned, hurt, and furious. Who could blame him? He'd been blindsided.

Bonnie and Leland were talking in the kitchen. He was doing his best to distract her, but she was a bright child. She knew something was going on. How do you tell an eleven-year-old her life was a lie?

Declan's parting words terrified her. Was he really going to talk to a lawyer? And what then? Would he ask for full custody of his daughter? A judge would probably grant him custody after the way she'd lied to him all these years. A sob tore at her throat. Bonnie was her life. She couldn't live without her.

"Are you going to hide in here all day?" Vivian's gaunt face reflected in the mirror.

"Thanks to you, I have to break Bonnie's heart."

Vivian's eyes blazed. "Someone had to make you tell Declan the truth. It was time."

"Truth?" She snorted. "What do you know about

truth?"

"I know what's right. Bonnie deserves to know who her father is."

"This is all your fault. How did you convince Janine to let you take Bonnie?"

Vivian shrugged. "Leland called in a favor and had a family court judge friend of his draw up some custody papers. They stated Bonnie was our ward, and we had the legal right to have her visit us." Her mouth creased. "Janine's a good friend. She didn't want to release Bonnie to us. It took a fair bit of convincing before she finally agreed."

Carrie Ann turned and faced her. "I can imagine the type of *convincing* you used." Her stomach churned with years of built-up anger and guilt. "Who do you think you are? Who made you judge and jury? Who gave you control over other people's lives?"

Vivian sagged, clutching the bathroom door handle as if she needed the support. "Everything I've done is because I love you, Carrie Ann."

"What do you know of love? Your idea of love is to dominate people, to make them do what you want. And if they don't, you shut them out."

Vivian shrank under the bitter onslaught, shoulders drooping, her body caving in on itself.

Outrage spewed out of Carrie Ann. "You never loved me. Don't you think I know how you felt?" She glared at Vivian. "Can you even imagine what it was like for me? I was five years old, for God's sakes. My parents had been killed in a fire. I had no one."

Tears streamed down Vivian's shrunken face. "I took you in. I cared for you."

"You call what you did, caring? I was devastated

248

by the loss of my parents. I needed love and understanding. And what did you give me?" Carrie Ann couldn't stop the venomous stream of accusations. "Rules. You gave me a list of rules." Her eyes burned, and her throat clogged with tears, making it hard to speak. "All I wanted was to be loved. I needed to be loved I…" The words faded and she sank, spent, onto the toilet seat.

The only sound in the small bathroom was the steady drip of water in the sink.

Vivian removed a tissue from the pocket of her slacks and wiped her eyes. "I gave you the best clothes, the latest toys, healthy food, everything you could possibly want."

"But not love."

"Do you really believe I didn't love you?"

Carrie Ann nodded.

"I loved you so much," Vivian said. "I'd have done anything for you. I still would."

"How come you never told me?"

Vivian heaved a sigh. "I tried to, but it was hard for me."

"Why? Why was telling me you loved me so damn hard?"

Vivian shook her head.

"Don't do this, Vivian. Not anymore. Tell me why you were so cold, why you never told me you loved me."

The drip, drip, drip of the tap filled the room.

"Vivian?"

Vivian drew herself up to her full height. She released her hold on the door handle. "I have always found expressing my emotions challenging." She shrugged. "Maybe I was afraid of letting others get too close, afraid of being hurt. I don't know."

"Bullshit," Carrie Ann spat. "I don't believe you. I was a child, and you treated me like one of your employees."

Vivian swallowed, her thin throat working as if something blocked it. "Have you examined your mother's effects?"

Carrie Ann blinked at the sudden shift. The small box was in her old bedroom in the closet beside her suitcase. She wanted to wait until she was home in Seattle before going through her mother's things. "I haven't yet. Why?"

"Look at your mother's things today. Right now."

Carrie Ann stared at her.

Lines of strain marred Vivian's pale face. Each breath was tortured, but her gaze was fervid. "Please."

"First I need to talk to Bonnie."

"Look in your mother's box, and then talk to her."

"But—"

"She'll be fine. I'll look after her. She's waited eleven years to hear the truth, an hour or two more won't make any difference."

The sheen of tears in her aunt's pale eyes made a lump rise in her own throat, and Carrie Ann nodded, unable to speak.

Vivian shuffled out of the bathroom.

"Vivian," she called after her.

The old woman turned to face her, her brows arched in question.

"How did you really convince Janine to let you take Bonnie?"

"I told you, Leland arranged for court documents

attesting to our custody rights as Bonnie's guardians. But even then, I don't think Janine would have let us take Bonnie if I hadn't told her you'd asked me to pick up Bonnie and bring her to Cooper's Ridge so you could introduce her to her father."

"In other words, you lied."

"Not really." Their gazes met again. "You'd already decided to tell Bonnie about her father, hadn't you? I mean, after spending last night with him."

Carrie Ann stiffened. "How did you—"

"I may be old, Carrie Ann, but I'm not blind. I see how things are between you two." The corners of her mouth twitched, and she left the room.

Carrie Ann shook her head. Vivian was full of surprises. She could only imagine the concerned-and-loving-aunt act she'd put on to convince Janine to let her take Bonnie. Once Vivian set her mind to do something, nothing stood in her way. Janine hadn't stood a chance. Vivian and Leland going to Seattle and picking up Bonnie explained her friend's frantic phone calls. She'd been trying to warn her Bonnie was on the way.

What was in the old shoebox? What was so important Vivian wanted her to look through her mother's effects now when she should be doing so much else? She left the bathroom and headed up the stairs to her room.

She sat on the hardwood floor, her back resting against the side of the bed and placed the battered shoebox on her lap. Taking a deep breath, she lifted the lid and set it aside. She picked up a photograph from the small stack of pictures lying on top. Two young girls, their thin arms draped around each other's shoulders, grinned back at her, their eyes filled with happiness. A small, spotted pony stood in the background grazing on a patch of tall grass, and she remembered Vivian telling her of the horse she'd had when she was young.

This was the first photograph she'd seen of her mother as a child, but she knew right away the small girl with two, white-blonde braids hanging past her narrow shoulders was her mother. The older girl in the photo with her auburn hair tied back in a severe ponytail, had to be Vivian. No mistaking the fierce look in her pale eyes.

The next three photos showed the same two girls smiling and happy. The close bond between them was unmistakable. Another photo, a studio portrait, taken a few years later, was of her mother as a girl of thirteen or fourteen, teetering on the brink of adulthood. Her long, shiny, blonde hair and slim build were the same, but the expression on her youthful face was hard, her eyes cold. Gone was the happy innocence of childhood; replaced by something darker, almost sinister.

She picked up the last photo. This one showed the two sisters, dressed in colorful party dresses sitting on a porch swing and squinting under the bright summer sun. Flowers bloomed in the background. Her mother appeared to be in her early twenties. Her youthful prettiness had blossomed into stunning beauty. Vivian must have been in her early thirties at the time the photo was taken, her face already showing the harsh lines marking it today.

The picture was disturbing, but she couldn't pinpoint what unsettled her. Holding the photo up to the light streaming through the window, she examined it more closely. The women's smiles were forced; her mother's blue eyes hard and cold. Vivian's wounded. Both women's bodies were stiff. A void separated them on the swing's seat, one she sensed neither wanted to cross. Gone was the closeness and happiness evident in the earlier photographs. Again, she wondered what had happened to cause such a drastic change.

She put the photographs down and looked at the small diary nestled in the box. Her mother's name, Caroline Jane Morgenstern, was etched in faded gold lettering on the cracked, red, faux-leather cover. A ripple of excitement trilled along her spine. Vivian had always been reluctant to discuss her younger sister. In spite of the questions Carrie Ann asked, Vivian managed to avoid providing any answers. This diary was her chance to find out what her mother had thought and felt.

Her hand trembled as she opened the book and turned to the first entry. The date at the top of the page indicated the words had been written when her mother was ten years old. *Just a year younger than Bonnie.* The first entries were written in a neat, childish hand. Tears filled Carrie Ann's eyes, and the words wavered in front of her as she read of the excitement and drama of birthday parties, Christmas gifts, and a child's hopes and dreams for the future.

As the months and years passed, the entries grew sporadic and then stopped. Nothing new was written in the diary until Caroline was almost thirteen years old. These new entries chilled Carrie Ann. Gone was the cheerful recounting of daily events; replaced with darker, angry, almost frightening thoughts, as if two different people had written them.

The writing was sloppy. Words were misspelled, the sentences long and confusing, filled with hatred and vitriol. A theme ran throughout—Caroline's growing hatred and jealousy of Vivian. Carrie Ann's stomach clenched as she read of her mother's scheming to exact revenge on her older sister.

She closed the diary, unable to read any more of her mother's angry ramblings, but the acrimonious words written so long ago were emblazoned on her mind. Had her mother really been such a vengeful person? Why? What had happened to cause her to hate Vivian so much?

A tap on the door startled her.

The door swung open, and Vivian stepped into the room. She sat on the desk chair and pointed at the photographs and diary spread across Carrie Ann's lap. "I'm sure you have some questions."

Questions? She had a million, but where to start? "Why didn't you tell me?"

"You have to understand." Vivian tucked her lips over her teeth. "Caroline was complicated. She was a striking child and grew up to be an even more gorgeous woman." Her eyes softened. "You look a lot like her, you know."

Carrie Ann held up the diary. "After reading this, I don't think that's much of a compliment."

A veil of sadness clouded Vivian's pale eyes. "I was an only child for the first ten years of my life. My parents had given up on having any more children, but then Mother discovered she was pregnant. From the moment she was born, Caroline was treated like a princess. She was so pretty, so delicate, everyone adored her." The corners of her mouth lifted. "I loved her too. She was my own little doll." Vivian's thin, veined hands twisted in her lap. "Something happened when she was eleven years old. It changed her forever."

Carrie Ann sucked in a tremulous breath. "What?"

"Our father contracted tuberculosis." Vivian met Carrie Ann's gaze, her eyes bright with unshed tears. "Times were different then. In those days, TB was incurable. If you became infected, you were removed from your family and home and sent to isolation in a sanitarium. You didn't have a choice. It was the law." She wiped her eyes with a tissue. "Most people never recovered from the disease. They died in those places."

"Your father?"

Vivian nodded. "I never saw him again. He was in the sanitarium a month before he succumbed."

A lump grew in Carrie Ann's throat.

"Mother was sick as well," Vivian continued. "I looked after her, tried to help, but..." Her voice fell away. "They put her in the san as well." Vivian's eyes were red-rimmed.

Carrie Ann inhaled a shaky breath. To lose her father, and then her mother so soon after, when she was so young must have been awful for Vivian. "But you and my mother were okay. You didn't get TB."

Vivian stared out the window, her gaze far away as if reliving those tragic times. "A few weeks after Mother passed away, Caroline began coughing. She ran a high fever. I couldn't let them take her to the sanitarium to die. She was eleven years old and all I had left." She met Carrie Ann's gaze. "I didn't tell anyone she was ill. I cared for her, bathed her, fed her, tried every remedy I could find. Nothing worked. She grew weaker every day. I feared I'd lose her." She shrugged.

"But then one morning, the fever was gone, and her health slowly returned. I was elated. I loved Caroline. She was all I had left. My only family."

"I don't understand." Carrie Ann shook her head. "You saved her life. Why was she so angry with you?"

Vivian aged before her eyes. "Caroline's body recovered. Her mind didn't. She was a different person after the fever. I took her to doctors, but no one could determine what had happened. The general consensus was the high fevers she'd suffered while in the throes of TB had affected her mind."

"How was she different?" Carrie Ann asked, though she knew. She'd read Caroline's bitter words in her diary.

"She grew sullen and secretive. She was always angry. Nothing I did was good enough." Vivian wiped her eyes. "The situation grew worse when I met Jonathon Bradstone." Vivian's eyes took on a hollow look. "We fell in love. He asked me to marry him, and I accepted. I couldn't wait to be his wife. And then Caroline…" Her voice trailed off.

Carrie Ann tried to imagine Vivian young and in love. She'd married Leland soon after Carrie Ann had come to live with her, but Carrie Ann had never seen any real affection between the two, let alone love. Vivian's voice drew her out of her thoughts.

"Caroline wanted Jonathon and set out to seduce him. She was so beautiful. What man could refuse her? They became lovers, and he called off our engagement and asked her to marry him. He told me she was his soul mate, and he couldn't live without her." She paused and blinked at Carrie Ann as if suddenly remembering she was in the room. "Caroline grew tired of him soon after. Once she achieved her goal, she didn't want him anymore. She broke off the engagement. Poor Jonathon was brokenhearted. He killed himself a week later."

Silence descended over the room. The old house creaked around them. Somewhere downstairs, Bonnie giggled.

"Caroline moved away not long after, and we didn't keep in touch, though I heard she'd married and had you." Vivian's voice was a thin thread. "You must understand it wasn't her fault. If Jonathon had really loved me, she wouldn't have been able to take him." She blew her nose. "When your parents died in the fire, the lawyer for their estate contacted me. Your father didn't have any living relatives, and your mother had named me in her will as your guardian."

Carrie Ann sank back against the bed. "You must have hated having to raise me. I was a constant reminder of Caroline's betrayal."

Tears once again filled Vivian's eyes. "I always wanted you, Carrie Ann; from the second I found out about you, I wanted you."

Carrie Ann fought back the flood of tears threatening to overwhelm her. "Why didn't you ever show you cared?"

"I was afraid you'd blame me for what happened to your parents."

"Blame you? Why would I blame you? The fire wasn't your fault. It was an accident."

Vivian dabbed at her brow with a shaking hand.

"I'm right, aren't I?" Carrie Ann was almost afraid to ask. "You always told me the fire was accidental."

Tears streamed down Vivian's lined face. "I tried

257

to stop her. You have to believe me."

A numbing cold seeped through her. "Tried to stop what?"

"Caroline contacted me." Vivian's voice was a hoarse whisper. "I hadn't heard from her in six years, but she phoned and wanted to see me. She said this was our chance to reconcile, to be sisters again. I left Cooper's Ridge right away and drove to Portland to see her."

Vivian shuddered. "The second she opened the door, I knew something was wrong. The house was a mess, books strewn across the floor, furniture overturned, glass shattered. There was blood on Caroline's nightgown." She inhaled a shaky breath.

"She held a knife in her hand. I asked her what had happened, but she wouldn't tell me. Instead, she led me into the dining room. The mess was even worse there, and then I saw your father lying in a pool of blood. I ran over to see if I could help him, but I was too late. He was dead. I told Caroline to call the police, but she acted as if she hadn't heard me. The knife was clenched in her hand and she stared at me with those awful vacant eyes.

"I…I asked her what had happened, and she said they'd had a fight. Simon had found out she'd had an affair with another man. He threatened to leave her, and she killed him. No one was ever going to leave her again." Vivian inhaled a shaky breath. Her hands gripped the sides of the chair as if to stop from keeling over. Recounting the terrible events of so long ago was taking a heavy toll. Her body trembled, and her face was a white mask of exhaustion.

Carrie Ann blinked away her tears. "You don't

have to tell me any more now. You should rest. We can talk again later."

Vivian continued as if she hadn't heard her. "I studied the woman standing before me, and I knew Caroline was insane. She needed help. I grabbed the phone to call the police, but she ran out of the room. I was afraid she'd hurt herself so I ran after her. She was in her bedroom, the door locked, but I smelled gasoline.

"And then the explosion happened. I guess I lost consciousness because the next thing I knew, I was lying on the floor in the hall. The smoke was so thick I could barely breathe. Flames crackled from behind Caroline's bedroom door. She was inside the inferno. I staggered to my feet and slammed against the door, but it wouldn't budge. Something was blocking it. Then I heard you crying."

"What do you mean?" Carrie Ann blinked. "I wasn't in the house that night. I was at a neighbor's."

"That's what I told you. How could I tell you the truth when the truth was so awful?" Vivian dabbed at her brow. "I found you in the closet in your bedroom buried under a pile of clothes. You must have crawled in there when you heard your parents fighting. There was so much smoke, but the flames hadn't reached your room. I carried you outside.

"I heard sirens in the distance. I saw your innocent face, and I knew what I had to do. I refused to let you live with the knowledge your mother had killed your father and then killed herself; far better for you never to know the truth.

"I called Leland. He knew who to bribe to make sure the fire was ruled accidental, and your parents' deaths became another senseless tragedy."

Carrie Ann rubbed her aching head.

"Don't make the same mistake I did." Vivian's voice was raw with emotion. "No matter what else she did, your mother loved you. She'd have been proud of the woman you turned out to be, proud of the mother you are. Bonnie is a wonderful child, and all because of you."

"Why are you telling me this now? After all these years?"

"I don't want any secrets between us anymore. It's time you learned the truth."

The truth. Carrie Ann snorted. "We have more in common than I thought. You've lied to me all these years, exactly like I've lied to Bonnie and to Declan."

"I did it for you, Carrie Ann, to protect you. Please believe me."

Carrie Ann's stomach knotted. She'd used the same words to justify not telling Bonnie about Declan. Was what Vivian had done any different? Didn't the fact she'd wanted to protect her niece show how much she cared? The same way Carrie Ann cared for Bonnie and wanted to protect her? For the first time, she understood Vivian, and with understanding, came the beginnings of forgiveness.

As if reading her thoughts, Vivian tottered across the room and bent down and wrapped her thin arms around her.

Carrie Ann stiffened at the unexpected embrace. *No more secrets, no more lies.* As the affirmation rang through her, she relaxed and hugged Vivian. "Thank you."

Vivian released her. "For what?"

"For bringing Bonnie here. You were right. She

needs to know the truth."

"It'll be okay. I promise." Vivian turned and shuffled out of the room.

Carrie Ann wiped her damp eyes and inhaled a deep, steadying breath and followed her aunt. *Here goes. God help me. Here goes.*

Chapter 24

"This isn't a good time, Declan." Vivian's voice echoed up the stairway.

Carrie Ann paused at the top of the stairs, her heart pounding as she listened to the confrontation below.

"I don't give a damn. I want to see her now."

She stiffened at his angry voice.

"I don't care what you want, young man." Vivian used her most authoritative voice. "This is my house, and I told you my niece does not want to talk to you."

"Fine. I'll talk to Bonnie."

Carrie Ann's heart froze, and she bounded down the stairs. "What do you want, Declan?"

"We need to talk," he bit off, his eyes hard. "Now."

"Declan." Vivian refused to back down. "I already told you, now is not a good time. Come back later when you've calmed down."

Carrie Ann's heart warmed at Vivian's pit-bull-like protection. The last thing she wanted was to fight with Declan. She had to talk to Bonnie. She opened her mouth to tell him to leave, but hesitated at the fierce determination in his dark eyes. He wouldn't leave until he said what he'd come here to say. "I'll talk to him."

Vivian's eyes were questioning.

Carrie Ann nodded. "It's okay."

"I'll be in the kitchen if you need me." Vivian walked away.

A strained silence followed her departure. Carrie Ann's mouth was dry, her palms damp.

"Let's go for a walk." Declan's face resembled a stone carving, but his eyes blazed.

Her heart beat a trip-hammer in her chest. She didn't want to go anywhere with him. But the challenge in his dark eyes changed her mind. He thought she was afraid of him. *Like everyone else in town.* The words he'd uttered yesterday reared before her. She'd hurt him enough. "Okay, I'll go with you."

Grabbing her coat from the hall closet, she followed him out of the house. They walked down the driveway and across the road to a narrow, dirt path almost hidden by overgrown vegetation. Her heart fluttered as she realized where they were going.

Walking single file, she followed him, shoving branches out of her way and stepping over roots and exposed rocks. The burble of running water reached her, and in another hundred yards, they broke through to a small clearing on the bank overlooking the river.

Their clearing.

The trail from her aunt's house was a private shortcut, one they'd taken countless times when they were teenagers. She perched on the same flat rock she'd sat on two days earlier when she'd followed him from the motel.

Declan remained standing, looking out over the rushing river, his hands jammed in the pockets of his jeans.

Water splashed and gurgled as the river flowed over rocks and around sweepers. She inhaled the fresh scents of damp moss, tree sap, and fish. Puffy, white clouds scudded across the soft blue sky, and streaks of sunlight filtered through the overhanging trees, dappling the ground.

"Well, are you going to tell me about Bonnie?"

She jumped at the sudden rasp of his voice.

His gaze drilled into hers.

"I already told you everything." She clenched her hands tight together, to stop the trembling.

"Tell me again."

"I found out I was pregnant just before we broke up. I was going to tell you, but we fought, and then you asked Skye to the prom. I tried to tell you a few more times, but before I could, Skye disappeared, and you were accused of her murder."

His mouth tightened. "You thought I was guilty."

She rubbed her hands over her knees. "I was confused. I didn't know what to think. Vivian and Leland were urging me to end the pregnancy. They said I was too young to raise a child on my own, and you couldn't help me. How could you when we all thought you were going to jail for the rest of your life?"

"So you decided to have an abortion."

She glanced away, unable to face his accusing eyes. "You don't know what my life was like. I was sixteen. I didn't want to have a baby. I was a kid myself. And you—"

"I was a murderer."

"No." She shook her head vigorously. "I never thought that, never."

"But you didn't think you could tell me you were pregnant with my child? You were going to destroy our baby?"

"No...yes...I don't know." She stumbled over the words. "Vivian arranged everything, and Leland drove me to Seattle to the women's clinic." Tears burned her eyes.

"But you didn't go through with the abortion."

"I couldn't."

A silence settled over them, all other sounds intensified. A crow cawed from the branch of a nearby fir tree, a fish splashed in the shadows of the deep pool beneath the fallen log overhanging the river, and the wind picked up, riffling the leaves of the tall cottonwoods.

"Why didn't you tell me about the baby?" he asked. "After I was cleared, why did you keep our child a secret?"

"At first, I was angry with you, but then..." She shrugged. "It was too late."

"You kept my daughter from me. All these years."

"I'm sorry."

"Jesus Christ," he exploded. "I don't fucking believe this." He glared at her, his eyes blazing. "You're *sorry*? Do you realize what you've done? You've stolen something from me I'll never get back. I've missed the first eleven years of my daughter's life." He clenched his fists. "She's my daughter too. I had a right to know, Carrie Ann. I had a right to know."

"I know." Guilt weighed heavy on her shoulders. "I'm sorry."

The pulse in his jaw beat a rapid tattoo.

"Declan," she tried again. "I'm sorry, I—"

"Sorry doesn't cut it." He kicked a rock, sending it scudding across the ground into the river where it landed with a splash. He wiped a hand across his face and pinned her with a piercing gaze. "Does Bonnie know?"

She bit her bottom lip until she tasted blood.

"I asked you a question," he demanded. "Does my daughter know about me?"

"No."

"Great." He ran his fingers through his hair.

"I was going to tell her. After last night and what happened between us, I was going to tell her."

He snorted.

"I was."

His eyes blazed. "Pardon me if I don't believe you."

"It's the truth."

His lips twisted in a sneer. "Yeah, and you're real good with telling the truth, aren't you?"

She opened her mouth to protest, but he was right. For almost twelve years she'd lied to him. He had no reason to believe her now.

Grabbing her hand, he hauled her to her feet.

"What are you doing?"

He pulled her behind him as he retraced their steps along the narrow, rocky path.

"Where are we going?" She struggled to keep up with him.

"To talk to our daughter. We're going to tell her who her father is, and you're going to explain to her why you lied to her all these years."

She stumbled, her stomach cramping. Bile filled the back of her throat. This wasn't the way she wanted to tell Bonnie, but the rigid lines of his face told her whether she agreed or not, Bonnie would learn her father was very much alive. Right now.

All too soon, they were back at the house. At the front steps, he released her hand and glared at her, his look scathing. "Ladies first." He gestured for her to go ahead of him.

Face heating at his censure, she walked up the steps into the house. Her legs shook, and it took all her effort to put one foot in front of the other. How would Bonnie react to hearing her father was alive? Would she forgive her mother for the lies she'd told all these years?

Declan strode behind her, the heat of his anger radiating off him, stirring the air like a living force.

Removing her coat, she hung it in the closet, and as if moving in slow motion, walked down the hallway on leaden feet to where she heard her daughter's voice. She paused in the doorway to the kitchen.

Bonnie, Vivian and Leland were playing a board game.

Bonnie tossed a pair of dice and moved her counter ahead several spaces on the game board. She grinned and let out a whoop as she passed another counter and took the lead.

A thick lump formed in Carrie Ann's throat, and tears filmed her eyes. Bonnie was so happy, so unaware her world had changed.

Bonnie looked up and her grin widened, her dimples dancing. "Mom, you're back! I'm beating Uncle Leland. I told him I was good at this game, but he didn't believe me."

Carrie Ann blinked back tears, her throat closed tight.

Unaware of her mother's distress, Bonnie chatted happily about the game.

Her daughter's voice washed over her in a blur, as Carrie Ann searched for the words to explain her lie.

"Mom? Are you okay?"

She forced a smile to her stiff lips. "I'm fine, honey."

Vivian and Leland watched her, their gazes worried.

"Do you want to play with us?" Bonnie asked. "We can start a new game."

Declan stepped into the room and stood beside Carrie Ann, his shoulder brushing hers. "Your mother has something to say to you."

Carrie Ann shot him a quick, sidelong glance, swallowed hard, and wet her lips.

Bonnie's gaze locked on hers. "Mom?"

"You remember Declan, don't you?"

Bonnie nodded. "He's your friend."

"Um, honey, I have something to tell you, something important."

Bonnie's smiled faded, and she put down the dice.

"Why don't you three go into the living room and talk?" Vivian's no-nonsense voice cut through the rising tension.

"But what about our game?" Bonnie protested. "We're right in the middle of it. I was winning."

"Don't worry, we'll save our spots," Vivian said. "Uncle Leland will help me make some hot chocolate for us all to drink when your mother and you are finished."

"Come on, Bonnie. Let's go in the other room." Carrie Ann cleared her throat to ease the croak in her voice.

Bonnie grabbed a green, stuffed frog from the chair beside her, and clutching the worn toy to her chest, she gripped her mother's hand as they walked out of the room, down the hall, and into the sunlit living room.

****

Declan followed, his gaze taking in every detail of Bonnie's young, gangly body and bouncing, blonde curls. *His daughter.* He had a daughter. He had a part in creating this beautiful child. She had his genes. Amazing!

Carrie Ann led Bonnie to the couch, and they sat side by side. She clasped Bonnie's small hand in hers.

He was too tense to sit, but he didn't want to frighten Bonnie, so he sat in the facing armchair and tried to appear relaxed.

Carrie Ann chewed on her bottom lip.

How many times had he seen her bite her lip when she was anxious? A memory of how he used to take her in his arms and comfort her when she was upset, how she fit, so soft, so right, rose before him. He thought of last night. She still fit perfectly. *Stop!* She'd lied, had been lying every second of every day for the past eleven years. Even after what had happened in his motel room a few short hours ago, when after all these years, he'd begun to hope again, she'd continued her deception. Only when Bonnie showed up, and she'd had no other choice, had she told him the truth. Even then, he'd had to drag it out of her.

"Carrie Ann," he prodded, his voice hard, wanting to wound her like she'd wounded him. "Don't you have something you want to say to Bonnie?"

Her eyes were huge in her pale face. Looking as if she were facing a firing squad, she nodded and turned back to her daughter. "Bonnie, there's something I need to tell you, something I should have told you long ago."

Bonnie watched her mother, her brown eyes wide,

her brow furrowed. Her fingers dug into the soft body of the stuffed frog on her lap.

A wave of guilt washed over him. Bonnie would be devastated when she found out her mother had lied all these years. How could he allow that to happen to his child? He opened his mouth to stop Carrie Ann, but then changed his mind. Better Bonnie learn the truth now than when she was older. *Was it? Was it better for Bonnie to learn the truth about her father, or was it better for* him?

"I told you your father died before you were born." Carrie Ann said the words slowly.

"I know," Bonnie chirped. "He was killed in a car accident, and you were so sad, but happy you had me to help you get through your grief."

Declan bit back a snort at the flagrant fantasy Carrie Ann had spun for their daughter, but then Bonnie reached under the collar of her shirt and pulled out a thin gold chain from which a tiny gold heart dangled. He forgot to breathe as his gaze zeroed in on the necklace in her hand.

"My dad gave you this necklace because he loved you, right, Mom? You gave this to me on my birthday last year, and you wanted me to wear it so I'd think of him and how much he would have loved me. That's what you told me, isn't it, Mom?"

A flood of bittersweet memories consumed him—how he'd saved for months to buy Carrie Ann the gold chain with the golden heart, how he'd wanted something concrete to show her how much he loved her. He couldn't believe she'd kept the necklace all these years. And she'd given it to Bonnie to remember her *dead* father. His gaze flicked to Carrie Ann, but her face was a white mask, giving no hint of her thoughts.

"You know I love you." Carrie Ann spoke as if Bonnie hadn't revealed the necklace. "More than anything in the world, right?"

"I love you too, Mom. We're a team. You and me."

Unexpectedly, a lump formed in his throat.

"What I'm going to tell you next is difficult." Carrie Ann's eyes were shiny with unshed tears. "You have to believe I never intended to hurt you."

"Mom?" Bonnie's lower lip trembled. "What's wrong?"

"Declan is more than a friend."

Bonnie's dark eyes fixed on him. Her light-colored brows arched.

His gut clenched at what the next words Carrie Ann uttered would do to this innocent child. "We," he began, surprised at how rough his voice was. "We, your mother and I, we dated, years ago, here in Cooper's Ridge."

Bonnie's eyes widened. "You and Mom dated?" She turned to her mother.

Carrie Ann nodded.

Bonnie studied him. "Weird. Mom never dates."

That was interesting news. Bonnie's shrill shriek drew him out of his thoughts, and he tensed, ready for the bombshell to drop.

"I know what this is about!" She squealed and turned to her mom. "You're going to tell me you and Declan are dating. Like Destiny's mom and her new boyfriend." She hugged Carrie Ann. "I think it's great, Mom. You should have a boyfriend."

Declan met Carrie Ann's gaze. A single tear leaked from the corner of her eye and slid down her cheek.

"No, Bonnie, that's not what I'm going to tell you." She inhaled deeply. "Declan is…he's your father."

"What? My father's dead. He died before I was born."

"That's not true. Declan is your father."

Bonnie's sprinkling of freckles were stark on her pale face. "You're my dad?"

He nodded. "I'm your father."

Bonnie eyed one parent, and then the other. Her cheeks flushed red, and she yanked her hand from Carrie Ann's grasp. "My father's dead. You told me he died." She glared at her mother.

"I…" Carrie Ann's voice faded.

"Your mother did what she thought was best at the time," he said. *What the hell? Where had that come from?* He slid his gaze to Carrie Ann. She was as startled as he was. Why was he defending her? Why didn't he tell Bonnie her mother had been lying to her all these years? "My life was complicated at the time, and she did what she had to do."

"Why didn't you ever contact me?" Bonnie's voice was tentative.

"I didn't know you existed until this morning."

Her eyes widened, and she jumped to her feet and spun on her mother. "You never told him about me? I don't understand. He's my *father.*"

Carrie Ann's face crumpled. "I thought I was doing what was right."

"You lied to me!"

"I—"

"Don't," shouted Bonnie, her eyes filled with tears. "Don't talk to me. Not anymore. Not ever."

"Please." Carrie Ann sobbed. "I love you, Bonnie."

Bonnie stared at her, her chest heaving, tears streaming down her smooth cheeks. "I hate you!" Her voice cracked as she screamed. "I hate you. You're a liar. I never want to see you again." She ran out of the room.

Declan listened to the pounding of Bonnie's feet as she raced down the hall and up the stairs, and then the slam of a door. He should be happy. He'd achieved what he'd wanted. Carrie Ann had finally told his daughter the truth.

Carrie Ann hunched on the couch sobbing into her hands as if she'd lost the only thing in the world that mattered. Bonnie's stricken face and bitter words ran through his head. He took a step toward Carrie Ann, wanting to comfort her, to ease her pain. But he stopped. She'd done this to herself. If she'd told the truth years ago, this wouldn't have happened. She deserved her heartbreak after what she'd done.

She glanced up with bleak eyes. "Are you happy?"

Her words struck like an arrow, and he flinched. "I'll be back later once she's calmed down." He closed his heart to the raw anguish in her eyes.

Carrie Ann nodded.

He walked out of the room and out of the house. The situation would be better once Bonnie had a chance to think things through. After all, she had a father now, a father who was very much alive.

Chapter 25

Carrie Ann sagged on the couch, too drained to shed any more tears. *I hate you.* Bonnie's parting words ran through her head in an unceasing litany.

"I gather your conversation with Bonnie didn't go well." Vivian stood over her holding a steaming mug in her hand.

"She hates me."

Vivian sat beside her and placed her hand on Carrie Ann's thigh. "She's upset. She doesn't hate you."

"You were right. I should have told her the truth years ago. Now look what I've done. She never wants to see me again."

"You told me the same thing hundreds of times. And look, you're here now." Vivian smiled. "Children say things when they're hurt. They don't always mean them." She held out the mug. "Here, I made you some hot chocolate."

Carrie Ann shook her head. She couldn't imagine eating or drinking anything.

"Come on, try a sip. I put in a little something extra. I thought you might need the sustenance."

Carrie Ann took the cup and sipped, struggling to swallow the hot liquid over the lump of ice stuck in her throat. Wiping her streaming eyes, she set the mug on the coffee table. "I need to talk to her."

"Leave her."

"I have to fix this."

"She needs time to absorb what's happened. You've just told her she has a father who's alive. Think how she must be feeling. Her life has changed. She'll need time to come to terms with the news."

"But she's my daughter. I have to try and make her understand."

"I'll check on her in a little while. Drink your hot chocolate and figure out what you're going to say when she does want to talk."

Every cell in her being urged her to go to Bonnie, but Vivian was right. Bonnie needed time to get over her shock. She sank back down on the sofa. "Okay." She picked up the cup of cocoa. "I'll give her some time."

"Good girl. I'll go and have a peek at her and make sure she's all right." Vivian struggled to her feet and shuffled out of the room.

Carrie Ann sipped the hot drink, her mind a torrent of conflicting thoughts. She hadn't expected Bonnie to take the news of having a living, breathing father well, but she'd hoped her revelation would go better than it had. If only Declan hadn't been watching with his accusing, bitter eyes. If only she'd had more time to figure out how to tell Bonnie the truth. If only—

A cough drew her out of her thoughts.

Leland stood in the doorway. "Do you want some company?"

"Sure. Come on in."

He sat across from her in the chair Declan had vacated. Withdrawing a small leather pouch and a black pipe from his pocket, he went through the ritual of filling the pipe with tobacco, tamping it down, and lighting it with a wooden match.

The sweet, pungent aroma of pipe smoke drifted over her. His quiet presence helped calm her ragged nerves. The strong shot of alcohol in the hot chocolate Vivian had given her didn't hurt either.

"It'll be okay, you know. Bonnie will get over this." Leland drew on his pipe.

"She's pretty upset." *I hate you. I never want to see you again.* A stab of fresh anguish filled her. The words were branded on her soul.

"It may take her some time, but she'll forgive you." A cloud of smoke swirled in the air above him. "Once she understands this means she has a father who's alive, she'll want to get to know him." His gaze met hers. "Have you thought how that will work?"

She let out a discouraged breath. Thought of it? It was all she'd thought of since Declan's threat to contact a lawyer. He'd want to be part of Bonnie's life. He lived in Dallas; she and Bonnie lived in Seattle. Her stomach lurched. She'd have to share her daughter. Would Bonnie spend Christmases and summer vacations with him? Her head throbbed. "You're a judge."

He nodded.

"What do you think will happen?"

He puffed on his pipe for several long minutes. "Family law isn't my specialty."

"I know, but what would a judge decide?" She wrung her hands until they ached.

"You're getting ahead of yourself. From what I've seen, you and McAllister seem to be, shall we say, getting along better these days? Is there a possibility you two could get back together?"

"No," she burst out. "I was just helping him solve Skye's murder. Besides, he hates me."

Leland's gray eyebrows rose.

"I'm telling you the truth. There's nothing between us. There never will be, I—" She stopped, realizing she was protesting too much.

His mouth quirked in a small, knowing smile. "And that's why you didn't come home last night?"

Her cheeks heated. Last night she'd been locked in Declan's arms, and today he detested her. What a difference a twist of fate and a few hours made.

"You do realize having sex with him was a mistake." He put his pipe in the glass ashtray on the table beside his chair and pinned her with a sharp look. "Surely you don't believe Bonnie is best served by you and McAllister getting back together. I mean, especially if he's convicted."

"He won't be." She shook her head. "He's innocent."

He smirked. "If I had a dollar every time a felon said the same thing."

"Declan's not a felon. He'll prove his innocence, and in the process find out who killed Skye." *From my lips to God's ears.*

"You're not thinking clearly, my dear. This situation has an upside. If McAllister goes to jail for murdering Skye Lawrence, you won't have to worry about custody of Bonnie. No judge would grant a convicted murderer visiting rights, let alone custody of a young child."

Her anger flared to life. "You're really something, you know? I would have thought a judge would be more concerned with justice than putting an innocent man in jail."

"No one's innocent, Carrie Ann."

She blinked, trying to make sense of his comment, but before she could dwell on what he'd said, he spoke again.

"I had a long talk with Sheriff Atkins. They found the vehicle that struck your car last night."

"Really? That's great. Who owns it?"

"The SUV was found abandoned twenty miles from here near Hedron. The vehicle had been stolen two days ago from the same area. The police are checking it for fingerprints as we speak."

She sank back, deflated. "What do you think the chances are whoever stole the SUV and crashed into me was stupid enough to leave his fingerprints behind?"

"Zero to none."

"I thought so." Another dead-end. "They don't have any idea who's responsible?"

"The sheriff and his men are still investigating." His eyes narrowed as he studied her through the haze of pipe smoke. "Is there something you're not telling me, my dear?"

She squirmed under the intensity of his penetrating gaze and looked away. An image of the piece of scarf, the word *Guilty* scrawled across the silk, flashed before her, and she shuddered. When she'd called the Sheriff's Office earlier this afternoon, she'd told the deputy she'd talked to about the crash, but she'd left out any mention of the torn piece of cloth. In spite of everything going on between her and Declan, she didn't want him to go to jail.

"Carrie Ann, what aren't you telling me?" Leland's voice was stern and authoritative, as if he were presiding over his courtroom.

She jerked back and fixed an innocent expression on her face. "I've told you everything."

His gimlet-eyed stare didn't waver, reminding her of the many years he'd spent as the town's prosecutor, ferreting information from the most hardened of criminals. "Are you sure?"

Her mouth tasted of ashes. "I'm sure." Before he could call her a liar, she jumped up from the couch and walked over to the window, staring out at the weak sunlight glistening on the lush green lawn and manicured shrubs. When her heart slowed and her breathing eased, she turned back to him.

He puffed on his pipe, his intense gaze raking over her, and she knew he didn't believe her.

"If I were to speculate, I'd say someone's trying to frighten you. According to the sheriff, the damage to your vehicle wasn't severe enough to cause you serious injury."

"That's what Declan said."

His face tightened, his dislike of Declan clear. "McAllister is still the main suspect in Skye Lawrence's murder. It's best you don't forget that." He set down his pipe and stood. "Well, I need to go into the office for a few hours and catch up on some work. Don't worry too much. Bonnie will come around. Give her time. She loves you."

Carrie Ann's nervousness vanished, and her throat clogged. "Thank you."

"You're a good mother, Carrie Ann. Bonnie's lucky to have you." He kissed her on her cheek and left.

She shook her head. *A good mother.* She doubted Bonnie would agree. Not after what happened today.

With a heavy sigh she picked up the empty mug. She needed some fresh air to clear her mind and help her figure out what to say to Bonnie. Her mouth twisted in a bitter smile. Cooper's Ridge, hell, the entire planet didn't have enough fresh air to prepare her for the coming confrontation with her daughter.

****

The pungent aroma of roasting meat and simmering gravy filled the kitchen when Carrie Ann removed the pot roast from the oven. She turned to the microwave and took out a bowl of steaming corn. Pot roast, roasted potatoes and corn, all smothered in a lake of savory gravy. Bonnie's favorite meal. She hadn't seen her daughter since the scene this morning, but Vivian had taken a plate of sandwiches and cookies to her at lunch and said she was quiet, but okay.

Carrie Ann hoped by making Bonnie's favorite food, she could convince her to leave her room and come to the kitchen for dinner. After they'd eaten, she'd try and answer any questions Bonnie had. Her stomach clenched, and she pressed her hand against her belly to ease the sudden, sharp pain.

She straightened her shoulders and headed down the hall and up the stairs. Taking a deep breath, she knocked on Bonnie's door. Her heart raced and she was certain Bonnie could hear its fierce pounding through the closed door.

No response.

She knocked again, louder this time.

Still no response.

She opened the door. "Bonnie? It's Mom. May I come in?"

The room was dark, the curtains closed against the

faint glow of the street light outside. "Why are you sitting in the dark?" She fumbled for the light switch and flicked it on, blinking against the sudden glare.

It took her a second to realize what she saw, and another, longer second to make sense of what she was seeing. The room was deserted. "Bonnie?" She walked over to the closet and peered inside and then looked under the bed. Where was she? She spun around and hurried down the hall to the upstairs bathroom. The door was open, the room empty.

She checked each of the bedrooms as an aching dread filled her. Running downstairs, she called Bonnie's name, her voice more and more frantic. The basement was her last hope, but Bonnie wasn't hiding in the dark, damp, cavernous space.

She collapsed onto a kitchen chair. Bonnie's dinner was cold, the gravy congealing into thick lumps. She couldn't think against her rising panic. Had Vivian taken Bonnie with her? She grabbed her cell phone out of her pocket and called the boutique. The phone rang and rang without answer. Next, she tried Leland's phone. Still no answer. She cursed and tossed the phone on the table. Vivian wouldn't have taken Bonnie without telling her. Nor would Leland.

Had Bonnie run away? Her heart stuttered. She was eleven years old. Where would she go? She didn't know anyone in town. She sat bolt upright. Bonnie did know someone in Cooper's Ridge. Picking up her cell phone with trembling fingers, she punched in numbers. When the call was answered, she said, "Where is she?"

"What?" Declan's voice was groggy as if he'd been asleep. "Carrie Ann? What's wrong?"

"Is she with you?"

"Who? Bonnie? Why would she be here?"

She ran her fingers through her tangled hair, hardly able to breathe. "I checked her room and searched the house. She's not here."

The faint noise of a television program playing in his motel room was the only sound for several heartbeats. "Okay. Calm down."

"Calm down?" she shrieked. "She's eleven years old."

"That's my point. She's eleven. How far could an eleven-year-old girl go at this time of night?"

His steady voice helped calm her racing heart. "I have to find her before something happens."

"You don't have to search for her on your own, Carrie Ann. I'm Bonnie's father. I'll help."

She choked back a sob. "I don't know where to look. What if—"

Declan cut in. "I'll be there in five minutes. Wait for me." He severed the connection.

She sat alone in the brightly lit kitchen, the pungent aroma of the food she'd prepared a painful reminder of her missing daughter.

****

Declan grabbed his coat and ran out of his motel room, leaving the door open behind him. He flew down the stairs two at a time and raced across the parking lot to his rental car. The second the motor started, he jammed his foot on the gas and squealed out of the parking lot. Keeping his hand pressed to the horn, he blasted through stop signs and red lights, going well above the speed limit until he took the turn to Winters Road on two wheels and screeched to a stop in front of Vivian's house. He leaped out of the car and froze.

Every light in the house was on. The front door was wide open, light streaming onto the porch. Carrie Ann, her hair a wild tangle around her pale face, her eyes dark hollows, hurried down the steps. "Thank God you're here. I called the sheriff. He's going to have a couple of deputies look for her in town." She flew into his arms.

He stumbled back a step, his body stiff and unyielding, his anger and bitterness too fresh and piercing. She'd lied and kept his child from him. But her anguished sobs knifed through him, and almost without realizing what he was doing, he wrapped his arms around her and pressed her against his heart.

The bitter weight of betrayal melted in the face of her anguished torment. This didn't affect just them anymore. They were Bonnie's parents. He had to put aside his resentment and work with Carrie Ann to find their daughter. Plenty of time for recriminations when Bonnie was safe.

She blinked up at him, her luminous amber eyes bright with tears. "I'm so worried. We need to find her, Declan."

Swallowing back a lump in his throat, he asked, "When was the last time you saw her?"

"Vivian checked in on her at noon."

"And you haven't seen her since?"

"I wanted to give her time to calm down. I didn't think she'd run away. She's never run away before."

"She's never had her world turned upside down."

"It's my fault." Her body shuddered with sobs. "If I'd told her the truth years ago, this would never have happened."

"Stop this." He shook her gently. "Blaming

yourself won't help. Right now, we have to find her."

Wiping her face with her sleeve, she nodded. "You're right. What should we do?"

"She can't have gone far. Cooper's Ridge is a small town. If she's run away, someone will have seen her." He took her arm and turned her toward the house. "Show me her bedroom."

"Why? She's not in her room. I told you. I searched the house."

He urged her up the steps and into the house, a chill of foreboding settling deep in his gut. He followed her up the stairs to Bonnie's room.

The bed was mussed. The pillow still held the small indent of her head. A book was open on the bed, and a half-empty glass of milk sat on the bedside table. A quilt lay in a heap on the floor, as well as a wrinkled pair of jeans and a purple sock. Nothing looked out of place, but what did he know? He'd only found out this morning he had a kid, and already she was gone. "Is anything missing?" He gestured around the room. "Did she take something with her?"

"Like what?"

He shrugged. "Clothes, a wallet, I don't know."

"I don't think so." She walked over to the closet and peeked inside. "I think everything she had with her is here. She doesn't have any money, unless Vivian or Leland gave her some."

"What about a coat? It's cold outside. She'd need a jacket or something."

She riffled through the clothes hanging in the closet. "I don't know. I think her pink hoodie is missing, but I don't know. This is my fault." Her voice was thick with tears.

"Blaming yourself won't bring back Bonnie."

He turned at the sound of Vivian's no-nonsense voice. She and Sheriff Atkins stood in the doorway.

"Have you found her? Have you found my daughter?" Carrie Ann asked. "Please tell me she's all right."

"Sit down, Carrie Ann," said Vivian.

"Why?" Her gaze flew between the sheriff and Vivian. "What's wrong?"

Vivian shuffled over to Carrie Ann and steered her across the room.

As if in a daze, Carrie Ann plopped onto the bed.

Sheriff Atkins glared with a narrow-eyed, suspicious gaze at Declan, and then he turned to Carrie Ann. "One of my men found this." He held out a green, stuffed frog, the fur matted and worn, one bulging, plastic eye missing. "Is this your daughter's?"

"Oh, my God," choked Carrie Ann. She pointed at the stuffed frog. "That's..." She swallowed with an obvious effort. "That's Binky, Bonnie's favorite stuffy. She was given the toy when she was a toddler and had to spend the night in the hospital because her tonsils were sore. She loves that toy. She wouldn't run away without taking Binky." Jumping up, she grabbed the stuffed animal from the sheriff and crushed it to her chest.

The sliver of ice in Declan's gut swelled into a solid block.

"She had the toy when I brought her lunch this afternoon." Vivian's voice cracked as, on unsteady legs she stumbled over to a chair.

"Where did you find it?" Carrie Ann looked at the sheriff.

"One of my deputies found the toy on the trail across the road from here, the one leading along the river. It was under a bush."

Carrie Ann hugged the stuffed frog tighter, tears streaming down her face.

Declan's breath caught in his throat. He and Carrie Ann had taken the same path this morning before they'd told Bonnie he was her father. His gut tightened. "How would she know about the trail? She's never been here before."

"I think I know the answer," said Vivian. "I saw Bonnie watching you and Carrie Ann from the front window this morning. She saw you two take the path."

"Where did she think she was going?" Carrie Ann's voice was strident.

"Does it matter?" Declan ached to be doing something useful instead of standing here talking. "The point is she's gone." His heart raced so fast he couldn't think. Had Bonnie taken her stuffed toy and gone for a walk to think things through? But why was the toy lying abandoned on the path? Where was she? He glanced out the window and shuddered. The sky was dark.

"Can you think of any place she'd go if she were upset?" asked Sheriff Atkins.

Carrie Ann shook her head. "She arrived here this morning. She doesn't know Cooper's Ridge at all."

"What about Leland?" Sheriff Atkins asked. "Could she be with him?"

A loud gasp filled the room.

Declan stared at Vivian.

The old woman's face was white as a sheet.

"What is it, Vivian?" he asked.

"Where's Leland?" Vivian asked. "Isn't he here?"

"I called his office, but he didn't answer. She wouldn't be with him, anyway. He'd have told me if he took her." A sob burst from Carrie Ann. "We have to find her. She's afraid of the dark. She'll be terrified."

Declan's stomach churned. Any child afraid of the dark would have come home by now. *If she were able.* The unthinkable words reared in his mind. His head throbbed as a band of steel tightened around his forehead.

"I have my men searching by the river," the sheriff said.

"You don't think she fell in the river?" Carrie Ann's voice was a thin croak.

As if drawn by some invisible force, Declan touched her arm, needing to connect with her, to share her anguish. "We'll find her. I promise, we'll find her."

She stared into his eyes, and he fought to keep his own fears at bay in the face of her desperate desire to believe him, to know he spoke the truth and Bonnie would be safe.

He must have done a good job because after a heartbeat, she nodded. "We'll find her," she whispered.

"I know we will." He prayed he wasn't speaking a lie.

"I'm going to head out and check a few places. We'll let you know as soon as we find anything." The sheriff walked out of the room with a heavy tread. The thump of his boots was loud as he descended the stairs and slammed the front door.

Declan glanced at Carrie Ann. "Stay here in case she comes back." He headed toward the door.

"Where are you going?" she asked.

287

"I'm not sitting here waiting for the sheriff and his men to find her. She's my daughter. I'm going to look for her."

"Not without me you're not."

He shook his head. "I'll be quicker alone. Besides, someone needs to be here in case she comes back."

"I can do that," Vivian said.

He turned to the old woman. Deep lines grooved between her brows, and her face was sallow, her cheeks gaunt. She looked as if she'd collapse any second. But her pale blue irises sparked with steely determination.

"I'm coming with you," Carrie Ann said again.

"No, you're not. I'm doing this on my own." The last thing he needed was Carrie Ann tagging along, her fear and trepidation fueling his own.

"Like hell you are. I'm her mother. When we find her, she'll want me."

"Are you so certain she will?" he asked, hating the harshness of his voice, but unable to stop his hurt from seeping out.

She staggered back as if he'd hit her.

He ground his teeth against the pain in her eyes. Finding Bonnie was the priority. He had an idea where she might be. He hoped to God he was wrong, but he couldn't silence the insidious voice in his gut telling him he might be right.

"You can't stop me."

He blinked, surprised to see Carrie Ann blocking the door to the hall. "What the hell do you think you're doing?"

Her face was pale, her eyes brimming with tears, but her mouth was set in a firm line. "I'm going with you."

For a brief second he considered shoving her aside. It wouldn't be hard. He outweighed her by almost a hundred pounds.

Vivian's voice cut through the tension. "For Heaven's sakes, you two, you're wasting time. Take her with you, Declan. She knows her daughter better than you. She'll know where she'd likely go."

The bitter truth in her words hit him, and he grimaced. He didn't know Bonnie. How could he when he'd learned of her existence only a few, short hours ago? He regarded Vivian's sallow face and shrunken, frail body. Did she have the strength to wait here alone in case Bonnie returned?

As if sensing his indecision, she said, "Go on. I'll be fine. I'll call you if I hear anything."

"Are you sure?" Carrie Ann stared at her aunt. "You don't look well."

Vivian dabbed at her forehead with a handkerchief, her hand trembling. "Don't be silly. Go find your daughter. Both of you."

"Come on," Declan said to Carrie Ann. "Let's get going." Hurrying down the hall, he raced for his car, flung open the door, and leaped inside.

Carrie Ann was right behind him, the stuffed frog clenched in her hands.

He started the car, backed out of the driveway, and sped down the street. The trees on the sides of the road passed in a blur as they raced down one street and on to another.

"Where are we going?" she asked.

"Rankin's Farm," he said, ignoring her gasp.

Chapter 26

"Why are we going to Rankin's Farm?" Carrie Ann's hoarse voice cracked. "Bonnie wouldn't go to the old farm. How would she even know of the place? Besides, it's too far. She couldn't walk all the way out there."

"She could be there if someone drove her."

"Who…?" The words died in her throat. "You don't think…" She gulped, fighting back icy fear.

He cast a glance at her, his mouth a rigid line.

She stilled, reading her worst nightmare in his bleak gaze. Her stomach heaved.

The little car flew over a bump and landed with a jarring thud, skidding on the gravel before the tires grabbed onto the road and raced ahead.

Her fingers dug into the vinyl armrest. "Why do you think she's at the farm?"

He kept his eyes on the road, his knuckles white as they gripped the steering wheel. "I'm not sure of anything."

She swallowed and spoke the unthinkable. "Someone took her. Is that what you think?"

His face was hard, his jaw rigid.

"Declan, speak to me. Tell me what you're thinking. Please."

He swerved around a pothole. "I told you, it's only a hunch."

"She wouldn't have gone with anyone. I've talked to her. Lots of times. She knows strangers can be dangerous." Her hopes lifted. "She's lost, that's all. She took the trail along the river and got turned around. You know how easily she could become lost. The bush is thick there, and the trail's hard to follow. The sheriff and his deputies will find her. She'll be fine." *She'll be fine.* She has to be.

His eyes met hers, bleak and cold. "Think," he said. "Why did she leave her toy on the path? If it's as important as you say, why would she leave her favorite, stuffed frog behind?"

"Maybe she dropped it and couldn't find it in the dark. That makes more sense than someone kidnapping her and taking her to Rankin's Farm."

"All the events happening lately revolve around that damn farm."

The certainty in his voice chilled her to the bone. "But—"

"I told you not to come. You should have stayed at the house."

"Maybe I should have. That would be better than driving all the way out here on a whim when we should be looking for Bonnie in town."

The car swung left as they turned onto the narrow lane to the farm. He drove into the overgrown clearing, skidded to a stop, and turned off the motor.

The cooling engine ticked as she stared through the windshield. A few stars twinkled in the night sky, but the moon wasn't up yet. The dark shape of the barn loomed overhead, the door gaping like a mouth. She shuddered and prayed her baby wasn't here; prayed the sheriff and his men had found her.

Declan dug inside a small storage compartment on the console between the front seats and removed a flashlight. It was too dark to see his face clearly, but she sensed the fear radiating off him.

"Stay here," he bit off and opened the door.

"But—"

"Stay in the car." A second later, he was out of the car and had vanished into the night.

Suffocating darkness surrounded her. She turned the keys in the ignition, pressed the button to roll down her window, and gulped fresh air. An owl hooted from somewhere nearby, the call haunting. She shivered and rolled up the window.

She couldn't stand waiting, doing nothing. The sooner they searched the farm and found it empty, the sooner they could leave this desolate place and look for Bonnie in town. Opening her door, she activated the flashlight App on her cell phone and shone the thin beam of light ahead as she stumbled through the overgrown grass and weeds to the barn.

What if Declan was right? What if Skye's murderer had taken Bonnie and was holding her in the old barn? Fear struck her, nearly knocking her to the ground. Lurching across the clearing to the open barn door, she stepped inside and was immediately assailed by the sweet scent of clover mingled with the sour tang of moldy hay.

She stepped on something hard, and it snapped with a loud, echoing crack. Another two steps and she froze, holding her breath, straining to hear over her racing heart. A low moaning emanated from somewhere deep within the vast barn. "Declan?" The hairs on the back of her neck prickled.

"Shhhh."

She spun around at his hoarse whisper.

He stood inside the door, his flashlight beam directed beyond her into the dark void of the barn. He raised a finger to his lips, and then turned and sprinted into the gloom.

Seconds passed and then minutes. Her heart pounded in her chest; her breathing was ragged.

"Carrie Ann."

Relief at the sound of his voice whooshed through her.

The beam of his flashlight struck her, and she blinked.

"Come here," he said.

She followed his light, stumbling over unseen objects until she saw him kneeling on the ground before a small, dark shape. "Bonnie!"

Bonnie lay on the floor, her knees drawn up, her arms folded across her chest. Her eyes were closed, her lashes dark on her pale cheeks.

Carrie Ann fell to her knees. "My God, Bonnie." She clasped her daughter's small hand. The hand was limp, the skin cold. A sob broke in her throat. "Is she…" She couldn't finish.

"She's alive."

His voice echoed as if from a great distance, and she scrubbed her face, wiping away tears, hardly daring to believe him. "She's okay?"

"She's in a deep sleep. Whoever kidnapped her must have given her something to make her sleep."

She cast a frantic look into the surrounding shadows.

"Don't worry. I checked. No one's here but us."

She squeezed Bonnie's hand. "Bonnie." She fought to steady her voice. "Wake up, honey. You're safe now. Mom's here."

Bonnie's pale lips parted, and she moaned, but her eyes remained closed.

Carrie Ann's heart caught in her throat. "Bonnie."

Declan placed a hand on her shoulder. "She's starting to come out of it."

She blinked back tears. "You were right. She was here. How can I ever thank you?"

He met her gaze. "You don't have to thank me, Carrie Ann. Bonnie's my daughter too."

Bonnie moaned again, and Carrie Ann swung back. She brushed a lock of golden hair off her daughter's damp forehead. "It's okay, baby. Mom and Dad are here. You're safe."

****

Mom and Dad are here. With each refrain, the block of ice in his chest dissolved, one drop at a time. He studied the child lying on the dirty, barn floor and his heart swelled. This was his child, his and Carrie Ann's.

Bonnie's eyelids fluttered, and she moaned again.

"We need to call the sheriff," he said. "Bonnie should go to the hospital. We don't know what the bastard gave her."

Bonnie's eyes opened, and she blinked, looking first at her mother and then him. Her brow furrowed. "Mom? Where…what happened?"

A swell of fierce protectiveness overwhelmed him. He clenched his jaw in a futile effort to stop a threatening flood of tears.

"It's okay, sweetie." Carrie Ann hugged her

tightly. "We're here."

"Declan?" Bonnie croaked, her dark eyes looking into his. "Are you really my dad?"

He swallowed. "I am."

Bonnie yawned, and her eyelids drifted closed.

He thought she'd fallen back asleep, but she opened her eyes and smiled. "I'm glad."

A tidal wave of emotion threatened to crush him. She was his daughter. The words sang through him. *His* daughter. He opened his mouth to tell her he loved her, but she was back asleep.

Carrie Ann's eyes shone. "I'm glad too."

Cat's eyes. He couldn't speak, but he could move, and so he did the only thing he could; he bent his head and kissed her.

Her lips were soft and welcoming.

He groaned when the kiss ended all too soon.

Their gazes met and held as a thousand unspoken words rose between them. He tore his gaze from hers and leaned down and placed a tender kiss on Bonnie's forehead.

Sirens blaring in the distance broke the silence.

"The cavalry's arrived," he said.

"We didn't call them. How did they know to come here?"

He shrugged. "I'm glad they're here. Now maybe they'll catch the creep who took our daughter."

The sirens increased to a frenzy, and red-and-blue lights flashed through the open barn door. The piercing wail ceased, and in the sudden silence, car doors slammed and men shouted.

Declan picked up Bonnie in his arms, holding her close to his chest, cradling her head. "Come on," he said. "Let's get her to the hospital."

"Thank you for saving my daughter."

"*Our* daughter."

She smiled and nodded. "Our daughter."

Grinning, feeling ten feet tall, and with his precious burden in his arms, he walked toward the flashing lights. He stepped out of the barn and stumbled, blinded by a bright spotlight shining in his face.

"Put the child down and get your hands up," blared a voice.

He wrinkled his brow and took another step, but froze when he heard the unmistakable sound of rifles cocking. "We found her," he called. "We found Bonnie. She's okay."

"Put the child down," commanded the disembodied voice. "Let her and the woman go, and put up your hands."

"It's okay." Carrie Ann moved to stand beside him. "It's me, Carrie Ann Hetherington. Bonnie's safe, but she needs medical help."

"Step away, ma'am."

"Declan?" She sounded uneasy. "What is this? What's going on?"

He shook his head. What the hell *was* going on? Why was he being treated like a criminal?

"This is your last warning, McAllister. Put the child down and walk away from the woman."

A sinking sensation filled his gut. Without taking his eyes from the glare of lights, he said to Carrie Ann, "Do what they say." He called out to the police. "I'm putting the girl down now. Don't do anything foolish."

"Declan, what is this?" Carrie Ann asked again, her voice trembling.

"You'd better do what they say. Can you hold Bonnie?"

Carrie Ann's eyes were huge in her pale face. She nodded. "Yes, but—"

"Here, take her and walk away from me. They won't hurt you. It's me they want."

She searched his face, her tear-filled gaze questioning, but she didn't say anything more. Taking Bonnie's limp body in her arms, she held her close to her chest. With a last worried look at Declan, she walked toward the bright lights.

A rush of feet, and he was tackled and thrown to the ground, a knee buried in the small of his back.

"Cuff him!"

He closed his eyes, tasting dirt where his face mashed into the ground.

A whirl of activity exploded around him. Car doors slammed, voices shouted orders. In the distance, more sirens approached.

He was dragged to his feet.

Rough hands roamed over his body, tearing at his clothes, digging in his pockets.

"He's clean, but you won't believe what I found in his coat pocket."

"Well, well, well," said a voice he recognized.

He blinked in the glare of bright lights and stared into the gloating face of Sheriff Atkins. The torn piece of Skye's scarf fluttered in the sheriff's hand. Declan stilled. Shit! In all the excitement of the day, he'd forgotten all about the damn cloth.

"We finally caught you, you bastard." The sheriff glared at him. "You're under arrest for the kidnapping of Bonnie McAllister and the murder of Skye

Lawrence, and that's just for starters."

What the hell? Declan opened his mouth to proclaim his innocence, but Carrie Ann spoke before he could get out a word.

"What's this about, Sheriff?" Her voice was shrill. "Declan helped me find Bonnie. Why are you arresting him?"

The sheriff ignored her as he glared at Declan. Spittle flecked the corners of his mouth. "I always knew you murdered Skye Lawrence, McAllister. Now I finally have the evidence to prove your guilt." He waved the scrap of silk in Declan's face.

"You have the wrong man, Sheriff." Declan shook his head, a band of steel tightening around his head.

"You criminals all say the same thing." The sheriff stepped closer and poked a hard finger in Declan's chest. "I hope they give you the death penalty."

A sense of déjà vu stole over him as the nightmare of twelve years ago repeated itself.

Two deputies stepped toward him, grabbed his arms and dragged him across the grass to a waiting police car. They shoved him into the backseat.

His head banged against the roof of the car, and he saw a flash of stars before he fell across the seat.

Carrie Ann called to him, her frantic voice rising above the melee.

Struggling to sit, he searched for her through the wall of activity outside the cruiser.

She stood where he'd left her, Bonnie and the stuffed frog cradled in her arms.

Their gazes met across the distance.

Her mouth opened, and she said something, but he couldn't hear her over the noise of the approaching sirens. He shook his head in frustration.

She spoke again. "What…done?"

Most of what she said was lost in the chaos, but he filled in the blanks for the rest. *What have you done?* Her words struck like a knife to his gut. He turned away, unable to look at her anymore, unable to bear her censure. Too late. Her accusing eyes and devastating words had seared into his soul.

A deputy climbed in the driver's seat, and another settled in the front passenger seat. With a wail of sirens, the car spun around and sped away from the farm.

He sank against the hard, plastic upholstery refusing to think what awaited him when they arrived at the Sheriff's Office. He was grateful for one thing— Bonnie was still asleep. She hadn't seen her father hauled away in handcuffs. He swallowed the lump in his throat and stared at the wire mesh protecting the driver and front passenger from him.

Chapter 27

"What evidence?" Carrie Ann fought to sound calm. "What evidence do they have Declan killed Skye and kidnapped Bonnie?"

Leland sat in his favorite chair in the living room, a smoldering pipe resting in the ashtray on the table beside him. "I talked to Sheriff Atkins. Someone called his office last night and left a message. The person who called said he saw Declan take Bonnie to Rankin's Farm."

"But he couldn't have. If someone saw Declan kidnap Bonnie, how would that person know where he took her? Did he follow him?"

Leland didn't answer.

"Leland? What's going on? What do you know?"

"I'm afraid I can't tell you any more than I already have."

"Why not?"

"This is official police business. I shouldn't have told you as much as I have."

"That's crazy. Whoever kidnapped Bonnie was the same person who phoned the police. Who else would know she was at the farm?" Carrie Ann huffed out her frustration.

He picked up his pipe and puffed. A spiral of fragrant smoke rose from the bowl and circled around his head. "I'm only telling you what the sheriff told me."

She crossed to the fireplace and stared at the flickering flames. This was a nightmare, but at least Bonnie was okay. After Declan had been driven away in the deputy's car, an ambulance had arrived and taken her and Bonnie to the hospital. The doctor had run a battery of tests and discovered she'd been injected with midazolam, a barbiturate used to induce sleep in patients before they underwent medical procedures. Carrie Ann's blood froze every time she recalled the doctor explaining the effects of midazolam. In high doses, the drug could be fatal. Fortunately, other than a headache and some dizziness, Bonnie was fine.

She'd stayed with Bonnie at her hospital bedside all night, watching every breath, every twitch of her daughter's eyelids. They'd released Bonnie this morning, and now she rested upstairs in her room. Vivian had offered to sit with her, giving Carrie Ann the first opportunity since the night before to talk to Leland and find out what was happening with Declan. "I still don't understand," she said. "Why is the sheriff so certain Declan did this?"

Leland exhaled a cloud of smoke. "How can you ask such a question? You saw the piece of scarf they found in McAllister's pocket."

"I explained all that to the sheriff. Why won't anyone listen?" Tears of frustration filled her eyes. *How many times did she have to say this?* "I found that cloth on the seat of my car where someone placed it when I was out at Rankin's Farm, before the SUV crashed into me. Declan had nothing to do with it."

He smirked. "So you say."

"It's true." She rubbed her aching temples. "I know

I should have told the sheriff about the cloth sooner, but—"

He raised his hand, stopping her. "It's time you quit defending him. Time you faced the truth." His gaze pinned her to her chair. "As sure as I'm sitting here, McAllister is guilty." He sat back, a smug expression on his face, and crossed one leg over the other and sucked on his pipe. "Besides, there's more. After the phone call from the witness to the kidnapping, the sheriff sent a deputy to McAllister's motel room. They found some very incriminating evidence."

"What did they find?" She couldn't imagine Declan possessing anything to connect him to Skye's murder or Bonnie's kidnapping.

"Another piece of the scarf Skye Lawrence was wearing the night she was killed."

She gaped, her mouth opening and closing, as Leland's shocking announcement sank in.

"It was hidden under a loose section of carpet in his motel room."

"I don't understand. Declan gave the cloth he found in the old barn to Jessup Caruthers, and Jessup turned it into the sheriff. The sheriff has the one from my car."

"The deputy found another piece."

"But that's ridiculous. Why would Declan have another piece of her scarf?" She held her breath, afraid of his answer, afraid what it would mean, especially now, when she and Declan seemed to be... Seemed to be what? A memory of how his stern features had softened, and his eyes had turned to molten chocolate when they found Bonnie safe in the barn flashed before her.

Leland pinned her with a hard gaze. "Think about it. Only the murderer would have had access to a section of Skye's scarf. McAllister's been found with three pieces."

Murderer. She reeled back as if he'd slapped her. Had she been wrong all these years? Was Declan a murderer? Could the father of her child be a cold-blooded killer? Again an image of Declan watching Bonnie in the barn rose before her, and with the image, a certainty arose within her. No matter what had happened in the past, one truth stood out—Declan loved Bonnie. She knew in her heart and soul his love for his daughter was strong. He'd never do anything to harm her. Carrie Ann had abandoned him once; she wouldn't desert him again.

Jumping up from the couch, she planted her hands on her hips and faced Leland. "Anyone could have put the piece of Skye's scarf in Declan's motel room." Her voice grew stronger with the certainty she was right. "The whole town knows he's staying at the Blue Horizon Motel. It's an old motel. I bet the locks are flimsy, if they even work at all."

"True," said Leland. "But the question is why would someone go to all the trouble?"

"I don't know." She closed her eyes to the image of Declan's haunted face as he was hauled away in handcuffs. His eyes had been flat and cold. She'd tried to talk to him, to tell him she'd help, but there'd been too many people, too much noise, and she had Bonnie to think of. "Is there any evidence to indicate Declan was involved in Bonnie's kidnapping?"

"I told you. The sheriff received a tip from someone who said they saw Declan put Bonnie in his car."

"Someone's trying to frame him like they did twelve years ago."

"One thing I've learned in my years in the legal field is you never really know someone. You don't know what darkness lurks inside a man, what he's capable of."

"I know Declan. I know he's innocent."

"The evidence suggests otherwise."

She rubbed her hands over her face. The nightmare was happening all over again—Declan accused of murder, everyone certain of his guilt. And now a kidnapping charge. She'd left him to face the accusations alone once before. Not this time. "I thought a person was innocent until proven guilty."

"The piece of Skye's scarf found in his motel room is the third section of scarf connected to McAllister. It can't be a coincidence." Leland tamped out the ash from the bowl of his pipe and set his pipe in the ashtray. "You and Bonnie should return to Seattle and leave this sordid business behind. Get on with your life."

Carrie Ann's heart sank. Leland thought Declan was guilty. Everyone in town thought he was. Declan was alone.

"Bonnie's asking for you." Vivian stood in the doorway, her face white, lines of exhaustion carved deep across her cheeks. Bonnie's kidnapping had taken a toll on her. She'd stayed at the hospital all night, offering silent support by her calm presence.

"Thanks for being here for me and Bonnie," Carrie Ann said. "Having your support at a time like this helps."

Vivian's eyes glistened with unshed tears. "You're

my niece. Bonnie's my great-niece. Family supports each other. I should have been there for you years ago. I let you down when you needed me the most; something I'll regret for the rest of my life."

Carrie Ann swallowed over the lump in her throat and walked out of the room and up the stairs to Bonnie's room.

****

Putting down the book she'd been reading to Bonnie, Carrie Ann studied her daughter. The child's face was pale. The doctor had warned Carrie Ann to watch for signs Bonnie was having difficulty breathing, one of many possible side effects of the drug with which she'd been injected. But Bonnie seemed fine. *Thank goodness for the resilience of youth.* "How are you feeling?"

Bonnie rolled her eyes. "You asked me the same thing a minute ago. I told you, I'm okay."

"I'm worried about you."

"I know, but I'm fine, Mom. Really."

"Good to hear, young lady," said a deep voice.

Carrie Ann glanced over her shoulder.

Sheriff Atkins stood in the doorway, twisting the brim of his peaked, felt hat in his big hands. He directed his comment at Carrie Ann as he strode toward the bed. "Your aunt let me in." His hard-eyed gaze softened as he studied Bonnie. "I'm glad you're doing all right, Bonnie. You gave us quite a scare last night."

Bonnie picked up her stuffed frog and clutched it to her chest. "I was scared too." Her young voice was barely above a whisper.

"We all were." Carrie Ann patted her daughter's shoulder. "But you're safe now, honey. You don't have to worry."

The sheriff picked up a wooden chair from the far side of the room and set it beside the bed before sitting down. "Are you up to answering a few questions, Bonnie?"

Bonnie bit her bottom lip and slid her gaze to Carrie Ann.

"It's okay, honey. I'm right here. The sheriff needs to know what happened last night."

"Why did you leave the house yesterday afternoon without telling anyone?" he asked.

"I was mad at Mom, and I wanted to get away to think."

Carrie Ann took Bonnie's hand in hers, holding her much smaller hand tight. "It's okay. You can tell the sheriff anything."

"Mom told me Declan's my dad, and I was upset."

The sheriff's thick, gray brows rose. "So you decided to run away."

She shook her head, her blonde curls bouncing. "It wasn't like that. I wanted to be alone." Her lower lip trembled. "I'm sorry, Mom."

"It's okay, honey."

"Why did you follow the path along the river?" Sheriff Atkins asked.

"I saw Mom and Declan go on the trail. I wanted to see where they'd gone. I know I shouldn't have, not without telling someone, but I was all mixed up inside."

"What happened next?"

Her fingers dug into the soft fur of her stuffed toy. "I was walking along the path. You know, not paying attention to anything. Then..." Tears filled her eyes.

Carrie Ann ached for her daughter. She wanted to

tell the sheriff to leave Bonnie alone, but she knew she couldn't. Bonnie had to tell what she knew so they'd catch the person responsible for kidnapping her. "Go on," she urged. "What happened next?"

"I don't know. One minute I was alone, and the next someone grabbed me from behind. I fought. I kicked him, but he jabbed me in the arm with something sharp. It really stung. The next thing I knew, Mom and Declan were there."

"Did you see his face?" the sheriff asked.

Bonnie shook her head. "I didn't see anything."

"Are you sure? You must have seen something." He shifted forward on the chair. "Was your father there? Did Declan McAllister kidnap you?"

Bonnie shook her head and burrowed her head beneath the blankets. "I told you. I didn't see anything."

Carrie Ann jumped to her feet and faced Sheriff Atkins. "I think you've asked enough questions, Sheriff. It's time you left."

He hesitated, clearly wanting to press for more information, but he nodded and lumbered to his feet. "Okay, but she'll have to give an official statement later."

"I'll bring her to the station when she's ready."

"He smelled sweet." Bonnie's small voice piped from under the blankets.

"Sweet, like what, Bonnie?" the sheriff asked, his gaze focused on the lump in the bed.

"Cherries, maybe?"

His gaze met Carrie Ann's.

She shrugged.

"That's good, Bonnie, real good. If you think of anything else, tell your mom, okay?" He nodded at

Carrie Ann and walked out of the room.

She hurried after him, catching him in the hall. "She doesn't remember much of what happened for a reason."

"And why is that?"

"The doctor told me the drug she was injected with can cause loss of memory."

"It doesn't matter," he said. "I don't need her to ID the perp. We already know who the guilty person is. I hoped she'd give me the nails to pound in his coffin and seal the deal."

"You're wrong, you know." She braced her hands on her hips and stepped into his space. "Declan didn't do this."

"I understand why you'd say he's innocent, ma'am, him being your *lover* and all, and the father of your illegitimate daughter, but you're the one who's mistaken. We have McAllister right where we want him. I've already asked the DA's office to go ahead with the conviction process."

"But he's innocent, don't you understand? He didn't do anything wrong."

He studied her for a long minute and shook his head. "You're a piece of work, lady. It amazes me a mother would choose her lover over her daughter's safety."

She opened her mouth to protest, but stopped. He wouldn't listen. He was so certain Declan was guilty, he refused to consider any other suspects.

With a final sneer in her direction, he turned and stomped away.

She sagged against the wall, overwhelmed by all the events of the past few hours.

Bonnie called, and she blinked back her tears and returned to her daughter.

Chapter 28

The basement of the Cooper's Ridge Sheriff's Office contained two jail cells. Declan was the sole occupant. He paced the width of the small holding cell, counting each step. Ten. Turning, he walked the length of the cell. Eleven steps. Almost a perfect square. He was locked in a ten-by-eleven-foot box, a cage complete with a tiny, wire-meshed vent up by the ceiling blowing a steady stream of frigid air, and a row of floor-to-ceiling, thick, steel bars spanning the front. He bunched his hands, squeezing until they ached, anything to stop from smashing his fist into the graffiti-marked, pitted, cement wall.

As far as this damn town was concerned he was guilty as sin. Eighty years ago, they'd already be building the scaffold. Crowds would be gathering to watch the hanging. Hell, for all he knew, they were.

Last night was a blur. The squad car he'd been shoved into had raced back to town, lights flashing, siren blaring, squealing to a stop before the Sheriff's Office. Two deputies had dragged him out of the back seat and escorted him up the steps into the station. They'd read him his Miranda rights, fingerprinted him, and taken his picture. He was marched downstairs to this cell and locked inside. And here he'd stay, they told him, until the paperwork to have him transferred to the county jail in Morganville was complete.

He stopped pacing and sat on the narrow, steel-framed bed bolted to the wall. Other than a rudimentary, stainless steel toilet and sink combination in the corner, the cot was the only place to sit. A plastic tray with a plastic plate piled with food and a plastic glass filled with water, sat on the cracked, cement floor. The food was cold, and if possible, looked even more unappetizing than when the deputy had delivered the tray earlier this morning. The thought of eating it, or any food at all, made him ill.

His mouth twisted at the acrid taste of bile filling his throat. For a brief moment last night after he and Carrie Ann had found Bonnie, he'd felt hope; hope for a future with Carrie Ann and their daughter; hope they could move past the anger and hurt and become a family. He pounded his fist into the thin, stained mattress, raising a fetid cloud of dust.

Last night, he'd demanded to see a lawyer, but so far no one had appeared. What did it matter? Sheriff Atkins had been smug as hell when he'd confronted him and read out the charges. Declan didn't blame him. Hell, even he saw how that piece of Skye's scarf in his pocket made him look. Why the hell hadn't he turned it in earlier? He scowled. He knew why. As soon as Bonnie appeared, and he'd found out he was a father, all other thoughts vanished. He punched the mattress again.

At least she was safe. How could the sheriff think he'd kidnapped Bonnie, drugged her, and left her in the derelict barn? He'd never harm her. She was his daughter, for God's sake.

He rubbed his aching eyes. He hadn't slept last night. How could he when he'd spent the unending hours since they'd stuck him in here pacing the damn floor of his cell?

A door at the end of the short corridor outside his cell opened with an earsplitting squeal. Heavy footsteps approached.

Assuming it was the sheriff, or one of the deputies coming to gloat, Declan didn't bother to lift his head.

"You're in a bit of a mess."

He jumped at the sound of Jessup Caruthers' gravelly voice.

The private investigator stood in the narrow hallway outside Declan's cell.

The fat deputy who'd given Declan his breakfast stood beside him, his hand resting on the gun holstered at his thick waist, as if he feared Declan would lunge through the bars and attack. When Declan didn't move, the deputy withdrew a plastic key card from a chain hooked to his belt and inserted the card in the door lock. The heavy door slid open with a loud click and the grinding of metal on metal. "You have fifteen minutes," he said.

Jessup stepped into the cell, his big body filling the cramped space.

The deputy closed and locked the door behind him, walked several steps down the corridor and leaned against the wall, his arms crossed over his burly chest.

Jessup's piercing gaze fixed on Declan. "You look like hell."

"What are you doing here?" He couldn't believe the guy was still around.

"You hired me to do a job. The job's not done." Jessup scanned the cell. "Nice digs."

Declan snorted.

"The sheriff thinks you killed Skye Lawrence."

"What's new? He's thought the same thing for the past twelve years."

"He also thinks you kidnapped Bonnie McAllister."

"That's what they're saying."

"Did you?"

Declan leaped to his feet, grabbed Caruthers by the collar and drew back his fist, ready to drive it deep into his face. His muscles bunched, but then he lowered his arm and released his grip. What the hell? This wasn't Caruthers' fault. He wiped a shaking hand over his mouth. "Get out of here," he muttered. "Leave me the hell alone."

Caruthers didn't blink. "Feel better?"

Declan wiped the sweat beading his brow. "Look, I'm sorry."

"You need to take it easy."

All his anger and frustration exploded out of him. "Easy? They think I'm a beast who murders women and kidnaps children. How the hell can I take it easy?"

"You're pissed. I get it. You have every right to be, but you have to calm down. Anger won't get you out of here."

Declan met his gaze. "Do you believe I did all those terrible things?"

Caruthers shook his head.

A wave of relief washed over him, and he sank onto the rumpled cot. "How do we prove I'm innocent?"

"I called your lawyer. He's working on having you released on bail. I'm not going to lie to you. The local authorities don't want to release you. They're afraid you're a danger to their fine community."

"Last night, when they arrested me, the sheriff said he had solid evidence against me. Do you know what he has?"

"They found another piece of the murder victim's scarf hidden in your motel room."

"Impossible!" Declan wanted to pace, but now there was even less room in the cell.

"This whole scenario stinks like bad fish. It's obvious someone's framing you."

"Just like before."

"Someone has a serious hard-on for you. They want you to go down for this, real bad."

"What about the kidnapping charge? What do they have to connect me to kidnapping my own daughter?"

"An eyewitness saw you. A tip was called in to the Sheriff's Office last night after Bonnie was reported missing."

Declan stared hard at the private investigator. "Who made the call?"

"They're not saying."

"But that's bullshit!" Declan jumped to his feet. "They can't hold me because some idiot said he saw me. He was probably riding high on a snout full of cheap hooch."

"They can, and they are. They're trying their damnedest to gather some hard evidence against you."

"Well, good luck. They won't find anything. I didn't do anything wrong."

"Unless someone plants something else to implicate you."

He stared at the other man, his mind spinning. *Unless someone plants something.* Like they had in the barn, and in Carrie Ann's car, and again in his motel room. A chill settled over him. He'd never clear his name. He'd never get out of here.

"Don't lose hope yet," said Caruthers as if reading his mind. "I have a few leads I'm following."

The deputy pushed away from the wall and approached.

Their time was up.

"I'll be back later today or tomorrow to fill you in. Stay strong, and for God's sake, keep your mouth shut. Don't say anything to anyone. They're itching to convict you."

Declan slumped on the cot. A sour reek rose from the thin mattress, even thinner pillow, and the gray, scratchy, wool blanket. He closed his eyes and fought to slow the wild riot of thoughts racing through his mind. Someone wanted him to go to jail for the rest of his life for crimes he hadn't committed. If he ever got out of here, he'd find the bastard. No, not if, *when* he got out of here he'd—

The screech as the door down the hall opened halted his thought. The soft tread of feet drew nearer. He didn't open his eyes. Let whoever his visitor was think he was asleep. Maybe they'd go away and leave him the hell alone.

The scents of roses and vanilla wafted in the air, subduing the ever-present reek of urine, vomit, and misery hanging over the cell like a dark cloak. He breathed in the scent, savoring the familiar smell and all the memories connected to it. For a brief second he forgot where he was, but then his eyes flew open.

Carrie Ann stood outside his cell watching him. "Hey." Her full, red mouth trembled in a smile.

His hungry gaze devoured the sight of her long, auburn hair gleaming under the fluorescent lights, her amber eyes sparkling with gold flecks. She wore tight-fitting blue jeans and a blouse the exact color of her eyes. She'd never looked more stunning. His heart thudded, and his mouth lost all moisture, but then he remembered where he was, and he jerked up. "What the hell are you doing here?"

Her smile faded. "I wanted to see how you were."

"How do you think I am? I'm locked in jail charged with murder and kidnapping." His voice was too harsh, his tone accusing, but he couldn't stop. He jumped to his feet, driven by the need to expend the fury threatening to detonate inside him. He stormed across the cell, turned and strode back, and again and again, unable to halt his frenzied pacing.

"I'm sorry." She shifted from one foot to the other, bouncing on the balls of her feet. "Being stuck in this cell can't be easy."

"How's Bonnie?"

"She's doing great. I can't believe it, especially after what she's been through. The doctor said Bonnie had been given a shot of midazolam. That's why she had a hard time waking up." She rubbed her arms as if she were chilled. "That stuff could have killed her."

Silence settled over them as he continued his endless pacing. Finally, he asked the question lurking in the forefront of his mind ever since he'd opened his eyes and seen her standing outside his cell. "Why are you really here?"

"I want you to know I'm going to do everything I can to get you out of here."

He snorted. "Did you bring a file?"

"I mean it, Declan. I'm going to prove you're innocent."

His heart swelled at her words, but he clamped off the spurt of hope. "No, you're not."

"I'm not?"

"You and Bonnie are going back to Seattle."

She shook her head. "You need my help."

"You can't help me. No one can. The best thing you can do is return to your life and forget me. Look after our daughter." The further away from him she was, the better. He refused to drag her and Bonnie any deeper into this nightmare. Look what happened the night before. He'd almost lost his daughter for the second time.

"You have everything figured out, don't you?" She stepped closer to the wall of metal bars. Her eyes blazed.

"Get the hell out of here." He turned his back on her. *Go. Go before I change my mind and beg you to stay.*

"I'm not leaving town. I did once before. I won't desert you again."

"You're a bloody fool if you don't."

"Well then, I'm a fool." She turned and walked down the hall toward the exit.

He couldn't stop himself. "Carrie Ann," he called.

She paused and glanced back.

"You didn't ask me." He gripped the bars, his knuckles white, his heart beating a mile a minute.

"Ask you what?"

"You didn't ask if I kidnapped our daughter."

"I don't have to."

Their gazes met.

"I know you didn't." She opened the door and disappeared through the opening. The door swung closed behind her with a loud squeal.

Even though he knew he should have pushed harder to make her leave town, he couldn't help the spurt of joy. She believed in him. He released his hold on the cold metal and backed into the middle of the cell, smiling his first real smile in hours.

Why hadn't he realized sooner? His smile widened. The sheriff had called his daughter Bonnie McAllister last night when he'd read the charges against him. At the time, he'd been too upset to notice. His chuckle filled the freezing cell, echoing off the cement walls. Carrie Ann had given Bonnie his last name.

A flood of warmth washed over him. He had a daughter named Bonnie McAllister! He couldn't stop grinning. He lay back down on the bed and thought of his wonderful daughter. Bonnie McAllister. With a smile on his lips, he slipped into sleep.

Chapter 29

Carrie Ann left the Sheriff's Office, drove through downtown and turned onto the highway. After two miles, she swung left onto a narrow, blacktopped lane. The track opened onto a large, empty, parking area. She halted before a chain link fence and regarded the baseball field in front of her.

How many Little League games had she played here? She'd watched even more ball games in the long, hot days of summer during high school. The local baseball team had been county champions one season. That year, the small stands had been filled to the limit, with everyone in town attending and cheering on the Cooper's Ridge Cougars.

The outfield, more weeds than Kentucky Bluegrass, was in desperate need of mowing. Bare patches of dirt covered the infield, nearly obliterating the bases. The green paint on the two wooden dugouts on either side of home plate was faded and peeling. The old concession stand leaned drunkenly to one side, its single window boarded shut. Graffiti covered the stained walls. Crushed soda cans and empty, torn, popcorn containers were heaped against the rusted, mesh fence. An aura of desolation surrounded the park. The Cougars must be losing these days.

Sheldon was late. He'd called this morning and begged to see her. At first, she'd put him off. She didn't want anything to do with him. Not after the way he'd lied all these years. But he'd insisted, and she finally relented.

She left her car and crossed the parking lot. Squeezing through the opening in the chain link fence, she stepped onto the damp grass of the infield and headed for the wooden bleachers on the far side. The bleachers' rickety steps creaked and groaned under her weight as she climbed to the top and sat on a scarred, wooden bench. The surrounding ballpark and empty parking lot were in clear view. Sheldon had wanted to meet here. He'd wanted someplace private where he could talk. This deserted ballpark certainly fit the bill.

Declan had been in jail twelve hours, and she still hadn't figured out a way to help him. This meeting with Sheldon had better not be a waste of time.

She'd called Jessup Caruthers as soon as she'd left Declan's holding cell. He'd told her Declan's lawyer was confident Declan would be released on bail in a day or two. *A day or two!* Would Declan survive in lockup that long? His incessant pacing reminded her of a caged animal. She'd expected anger, even outrage; but instead, the sour smell of defeat emanated from him. He'd given up. The dull, beaten look in his eyes frightened her more than anything.

"What took you so long?"

She jumped, startled out of her thoughts.

Sheldon appeared from under the bleachers and slowly mounted the steps and sat beside her. His cheeks were flushed, and he was out of breath as if he'd been running.

"I didn't see you arrive." She looked at the empty parking lot. "Where's your car?"

"I parked down the road a ways and walked." He hunched into his coat, and his gaze darted around the ballpark.

"Is everything okay?" She followed his gaze, but couldn't see what he was looking for.

"I hope so." He stared at the entry road to the park. Beads of moisture shone on his high forehead, and his hands tapped a rapid beat on his thighs.

"Are you expecting someone?" She wanted him to get to the point. Declan was in jail. Every minute counted until he was free.

He withdrew a handkerchief from his coat pocket and dabbed his face. "You didn't tell anyone you were coming here, did you?"

"You told me not to."

Some of the tenseness seemed to leave his body, and he slumped, but his gaze kept darting between the parking lot and the entry road.

"What's going on?" She frowned at him. "What's so important you had to see me right away?"

He cleared his throat. "This whole mess started a long time ago when I was a scrawny, pimply-faced kid whom everybody and their dog picked on. I was an outsider, but I wanted to be like everyone else. Just once." His eyes were imploring. "You don't know how much my life sucked. I didn't have any friends. No one liked me." He wiped the handkerchief over his reddened eyes. "Sometimes I wondered if even my parents cared for me."

"You had Declan." Her eyes stung as a rush of unexpected pity filled her. "He was your friend."

"Was he? Or did he just feel sorry for me?"

"He was your friend. We both were."

He met her gaze, his watery eyes searching. "I see that now." He drew another deep breath and released it with a loud whoosh. "When I was sixteen, I..." His Adam's apple bobbed in his thin throat. "I bought some drugs. I wanted something to relax me, to make me..." He shrugged. "Make me more likable."

"We all tried drugs then. Smoking dope wasn't a big deal." She tried to ease his mind.

"You don't understand." He wiped his gleaming brow again. "I bought some pills from a kid at school. I'm not sure what they were, but he promised they'd give me a high I wouldn't forget. I snuck some booze from my dad's liquor cabinet. I thought..." He shrugged again. "I don't know what I thought."

She glanced at her watch. What did this have to do with Declan sitting in a jail cell? "Look, Sheldon—"

He cut her off. "Let me finish. Events sort of happened. I didn't mean to hurt anyone." He rubbed his hair, tousling the thin strands into orange spikes. His leg bounced up and down in a rapid tattoo shaking the bleachers.

Fingers of unease rippled along her spine. "What did you do, Sheldon?"

"You have to understand. I was drunk and stoned out of my mind. I didn't know what I was doing. I didn't see the other car."

"You hit someone?"

He nodded.

"Oh, my God. Was anyone hurt?"

"I heard the other driver was in the hospital for a while."

"What do you mean, you *heard* the driver was in the hospital? Didn't you stop and help?"

322

"I couldn't. I wanted to, but I couldn't. You have to understand, if my father found out I was drunk and stoned and driving and…and I hit someone, he'd have killed me. The police would have arrested me. I'd never be able to join the family business, not with a criminal record." He stared at her with pleading eyes. "Don't you see? I couldn't let one, stupid mistake ruin my life."

"So you left the injured driver of the other car lying on the road?"

"I called the police anonymously. I told them there'd been an accident and to send an ambulance."

"But you didn't stay to help."

He shook his head.

She nodded. "Okay, you made a mistake, but this all happened a long time ago. What's it got to do with what's happening now to Declan?"

He fumbled in his coat pocket and pulled out a crumpled pack of cigarettes and a shiny metal lighter. His hands shook as he tugged free a cigarette and placed it between his lips and flicked the lighter. When the cigarette finally glowed to life, he sucked in a breath, inhaling smoke deep into his lungs. The nicotine seemed to calm him because after two more puffs, his breathing slowed, and he continued his sordid tale. "I thought I was in the clear, but two weeks after the accident, Judge Winters called. He told me he'd seen what I'd done, and I was facing criminal charges. He was going to have me arrested." He blew out a cloud of smoke. "I freaked. My life was over.

"But then he said he could make the charges go away. He'd snap his fingers, and the entire mess would vanish as if it never happened. But he exacted a price for his silence." His throat worked. "He wanted me to do stuff for him."

She jumped to her feet. "I don't believe you. Leland would never resort to blackmail. If he saw someone commit a crime, he'd have him arrested."

"I knew you wouldn't believe me." Sheldon stood and tossed his cigarette on the bleacher floor and stomped on the butt, grinding it beneath his boot. "Tell Declan I'm sorry." He lurched toward the steps leading to the ground.

Her mind whirled. Was he telling the truth? He couldn't be, but what if he was? "Sheldon, wait!"

He paused, but didn't look back at her.

"What sort of things did Leland ask you to do?"

He shrugged. "Little things at first—running errands for him, passing on information I learned from kids at school—nothing terrible. I helped him make Cooper's Ridge a better town. I mean, I wasn't hurting anyone, not really."

An uneasy foreboding filled her. "What else did he ask you to do?"

He sank onto the bench, his shoulders hunched as if he were in pain.

"The night Skye was murdered, Judge Winters told me to find Declan and drive him back out to the farm."

"You're lying." The words exploded out of her, but a cold tremor washed along her back, and she shivered.

"I swear, I'm telling you the truth."

"You're not making any sense. Why would Leland ask you to take Declan back out to the farm?" She tried desperately to think over the pounding in her head.

"Don't you get it? He wanted Declan to look guilty. He wanted people to think Declan murdered

Skye."

"*You* set up Declan."

"Do you think I wanted to betray my only friend? I didn't have a choice. Judge Winters said he'd tell the sheriff about the accident, and I'd go to jail if I didn't help him." He choked on a sob. "I couldn't face prison." His eyes, red-rimmed and filled with tears, turned pleading. "Do you know what they do to guys like me in prison?"

"That's not all you did, is it?" Anger flashed over her in a hot wave. "You called the sheriff last night and told him you saw Declan kidnap Bonnie."

Guilt was written all over his pale, freckled face. "I didn't have a choice. Judge Winters made me call the sheriff, and he told me what to say."

She rubbed her temples. "Why are you telling me this now?"

"Declan's my friend. I can't stand by any longer and watch him go through hell for crimes he didn't commit."

"Yet you were content to watch him suffer for the past twelve years."

His mouth opened and closed like a fish fighting for air. "Carrie Ann, you have to understand. It was—"

"You disgust me!" She yanked her cell phone from her pocket.

"What are you doing?"

"I'm calling the sheriff." Her fingers shook, and she cursed as she hit a wrong digit and had to redial. "You're going to tell him what you told me. After that, you can go straight to hell as far as I'm concerned."

Tears leaked from his eyes. "I deserve all the punishment coming to me, but please don't call the sheriff. I'll talk to him. I promise. I'll tell him everything. Just don't call him."

"Why don't you want me to call him?"

He sniffed and swiped his face with his sleeve. "I don't want Judge Winters to know, not until it's too late for him to do anything about it. I know him, Carrie Ann." A visible shudder ran through his thin body. "Leland Winters is a monster. He'll stop at nothing to silence me if he thinks I'm going to rat him out." Fear radiated off Sheldon in palpable waves.

She narrowed her eyes, studying him, trying to discern the truth. Was he lying? He had to be. Leland was highly respected in Cooper's Ridge. He'd been the Judge for the county for years. Before that, he'd been the District Attorney. Everyone trusted him. Everyone respected him. Sheldon, on the other hand, had been caught in one lie already. Why should she believe him now?

"I'll turn myself in. I promise." He held his hands out before him in a pleading gesture. "I'll go to the Sheriff's Office right now. Please, give me this chance to make up for what I've done." Guilt and fear were written across his homely face.

She lowered the phone. "I don't know why I'm doing this. You sure as hell don't deserve any consideration, but this is your chance to redeem yourself. Make it damn good."

He nodded, looking like a prisoner granted a reprieve from execution.

Disgust filled her. Unable to look at him a second longer, she climbed down from the bleacher and headed across the field to her car.

"Where are you going?" he called after her.

"To talk to Leland."

"Don't!" The word burst out of him.

She turned, frowning.

He ran toward her, a frantic look on his haggard face. "Stay away from him, Carrie Ann. Please. He's dangerous."

A shiver rippled along her spine, but she forced a chuckle. "I've known Leland most of my life. He won't harm me."

"You still don't get it, do you? Leland Winters is not the man you think he is." Sheldon's pupils were huge, the whites of his eyes streaked with fine, red lines.

The shiver of unease morphed into a full-blown shudder. "I'll be okay." She put steel into her voice. "You just make sure you talk to the sheriff."

"Please don't say anything to Judge Winters. Wait until I talk to the sheriff."

"I have to find out the truth." She turned on her heel and walked to her car. As she started the motor, she saw him standing in the middle of the deserted baseball diamond. Even from where she was parked, the distress written across his face was visible.

Again a wisp of unease tugged at her, but she brushed away her worry. Sheldon was lying. He'd lied before, and he might be lying now. Could she trust him? Would he go to Sheriff Atkins and tell him what he knew? She rubbed the back of her neck. She'd give him the chance, but if he reneged on his promise, he'd better watch out. She'd hunt him down and make him confess.

Chapter 30

Her head throbbed, her legs were heavy; each step was a monumental effort as Carrie Ann walked down the hall to the living room. Her mind had been spinning all the way from the ball field. How do you ask someone who'd been like a father to you if they'd framed the father of your child for murder and kidnapping? The thought made her ill.

She paused in the doorway.

Leland reclined in his chair, smoking his pipe and reading the newspaper.

Vivian sat on a matching chair, her eyes closed, possibly asleep. A cheery fire crackled in the fireplace. Two table lamps were lit, casting a warm glow over the cozy scene.

Taking a deep breath, she stepped into the room.

Leland glanced up. A warm smile creased his face, the lines radiating from the corners of his eyes deepening. But then the smile faltered. He raised a finger to his lips and nodded toward Vivian.

Vivian's chest rose and fell with each shallow, rasping breath. A line of drool leaked from the corner of her slack mouth. Dark hollows underlined her sunken eyes.

All thoughts of accosting Leland with Sheldon's accusations vanished and Carrie Ann swallowed a lump in her throat. Unable to avoid the obvious any longer, she quietly asked, "How long has she been sick?"

Leland sucked on his pipe, the sweet-smelling smoke swirling around him in a cloud. "She hasn't been well for a long time. I finally convinced her to go to the doctor a few months ago, but she'd waited too long. There was nothing the doctors could do."

"What's wrong with her?"

"Cancer."

"How bad is it? Can't she be treated?"

He shook his head. "The cancer's spread everywhere—her lungs, liver, bones."

"I didn't know."

"She didn't want you to know. You know your aunt. She doesn't want anyone's pity."

"How long does she have?" Carrie Ann blinked back the sting of tears.

"They gave her three months. That was two months ago."

Carrie Ann reeled as if she'd been punched.

"Her illness is why she was so determined you come home. She wanted to see you again and meet Bonnie before—" He choked on a sob.

"Carrie Ann, I didn't hear you come in." Vivian's thready voice cut through the pall of sadness and regret. "I must have fallen asleep."

Carrie Ann wiped away her tears.

"What's wrong?" Vivian asked, her brow furrowing. "Why are you crying? Has something happened?"

Carrie Ann glanced at Leland.

He shook his head, his warning clear.

She pasted a smile on her lips. "Nothing's wrong. How's Bonnie?"

"She's sleeping, poor thing." Vivian chuckled. "I think I tired her out playing crib. I swear, I've never met anyone so determined to win."

In spite of her sorrow, Carrie Ann beamed. "She gets her competitive spirit from her father." Her humor died as she remembered where Bonnie's father was and Sheldon's shocking confession. She studied Leland, searching for some indication he was the brute Sheldon had painted him to be. But all she saw was the same warm, compassionate man she'd always known.

"How's Declan?" asked Vivian.

"He's as well as can be expected for someone sitting in jail facing charges for crimes he didn't commit."

Leland puffed on his pipe, watching her with a steady gaze. A frown deepened the furrow between his gray, bushy eyebrows.

"He's innocent." She enunciated each word clearly, as if by doing so she'd convince him of Declan's innocence.

Leland shook his head. "I know you want to believe that, my dear, but the facts say otherwise."

"I had a long talk with Sheldon Dubrowski." She searched his face for some reaction.

A shadow darkened his eyes. "Dubrowski." He scoffed. "I can't imagine you'd want anything to do with him after the way he's lied all these years."

Carrie Ann leaned forward, her nerves thrumming, keeping her gaze on him. "We had quite a chat."

"I wouldn't believe a word he says," said Leland. "I've never liked the boy. I always thought he was shifty."

"He said you told him to lie so everyone would

think Declan murdered Skye. He also said you told him to call the police and tell them he saw Declan kidnap Bonnie last night."

Leland's eyes were hard, but he chortled. "Ridiculous."

Vivian struggled to stand, her hand gripping her chair for support. "Carrie Ann, what is this? What are you accusing Leland of doing?"

Carrie Ann ignored Vivian, watching Leland, searching for the truth beneath his bluster. "Is it true? Is Sheldon telling the truth?"

"You don't believe me?" He set his pipe in the ashtray and placed a hand over his heart. "You've crushed me to my soul."

A chill seeped through her bones. "It is true, isn't it?"

"Of course it's not true," sputtered Vivian. She turned to Leland. "Tell her, Leland, tell her she's wrong. You had nothing to do with any of this."

"Stay out of this, Vivian." Carrie Ann ignored her aunt's outraged gasp. "Tell me the truth, Leland." She saw his mind working as he made up another lie.

"There are two problems with what you're saying." He kept his gaze steady as he raised a finger. "One, no one will believe anything Sheldon Dubrowski has to say. He's a proven liar." A small smile lifted the corner of his mouth. "And two"—he raised another finger—"you don't have any proof."

She sagged back on the couch as if he'd slapped her. "So, what Sheldon told me is true."

"What's going on here?" Vivian's anxious demand pierced the room's tension. "Leland, what is she talking about? What did you do?"

He closed his eyes, breathing deeply. His fingers drummed a steady beat on his knees. When he opened his eyes again, defeat and maybe a hint of relief filled his faded, blue eyes. "Yes, it's true. It's all true."

Vivian spluttered.

Another thought occurred to Carrie Ann, leaving her shaken, as the nightmare kept getting worse. "Did you kill Skye Lawrence?" She held her breath, hardly believing what she asked.

He stared at the logs burning in the fireplace for a long minute. His body seemed to shrink, transforming him into a frail, old man before her eyes. "It was an accident." His voice was barely above a whisper. "I didn't mean to kill her."

Her breath rushed out in a blast of air.

"My God." Vivian's gasp filled the room. "Leland, what have you done?" Her face lost all color, and she swayed, her thin legs wobbling. Her hands grabbed for the arm of her chair, missed, and she crumpled to the floor.

"Vivian!" Carrie Ann rushed to her side and gripped her hand, so frail and cold, and fumbled for a pulse. Thin and thready, but still beating. She shot a glance at Leland. "Call an ambulance."

He sat in his chair unmoving, his face expressionless.

Vivian moaned, and she spun back to her aunt.

The elderly woman's eyelids fluttered open, and her chest heaved as she fought for air. She struggled to sit up, but groaned and fell back on the floor.

"Leland," Carrie Ann called again. "Help me get her into her chair."

He didn't budge.

Vivian tried again to sit up, but she was too weak. Her breathing was labored, her face ghostly pale.

"Let me help you." Carrie Ann grasped her aunt by her thin, upper arms and lifted her onto the chair, shocked at how little Vivian weighed. "Stay here while I call an ambulance."

"No." Vivian struggled to breathe, her narrow chest heaving. "My purse," she wheezed. "Pills...hall..."

Carrie Ann ran to the front hall and retrieved Vivian's purse from the bench beside the door. She fumbled with the clasp and rifled through the contents until she found a small vial of prescription pills. She retraced her steps and hurried over to Vivian. "How many pills?"

"Two." With a trembling hand, Vivian placed the small pink pills under her tongue. She laid her head back against the chair and closed her eyes. Within minutes, her breathing eased and color returned to her lined cheeks. She opened her eyes. "Thank you, my dear. I'll be fine now."

"You need a doctor. I'm going to call an ambulance."

"No," Vivian said, some of the old steel in her voice. "I don't want a doctor."

Carrie Ann bit her bottom lip. Vivian was in distress, but she knew by the determined light in her aunt's faded eyes she'd refuse medical attention. "Are you sure?"

Vivian touched her hand. "A doctor can't help me. Not anymore."

Their gazes met and Carrie Ann blinked against a fresh sting of tears. "No! You can beat this. All you need is to go to the hospital. They'll help you."

Vivian's mouth curved in a tremulous smile. "I've never told you I love you, have I?"

The lump in Carrie Ann's throat made it impossible to speak.

Vivian's eyes met hers. "I do love you. Bonnie too. I want you to know how much I care." She panted, fighting for breath. *Before it's too late.* Vivian left the words unsaid, but her intention was clear.

"You're going to be fine. I'll call your doctor, and he'll help you."

Vivian squeezed her hand. "You're a good girl. You always were." She turned to Leland, and her expression hardened. "Is this true, Leland? Did you murder Skye Lawrence?"

Still staring at the flickering flames, he spoke in a flat, singsong voice. "It was an accident. If she hadn't decided she was in love with McAllister, none of this would have happened. It's all his fault."

Carrie Ann stumbled to the couch and sank down, wishing she could disappear into the soft cushions.

"What did you do to the poor girl?" Vivian's voice was a harsh rasp.

"We were lovers."

Carrie Ann sucked in a breath. "She was just a kid. You were…"

He nodded. "An old man. I know. I couldn't help myself. She was so pretty, so fresh, and we were in love."

Vivian's derisive snort filled the room. "You were a pedophile."

His face paled, but he kept talking, almost as if he was relieved the sordid tale was finally coming to light. "Skye wanted to end our relationship. She said she loved McAllister. Love." He sneered. "What did she know of love?" He rubbed a shaking hand over his gray hair, and for the first time since he'd begun his confession, he met their gazes. "I couldn't let her go, don't you see? She would have told everyone. I was the County Judge. What would people say?"

Carrie Ann's stomach churned as with each damning word, Leland revealed the monster he'd hidden so well all these years.

He no longer looked at Vivian or her, but somewhere deep inside as if he'd forgotten they were in the room. "We fought." His voice was eerily flat. "She hit me." He blinked, as if affronted anyone would do such a thing. "She shouldn't have done that. I hit her back. I had to stop her. Don't you see? I couldn't let her keep hitting me."

A log shifted in the fireplace, sending up a shower of sparks.

Leland's teary gaze met hers. "I couldn't allow her to tell anyone about us. Some people wouldn't understand our relationship. Don't you see? She forced me to kill her. I didn't want to. I loved her."

"You murdered her and buried her in the clearing behind the old barn. You left her in the woods like she was a piece of garbage." Carrie Ann let her disgust show in her voice.

"I panicked. I didn't know what to do."

A heavy silence descended over the room.

Vivian sat unmoving in her chair, one hand pressed to her mouth, the other to her chest, her face white and drawn.

Leland picked up his pipe and busied himself knocking the cold ashes into the ashtray. Opening a small, leather pouch, he filled the pipe bowl and tamped the tobacco down. Picking up a box of wooden matches from the table, he removed one, struck the match head against the side of the matchbox and sucked in air as he held the flame to the bowl, lighting the pipe. A spiral of smoke circled the air above him.

As the aroma of his pipe smoke wafted over her, Carrie Ann sat up with a start. "What flavor of pipe tobacco do you use?"

"My tobacco?" He puffed out another cloud. "Nice, isn't it? I order this special from Virginia. It's a blend of cherry with an underlying hint of oak."

"You did it, didn't you? You kidnapped Bonnie. She smelled your pipe tobacco when you took her." It was hard to breathe, even harder to talk. "Why did you kidnap her? She's your niece."

"I didn't harm her. I just wanted to frighten you, so you'd go back to Seattle."

"You shot my tire out the day I arrived, and you slashed my tires, and keyed Declan's truck." She stared at him. *Who was he?* He looked like the man she'd known most of her life, but the terrible things he said, the things he'd done. She gasped. "You rammed my car the other night. You tried to kill me."

"I'd never hurt you, Carrie Ann. I love you. I always have. I did all those things for you."

"For me?"

"I wanted to keep you away from McAllister. I thought if I frightened you enough, you'd leave and never see him again, but you're too stubborn. You couldn't let it go."

She sat back, too stunned to respond.

"Anyone with eyes can see the attraction between

you two. I had to get you away from him like I did before. I couldn't let him ruin your life." His gaze was unblinking and steady.

She shivered at the madness in his eyes.

"McAllister isn't the man for you." He shook his head. "Look at his family. His father was a no-good, drunken, mean son of a bitch. His mother wasn't much better. They weren't good people. Not like us. You deserve so much better than Declan McAllister."

"So you framed him for Skye's murder and kidnapped Bonnie, and framed him for kidnapping."

"Everything I did was for you, Carrie Ann. You have to understand. I love you. You're my niece." He puffed on his pipe, then pinned her with an earnest gaze. "No one needs to know. I've set up the scenario perfectly. McAllister will go to jail for the rest of his life, and you'll finally be free of him. You and Bonnie will both be free. Our family will be free. It's what we've always wanted."

"I don't know what you thought you were doing, but you didn't do any of this for me." She grabbed her cell phone. "The sheriff needs to learn the truth."

"He won't believe you." He grinned, exposing his teeth, looking almost feral. "Do you think anyone will believe you? I'm a respected County Judge. The whole town knows you fathered an illegitimate child with a vicious murderer."

"Vivian heard what you said. She'll back me up."

His smile didn't falter. "I don't think so, my dear. My poor, sick wife will say whatever I tell her to." He smirked. "She doesn't want this to get out any more than I do. Her husband a convicted murderer and a kidnapper? Think what the town would say." He shook his head. "Oh no, my dear wife will say nothing. You can count on her keeping her silence."

Carrie Ann glanced at Vivian, and her breath rushed out of her chest. Her aunt's face was ashen. Her eyes, deep hollows in her ravaged face, were fixed on Leland.

"Vivian?" Carrie Ann shook her head, not able to believe her aunt would continue to support Leland. "You're not going to let him get away with this, are you?"

Vivian's bloodless lips moved, but no sound emerged. She stared at Carrie Ann, her eyes pleading, as if begging forgiveness.

Carrie Ann collapsed on the couch. Leland was right. If Vivian didn't back her up, no one would believe he was responsible for all those terrible crimes. It would be her word against his. Even if the sheriff believed him, Sheldon's testimony wouldn't be enough. Declan would be convicted of crimes he didn't commit and spend the rest of his life in prison.

Chapter 31

Carrie Ann wiped tears from her eyes.

Leland crossed his legs and smoked his pipe. A smug smile played across his lined face.

Declan was in a jail cell charged with murder and kidnapping. If she didn't do something, he'd go to prison for the rest of his life. Leland was right. No one would listen to her. He was a respected judge, and who was she? A woman who'd had a child with the accused. Somehow she had to make the sheriff believe her.

"No." Vivian's single, shouted word reverberated in the tension-filled room.

The old woman stood on shaky legs, her hands gripping the back of her chair. The pallor on her gaunt face showed how much effort it cost her to stand, but her eyes blazed.

"I won't do it, Leland. I won't lie for you. Not anymore."

He chuckled. "No one will believe you. You're a sick, old woman. Your cancer has affected your mind."

"They'll believe me when I show them the piece of Skye Lawrence's scarf you have hidden in your secret drawer in the desk in your den."

"She's right." A deep voice spoke from the doorway.

Carrie Ann spun around. "Declan!" She jumped to her feet and ran to him. He opened his arms, and she slid into his embrace. "You're out of jail."

"Thanks to Caruthers. He found a used syringe in your uncle's car. Turns out, the needle still contained remnants of the drug used to inject Bonnie."

He smelled so good; felt even better. She burrowed deeper. "Leland—" Where could she even begin?

"I know." Declan caressed her hair with the palm of his hand. "We were in the hall. We heard everything."

Jessup Caruthers stepped into the room, followed by Sheriff Atkins and Deputy Beau. Jessup nodded. "Everything."

The sheriff, his face grim, strode over to Leland. "Leland Winters, you're under arrest for the murder of Skye Lawrence and the kidnapping of Bonnie McAllister." He removed a set of handcuffs from his belt.

Leland set his pipe in the ashtray. "I knew this day would come." He heaved himself to his feet. "You won't need those cuffs, Sam. I'll come with you."

The sheriff hesitated, but he nodded. "Let's go, then."

"Wait." Carrie Ann stopped them. "I have to know, Leland, why did you keep those pieces of Skye's scarf all these years?"

"I wanted something to remember her. The scarf was the last gift I gave her. She loved that scarf." He bowed his head. "I loved her."

Declan snorted.

"Why did you put a piece of scarf in the barn for Declan to find?" Carrie Ann figured she'd take advantage of her uncle's willingness to explain. She needed to know the truth…all of it.

"I thought if McAllister showed up with a piece of Skye's scarf, the sheriff would have to charge him with her murder, and you'd leave."

"What about the piece you put in my car? The one with *Guilty* written on it."

"I wanted you to think McAllister put the cloth in your car." He snickered. "My plan worked better than I hoped. When you gave the cloth to him, and the sheriff's man found it in McAllister's pocket, I knew it was only a matter of time before he was arrested."

"It's time, Leland." Sheriff Atkins gestured. "Let's go."

"One more thing." Carrie Ann would never have peace until she knew the whole, terrible truth. "Why Rankin's Farm? Why did everything revolve around the old farm?"

"The farm was special. Skye and I used to meet there so no one would see us together." He shrugged. "I thought it a fitting place for her to spend eternity. She liked it there."

Carrie Ann shivered at the madness in his eyes.

Declan lunged at Leland, grabbed his collar, and lifted him off his feet. "You fucking bastard," he spat in the old man's face. "You killed her, and then you left her there."

"She was the love of my life." Leland said it as if that explained everything.

Declan's knuckles whitened, the muscles in his arms bulging as he twisted Leland's shirt tighter.

Leland's face turned red, his mouth opening and closing as he fought for air.

"Declan, no!" Carrie Ann tried to intervene. "Let him go. He's not worth the trouble."

Declan ignored her. "You killed her, you son of a bitch."

Sheriff Atkins and his deputy lunged forward, each man grabbing one of Declan's arms, fighting to ease his grip.

"This won't help, McAllister," Sheriff Atkins said. "You gotta let him go."

With an explosion of air, Declan shoved Leland away.

Leland reeled, his hand at his throat, gasping for air.

The sheriff grabbed his arm. "Let's go, Leland."

Leland yanked free and stumbled over to Vivian.

The old woman stood as if carved from stone, her face white, her eyes haunted.

"I apologize, Vivian. I'm afraid I've made quite a mess of this. It wasn't supposed to end this way."

She flinched, but held his gaze. "I hope you rot in hell for what you did."

His face fell, and he turned to Carrie Ann. "Take care of her." He straightened his shirt, tucking the tail into his pants, sucked in his stomach, and walked with a heavy tread out of the room.

Deputy Beau hurried after him.

The sheriff started to follow, but halted when Carrie Ann called to him.

"Sheriff Atkins, what's going to happen to him?"

"He'll be officially charged and held in the county jail." His mouth twisted. "I doubt he'll spend much time in custody. His lawyer will have him released on bail by the end of the day. I imagine they'll try for a diminished capacity defense." His brow furrowed. "If his legal team is any good, they'll have him plead down to a lesser charge. He could get away with a minor conviction, and be out in a year, two at the most." He shook his head. "I still can't believe he confessed to murder and kidnapping. We've been friends for years. I never suspected a thing." He turned to Declan. His lips pressed together as if he were trying to staunch his next words. "I guess I owe you an apology."

Declan was silent.

The sheriff shifted from one foot to the other, twisting his felt hat in his big hands. "I was sure you did it." He shrugged. "I was wrong. I'm sorry."

Declan's mouth tightened. His hands at his sides clenched and unclenched. Sparks flashed from his dark eyes.

Carrie Ann tensed, waiting for him to show the sheriff how furious he was after the years of suspicion and hostility he'd faced because of this man's certainty he'd committed a crime.

Declan walked toward him, his eyes never leaving the sheriff's.

The sheriff's face paled, and he stumbled back a step.

Carrie Ann held her breath.

The two men faced each other.

Seconds ticked into minutes. Finally, Declan released a long breath. "You were just doing what you had to. Leland did a pretty good job framing me."

The sheriff's relief was palpable. "I shouldn't have been so quick to judge. Again, I'm sorry. I'll make sure word gets out you're cleared of all suspicion in the Lawrence murder and Bonnie's kidnapping."

"Your help would be appreciated."

The sheriff nodded and left the room. His footsteps

echoed on the wooden floor in the hall followed by a low rumble of voices. The front door opened and closed.

A grin wreathed Jessup's blunt face. "Well, Declan, your name's cleared once and for all. I'm happy for you." He held out his ham of a hand.

Declan shook his hand. "Thanks for your help. If you hadn't found the syringe Leland used to sedate Bonnie hidden in his car, I'd still be sitting in the Cooper's Ridge County Jail."

"We'd have figured out something else."

"How did you know to come here?" Carrie Ann was amazed at their timing.

"Sheldon told us," Declan said. "He was worried about you confronting Leland. With the syringe Jessup found and Sheldon's statement that he'd helped Leland cover up his crimes all these years, the sheriff had to release me."

Jessup nodded. "We convinced him to come with us and arrived just in time to hear Winters' confession."

"I'm glad it's over." She still couldn't believe it.

"I know what you mean," Declan said.

Jessup's usual intimidating scowl transformed into a grin. His gaze settled on Carrie Ann. "Take care of him. He's a good man."

A rush of warmth filled her. "I know."

"I'll send you the bill for my services." Jessup gave a final nod to Vivian, then left the room.

"The nightmare's finally over." Carrie Ann couldn't suppress a joyous grin. "It's going to take some time for me to accept that."

"With Sheldon's testimony and Leland's confession, his conviction should be a slam dunk," said

Declan.

"How could Leland have committed all those terrible crimes?"

"You heard him." Vivian spoke for the first time since Leland had left the room. "He thought he was doing what was best for you." She shook her head. "I blame myself." She sank onto her chair.

"You didn't know what he'd done." Carrie Ann's eyes narrowed. "Did you?"

"I knew he and Skye Lawrence were lovers. I followed him out to the old farm one day, and I saw them together."

Carrie Ann stiffened. "You saw them? Why didn't you call the police? Skye was just a child."

"Life was different back then. Leland was a respected man. I couldn't turn him over to the police. If anyone had found out, his career would have been over, and his life would have been ruined." She turned pleading eyes on Carrie Ann. "Yours too."

"He murdered her. Why didn't you go to the police then?"

"I didn't know he killed her. Everyone blamed Declan. I thought he was guilty."

"What about when you found the piece of Skye's scarf in his desk? Why didn't you come forward?"

She shook her head. "I wasn't sure it belonged to Skye. I didn't know until the first piece showed up, and Declan had it. I guess I hoped I was wrong and Leland hadn't murdered the poor girl."

"So you let Declan take the fall." Carrie Ann's stomach churned.

"It wasn't like that." Vivian closed her eyes and laid her head against the back of the chair, as if it were too much effort to support her head. "Declan was wrong for you. You were my only niece. I couldn't let you ruin your life." She coughed, a long rasping hack, thick with phlegm. She wiped her mouth with a tissue and met Declan's gaze. "I'm sorry." She wheezed. "You didn't deserve to be blamed all these years for a crime you didn't commit." Sweat beaded her forehead as she fought for breath. "Can you ever forgive me?"

Declan watched her for a long, drawn-out minute. He nodded, the simple gesture saying more than words.

"Thank you." Vivian turned to Carrie Ann. "What about you? Do you forgive me?"

A lump rose in Carrie Ann's throat. She kneeled on the floor before Vivian and clasped her heavily veined hand. "You were doing what you thought was best."

Vivian's lips tightened. "So was Leland."

"There's a big difference. You didn't kill anyone."

"I didn't shoot anyone, but I as good as loaded the gun and pointed the barrel." Her eyes drifted closed again. Tears leaked from her eyes and streamed down her weathered cheeks.

Declan crouched beside Carrie Ann. "Vivian, you were right. I wasn't good enough for Carrie Ann, not back then. I was too filled with anger to truly love anyone."

Vivian struggled to open her eyes. "You've grown into a good, decent man." She drew a shaky breath. "Look after my girls." She collapsed in the chair, her pale face turning gray as she fought for breath.

"Call an ambulance," Carrie Ann yelled.

Vivian's hand gripped hers with surprising strength. "No," she panted. "I don't want an ambulance. Let me go." Her gaze bored into Carrie Ann's, her meaning clear.

Carrie Ann shook her head. "I can't. The doctors—"

Vivian cut in, her voice surprisingly calm. "The doctors can't help me. Not anymore. Let...me...go..." Her voice faded on the last word, and she collapsed back onto the chair, her lips blue.

"The ambulance is on the way," said Declan.

Carrie Ann studied her aunt's still form. Her skin was waxen, the corners of her mouth lifted in a small smile as if she'd finally found peace. "She's gone."

****

Declan regarded Carrie Ann. Lines of strain from the past few days' events were written across her face. First she'd had Vivian's funeral to arrange, and then the unending questioning by the sheriff's investigators as they made their case against Leland. Sheriff Atkins' prediction that Leland would be released on bail hadn't panned out. Not yet. Leland Winters continued to occupy a cell in the county jail.

Sheldon had been charged with obstructing justice, as well as a dozen other charges. He'd asked to see Declan, but so far he had refused. He didn't know if he'd ever speak to his so-called friend again. Not only was Declan angry for the way Sheldon's actions had ruined his life; he was furious at how the man's cowardice had affected Carrie Ann.

"This has been hard on you." He searched for the right words. "I shouldn't have run away all those years ago. I should have stayed and fought back; fought to prove my innocence; fought for you, for us. Then none of this mess would have happened."

"We both should have done things differently."

Tears gleamed in her eyes. She cleared her throat. "I shouldn't have kept Bonnie from you. I should have told you the truth long ago."

"You did what you thought was best at the time." He narrowed the distance between them until he felt her warmth, smelled the floral fragrance of her hair. Their bodies brushed. An electric current sizzled through him. He caressed the back of her neck.

She edged closer. Her breasts grazed his chest, her hips pressing against his; yet, they were still not close enough.

He skimmed his lips over hers, and then he deepened the kiss, tasting her sweetness.

Her hot breath slid across his cheek. She took his earlobe between her teeth.

He moaned, low and deep and with trembling hands, cupped the soft mounds of her breasts. Then he did the hardest thing he'd ever done. He stepped away from her. Eying her passion-glazed eyes, he cursed under his breath. Digging deep for strength, he said, "Not here, not now."

She opened her mouth to protest.

He placed two gentle fingers over her lips and leaned in to whisper in her ear. "I can't do what I want to do to you here. I don't only want sex, Carrie Ann. I want to explore every inch of you, body and soul." He lifted his head and met her gaze. "Do you understand what I'm saying?"

Her eyes glowed.

Cat's eyes.

She licked her lips, rosy from his kiss.

He dug his nails into his palms, fighting for control. "I love you, Carrie Ann Hetherington. I want

you and Bonnie in my life. I want us to be a family."
His heart thudded so loudly he feared he wouldn't hear
her answer. He feared he would.

Her gaze searched his.

He couldn't breathe. What would he do if she
rejected him? The silence lengthened, and something
inside him shriveled. His shoulders slumped. He pasted
a smile on his stiff lips and backed away. "It's okay. I
get it. No problem." He searched for an escape route.
He had to bolt before he lost all control.

"Declan?"

He shook his head. "No, it's okay, really. Look, I
have to go." He spun on his heel and started moving
away from her, each step drilling another painful shard
into his heart.

"Where are you going?" She called after him.

He focused on the open door and escape.

"You always run away, don't you? That's what you
do. You don't stay and fight for what's important."

Her words burned through his pain. He stopped and
turned back, frowning.

Tears gleamed in her eyes turning the amber irises
golden. "I thought you wanted to be a family."

"I do."

She smiled and held out her hand. "Well, then,
come on. Let's go and tell our daughter the good news."

"Good news?"

"Didn't you just ask me to marry you?"

The suffocating weight in his chest eased. He
opened his mouth, but closed it again, not wanting to
say anything to change her mind. He nodded and kept
nodding as a grin started to form.

She walked toward him, her gaze never leaving his.

"I love you, Declan McAllister. I always have. I always will."

I love you, Declan McAllister. Her words sang through him like an aria. In the next second she was in his arms.

****

He stood by the open door, watching as Carrie Ann woke Bonnie. His heart thudded in his chest. He couldn't hear what she said, but Bonnie sat up and regarded him with her dark brown eyes.

He gulped.

She smiled, her dimples dancing. "Hey, Declan."

He nodded.

"I'm glad you're here."

He gulped again. His feet felt stuck to the floor.

"Aren't you going to come in?" A smile wreathed Carrie Ann's face.

He nodded again and ordered his feet to move. The distance to the bed from the door took forever to cross, but then he was beside the bed looking down at his daughter. He shoved his hands in his pockets to hide their shaking.

"Do you play crib?" Bonnie pointed to a wooden cribbage board on the table beside the bed.

He nodded. *Say something. She's going to think her father's an idiot.*

"Good," she chirped. "Do you want to play a game?"

He turned to Carrie Ann.

"Go ahead. I warn you, she's good." His wife-to-be dragged a chair closer to the bed and motioned for him to sit.

He smiled at Bonnie. "Thanks."

She grinned back. "You won't be thanking me for long. I'm going to kick your butt."

"Really? I don't think so. I'm pretty good at this game myself."

She giggled. "Okay. Let's go."

He met Carrie Ann's gaze.

The soft light of love glowed in her amber eyes.

He glanced back at Bonnie. Her cheeks were flushed, her golden curls bouncing. *Sometimes life does work out. Sometimes life is pretty damn good.*

A word about the author...

C. B. Clark has always loved reading, especially romances, but it wasn't until she lost her voice for a year that she considered writing her own romantic suspense stories. She grew up in Canada's Northwest Territories and Yukon. Graduating with a degree in Anthropology and Archaeology, she has worked as an archaeologist and an educator, teaching students from the primary grades through the first year of college. She enjoys hiking, canoeing, and snowshoeing with her husband and dog near her home in the wilderness of central British Columbia.

Ms. Clark's previously published book, *My Brother's Sins*, also a romantic suspense, was published in February 2016 by The Wild Rose Press, Inc.

Visit her on Facebook:
    https://facebook.com/cbclarkauthor
And follow her on Twitter:
    https://Twitter.com/cbclarkauthor